The Middle Room

Also by Stephen Reardon

The Equal Sky

Stephen Reardon

The Middle Room

© Stephen Reardon 2009

This book is sold subject to the condition that it shall not by way of trade or otherwise be lent, resold, hired out or otherwise circulated without the publisher's prior consent in any form of binding or cover other than that which it is published and without similar condition being imposed on the subsequent purchaser.

Stephen Reardon has asserted his right under the Copyright, Design and Patents Act 1988 to be identified as the author of this work.

First published in 2009 by Lulu.com
ISBN 978-1-4092-5564-2

Cover design by Constantine Lourdas
www.lourdas.co.uk

For Jane and my mother

The Middle Room is a work of fiction. Its central characters and plot are entirely fictitious and any resemblance to persons living or dead is coincidental and unintended.

1

I don't remember the detail like Rhoda says she does, but she always puts on a good performance for an audience. Well, she's an actress, after all.

She does Pa to a tee. 'What's *Madame* doing, now? Never does as she's told. Never comes when she's called. She does it just to provoke me, doesn't she? Well if she gets killed it will just about serve her right.'

'Don't take on, Charles. She'll come down in a minute. They're still a long way off, aren't they?' says our mother back to Pa. Rhoda does that weary, weary voice which now is the only way I can recall Mother sounding. Was I beginning to recognise it even then?

'Where the dickens are you, *Madame*?' Rhoda goes out into her hallway and shouts up the stairs. She does my father putting on a funny French accent. He always did that when he addressed our grandmother as *Madame*. I suppose it was meant to irritate her. But she either ignored it or would speak back to him in her fastest *Lilleoise* and that would really annoy him.

I probably remember it because the story has been told so often since. We were all huddled on the stairs that night. My poor mother at the bottom on her own, then we two girls, my sister Rhoda and me, the baby of the family – I can only have been about two. I expect I was clutching her rather more tightly than she was holding me. I usually did. Then, one above us was our brother Leonard, a name none of us liked very much, including Mother who'd chosen it. He was older than me, but younger than Rhoda, and would have been deliberately digging his knees into her back.

Pa must have stepped over us all to call again from the landing above.

The door to the middle room opened and there was

Grandmother, framed in a curious light shining in through the big bay window.

'You should have left the curtains drawn,' Pa barked at her. 'Still, at least you turned the gas down.'

My grandmother ignored him and called down the stairs, but to no-one in particular, in her wonderful heavy French accent – well I always thought it was wonderful – 'It is *magnifique*. A *montgolfière* of such size. We used to see them every day, leaving Paris. But never of such size. And such a light in the sky, yet there is no moon.'

There was a heavy thud and then another. It came back to me really vividly all those years later, listening to them again and again, night after night. Rhoda says it made the glass on the gaslight by the front door tremble. I must have held Rhoda too tightly because she pushed me away banging the side of my face on the banisters. I do remember that.

'I told her, they're not balloons, Grandmother, they're Zepps,' Leonard always reminds us if he's there listening to Rhoda's performance. He's such a know-it-all. 'It was the last Zeppelin raid of the war – 1917. They were going for Hendon aerodrome. And afterwards Paddington Station. A man was killed in Praed Street when his own piano fell on him. And it was an aurora borealis that night. Pa didn't know whether to draw the curtains after all or gaze up into the heavens himself in wonder.'

I strain to remember the strange lights too, and the balloon or whatever it was Grandmother was so ecstatic about and the heavy explosions shaking the house more and more so that even Leonard would have fallen silent and stopped plaguing Rhoda.

Then a stillness, Rhoda says. As if the house had taken a deep breath and held it. Then someone, a policeman I suppose, going down the road on a bicycle, shouting 'All clear, all clear.' And then I expect Mother fell to coughing. She must have kept it in for an unbearably long time. Perhaps the noise of the bombs and her fear would have had the effect of switching off her bacilli for a brief respite, who knows?

Afterwards, as I stopped being a baby and got on with being a girl, I came to know much more than any of the others about Grandmother's montgolfières. That's what she always called balloons.

I was the only one of the three children she had any time for, and even from the beginning, the only one she invited into the middle room with any kind of good grace. She positively banned Rhoda, but admittedly that was after she had found her there going through her things. Looking for props for one of her school performances, Rhoda always maintains, but she could have asked. She probably knew she would be refused, that's about the size of it. And she never could abide anyone who would not succumb to her winning charm. Many did, but Grandmother was certainly not one of them.

Even now I don't know why she and Pa did not get on, either. Not one big reason, I don't think. Rhoda always says darkly, 'Josephine Lucie cramped Pa's style,' but I've never understood what she means by that. She's always throwing these lines away in this voice or that voice, as much as to say, 'if you don't know what I'm talking about, I'm not going to explain it to you.' Rhoda would never have dared call her Josephine Lucie even behind her back. Not while she was alive anyway.

Perhaps Pa just resented the necessity that had brought his mother-in-law to live at Coatwood, selling up her general store in Essex and lugging her heavy French furniture over by Pickfords, only to find that half of it wouldn't fit into the house and had to go into the repository. Just because Coatwood had a name not a number, I suppose; she probably thought it would be grander.

Pa had moved the family out there from Palmers Green because it had an open aspect at the back, looking onto parkland. The fresh air would be good for Mother's 'health'. Her tuberculosis, was always called 'her health'. It's odd, that, when I think about it now. I expect he wanted to get away from the neighbours too. TB always had that 'something not quite nice' air about it. The music teacher wife of a schoolmaster wasn't supposed to get consumption even though there was an awful lot of it about.

So Grandmother came to nurse her, I suppose that was it. And her presence must have been a constant reminder to Pa that his beloved wife was going to die. That's what I think. He wanted to be able to manage all by himself but he knew he couldn't. Knowing Pa, he would have wanted a paid nurse in, I expect. One he could intimidate. But he couldn't afford it, so he had to make the best of it when Grandmother decided to move in. He and Mother went up a floor to the attic room where it was easier to keep the windows open all the time and Grandmother had their room which became 'the middle room' to distinguish it. Neither she nor Pa, it seems, ever contemplated calling it 'Grandmother's room'. I suppose neither of them wanted to give the arrangement any such permanence.

I loved her being there, much more than Rhoda and Leonard

did. I suppose I was so little when she arrived she seemed always to have been part of the house. When I went to school it was as good as having a rabbit of your very own, having a grandmother who came from France and spoke in a funny way. Children in my class would try and mimic her, just like Rhoda did, but not half so well, of course. But somehow a French accent always sounds so noble, even when you're making fun. Not like a German one. But then, we hadn't been at war with the French.

So I was the only one, really, who set foot in the middle room, apart from my mother occasionally when she was well enough to leave the bedroom she still shared with Pa. Even so she never stayed long. It was too warm in there and in the rest of the house. Her bedroom windows in the attic were always wide open, winter and summer alike. Sometimes Pa would come down to breakfast with frost on his moustache. Grandmother took all her own meals in the middle room. I don't know whether that was from choice or because there wouldn't have been enough room round the table in the breakfast room downstairs. She used to prepare my mother's meals before Pa set about ours so she probably couldn't be bothered to come all the way back down to sit and be civil to him.

I would get called into the middle room quite often to have tea with her and as I got older and bolder I would try and make it happen when I thought it wasn't going to otherwise, usually by knocking and asking her to examine the contents of Mother's spittoon when it was my turn to bring it down and empty it.

Grandmother was a wonderful cook. Pastries and cakes were her speciality, but then, of course, she had trained in that grand house in Paris. But she could do everything else as well, or so it seemed to me although she was always bemoaning the lack of *'choses de qualité'* at home. She had her own money, of course, from the business, at least at first, but whether she didn't offer it to Pa or he was too stubborn to accept it, I don't know. It was probably because *'choses de qualité'* weren't to be had in our part of north London whether you had money or not. Pa's money all went on doctor's bills anyway. Rhoda says the food budget had to be cut back especially whenever Mother went away. Rhoda would have known that because as she got older Pa pressed her into taking over more and more of the kitchen duties, very reluctantly needless to say, until I was of an age to take over.

It's when I ask Rhoda why Grandmother didn't do the cooking that she starts talking about Josephine Lucie 'cramping Pa's style'. He used to make us cut the boiled eggs in half between two egg cups anyway, so I suppose money did get a bit tight. I've given up asking that kind of thing now. You can never get a straight answer out of Rhoda.

Still, I know all about the *montgolfières*, which is more than she does. And éclairs.

2

'Perhaps you would like to help me make some éclairs?'
Everyone would be out, except for my mother in her sick room. Grandmother would have seen me with a basin of eggs from the house three doors up where they kept chickens. At first when she would suggest this I must have looked anxious. The eggs were mainly for my mother and Pa would know how many we were supposed to have had when he came to settle up at the end of the week, but Grandmother would brook no argument.

'Don't worry Florence, I will replace them. Your father will not need to know. At any rate, we only need two. Éclairs should be of such lightness.'

They always were too, and although he would give me a fierce look Pa never called me to account for the missing eggs. I would sift the flour, while she deftly separated one of the egg yolks and then I would beat it in with the other whole one. Grandmother had already melted butter and added a little water. In would go the flour and when she judged the mix not too hot, I would add the eggs and some vanilla from a little bottle. She would always tut tut as she handed me the bottle. I assumed this was because the vanilla essence was not *chose de qualité*.

I was always amazed that so little could make so much. Grandmother would sometimes top the éclairs with a little glacé icing, but very often we would eat the pastry rolls just as they came, unadorned, from the oven and whisked upstairs to the middle room before the others came in.

'Imagine, Florence, just imagine. The table, some sweet wine poured. A Muscat would be good, perhaps a Montbazillac. Today we will have a filling of *crème anglaise*.'

I found the imagining as good as the real thing, partly because

I had no idea what any of these things tasted like, and partly because the action of the éclairs melting in my mouth was the trigger for Grandmother to recount another episode from her history. Gradually I collected these together to make a picture part real and part imagined, just like the éclairs. Cake always seemed to take her back to her Paris and the big house.

'Before the war,' she would say as she watched me critically, rolling crescent and horse-shoe shaped dough for croissants, or creaming yeast and sugar together for French buns, 'our kitchen in the *dix-septième* made these all day. Just a few and then a few more if they were consumed or if they were not and became tired. Always the gentlemen who came and went should have a croissant offered with their *café noisette.*'

From what she said, or rather didn't explain, I assumed that the war with Germany must have started in France years and years before and had been going on ever since until 1918. I said something which revealed this misapprehension to Leonard when I was nine or ten and Leonard being Leonard pounced on it with scornful delight.

'Where'd you get that crackpot idea from?' he demanded. But I bit my tongue rather than let him realise that there might be something more than chores involved when I was closeted with Grandmother in the middle room. Leonard was a voracious acquirer of knowledge and, no doubt, would have found some way of plundering Josephine Lucie's recollections if he had suspected for one moment that they were at all interesting. I wasn't about to risk sharing *my* grandmother with Leonard. Anyway he couldn't bear not to put me right. 'The Germans, Prussians they were called then, gave the French a good hiding years before the Great War. That's why the French had to give them Alsace and Lorraine. And that's a lot to do with it. And now we've given the Germans a good hiding back so that shows we're better than them and the French put together.'

Some kindly spirit stopped me asking Leonard who Alsace and Lorraine were. That would have been too much for him and, in any case, I wasn't entirely sure about his schoolboy judgements on the Great War even then and even though he was an older brother. There were far too many fathers and brothers around and about, missing limbs and eyesight, it seemed to me, for anyone to have had the better of a good hiding. But then he said something that made me take notice. 'The French had to eat cats and rats and the animals in the Paris Zoo, too.'

'When?' I asked, whole afternoons of new questions and new

cooking with Grandmother suddenly beginning to jostle for shape in my head.

'At least fifty years ago. 1870. Siege of Paris,' said Leonard dismissively. 'Ask Pa if it isn't the truth.'

But I had someone better to ask. I waited to drop my new found knowledge into one of our teatime conversations, knowing what could draw Grandmother out depended on what she decided to cook and the ingredients to hand. I wasn't sure what would be an appropriate accompaniment to cats, rats, or even the animals in the zoo and despite my bursting curiosity I knew better than to try and link them to éclairs.

The opportunity came one afternoon when, for lack of illicit eggs, we fell back on simple iced biscuits. Grandmother, I suppose feeling a little disappointed at the lack of artistic satisfaction in this, tut tutted more than usual and rummaged around in the interior of her heavy chiffonier. After a minute or so she stood up clutching a tin box and opened the lid. '*Voilà*,' she said.

It contained an assortment of pastry cutters all in animal shapes, a lion, a camel, an elephant, a giraffe. Lots. Some I couldn't recognise immediately from the tin designs. I picked them out one by one as Grandmother intoned their names in French. She didn't know what some of them were meant to be either.

'They are for the *Arche de Noé*. I would make her out of brioche with a lid to lift off and so all the animals in biscuit *deux fois deux* inside. And see…' she turned the emptied box upside down and tipped out a rubber mat indented with little moulds of the same animals. 'This is for doing them in chocolate sometimes. We had a shape for the boat to make in chocolate too, but I don't have it now.'

I knew the moment had come. Holding up one of the unrecognisable creatures, I said, 'What do you think this one could be, Grandmother? Is it a cat? Or a rat?'

'A rat? A biscuit rat would not be good, Florence. We will just make elephants and lions today, I think.'

'Did you ever eat a rat, Grandmother?' I asked as carelessly as I could and then added with a rush, 'In the war? In Paris?'

I remember she looked over my shoulder as if she were looking through the walls of the middle room and beyond. Then she looked back at me, making up her mind about something, I thought, and it certainly wasn't a rat, biscuit or otherwise.

'Perhaps I should tell *you*. I should tell someone about it and why not you, Florence?'

3

After all these years now I feel I should be telling it all, just as she told me, so that it won't be lost. It was the same with those wretched bombs in the City night after night after night. Every time they started up they just took me straight back to that night on the stairs at Coatwood and my grandmother lit by the Northern Lights.

I should have been worrying myself sick about Freddie with his unit up there in the thick of it, really up there, on the roof of that wretched Bank of England or the Stock Exchange or wherever they put him, with his bucket of sand and his stirrup pump. He laughed it off. Said at least the boys at Dunkirk only had the Germans trying to kill them. Those nights in the City they'd be just as likely to cop it from our anti-aircraft shrapnel. And there I was, in a tin hat and an armband, my heart in my mouth, filling up my mind with Josephine Lucie's biscuit rat. Laughing out loud when I remembered some of the things. But I had to remember, had to get it all straight. Our lives seemed so fragile suddenly. All today and no tomorrow until it came.

Grandmother would have agreed with that. She creamed and thickened what must have been, for her, a disappointing present by continual little additions of her past, just as she would add more butter to a cake filling to make it firmer and richer. But this was for her benefit alone. As a little girl growing up, listening and learning in the middle room at the edge of her table, I gleaned what I could and made a picture of her in my mind that may or may not have borne any resemblance to reality. But until that time with the biscuit rat, she rarely explained, hardly ever told it as a story for someone else to understand with a beginning, a middle, and perhaps even an end.

In fact she could be infuriatingly non-forthcoming at times. I remember once Leonard was sitting at the kitchen table labouring over his homework. Pa was gnawing away at him over it as he always did, and Rhoda, at the other end, was making annoying eyes at Leonard to make matters worse. It was awful having a schoolmaster for a father even though none of us went to the school he taught at. It was history Leonard was doing and, I suppose to deflect Pa's unwelcome scrutiny, he asked him, 'Do we have any ancestors who won any medals in a famous battle?' Apparently someone in Leonard's class had been asked to read out something he'd written about a great-uncle at Balaclava. Pa said he didn't know. He didn't think so.

But then Grandmother, who was moving quietly in the background getting Mother's tea ready and had been ignoring everyone else, as she usually did when she had to make a foray into the occupied kitchen, said, 'Your great grandfather fought at Waterloo and he had a medal already from before.'

Leonard looked accusingly at Pa for some kind of confirmation. Pa looked perplexed.

'Well I never heard that,' he said and then to Grandmother, 'Is that something my father told you, *Madame*, for he never told me such a thing.'

'And what would your father know of such a thing, Charles? Why would he concern himself with my family?' said Grandmother, a bit hoity-toity, I thought, as if to imply that no-one in Pa's family would ever concern themselves with hers, especially him.

'*Your* family, *Madame*?' he said, the penny beginning to drop.

'Yes, *M'sieur*. Mine and little Florence's here, I am sure. And Leonard's as well, if he will have them.'

Leonard was near beside himself by this time. He really did not know what to make of the awful truth that was beginning to dawn on him. Grandmother glided on magnificently, only too well aware of the impact she was having.

'My grandfather, your *arrière grandpère*, Leonard, he was a *cuirassier* in the Emperor's army. He had a medal at Borodino from the hand of the Emperor, for his courage and on the way back from *Moscou* he had to eat his horse. And afterwards he was at Waterloo.'

'But Grandmother, he was French,' said Leonard. 'They were the enemy, like the Germans.' He tailed off.

'Even so,' said Grandmother with great serenity, 'But he was your great grandfather and you should be proud of him like me. He was very courageous.'

As she swept out with Mother's tea, Rhoda says she remembers Pa muttering under his breath, 'And he ate horse. Typical Frenchman.'

So my late afternoons in the middle room took on an additional character. I don't know whether Grandmother had been trying up till then to turn me into a *patissière*, as she called herself, or whether I had simply been there to let her live a little in her past. The éclairs, the almond paste, the *tarte aux poires et chocolat*, the croissants, perhaps they were like bookmarks in her head. Places kept by pastry.

But after the episode of the biscuit rat I became her confidante. I must have started thinking of her as Josephine Lucie then, although even now I cannot bring myself to call her that out loud. And I knew then she had not chosen me to carry her past on simply because I was a dutiful granddaughter. It had come to her in that moment, with the Noah's Ark animals. I think she must have been looking for someone for a long, long time. And who else was there in her life by then? Mother was dying. Grandmother knew that, even though it was never discussed in front of us children, even as a remote possibility, so there would have been little point in choosing her. Pa would clearly not have been interested or patient enough. He had no time for the French. It didn't take much working out that he did not regard Mother as French. Well her father had been English, hadn't he? Grandmother and her forebears were an irritating accident.

Leonard was too much like Pa to have been any use to her. And Rhoda? I think Rhoda would have done just as well as me, probably better. She always was one for learning a part and remembering it, much better than I ever will be. After all, she became a proper actress, didn't she? In the West End in the raids. The show must go on and all that. She's welcome. But Josephine Lucie just didn't trust Rhoda to please anyone but herself, so she certainly wouldn't have asked her to be the guardian of her history.

Then, of course, there was Maurice. Out of the question, I can see that now. Maurice was Grandmother's son, Mother's younger brother. Josephine Lucie always called him 'Mow' reece' in the French manner, but we all called him 'Uncle Morris' like the dancers. He was charming and funny, very handsome and a total rogue. We children adored him, so did his sister and mother. But much as his mother loved him she saw all his imperfections as clearly as if they had been hung round his neck on a board. She would never have burdened him with anything precious and expect him not to pawn it.

Pa, needless to say, couldn't abide him.

4

'Perhaps I should tell you. I should tell someone about it and why not you, Florence?'

I cut out a biscuit elephant, deliberately losing its trunk in the process so that I was forced to eat his remains of deliciously uncooked dough.

Grandmother continued, almost as if I were not there at all, 'She will have to hear some things of course.' She looked at me sharply, 'How many years have you, Florence, ten, eleven?'

'Twelve, next birthday, Grandmother,' I said. I remember being a little cross that she should have to ask. It was another of her careless slips that told you she didn't really regard the Coatwood household as home and family. She was just there for her daughter.

'It is enough,' she said. 'A girl has to know things some time. But none of this goes out of my middle room except in your head, Florence. And then one day, you will pass it on to someone with some history of your own, *n'est-ce pas*? And so we will both be more complete.'

It was one of those moments when nothing that ever happens afterwards seems to be quite connected to what had gone before. A growing-up moment perhaps. I can still bring back that surge of excitement I felt then, just by thinking about it now. For the first time, I suppose, I remember not feeling quite safe with a family grown-up. So, that's probably when I started thinking of her as Josephine Lucie. Not as Rhoda and Leonard do, to dismiss her. For me she became a little too dangerous to think of her as my grandmother. I had an odd feeling she could get me into trouble, a bit like Pa's eggs, only more so.

'So what have you to say about it?' Grandmother said, speaking to me for the first time as Josephine Lucie. There was no question though. I knew I had no choice in the matter, and in any case, what were these things a girl needed to know? They might be those things Rhoda got all superior about with Leonard and he pretended not to be interested in anyway when she wouldn't tell him anything. If so this could be really dangerous. Rhoda would never forgive me for knowing something as big as that, whatever it might be. In fact – unthinkable horror – she might even tell Pa.

'What is it?' I said, 'A secret?'

'Well, there is a secret, Florence, which I will perhaps tell to you, but perhaps not all at once and not now at first. It was a long time ago and secrets sometimes become decayed and fall to dust when we breathe on them. And after so long who are they secret from, in any case? No, it is a woman's life, my life that is still the true secret hidden from me, where it should have gone. Our lives change their path and at first you don't see where it has wandered. You did nothing, but you look around and it is over there. You run to catch it to bring it back, but you cannot go back. You cannot even remember where you were going.'

Somehow I didn't think this was the secret Rhoda was keeping from Leonard. The decayed pile of dust secret sounded interesting though. I was still learning how to manoeuvre Josephine Lucie into position but felt I hadn't done too badly so far.

'So are you saying you are sorry for your life, Grandmother?' I asked her.

'I suppose. Your mother. My dead husband Edward Burnell, your grandfather, Florence. Maurice. I wish always…But if I tell you how it was in Paris in the beginning, then you will recognise in your own life as it comes when the paths are going to change before it is too late. Before they become a secret from you as they did from me.'

Yes, life not quite connected to what had gone before. I certainly recognised this change of direction anyway, and I think I've seen a few others coming since. But who knew what this war would bring me? Maybe those of us left at home should leave direction to the men. But then, in a tin hat at two in the morning listening to them bombing hell out of Freddie and his unit only a dozen miles away, I couldn't really feel left at home. Ruby at work could be very cutting because her George was overseas somewhere and Freddie wasn't. I suppose that's why she thought she could take the men on the searchlight on the allotments their tea in the middle of the night when she was meant to be on fire watch like the rest of us. No, I shouldn't think like that. Ruby was all right.

Still I remember I couldn't believe what Josephine Lucie had just said to me. Pa never said anything to any of us that could remotely be called confiding. It just wasn't done and I certainly would never have had the temerity to ask my mother a personal question about her life. When Pa and Mother were together with us in the same room which, because of Mother's health, was already a rare occurrence by the time Josephine Lucie had taken me under her wing, they spoke to each other in meaningful silences and addressed us children almost entirely with inconsequential questions about school.

Thinking about it now, I suppose I might have used my sessions with my grandmother to ferret out more about what was going on then at Coatwood. But I can see she wasn't really interested in anything there except Mother's slow dying and the occasional respite from it afforded by Maurice's visits.

Yes, the adorable Maurice. She'd just put him on her tantalising list of sorrows. Moreover, there was this dead grandfather, Edward Burnell. He sounded promising too.

And then there were still the rats.

'Paris, in the beginning, Grandmother?'

So there was to be no going back now. Josephine Lucie had already said too much for that to be a choice. She had mentioned grown-ups' names to me. People in the family. She had annointed me with the promise of guilty knowledge, knowledge beyond Rhoda's wildest dreams or Leonard's remotest understanding. But Paris was plenty to begin with.

'Was that where you were born, Grandmother?' I asked her.

'No,' she said, 'I was born at Orgelets, a village on the Sambre canal. I think about 1850. My father was a farmer with cows and sometimes he was *Monsieur le Maire*. So ask me something besides, Florence. This is the way we shall proceed.'

I thought about it. Canals and cows didn't sound very interesting.

'So when did Paris begin, then?' I tried.

'My father and I had a great quarrel when I was not much older than you. Perhaps thirteen or fourteen of age. He sent me to Lille to a grand branch of our family, but despite all, I worked in the kitchen. I was like *Cendrillon*, but without a charming prince to save me. So I saved myself. On the train to Paris.'

This was more like it.

'All by yourself, Grandmother? You must have only been...about Rhoda's age?' I said.

'It is difficult. How many years has Rhoda now? Sixteen?

Seventeen? Maybe I was not yet twenty. I know I did not decide to come of age until the year of the Great Exhibition. But perhaps then I was only truly seventeen No, there was a *Monsieur* on the train who was very kind. I told him I was a true *patissière*, almost, and was going to a big house in Paris. I think he knew it was not true because I did not know the *arrondissement* when he asked me. So he said all the grand houses were in the *dix-septième*, gave me his card and said he too had a big house in the *dix-septième* and besides he was very fond of *pâtisserie*.

This was wonderful. I pressed on regardless.

'Wasn't your father very angry? You had run away hadn't you?' I said.

We didn't have a live-in servant at all now, not even a maid of all work, because of Mother's health and the bills it incurred, just Mrs Croucher who came and broke things three times a week. Leonard said she should pay us, not the other way round. But I did know enough about servants to know that what Josephine Lucie had done showed a dangerous disregard for the rules.

'I did not speak to my father again after I went to Lille. He had not sent me there to work in the kitchen, I imagine, but he did not care enough to prevent it either. This is what I mean, Florence. Mostly we find that a man will choose a route for us. If you are not careful, it will be a route you do not want. I did not want to accept my father's route for me and I was young enough for my anger at him to make me strong. But just as I was happy to turn away from one man, my father, I was just as happy, nevertheless, to turn to another one, a stranger on the train to Paris. Can you believe?'

Indeed I could believe. It was, I remember, as if my grandmother's greyness and years were melting away. From then on my grandmother was for downstairs with Pa and the others and up in my mother's sickroom. Here in the middle room she was becoming my friend, Josephine Lucie. I determined no-one must suspect our special relationship, because then somehow it would be spoiled. If Rhoda worked out that our grandmother was favouring me for something, she would find a way to stop it, just to spite her. If Leonard thought he might be missing something the least bit interesting he was likely to come and tramp all over it and ruin it too. And if Pa thought I was spending too much time alone with *Madame* whom he considered a barely necessary nuisance he would just find me more things to do for Mother. I burned to take all my new found liberties in one huge go but I was jealous and secret enough to know that only by conserving them and eking them out would they pay off.

Josephine Lucie was in no rush either, I seem to remember. One minute we would be talking about Paris in the Second Empire and the next she would abruptly change the subject and bring it back to 1925 and the mundane present. But I suppose that means she was right about the past and present. She could remember all that as if it were still the present and she could recall her grandfather who had fought at Waterloo.

Yes, it was the Blitz that really started, not so much to bring it all back, but put it all in order so to speak. Especially because of the things that started to happen then.

The ARP warden was getting very acid with me, I remember, about 'day dreaming'. I'd be miles away. In Paris, most likely, when we were supposed to be doing our drill. Pompous ass. Him thinking I'd be impressed with his manly authority. He'd have liked me to take a shine to him. What a nerve! His wife worked in the cash kiosk at the Home and Colonial. It would have been all right if we could have put out a proper fire. But of course weren't allowed to light any in the blackout. I must say I couldn't get very worked up about pointing my stirrup pump at an empty sand bucket in the dark to make it ring if your aim's true. It made us girls laugh anyway, because it sounded just like someone piddling in the latrine.

This will be my history one day, I thought. It might be already. As soon as you've done something or thought something, it must instantly be history. In fact, it's all so instant perhaps there's no real past at all, nor a future either come to that. We just make it seem that way in our heads. Stops us going mad, I expect. Imagine. The wretched Blitz, then back to Coatwood, and then back to Paris, and even Waterloo. But all of it going on all the time in a few people's heads, Josephine Lucie's, and then mine when she told me. Even Freddie's if and when I ever decided to tell him the bits he didn't know.

And if he didn't get himself killed. Imagine that. Getting killed in the Pay Corps. It would be so unfair.

'So you went to his house, did you? This man you met on the train?'

I risked missing off 'Grandmother' at the end of the question, to see if I would be rebuked or not. Josephine Lucie appeared not to notice at any rate.

'But of course. I had nowhere to go and very little money. I did not know Paris. I don't think I had ever stayed anywhere besides the house of someone in the family. It was just beginning to occupy me on the train, this problem, when Monsieur addressed me.'

'What was he called?' I already had a picture of him in my head, tall, blue-eyed, laugh lines around his mouth and a really lovely suit. I don't suppose it was the right kind of suit for the time, but as far as I was concerned Monsieur was the spitting image of the adorable Maurice.

'He was Monsieur Adolphe de Marquise. I thought he had been sent by God to look after me.'

Of course, it didn't mean anything to me then when she said his name. Not like it does now. Apart from Hitler, her Monsieur de Marquise is the only person I've ever heard of called 'Adolph'. But I didn't know about Hitler then.

It's funny. When we first started hearing about the Nazis, I remember thinking 'Why's he got a French name?' You change your ideas, don't you, about people's names and things? Rhoda and I danced with those young German officers that first night in Cologne with the Co-op holidays before the war. Well, we had to do something to cheer ourselves up. Rhoda commented on their lovely black uniforms with white trimming. They seemed really nice then.

'So you went with him when you arrived in Paris, did you?' I asked her.

'I was still very young and I had nowhere else to go. If I had been older and more acquainted with the world perhaps I would have pretended more to have an address. Then where would I have spent that first night, I wonder? At the *Gare du Nord* I shouldn't be surprised. And what would have become of me after? A woman of the night, as they say.'

Now I know what she meant, but I didn't then. I remember thinking that must be something like a bat. Women in long black cloaks who slept upside-down at railway stations.

So Josephine Lucie had become an addition to Monsieur de Marquise's house. An *hôtel* she called it. But as one afternoon followed another I began to realise this was not the kind of hotel where we once stayed with Pa and Mother at Seaview before she became ill. It was a private house, a grand establishment. Monsieur seemed to entertain a great deal. Gentlemen would come to talk, play cards and, it seemed to me, consume enormous quantities of food and drink, much of it prepared by Josephine Lucie.

'His mother lived in an apartment in the house. She was quite old and rarely came down to the salons. But because she was there it must have helped Monsieur's friends when they met with ladies there during the day,' Josephine Lucie told me, adding by way of explanation, 'This is the middle room, remember, Florence. Not outside this room. These ladies had husbands of their own, you know, and some of Monsieur's friends, they had wives too. But it was Paris, of course. Such things do not occur in Edgware.'

I wasn't so sure of that. I'd heard Rhoda more than once saying to Amy Stringer, queening it over her because her father was the butcher, that Mr Tozer, the insurance man, had more than one wife on his round. As he called at several of the houses in our street I wondered whether any of them lived near us.

One day, I suppose growing bored with éclairs with imaginary fillings, Josephine Lucie had decided to introduce a little magic into the proceedings.

'Today we shall make some *oeufs mouilleux*,' she said. 'They are not hot so you can decorate them for the table, perhaps a nest of salad *frisée* or a robe of *gelé*. But even so when the guests open them for their hors d'oeuvre there is always a sound of happy surprise, even when they have had one before, because the yellow flows as if it was still breakfast.'

I tried to look happy at the prospect of plundering more of Mother's eggs although my worst fears of Pa's wrath had not been realised and by now his frown and disapproving snort at the depleted bowl on the kitchen table seemed not so much aimed at me as at Josephine Lucie upstairs in the middle room.

She swept on serenely, however, uninterested in either my discomfiture or his distemper.

'*Oeufs mouilleux* were Monsieur Machin's special dish. He would pride himself on making sure that perhaps as many as twenty would arrive at table in perfect condition. Cold from the ice water but the white firm, and the yellow, as you see…' She pierced my first one vertically with the point of her kitchen knife and I too uttered the happy cry of surprise and wonder that had so often rippled round that *hôtel* table in Paris as the yolk ran cold onto the plate.

Monsieur Machin's name was becoming familiar to me by this time. Josephine Lucie mentioned him with the same quiet, firm pride that she did when talking about her patron, Monsieur de Marquise. But this was the first time I'd had something so especially his, running about on the plate in front of me, so I decided it was time to explore him further. 'He was the cook, wasn't he,' I said innocently.

'But no. I was the cook, if you prefer. Monsieur Machin was *chef de cuisine*, the master, a great artist. He had his own *hôtel restaurant* before the revolution of 1848. It was said that Louis Philippe himself would dine at Machin's. This is perhaps why it was burned by the people and he lost everything, poor man. Monsieur Adolphe's father had been a great patron too of Machin's and took him under his roof.'

I have to say they didn't register with me at all, then, the names and dates. I just had this vision of an enormous man with a huge moustache in chef's whites, like the plaster one that used to hold the blackboard outside Stringers the Butchers in the Broadway, desperately beating off the mob with a frying pan and trying to douse the flames with soup.

'So you didn't mind working in the kitchen there, then?' I asked her. 'I thought that was why you ran away from your family in the other place.'

'Lille, yes. But this was altogether different. Monsieur Adolphe treated me like his *protégée*. The kitchen for him was a place of learning and culture. He regarded Monsieur Machin as much as a *philosophe* as a chef. It is my opinion that when he put me into the kitchen it was as if he was sending his daughter to the Sorbonne, if such a thing is possible. Besides, I was not all the day in the kitchen. More and more I would receive and serve the gentlemen and their ladies in the *salons* when they came to pay calls, which was almost every day. I would make sure they had fresh *jeu de cartes*, and sometimes I would deal them if they were playing *vingt-et-un*. I remember just before the Great Exhibition, Monsieur had a new roulette wheel put in the small *salon* and he taught me to spin the ball.

'That was a marvellous time, the Great Exhibition. The year I decided to be twenty-one. It is sometimes good not to know when you were born. It is like not knowing when you are going to die, so you can decide your life without a fence round it.'

I'd never thought about having a deathday before Josephine Lucie said that to me. But I've often thought about it since. We've all got one, and once or twice on fire watch I thought mine might not be far off. Still there wouldn't have been a deathday cake. Couldn't get the sugar.

5

'I haven't baked a cake,' I said to Maurice. I couldn't think of anything else to say. He laughed. Same old, adorable Uncle Maurice.

'You used to. You and Mama were always at it in that room of hers, weren't you?'

'So, not in uniform, then?'

'Too old, Florence, too old. God, I'm nearly as old as your father.'

I'd never really thought of Maurice being from Pa's generation and when I think about it, he wasn't really. He was Mother's younger brother and she was younger than Pa. Still I suppose she'd be in her sixties now. No, Maurice wouldn't be in uniform, would he? Even so he looked so young and still so handsome, you'd expect him to be flying a spitfire or something. Either that or he looked like someone who ought to be in uniform but had managed to swing the lead. That would be more like the adorable Maurice.

His mother loved him and so did mine. Pa, however, used to grind his teeth whenever Maurice came to visit, always unannounced. Now I come to think of it, that's just how he turned up that day – unannounced, as if you could not be trusted with the knowledge in advance.

The first we'd know about it would be the sound of his motor car drawing up outside Coatwood. There were very few motor cars came along our road then. Even Mr Tozer only had a bicycle. I've always supposed that it was the motor car that made Pa grind his teeth. Not that Pa would have wanted a motor car himself, except to take Mother to the sanatorium when she had to go away. That must have been it. Pa would have taken Mother by taxi at a pinch, but she would always have arranged beforehand with Maurice that he would take her. And Rhoda, of course, to 'settle her in'. Pa never got to go. I imagine he wouldn't give Maurice the satisfaction and so stayed at home, bereft of the wife he loved and grinding his teeth. Maurice would 'take Rhoda for tea' on the way back.

'I was just in the area on a bit of business,' Maurice said. 'I thought I'd look you up, see how you were. It's been a long time.' It didn't sound very convincing, even from Maurice. It had been a very long time indeed. I'd not seen hide nor hair of him since Josephine Lucie's funeral.

'I didn't know you knew where we lived,' I said.

'We? Oh yes you're married now aren't you, to... er?'

'Freddie, he's in the Pay Corps, up in the City, so I have him billeted at home, except when the air raids are on, which is most of the time.' It came tumbling out. I usually didn't mention Freddie's job to anyone if I could help it. The girls I worked with at the post office thought Freddie had a cushy number and that I must have had some influence to have him at home. Their men were all away. Two in the Navy, one in Egypt and Hilda Crease's fiancé was in the Signals in Singapore, with my brother Leonard, as it happened. We weren't supposed to know where they are, but we did. It helped, being in the post office.

'The City's no place to be if you can help it at the moment,' said Maurice. It was as if he could read my thoughts. I'd forgotten that about him, but it all came back. It was one of the reasons, I think, why girls, women, felt drawn to him. So many men just have no idea what we're thinking, when it's important that they should.

'No,' he said, picking up the earlier thread. 'I ran into Rhoda and she told me where you were.'

I wonder if he had just happened to be 'in the area on a bit of business' when he'd run into Rhoda. Something in the way he said it made me think that he might run into her quite often.

His big Austin was turning a few heads down the Gardens. A middle-aged civilian stranger with access to petrol on my doorstep would set all the tongues wagging, I knew. Not the doctor – he was known by sight. So who then? Police? It didn't bear thinking about.

'You'd better come in Uncle Maurice,' I said. 'I'll have all the neighbours quizzing me as it is.'

'We can dispense with the "Uncle" now, can't we Florence? Bit too grown up for all that now, aren't we? I never did feel like anybody's uncle, anyway, even when you were kids.'

Certainly not Rhoda's, I thought.

'I've got some tea and a few biscuits in the motor,' he said.

'Shall I fetch them in? Silly question.'

Tea and biscuits weren't the half of it. I really began to panic about the neighbours, and on a Sunday too. I'd never hear the last of it if Ruby spotted him. Still, I wasn't about to turn any of it down.

'I can't possibly pay you for all this,' I said foolishly.

'Never asked you to, did I? What's a bit of bully beef in the family, *cherie*? Not *chose de qualité* after all's said and done.'

I started. I'd forgotten, too, how like his mother he could sound.

Maurice followed me into the kitchen where I'd stacked his offerings on the table. 'Nice little place you've got here then. What would you call it…a flat?' he said.

'The landlords call them "maisonettes",' I said, putting the kettle on.

'Oh, very *chic*' he said archly. 'Do you think my mother would have approved?'

Why did I think he was deliberately working the conversation round to Josephine Lucie? That was twice he'd mentioned her since he'd arrived, to say nothing of his throwaway French phrases.

'I don't think I've seen you since we buried her,' I said, interested I suppose to see where things might lead. 'Do you see much of Rhoda, now? You said you'd run into her.'

Why do I think he ignored that last question deliberately?

'That was a bad day, wasn't it Florence? My mother's funeral. Damn rain, excuse my French, and having to open up poor Lottie's grave for it, too. Why your father didn't buy two plots when Lottie died beats me. I'd have helped if it was the money. So where's he going to go when he goes?'

Somehow I didn't feel like telling him that the last thing in the world Pa would have thought about in his angry desolation when Mother died, was where to bury Josephine Lucie when the time came. Whatever else it was, it was an act of great selflessness that he gave up his place so that mother and daughter could be together. I wonder if Mother had made him promise it? After all, Josephine Lucie was not so much his responsibility as Maurice's. I thought, I must ask Rhoda sometime. More to the point I'd ask her if she'd been seeing Uncle Maurice. She'd been keeping it very dark indeed if she had, which would hardly be surprising for most people, but Rhoda is not most people. She can't resist being tantalising. It comes of being in the theatre and being cast as the *femme fatale*.

'I suppose your father has still got my mother's things at

Coatwood, has he?' said Maurice, as we waited for the kettle to boil.

I said, as far as I knew, the middle room was much as she'd left it. Maurice had taken what he had wanted, which wasn't much, immediately after the funeral. I knew there were a few bits of her furniture still there, the French style not being to many people's taste these days. I had been allowed a few little pieces of jewellery and had made sure of the Noah's Ark animal shapes.

'I can't quite remember now,' said Maurice in a casual kind of voice that was meant to suggest that whatever it was he couldn't remember, wasn't all that important anyway, 'whether she had any pictures on the wall.'

I thought, 'Pictures on the wall? Whatever are you after, Uncle Maurice?' I was instantly on the alert.

'There was a wedding photograph, taken in a garden somewhere. It must have been of their wedding, she and your father,' I said, pretty sure that wouldn't be it: Maurice had something else in mind.

'Wasn't there a portrait of a man? An oil painting?' he said, so matter-of-fact. So this picture was why he was 'just in the area on a bit of business'.

'Not that I recall, Uncle Maurice,' I said, 'But didn't she have a lot of stuff in store?'

'No, it wasn't with that stuff. I auctioned most of that after she died. I'd have remembered,' he said, as if he were musing to himself.

I poured our tea and half-heartedly went to open one of the precious packets of biscuits. I had a vision of Freddie coming home and finding them broached.

'Not unless you're having one,' Maurice said, reading my mind again. 'Save them for your old man. What's he like?'

I told him about Freddie and his books, his taking me to concerts before the war, before we were married. God that made it sound so long ago. It was only the year before.

'I like a bit of culture, myself,' said Maurice. 'Have you seen Rhoda's new play?'

'No,' I said. 'Actually, I've never seen Rhoda performing on stage. She always seemed to be a long way away when she was getting started. Outside London. Too far to go really.'

I felt embarrassed. Why didn't I just say that Rhoda and I fell out during that holiday on the Continent, and just drifted apart? She didn't even turn up to my wedding, although I suppose it was a bit of an unexpected rush. Just Freddie's mum and dad and the registrar. Pa had just been evacuated with the school. Leonard had already joined up early and gone abroad. Why did he do that, I wonder? He was older, he needn't have gone. Always wanted to be a soldier, I suppose. Ever since the cadets.

'We should all go and see her. The theatres are open again. That didn't last, thank God. Closing them down like that. We could take in a matinée before the sirens go. Would Freddie be able to get away?'

I wasn't sure. We drank our tea. I asked him about his wife and he told me they were divorced – something else Rhoda hadn't mentioned. Still, I never liked her. She was very plain and bossy. I assume Maurice married her for her money: it couldn't have been for her looks.

'So when did you last see this picture, then?' I heard myself saying and wishing I hadn't.

'I don't remember. It must have been before my mother moved in with you.' He sounded a bit vague, as if he were trying to get me to help him out with the answer.

'What was he like, this man?' I asked

'I don't know...old-fashioned nobleman. Lace collar, that kind of thing.'

'Have you asked Rhoda?' I asked him.

He looked at his watch in a best be-off kind of way. 'It's not really important,' he said.

It blooming well is though, I thought.

6

'It is not so important, Florence.'

'What isn't, Grandmother?' I asked. We were not in the middle room. I was in the hallway and she was calling down from the first landing, so I addressed her properly as if the family might be able to overhear, which they couldn't because they were all out somewhere. Even Mother was away at the sanatorium or the hospital, I forget which now. She'd been gone some weeks, I think. I know I was getting used to her cough not being there and feeling guilty at the sense of relief from it.

Josephine Lucie beckoned me up and retreated into our sanctum.

'What isn't important?' I repeated breathlessly as I ran up the stairs and followed her in.

She busied herself for a while at nothing at all, rearranging things on her mantelpiece and then putting them back the way they had been before, deliberately making me wait.

'It is not so important, whatever you are doing down there when I am preparing myself to tell you about, about...' She stopped impatiently, as if her lack of a real reason for calling me up to the middle room was all my fault. I said nothing which made her crosser.

'About Louis Gaillet, for example,' she said, slightly too triumphantly, as if I was supposed to think she hadn't just that instant called him to mind.

'Was he your sweetheart?' I asked, jumping straight in and not indulging her with the usual cat and mouse build-up of my questions and her answers. I wasn't going to let Josephine Lucie get away with a sulk that was not of my making.

She settled herself down into the cushions of her couch. 'We shall not cook today, Florence,' she said. 'There are no eggs, because Charlotte is not here and your father does not send you for them. Why you should not eat eggs because your mother is not here is a mystery which only your father understands. Above all, I have no butter or sugar because I am a *vieille étourdie*. That is to say, Florence I forget to go to the Broadway. As you know, nothing in the *pâtisserie* can commence without butter, sugar and eggs, just as nothing in the kitchen can commence without *les echalottes* and *la sueur* as César Machin was always telling me, that is to say with onions and some sweat.'

I was tempted to ask if the great chef had cooked rats with sweated shallots, but Josephine Lucie had still not taken the bait on the rats, so to speak, although it was obvious that she always heard my oblique references to them perfectly well and deliberately chose not to respond. I was pretty sure, however, that she was saving them up, so I was not too concerned. Apart from the rats she would sometimes let me dictate the course of her history with my questions, or else would set sail herself in a direction of her own. Today it was to be Louis Gaillet, whoever he might turn out to be.

'And no, Florence, he was not my sweetheart. For one thing he was too old to be a sweetheart. He had perhaps thirty years when I came to the *hôtel*. But he wished to be my lover. Does this shock you, Florence? Perhaps you do not understand yet what this means? But naturally, we are in my middle room where nothing escapes outside.'

I suppose looking back I didn't really understand what she meant about Louis Gaillet although I remember hoping with every fibre of me that it would turn out to be about Rhoda's secret that she tormented Leonard with. But then where would I be? Nothing went out of the middle room. Still, thirty seemed awfully old and I said so.

'Well, he was not as old as Maurice is now, and he is quite beautiful, would you not say?' Josephine Lucie suggested.

Younger than the adorable Maurice? Hardly any age at all then. Louis Gaillet instantly usurped the place of Monsieur Adolphe in my imagining, blue suit and all.

'He wanted to take me to his bed, but not at his own house and of course not under the roof of his friend Monsieur de Marquise. He would never have permitted it. He suggested we should go to the *Ile de la Cité* to a place of assignation on my free afternoons.'

It's so difficult, looking back with hindsight, to remember what I thought they would do in bed together, now that I do know. Josephine Lucie just managed to create a picture of her life out of these fragments that had more to do with noise and smell and cooking than a real vision. Even now when I think about what she told me, the image is the same. The bed in the place of assignation is not clean, the sash window is broken and propped open with a walking cane, like mine was on hot summer days at Coatwood. A smell of cooked cabbage comes through it from an unseen courtyard outside. Sometimes an undesirable Louis Gaillet lies on top of the bed in his braces and boots. Sometimes there is frost on his moustache despite the heat of the afternoon. I did not want to ask Josephine Lucie whether she ever did go there with him. I wanted her not to have done. My imagination would not permit it.

'It is not so important, *chérie*,' she said answering the question I would not ask, in a way that let us both off the hook. 'When a man does not love you and you do not love him, there is a balance, and if you both love each other, it is the same, you can talk. It is when one person does and the other does not, that it becomes a silence.'

'So what happened to him, Louis Gaillet?' I asked, putting a space between him and Josephine Lucie that I wanted to be there.

'He came to play at the *hôtel* frequently. His wife was sick like your darling mother and of course eventually…'

Eventually they died. But it was always left unsaid.

'Monsieur Gaillet was also one of the private dinner circle,' Josephine Lucie said after a while, as if it had been an afterthought. 'I suppose that is why he felt that he could ask me to go to bed with him. Most of the men who came to Monsieur Adolphe's knew that I was under his protection. They were far too polite to say anything to me even though they desired me with their eyes. But Louis Gaillet was so close to Monsieur Adolphe he was like his brother. It was as if everything and everyone in the *hôtel* belonged a little to him. To him and the other private diners. I sometimes think now that perhaps the *hôtel* did indeed belong to them all in some part. Of course it had belonged to Monsieur Adolphe's father before, but who knows when the money runs out? In all the time I was there I never saw any money pass, but I have cause to know that the kitchen bills alone were large. When the gentlemen played cards and roulette, always something went to the house, I think, but it was not the way Monsieur made his living.'

I thought this was all getting a little tedious. Who cared how Monsieur made his money as long as he had pots of it? Time to move on to the rats, I thought, now that Josephine Lucie had managed to talk herself into a better frame of mind. The private dinner circle sounded just the kind of people who would sit down to something a bit whiskery, provided the great Monsieur Machin had dressed it up with a quality sauce.

'Why were these dinners private? Was it something secret?' I asked hopefully. Josephine Lucie was already beginning to lift the corner of a curtain in our conversations, giving glimpses of things sweet and dangerous, and not properly understood by me.

She thought about my question. 'At first I used to think it was just that they wished to be discreet. It was about art, you know, paintings. The four of them would have a private dinner in Monsieur Adolphe's *cabinet* once a month. It was always the same four. Monsieur of course, Louis Gaillet, Gaston Béranger, and the other one was…I don't remember his name, it will come to me, it is not so important.'

Where to now? Food or art? I plumped for food. If I'd known what was to come I would have gone for the art. Of course Josephine Lucie was never averse to discussing the cuisine, either.

'Monsieur Machin would excel himself for the private dinner,' she said wistfully. 'He would go to the markets personally. Early to *les Halles* for the meat and the fowls and then very often he would go again to meet the fish train from Boulogne. It came into the Gare du Nord at about eleven o'clock in the morning in time for the Paris *déjeuner*. Monsieur Machin would never have yesterday's fish, always today's fish. "I want to see their eyes still blinking in the light," he would say. Usually he would obtain soles or a great turbot. "The sole is the prince of fish," he would say, "but the turbot is the king." He would put it in the oven with onions cooked in butter to rest on and then more butter on the top. Just butter and onions. No wine. He would put the fish in a long dish, when it was tender, and only then put white wine and cream and yet more butter with the onion bed and cook and cook it until the sauce was thick to pour over the turbot. It goes back in the oven until it has a wonderful shine with the sauce. Then at both ends of the long dish he would make a little hill of fried scallops to serve with it. Have you ever tasted fried scallops, Florence? I don't suppose so. One does not see them in the Broadway, and in any case, a father who cannot always bring himself to serve eggs to his children, will not find it in his heart to give them *coquilles Saint-Jacques*.'

Josephine Lucie alone served at the private monthly dinners, she told me. None of the servants in the *hôtel* was permitted to be present it seemed and by now her position as *protégée* meant that she was somewhere between housekeeper and an eldest unmarried daughter. Monsieur's ward perhaps. I'd just started reading about wards and their improbable adventures in my first borrowings from our local Carnegie library.

'During the dinner they would talk about a picture, who had

owned it at one time, who had it next, and so on. Sometimes the picture they were talking about would be there in the *cabinet*.'

I was curious to know why it was all such a secret. It all sounded pretty boring to me, talking about pictures over dinner, although the food sounded wonderful.

'Well, Florence,' said Josephine Lucie in a matter-of-fact kind of way, 'I suppose it was all a big secret because the pictures were not as they seemed. They looked like old masterpieces, as far as I could see, but in fact they were being painted by a man who had a studio near the Luxembourg Gardens.

'Well, what was so secret about that?' I asked her, not grasping the point of her revelation.

'But it was not quite honest what they were doing, Florence. The one whose name I cannot for the moment recall, he had a fashionable gallery near the Opera. He would often sell these paintings there, pretending that they were the work of an old master. Monsieur Adolphe was a buyer and seller of pictures and had a fine reputation. He was respected for his knowledge in such matters. The man with the gallery would invite customers for a *vernissage*, you know, a *soirée* to buy pictures, and Monsieur Adolphe would be there to say that this particular one was undoubtedly by such and such an artist, and therefore worth a great deal of money.'

'But it was not.'

'No, indeed, Florence, it was not.'

'So it was a kind of trick? Almost like stealing?' All thoughts of rats had well and truly disappeared.

Josephine Lucie sighed heavily. 'Without doubt, *chérie*, but I did not think about it too much at first. In any case it was not clear to me in the beginning what they were doing. Monsieur Adolphe did not explain it to me, I just served the dinner at table and listened with half my ear. So after a time it became natural to me, what they were talking about. They did not make it sound a bad thing, only a normal business affair, you know.'

'And what did the other one, the one who…liked you, what did he do?' I did so want him to be despicable, the one who wanted to take Josephine Lucie to a room smelling of cabbage for the afternoon.

'Ah well, I discovered what Louis Gaillet and Gaston Béranger did from time to time, because they would find it so amusing to discuss at the dinner when it had gone well. Monsieur Adolphe, as I have said, Florence, used to buy and sell pictures. He was well known. He would arrange for a false picture to go to an auction, not always in Paris, you understand, sometimes even here in London. I told you, at the dinner they would discuss its history, but this was a fabrication, I discovered, to make the painting seem veritable. You see, Florence, an old painting does not have just to look old, it has to sound old as well, and truthful. It has to have a good history to tell. So the four of them would put together a history, one adding something and then another. Then they would all ask questions, question after question, like policemen, so that the story became stronger and stronger. Because you see, Florence, they were all connoisseurs, so knowledgeable that it seemed that they made the false pictures truthful, when I think about it now. Louis and Gaston would go to the auction and bid against one another to make the price go higher. Monsieur Adolphe would make sure that there were other people who wanted to buy the picture also and *voilà* somehow they would always be successful.'

'How did you feel about Monsieur Adolphe doing something wrong like that?' I asked. I knew by now how Josephine Lucie idolised him.

'I don't know, *ma chérie,* I don't know. He used to say there were many fools in the world and one should not disappoint them.'

7

'There are some fools in the world, Florence Duck.'

Typical Freddie. Some bee in his bonnet he'd been brooding on all the way home. He was standing on the step in his forage cap and great coat, his breath smoking in the chill night air. I could smell him as soon as I'd opened the front door and then thinking, even through my joy at seeing him for the first time in a couple of weeks and in one piece, as I clasped him round the neck, 'Golly, you stink Freddie,'

He smelled of brick dust, damp plaster, unchanged vests, and to be honest, slightly of pee. What Pa used to call 'a melancholy whiff' whenever we went upstairs on the tram.

Freddie dumped his kitbag in the hallway and virtually carried me through to the kitchen. 'You know what I'm thinking, Florence Duck? I'm thinking about a nice hot bath…the two of us and then a bed snuggle and sod the Luftwaffe.'

All three suggestions appealed to me, although, Freddie ponging the way he was, I was less sure about the first one than he was.

'You have the bath first,' I said, trying to sound as Gloria Swanson about it as I could, not wishing to dampen his ardour. All the same, he looked a bit crestfallen, poor thing.

'I'm not sure the ascot will run to a whole bath full and besides, we're only supposed to fill it up this high…' I said lamely. 'You get in first in case the gas runs out and then, if it doesn't we can top it up a bit and I'll get in with you. Anyway, Freddie, it's perishing in the bathroom, I'm not sure if there's oil for the stove.'

However, there was just enough paraffin in the reservoir to get a smoky glow going in our tiny bathroom, so while Freddie soaped himself with a new bar of army ration he had in his kitbag, I was able to rub his back in just my knickers without actually freezing to death and so that he didn't feel entirely rejected.

In a while he noticed the rather unpleasant scum he had created on the bathwater. 'Look at me,' he said reprovingly. 'I'm filthy. Probably not such a good idea you getting in this with me. We've all been on the go for a while. No time for proper ablutions. Except shaving, of course. Have to shave even if you're facing a firing squad. Cold water, mind.'

But rubbing Freddie's back in the fug and glow of the Aladdin stove made a tiny world I found I didn't want to leave ever, a world without nagging anxiety just for a change. 'Let's fill it up again,' I said. 'And sod the Gas Board and sod the King's red line.'

Then, of course, the sirens went off, didn't they? Just when we'd climbed pink and naked under the covers.

'Oh Freddie,' I groaned, 'I'm on the fire watch rota tonight.'

'Sod the fire watch rota,' said Freddie, 'You've just had a bath. You'll catch your death up at the shelter. You've still got frog skin. Anyway,' he added, 'I've not been to bed for days thanks to bloody Göring. I'm bloody well having the night off with my wife.'

'Why are there some fools in the world?' I said later, as we lay there in the dark with the blackout open, listening to the docks getting another pasting over the glowing horizon to the south east, and probably Willesden marshalling yards to the south west, nearer to.

'What?'

'When I came to the front door you said, "There are some fools in the world." It was the first thing you said to me, beast! Who did you mean?' I asked.

Freddie propped himself up suddenly on one elbow and looked down at me. 'This bloody war. It brings all the fools out of the woodwork like a lot of, I don't know what, like a lot of beetles. About as much brains as beetles, some of them.'

'Like who?'

'Like Harry Bayliss for one,' said Freddie.

'But you like Harry Bayliss. You're always saying.'

'All the more reason the daft ha'porth shouldn't get himself killed.'

I sat up. 'Harry's not been killed?'

'No thanks to him, he's not been,' Freddie said.

I felt a chill down my spine and it wasn't from the frosty bedroom. All the same, I lay back and pulled the eiderdown up to my chin. 'What have you all been up to, Freddie?' I whispered. 'You don't get killed in the Pay Corps, do you?'

'Not if I can help it, Florence Duck,' he said.

'What then?' I whispered, not really wanting to know and not being able to bear not to.

'You're not to worry yourself, Florence. I couldn't be doing with that.' He stared out of the window, dimly lit by the flickering firelight of the distant bombing. 'It's quite funny really, I suppose, in a funny sort of way. It is a bit like the front line up there in the City. Dad's front line, though. You know, Cambrai and Ypres in the last lot. Everything standing still, being bombarded night after night and not being able to go anywhere. Just taking it. And then suddenly, like today, the sergeant says to our platoon, "You horrible lot can stand down tonight, get yourselves a sh...get yourselves back to billets, get some shut-eye, if jerry will let you. On parade nine ack emma tomorrow." Well I'm billeted at home, so here I am. I expect Harry Bayliss is in some shelter somewhere in Haringey or wherever his billet is. He comes from Oldham. He won't be seeing his girl for a while. He's the one got us stood down, I reckon.'

'Why's that?' I asked.

'Last night,' said Freddie, 'last night we'd settled up the day's leave payments and squared the books by about seven o'clock. The sirens were already going off, so there was no question of getting the cash into the night safe at Finsbury Circus. In any case, we haven't been banking it, with this lot going off night after night. You'd never know whether the bank would still be standing in the morning. So we've drawn rifles and ammunition and taken it up the road to an office that's been requisitioned, that has a strong room of sorts, but where we could get at the money in a hurry if it got hit. So two of us sit and guard the money with fixed bayonets, two get some sleep of sorts and two take to the roof fire watching. We do this turn and turn about all night. About three o'clock in the morning Harry Bayliss and I are due to go up on the roof when the sergeant says, "You two, go and fetch the tea from the mess point." Well the mess point is a good quarter of a mile up the street back at Finsbury Circus, or by now what's left of it. Anyway, we stuck our noses out of the door.'

He paused, as if still gathering himself in his head to run up that dreadful, deadly, blazing street, I know. But he put his arm round me instead. 'Not to worry, Florence Duck, not to worry. Here safe and sound, you see. Well Harry and I dodged up the road from doorway to doorway. So much noise and smoke and whatnot and the funny thing was, there wasn't a soul about except us. "Where are they all?" I shouted in Harry's ear in one doorway we'd stopped in. "All who?" he shouts back. "All the buggers making this damn racket," I said. He didn't get it. I thought it was funny anyway. So we made it up to the Circus and the main office was miraculously still standing, not a scratch on it. You'd think the buggers could drop a bomb where it really matters, wouldn't you? Filled the big enamel tea jug at the mess point, about two gallons, and set off back down to the lads with the money. It was a bit hairy going back because we couldn't really run without spilling the tea. There was no damn lid to the jug. "You'd think they'd give you a jug with a lid in wartime, wouldn't you?" I said to Harry, when we stopped in the first doorway. The shrapnel from the ack ack was coming down on the roadway like hailstones, I kid you not. It was bouncing and ringing as if huge sacks of loose copper was being dropped. I remember thinking it sounded like money. While we were getting our breath, Harry says should we have a swig out of the jug before it gets cold? And I said, "More to the point, we should have a swig before a blasted lump of ack ack shrapnel falls smack through the bottom of it and lets the tea out all over the roadway. We'd probably be put on a charge for losing it too." I don't know if it was the thought of losing the tea or being put on a ridiculous charge over it, which would be typical I may say, but when we set off for the next bit of cover, not that there was much by now with all the blazing masonry and whatnot, Harry takes his tin hat off and sticks it over the jug of tea. So we lugged it back to the unit. Straight off the sergeant wants to know where Harry's tin hat is and I told him how Harry had put the mess tea ration before all thought of personal safety. And when I thought about it again, Florence Duck, it was true wasn't it? He did put his life on the line so his mates could have their tea.'

'You both did, by the sound of it' I said.

'Yes but I didn't put my tin hat over it. Harry's a fool. The kind of fool that wins a posthumous VC.' But there was a kind of bitter affection in his voice. You were hearing that a lot from the men, then.

'So you got the night off instead of the guardroom?' I asked.

'Yes. The officer got to hear about the heroic tea rescue mission and gave us both a pass. I think he thought we were both starting to crack up and needed a night off.'

Somehow I don't think that was the reason. I don't think Freddie was telling me the half of it. But the men didn't, did they?

They'd just joke about it and we'd all have a good laugh.

Later I remembered my unexpected visitor.

'My uncle Maurice came round on Sunday,' I said. 'In a motor. A big one. Well, quite big.'

'Good Lord,' said Freddie. 'He's a bit of a ghost from your past, isn't he? What did the old rascal want? Get his hand in your knickers again? Let me catch him round here when I'm away at the front, that's all I have to say.'

'I never said he did that, Freddie. Not to me. Not my knickers at any rate.'

'Rhoda. You said he did it with Rhoda.'

'No I didn't! Did I? When did I?'

'Perhaps it was your brother Leonard said it,' said Freddie. 'Anyway I see you're not denying he had something on with Rhoda.'

Sometimes Freddie can be really provoking. Well, so can I.

'Maurice is adorable,' I said. 'Always was, and still is, from what I can see. Any girl would be glad to have his hand in her knickers. He brought biscuits and corned beef and things.'

'Ah ha!' said Freddie. 'I rest my case, m'lud. Maurice is a black marketeering sex fiend. I shall have to meet him and have it out with him, that's all there is to it.'

'Well you can if you want to,' I said. 'He wants us to go to the theatre and see Rhoda's play.'

'Have they reopened then?' said Freddie. 'I'm not sure when I can get another pass. Anyhow, I thought you and Rhoda weren't speaking.'

We weren't. Not since the trip with the Co-op holidays and afterwards Rhoda let Pa think the worse of me to save her own skin.

'Oh well,' said Freddie, 'there's a war on. Perhaps it's time to let bygones be bygones.'

'Maybe,' I said. But I knew it was Maurice I really wanted to see again, not Rhoda. I wanted to know how much he knew about his mother's painting. More than he'd let on to me I felt certain. But did he know what I knew? That it might be the genuine article, and there again it might be a forgery.

8

'Monsieur Adolphe knew this one wasn't a forgery, Florence. He told me it was a *chef d'oeuvre* of enormous value.'

Pa had gone with Rhoda to visit mother in the sanatorium. Leonard was out, up to no good somewhere, so Josephine Lucie had bustled downstairs to make pancakes, *crêpes* as she called them, on the large kitchen range, having sent me ahead to scout for eggs in the larder. There were nearly a dozen in the bowl but my anxiety at letting her pilfer them must have shown.

'Pouf, pouf, Florence,' said my grandmother, as she had become again as soon as she had embarked on this raiding party outside the middle room, 'Your father cannot suppose that you have eaten all these eggs this afternoon while he is seeing Charlotte. In any case, they are not of a true freshness. It is nearly a week since she went away this time, so I know you have not obtained them today or yesterday. We will be doing him a service in consuming them at once. If he dares to mention it, you may tell him I said they were bad, which, indeed, they may be.'

So we set to work, beating, spreading, heating, skimming until we had a stack of *crêpes* and a worryingly depleted bowl of eggs.

'Bring them up to the middle room and we will fill them with what I have. The thin peel of an orange and its juice is very good. Chocolate I think I have. Some cognac would be very good too, but sadly I don't have, and I don't think your father has.'

I was mightily relieved to hear this.

'César Machin used to make *crêpes à la cévenole*, with *marrons glacés* and white rum, but these things you cannot get in the Broadway. They are *choses de qualité*.'

Back in the middle room, sticky with the fillings she managed to concoct, some sweet, some savoury, and an extraordinary one I produced, combining Marmite and marmalade, which she did not exactly disapprove of herself, but declared to be 'not truly French',

Josephine Lucie suddenly resumed our conversation about the paintings.

She picked up her thread in mid-thought, as if only a moment had passed, instead of the days or weeks it must have been. She also carried on as if she had been talking all the while in my absence and I must catch up as best I could.

'Knew what wasn't a forgery?' I said, dropping the 'Grandmother' again as we resumed the equality of the middle room.

'Why, the portrait, the portrait. I told you, did I not? The man with the lace collar. Such a collar. Not over his shoulders like this. No, standing up like the collar of a coat turned up against the wind, like this, so that the waves of his hair fell into it and his pointed beard seemed to be a part of it in the front. Such a collar. I would say the lace was French, of course, from near my home of Orgelets. I have seen such lace made in the country between the Sambre and Cambrai. He had a French name, Monsieur Adolphe said, this gentleman with the lace collar, but he was an English milord, even so. His name was George Villiers.'

The way Josephine Lucie said it, sounded French to me then. Now, I know, you're meant to say it like the street that runs down the side of Charing Cross station to the river.

'So he didn't have to worry about tricking people into buying this one, if it wasn't a fake,' I said.

Josephine Lucie took another bite of my yeast extract and marmalade *crêpe*. 'Monsieur Machin would…have…found this interesting, Florence.'

I was within an ace of mentioning rats, but in the instant she returned to her story and the opportunity was lost.

'It was not so simple, *chèrie*. In fact it was more difficult than any of the false ones, because Monsieur Adolphe could not say how he had arrived at this picture. It was not so easy to create a provenance, a story, for a true painting. Who might not know the truth when there was a truth beyond the one they all invented in the *cabinet* after dinner? Someone might stand up at an auction and proclaim such a truth.'

'Why couldn't Monsieur Adolphe say how he had got hold of the picture?' I asked.

'Because for one thing, perhaps it had been stolen,' Josephine Lucie said.

She had already told me her benefactor was very much sought after for his opinion by those who collected paintings for their own pleasure and valued his advice at the auctions. But it seemed too that there were other people who wished to use him as a go-between to reach the collectors. Small-time dealers of one kind or another, many from outside Paris, would bring their discoveries to him, knowing that his opinion would command a better price than their own. For much of the time, therefore, Monsieur de Marquise would find himself patiently sifting through the dingy dross of provincial house clearances and widows' effects, hoping to find the occasional gem, or more often, a work he could pronounce to be a gem. Mostly this activity was conducted via the backdoor of the gallery near the Opera, owned by the member of the *cabinet* diners, whose name Josephine Lucie could not at once recall.

I suppose the gems, and even the paintings that might be passed off as gems, were pretty few and far between, so forging them entirely must have seemed a logical way of satisfying the demands of the foolish. I should think that Monsieur de Marquise thought that he was providing a very necessary service.

The portrait of the gentleman in the Cambrai lace had appeared at the backdoor of the Opera gallery as part of a job lot of paintings put together by one of Monsieur de Marquise's occasional country *bric à brac* men.

'I remember it very well, because I was in the kitchen when one of the young men from the gallery came running into the courtyard. He was out of breath because his *patron* had told him to run all the way to the seventeenth from the Opera, through the Parc Monceau which is all uphill, you know. I took him straight away up to Monsieur Adolphe and heard the young man say that Monsieur…what *was* his name, said that it was imperative that he came at once to the gallery, because something *extraordinaire* had happened and it could not wait.'

'What was it? What had happened?' I asked, swept along by the sudden pace of her story. It was as if we all had to run back down through the Parc Monceau. I plainly saw Monsieur Adolphe cantering in Maurice's lovely blue suit, clutching a Homburg to his head, like the one Pa wears to his meetings.

There was a sound at the door of the middle room. Not quite a knock. Something between a knock and the opening that didn't wait to be invited in. It was Pa. Rhoda was hovering behind him.

'Something has happened, Charles,' said my grandmother, echoing Josephine Lucie's words moments earlier.

It was Mother. Monsieur Adolphe's painting would have to

wait. I felt cheated, yet ashamed to be angry.

'I shall go to her, of course. Florence will come with me for the bus. I cannot wait for Maurice.'

9

'I can't wait any longer for Maurice,' said Freddie impatiently. 'I need to get the bus back to Victoria before the Luftwaffe arrives.'

'They might not come tonight,' I said. 'Besides you can walk across the park from here quicker. Good for you. Shake off some of that Naafi stodge.' I poked him through his battledress.

He was inclined to be grumpy.

'I've only got about another half an hour,' he said. 'And I had to wangle that with a week's fag ration.'

'But you don't smoke them. You only smoke a pipe.'

Freddie looked at me witheringly. I hoped he wasn't going to give me a lecture on exchange and barter during wartime. Like one of those silly Ministry films. He saw my look and thought better of it.

'You're just as irritating as that uncle of yours has turned out to be, Florrie Dee. It must run in your family. What's taking him so long? That minx Rhoda, I suppose. He's probably smearing her with cold cream to get her makeup off.'

'You hope,' I said. 'You can't get cold cream anyhow.' All the same, it was a thought I wished he hadn't planted in my head.

'I bet Rhoda can,' said Freddie.

We're standing in the gathering gloom outside the theatre in Shaftsbury Avenue. The theatres hadn't long reopened. We'd all been to the Saturday matinée to see Rhoda. She was quite good – well, very good really, I suppose, but I can't forget she's Rhoda.

I wasn't sure what I was going to say to her when she emerged. I'd hardly spoken to her since the Co-op trip, but knowing Rhoda she probably wouldn't notice. She'd make out she hadn't noticed, anyway. There, she wasn't even here and she'd put me out. I knew what it would be like. She'd sweep up to us in a cloud of black market *Je Reviens*, ignore me, embrace Freddie loudly, so that all the eyes in the street were on her and then, when they were all looking, make some comment about him not being a guards officer. Then she'd mention my frock.

'Freddie, darling, did you just love me?' Rhoda engulfed him.

'Hello Rhoda,' he said carefully disengaging. 'Not bad, not bad.'

Good for you, Freddie, I thought. Just a touch grudging.

'What's this, then? No pips. Not even a stripe or three?' Rhoda stepped back, looking him up and down as if she were still playing to the gallery. 'Oh Freddie, darling! The bloody Pay Corps!'

'Don't knock the Pay Corps,' said Maurice, stepping forward and taking her arm, 'They've been winning a few medals in the City from what I hear. And catching a few spies.'

'Careless talk, careless talk, Maurice old chap,' said Freddie, but not entirely joking, I could tell. They'd only met for the first time this afternoon and I could see that Freddie didn't find Maurice quite as 'adorable' as he had been made out.

'Quite right, Freddie, quite right,' Maurice said in a conciliatory way, which I knew wouldn't improve Freddie's impression of him. 'Now what's it to be? Bit of a bite at the Corner House? I suppose a poached egg would be out of the question, but we might get some toast and dripping, eh?

'I'm awfully sorry, old man,' said Freddie – I wish he wouldn't put that on with people he thinks he's taken a dislike to – 'Haven't got a late pass I'm afraid. Don't want to ruin a delightful afternoon by ending up on a charge.'

No Freddie, you beast, I thought, don't leave me in the lurch with my sister. How am I going to quiz Maurice about Josephine Lucie's painting without arousing unwanted interest if you're not there to sidetrack Rhoda? I pinched him secretly under his arm.

'Can't be helped, Florence,' he said, 'Got to dash,'

A bus loomed into view. Freddie pecked me on the cheek, shook Maurice's hand rather too fiercely and snapping to attention gave Rhoda a perfect salute. Then with a shout of 'Taxi!' he leapt on the open platform as it drew level with us and was gone. Bastard.

'What a pity,' said Maurice, really sounding as though he meant it, I thought. 'So it's just the three of us for the Corner House, then?'

High tea at the Coventry Street Corner House by Piccadilly Circus ran to some nameless tinned fish, toast, tea and a trio playing *I dreamt I dwelt in Marble Halls*. As I had foreseen, Rhoda behaved as if we saw each other every day. Actually that suited me. I had no particular desire to start raking over the coals with her.

'I meant to ask you, where did you get that sweet frock, Florence?' she said rather too loudly so that the people on the next tables paused to take it in too.

I wanted to smack her.

'It's just an old thing that I've altered a bit here and there. You know how it is these days. Make do and mend,' I said.

'No, really? Can you do that? I never had the patience,' Rhoda said.

She started on the subject of my husband, the Pay Corps private.

'Lovely salute just then, Florence. I didn't think they taught them that sort of thing in the Pay Corps. I must get to know him better. I don't think I've seen him since your wedding and only a few times before that. You two were far too lovey-dovey for me to get near him then.'

I should have let it go, but I didn't. 'You weren't at our wedding, Rhoda.'.

'Wasn't I, darling? I expect I was on tour. Register Office wasn't it?'

'You didn't even invite me,' said Maurice. 'I'd have come.'

'I don't suppose I had your address,' I said, 'Anyway, it was all a bit of rush…'

'There you are then,' Rhoda said smugly. 'Turned out to be a false alarm, did it darling?'

I blushed of course. And I was so angry for letting Rhoda do that to me. She of all people. But there, she always has and always will.

'No,' I said, 'not that kind of a rush. Everyone knew the war was coming. Freddie knew he'd be called up and might have to go away. Lots of people did it, didn't they?'

'And ended up in an office in Victoria in the Pay Corps,' said Rhoda in a voice that was used to carry to back of the stalls.

'Shut up Rhoda, love,' said Maurice, quite fiercely. 'We've already been ticked off for careless talk once today.'

Rhoda actually looked a little chastened. 'Well, who cares about the silly old Pay Corps?' she said in a quieter voice. 'Careless talk doesn't mean them, surely?'

'You'd be surprised who'd be interested in them,' said Maurice.

I was really grateful to him then, but I have to say I was rather surprised that even the adorable Maurice should come to Freddie's rescue like that after only one meeting and most of that in the dress circle.

We were all silent, even Rhoda.

'Did you think any more about that thing of your mother's, you were asking me about? I said to Maurice. I deliberately didn't say 'painting' in front of Rhoda. Maurice might not want her in on the act and I certainly didn't.

'Oh, has he been on to you about her stuff?' Rhoda said. 'I told him that if anyone knew about Josephine Lucie's things in that room of hers, you would, Florence.'

'No,' said Maurice, 'I haven't. Have you?'

'No,' I lied.

We were interrupted by a rather nice looking man in Free French uniform, although I thought he looked a bit old for it. I put it down to his being an officer. Some of the senior ones have to be older, don't they?

'I ask your pardon ladies,' he said, bending ever so elegantly towards Rhoda and me, 'but I believe I am acquainted with Monsieur Burnell.'

Maurice rose and shook his hand.

'Yes of course,' he said, 'Capitaine Gaillet, how good to see you, what brings you here? Not the pilchards surely?'

He invited the captain to join us and launched into perfect French. Well, it sounded perfect to me. I'd totally forgotten that Maurice was bi-lingual. Mine is no better than schoolgirl so I didn't catch what they were saying. But the captain's name rang a huge bell with me, especially as Josephine Lucie's painting was fresh in my mind. Still, it might be a common enough name in France.

'How do you know my uncle, Captain?' I asked, needing to bring the conversation back into English.

'Excuse me...' he glanced at my hand, 'Madame. I had supposed your family would all speak French as well as Monsieur Burnell. From what he has told me you are all half French, are you not?'

I didn't think Pa or Leonard would have signed up to that for one moment. I smiled inside myself at the thought of it.

'Monsieur Burnell has been assisting the Free French headquarters, Madame. His facility with the French tongue and his contacts have been invaluable in helping us get the materials we need to set up our arrangements in London.'

I bet they have, I thought – and how suitably vague – not

much careless talk there.

Rhoda asked him if he had come out at Dunkirk, but apparently he had been in London all the time, in the French embassy as a military attaché of some kind, and just hadn't gone back when France fell.

He looked at my wedding ring again. 'Your husband is serving, Madame?' he asked.

I just wanted to laugh. He made it sound as though Freddie might appear at the table with a jug of hot water for the tea.

'Isn't that careless talk, Captain?' I said and looked him in the eye from under my hat. He was rather nice, in an older kind of way. 'We've just been reproving ourselves for careless talk.'

'Her Freddie's a private in the Pay Corps,' Rhoda said cuttingly, not bearing not to be the centre of attention. 'You've just missed him, as a matter of fact. He came to see *me* at the matinée.'

So then, naturally, the conversation for the next twenty minutes or so all centred around her. I didn't mind that, but I was irritated that we were moving farther and farther away from Josephine Lucie's painting. I had no idea when I might see Maurice again to pump him, if I didn't take this chance. And what had he been saying already to Rhoda? I couldn't tell whether he'd actually mentioned the painting to her or not. If he had, she didn't seem very interested. Still, perhaps I was making too much of it all. Perhaps it really wasn't that important to him. Who could tell?

'So he is in London, Madame?' There was a brief lull in Rhoda's flow and Captain Gaillet addressed me directly. I wasn't sure who he meant, actually. I think I was miles away. It was Maurice who answered him. He sounded really apologetic.

'Yes. Shame. He only had an early pass apparently. Had to rush back to Victoria.'

'That is very fortunate for you, Madame, when you are able to go with him to the theatre, as you have today.' Captain Gaillet seemed inclined to pursue the matter of Freddie's furlough. It seemed a bit odd, but I supposed he was just being polite. Politeness is second nature to the French, isn't it? The first one is rudeness. That's what Pa used to say to my grandmother. Still, I began to think that he was really sorry to have missed Freddie. I couldn't imagine why. Presumably taking tea with an officer, even a Free French one, Freddie would have had to sit to attention or something.

Then he said, 'It has been so nice to meet you. Monsieur Burnell has told me a great deal about his French mother, your grandmother. I should very much like to hear your stories of life with her.' He stood up to go, made a little bow and continued, 'Perhaps we could meet again, and you could introduce me to your husband too, if that is possible.'

He didn't exactly exclude Rhoda from this invitation, but I had the distinct impression that she wasn't really included. If Rhoda had the same feeling, she certainly didn't let it get in the way of accepting.

'That would be delightful *mon Capitaine* darling. Maurice shall arrange something.'

Captain Gaillet murmured something appropriate and took his leave. Maurice walked with him to the door, talking animatedly to him in French. As I watched them cross the restaurant I had a funny feeling that Captain Gaillet hadn't run into us all by chance. For one thing he hadn't taken any tea.

Rhoda had to rush then for her evening performance. The sirens hadn't gone off. The Luftwaffe were late tonight. Maurice didn't offer to go with her. He said he'd see me to the tube.

'You know, Florence,' he said, as we crossed Leicester Square so that I could get the Northern Line, 'it's not quite true that I haven't been thinking about that painting of my mother's. I have. In fact it was friend Gaillet who first started me off on it shortly after we'd got together.'

'Why, what does he have to do with it?'

'No, no. He doesn't, of course. We were just talking about pictures in general and he described something which put me in mind of that one of my mother's, so I told him about it. He said he'd like to see it if that were possible. I would like to know what happened to it.'

'Does Captain Gaillet know about pictures then?' I said, sounding as innocent as I could.

'From the way he was talking he sounded pretty knowledgeable,' said Maurice. 'But then, what do I know?'

We reached the entrance to the tube as the sirens began to wail. Anxious passengers like me jostled with those people clutching bags and blankets just hurrying to take shelter.

'I'll fix something then, now that we've broken the ice after all this time,' said Maurice. 'All right if I leave you here?'

10

'I will have to leave you here, Florence,' said my grandmother. 'This is no place for a child.'

It was a long way by two trams and a bus to the sanatorium. Fortunately Pa had managed to persuade her that it would be far too late to set off that afternoon. Regular visiting time would be long over and the prospect of the return journey after dark proved too daunting, even for her. So the pair of us had set off at the crack of dawn the next day.

I had no real idea what to expect, but I was full of fears and forebodings. Pa had shooed me out of the middle room and closeted himself with Grandmother with the door firmly shut. I was incensed at this, but also panic stricken at what might have brought about his violation.

Rhoda was, of course, totally Rhoda, especially when Leonard arrived home, late and sheepish, reeking of Players Weights, only to find to his delight that no-one had been interested for once in his whereabouts. I didn't know whether to believe her or not. I certainly didn't want to.

'It's completely ghastly,' said Rhoda. 'Mother's bed was outside on this horrible, rusty iron balcony and the bedclothes were sodden from the rain.'

'Why?' said Leonard.

'That's where they put them. It's supposed to be good for them. Like Pa and mother sleeping with the windows open all the time.'

'Yes but they don't get wet from the rain in their bedroom,' said Leonard, sounding as appalled as I felt. 'Is getting wet part of it too?'

'I suppose it must be, because Pa was furious and wouldn't be quiet until he saw the head doctor – superintendent he called him. It sounds just like a zoo or something. Anyway, Pa went into his office and shut the door, but I could still hear him ranting for a bit. And then it all went suddenly quiet. Then he came out looking very pale and I heard the doctor call after him, 'I mean it – her only chance.'

'So how was Mother?' I ventured.

'Well I wasn't allowed anywhere near her. I had to stand by the door. Pa went out onto the balcony, but he wasn't allowed to touch her or give her a kiss or anything.'

'But we go near her at home and we're all right,' I said. 'I empty her jug thing and everything. I know it's always covered over.'

'Completely ghastly,' said Rhoda, taking the centre stage again as if no-one else had spoken. 'These two women went by while I was standing by the door. Visitors I suppose, but they were really common. One said to the other one, "and she 'as to take it 'erself, when the gong goes. They all of them 'ave to at the same time when the bleedin' gong goes. 'As to stick it right up 'er…' Rhoda stopped and looked at us to make sure she had our undivided attention.

'Up her what…?' said Leonard.

'Up 'er arse,' she concluded triumphantly.

'Stick what up?' I said lamely. I was totally lost, but the atmosphere Rhoda conjured up with her acting left me sinking into a pit of terror.

'Thermometer, was it?' said Leonard. 'Couldn't have meant anything else, could they?'

'I thought they put those under your tongue,' I said. 'They did when I had the measles.'

'And what was the gong all about? Sounds very rum to me, Rhoda,' said Leonard.

Pa's appearance in the kitchen put a stop to Rhoda's production of the horrors of the sanatorium, and needless to say, I was left replaying the lurid scenes she had put in my mind, over and over, not knowing whether they were my own exaggerations or hers.

By the time Grandmother and I were at the gates I was on a knife's edge.

'Rhoda went in with Pa, Grandmother,' I said.

Part of me wanted to sit on one of the benches just inside the gate, along with those others, mainly children, who had been abandoned at a safe distance. But part of me, too, felt it had been a long journey, wanted to see it through, needed to see for myself if Rhoda was right.

'Rhoda goes where Rhoda will go,' said Grandmother in a fierce whisper, mainly to herself, adding, 'Like my middle room when

I go to the Broadway.'

'I'm sure that was only the once, Grandmother,' I said. Why I felt I had to defend Rhoda I can't imagine.

She did not reply and we continued walking up towards the entrance anyway. There were separate groups of men and women in the grounds, apparently working even though there was a bit of a drizzle in the air. There was a long row of what I took for garden sheds over to one side and the workers had garden tools, rakes and hoes and wheelbarrows, which were presumably stored in them.

I was puzzled. They didn't look like gardeners. There were so many of them for one thing. I thought they looked more like prisoners. Some of the men were smoking and drinking out of bottles, while two were obviously keeping a lookout, like Leonard and his friends in the Dollis Brook pipe culvert after school. It dawned on me then that they must be patients. My grandmother confirmed this when I asked her.

'Why are they making them work in the grounds?' I asked. They were obviously being made to do it. You only had to look at them. 'Can't they afford the bills or something?'

'I cannot say, Florence. I shouldn't think so. It is perhaps part of the treatment. Fresh air. Exercise. I should hope so, anyway.'

'Mother hates gardening. Pa does it all. Do you think they make Mother…'

'I don't know, I don't know, I don't know,' said my grandmother sharply. I glanced into her face, startled, and saw that her eyes were brimming. I remember feeling mortified. That and more panic about what we might find. This was not middle room business. This was Grandmother, not Josephine Lucie. Personal family questions about grown-ups were out of bounds.

'You should have left the child at the gate, if she had to come at all,' said the starched dragon in the cubby hole in the polished hallway.

Grandmother turned to me. *'Qu'est-ce qu'elle m'a dit?'*

This was a ploy I recognised. She did it when she wanted to get rid of people who knocked at the door unasked, or bus conductors of the kind Pa called 'insolent'.

'I'm afraid she's French,' I said apologetically. 'That's why I have to stay with her.'

It did the trick and we were pointed upstairs to the female ward corridor, but not before I had been sternly warned to remain at the cubicle door and to 'listen for the gong'. So far Rhoda's account couldn't be faulted.

Mother was very pale, sitting in a chair by her metal bedstead with the window open, of course. She didn't notice me at first, by the door, but Grandmother mentioned my name and she turned her head towards me and smiled. Grandmother said something else I didn't catch, and Mother said, 'Speak English, *Maman*, I'm too tired. Have you brought the Ovaltine? They say I'm to have Ovaltine.'

Grandmother had not brought Ovaltine. I knew that for a fact.

'Oh dear,' said Mother a bit tearfully, 'I was sure I mentioned it to Charles. They nag one so about it here. I wouldn't want them to think we can't afford it.'

I could tell that she was controlling herself with great difficulty, stopping herself from breaking down altogether. I felt sorrier for her than I ever had before. Mother had been ill for as long as I could really remember and I had grown so used to it, the routine, that I never really thought anything would change. Now for the first time I knew things were changing and not for the better. Nothing was said. Nothing was ever said to us. It made whatever it was Pa had said behind the closed door of the middle room all the more frightening to think about. Whatever it was had brought my grandmother scuttling across half of Middlesex on the public transport to be at her daughter's side. My heroines from the Carnegie library were always trying to be strong, but it was very difficult for me when I didn't know what I was supposed to be strong about. I didn't feel at all strong, just very frightened and confused.

Grandmother sat holding her hand. They had both stopped talking. The effort only seemed to make mother cough anyway. I lent against the doorway feeling terribly bored on top of all the other emotions milling about inside me. I felt guilty about that too. On either side of me the corridor remained empty and chill, while beyond me, in the little room, the two women sat motionless and silent, only the movement of the blind above the open window signifying that the scene was anything other than a ghastly illustration from the *Girl's Own Paper*.

Unmistakably the gong sounded. Grandmother rose and kissed my mother on the forehead. Then Mother turned her head towards me. 'Goodbye Florence. It was lovely to see you. I shall be home soon, I expect. Give my love to Leonard and everyone.'

I couldn't bear it any longer. I called to her. 'Do you have to do the garden, Mother?'

She smiled. 'Not yet, Florence. When I am stronger I shall. I'm only on vegetable peeling. I can do that sitting down, mostly.'

I was appalled. Mother did no work at home, the rest of us did it, even Pa. I couldn't see why she should be made to in a place like this. It didn't seem decent somehow.

'But why do you have to, Mother?' I persisted.

'It's something they call "graduated labour". It's good for me. Keeps me strong,' she said, reaching for her spittoon with one hand and waving us away with the other, as the coughing took hold of her again.

As Grandmother and I walked down the drive towards the main gate I could see some of the men patients who had been doing the gardening sitting in the doorways of the little wooden huts I had noticed earlier. It dawned on me that these allotment sheds were where they slept. I shared my thoughts with Grandmother in a horrified whisper, as if to have said anything out loud would incur an unseen wrath which would somehow be taken out on Mother. By the same token, I did not mention the question of Mother's release from that malevolent institution until we were well out of it and on the first leg of the journey back home.

To my surprise Grandmother was inclined to be confiding. The visit had shaken her, I could see. Whatever it was that Pa had said to make her rush to the sanatorium had clearly been confirmed by going, and she desperately needed to talk. If Maurice had been the one to take her in his motor I doubt if I would ever have got to know anything. As it was, on that journey home she almost relapsed into Josephine Lucie and the bus almost became the middle room. When I asked her if Mother would indeed be coming home soon, and better, she chose to ignore the questions and to raise another set of possibilities and unknown quantities, just as Josephine Lucie would do behind our closed door at Coatwood.

'They are going to give my Charlotte a new treatment,' she said.

'Not gardening, you mean?'

'They are going to collapse her lung, the one that has the infection and when it has rested it will be better and they will *gonfler* it again.'

She didn't sound very enthusiastic, and I began to feel apprehensive about this new treatment. The whole thing was already more information than would ever have been revealed in normal circumstances to a mere child. How on earth would I be able to deal with it to Rhoda's satisfaction? Pa wouldn't have told her anything about collapsing lungs, or else she would have been dancing all round the subject to keep Leonard and me on tenterhooks. I had to press home this advantage. I wished I hadn't.

'How do they do it? Collapse her lung?' I asked.

'Evidently with a big needle through her back.'

I felt sick. I imagined Mother being taken to a garden shed and heard a gong sounding, although the gong did cheer me a little. At least she wouldn't have to collapse it herself and especially not via her….bottom.

'Is it…is it dangerous?' I asked.

'Lungs, *montgolfières*. They are the same I imagine. Yes it will be dangerous.'

11

'Yes it will. It will be dangerous. I don't want you coming up at night and that's flat,' said Freddie. 'Why can't you meet them during the day like we did the last time?'

The pips went again. I fumbled with the coppers and pressed button A.

'Are you still there Freddie?'

He was.

'I don't know why you're so suddenly taken up with Maurice and Rhoda. There's something a bit unsavoury there if you ask me. He's old enough to be her...'

'...Uncle. Yes I know, Freddie, but he *is* adorable. And it has to be the evening because Captain Gaillet wants to take us all to a French restaurant in Jermyn Street and it doesn't do anything at midday. Maurice says the food is really good if you go there with the Free French. And it'll be off ration and we won't be paying.'

'And why on earth is this Frenchman so keen to meet me? Or is it you he's got his eye on? Not that I'd blame him, Florence Duck. But all the same...'

'Look Freddie, I can dive down the tube if the sirens go. We all can. I can sleep down there if necessary, but it won't be. The last time it was the best place to be. The trains still run out of Town and you don't come out in the open until East Finchley. I don't think Hitler's interested in East Finchley.'

'Well, it's where all the Jews live, Florence Duck, so I wouldn't be so sure.' Freddie snorted at his own wit at the other end of the phone, but it was enough to topple him off his high horse. 'I don't suppose for one moment I'll be able to get a late pass,' he said, thereby conceding that the invitation could be accepted, by me at any rate. 'I'll try and wangle something but you'd better leave the date open until the last minute. But I know I won't be able to make it though, so don't bank on it.'

Maurice had phoned me at work, a crime so heinous my stomach turned to water when Mr Webber, the Postmaster, came to his office door and said there was a call for me.

'He says it's someone from the War Office,' he said, giving me a searching look as he indicated the accusing receiver lying on his desk. 'I hope it's not a personal call, Mrs Draper.'

'I don't know anyone at the War Office,' I said truthfully. 'I hope it's not about my husband. The War Office wouldn't phone about him, would they?'

Mr Webber clearly had no intention of leaving the room while I took the call so I had to stifle a shriek of panic when I heard Maurice's voice at the other end of the line.

'I heard that,' he said. 'Who is it? The boss? Is he still there?'

'Yes,' I said guardedly.

'Well you'd better not call me Uncle Maurice then. Just say yes and no in the right places. I do quite a lot of this and that for the War Office in a manner of speaking, so you needn't act too shifty.'

Maurice proceeded to issue Captain Gaillet's invitation to Freddie and me. He gave me a telephone number where I could reach him with our reply, which I wrote down on my pad. Mr Webber tried hard not to look as though he were squinting at it upside down.

'Is he still there?' said Maurice.

I said he was.

'Well, when he asks you what the call was all about, just look him in the eye and say you aren't at liberty to say.'

'I don't think I can,' I said.

'Well then, tell him that he may be getting a communication from the Postmaster General's Office which will explain everything, but until then your lips are sealed. 'Bye.'

I hung up slowly, trying not to catch Mr Webber's stern eye.

'And what, may I ask, was all that about?' he said acidly.

'They want me to vouch for someone I know, who's going to work there. I said I would. It's because I'm a civil servant I suppose.'

Mr Webber opened and closed his mouth a couple of times. 'Well it all sounds highly irregular, highly irregular, Mrs Draper.'

'I expect it's because of the war,' I said sweetly.

'You wouldn't still be a civil servant if it weren't for the war,' he retorted. 'Married women! Hitler's got a lot to answer for. This acquaintance of yours you're vouching for is also married, I presume?'

'I'm not at liberty to say, Mr Webber,' I said and scuttled out with as much dignity as I could muster, trying not to giggle.

I waited for Freddie outside the Hippodrome Corner exit to Leicester Square tube station. He was still nervous about my coming up to town during the air raids and didn't want me to be out of sight of the underground until he got there.

However, he came bounding up the stairs, gave me a huge hug and kissed me so hard he knocked my hat over one ear.

'You've lost your grumps,' I said. 'I thought you said there was no chance of your getting a pass.'

'It's quite extraordinary,' Freddie said. 'I took my chitty to the guard room expecting to get bawled out for insolence, especially as the sergeant-major just happened to be there, but he looked at it and said I had to see the officer about it.'

'And?'

'And so I marched into the Major's office, lef'right,lef'right, lef' right, off cap, all right, stand easy. And the Major says to me, "Oh yes I know about this, Draper, back on parade nine-thirty sharp." Absolutely frightening!'

'Why?'

'Well, he knew my name for a start.'

'Oh Freddie, you fool. Anyway I suppose half past nine is better than nothing. Perhaps you'll have to forego the brandy and liqueurs.'

'No, Florrie Dee. Nine-thirty *tomorrow morning*. He's given me the whole night off. I can't imagine why. There'll be hell to pay with the chaps. They'll think I kissed his arse or something worse.'

Suddenly I had a lovely warm feeling in my tummy. I nearly suggested we turned back down the tube, headed straight for home and sod Maurice and Rhoda and the Free French.

'Freddie, that's wonderful. If I'd known I'd have used the soap.'

He squeezed my arm under his. 'You're a bad girl, Florence Duck, so you are.'

'I hope so, sir, and thank you kindly,' I said.

The restaurant where we were to meet, just off Jermyn Street, was not the kind of place Freddie or I would have dared set foot in even at the best of times. Freddie would have spent the whole time surreptitiously counting his wallet under the table. The Corner House was the most we generally aspired to on high days and holidays, and if we did need a bite to eat out it, was mostly a Lyons teashop that would fit the bill. Haddock and chips or steak and kidney pudding and mash. It seemed a long time ago, 'before the war'. When you said it like that. Another world.

A waiter took our coats. Freddie's army great coat of course, and mine, the long, cream wool one, fitted at the waist, with the double lapels. I had bought it for a guinea to take on the ill-starred trip with Rhoda. I was a bit reluctant to let it go to the cloakroom. I'd hate anyone to be given it by mistake – or on purpose. You can't be too careful these days especially with a good coat like that. We didn't know whether we were supposed to give up our gas masks with the coats, but the waiter said keep them with us, when we dithered. He sounded French, but he was quite old, they all were, so he'd probably been there for years.

'Are you sure this French chap's picking up the bill?' Freddie whispered anxiously as we were taken over by the head waiter and filed after him to our table in the far corner. Most of the men at the tables we passed were officers, but as neither they nor Freddie were wearing hats, I suppose, thank God, he didn't have to salute them all. We got some curious glances from some of them though. Looking at the women with them I rather wished I'd kept my coat on as it was by far and away classier than the frock I had on underneath it. For once I wished I were in uniform like some of them were. A girl can be anyone in a uniform. Mind you, Freddie could be anyone in a uniform too. He looked bookish and interesting, I think, even if he was a private in the Pay Corps. Like a don or a poet. Perhaps that's what the glances were about. I'm sure hundreds of ordinary soldiers are far from being ordinary in real life. Real life. What was real anymore?

We were the first to arrive, which flustered me a bit, as I didn't know where we should sit, next to one another, or opposite, or on either end. One side was a padded banquette running the length of the mirrored wall. The head waiter obviously expected me to sit in there so I did. Freddie chose to sit opposite. Another waiter arrived bearing an armful of menus, and a wine list which he gave to Freddie.

'Would you care for an aperitif?' he said, addressing us both at once and we both answered over one another, of course.

'No thanks, we'll wait for the others…' Freddie began to say.

'…Yes please, I said.' We both looked confused and went red.

'Gin and tonic, madame?' said the waiter, ignoring Freddie.

I nearly said 'yes please' again which would have left him thinking I had no mind of my own, and then Josephine Lucie came majestically to my aid.

'You don't by any chance have any *Muscat de Beaume de Venise* left, do you?' I heard myself say, and fair dos, I think the 'any left' thought was inspired. The waiter had to struggle not to beam.

'I'm sure we do, Madame,' he said. 'Sir?'

'I'll just have a bottle of Worthington then,' Freddie said. 'Thanks.'

The waiter glided away.

'What's that when it's at home?' said Freddie, 'Something expensive by the sound of it.'

I gave him my exasperated look.

'All right, I know, I know. We're not paying. But the chap's not even here yet and you're opening the champagne,' he said.

'It's not champagne,' I said. 'It's a very classy sweet white wine. "Something of the rose, something of the flowers of orange, and something of the evening sun".'

'Crikey, Florrie Dee, where'd you dredge that from?'

'From my French Grandmother, of course. Who else? She always said it was what any lady should ask to be served in a situation like this. It's a *chose de qualité*'

'A thing of quality? What did she mean by that?' said Freddy, intrigued.

'Something you could not get in the Broadway,' I said.

Maurice and Rhoda arrived together. She actually had a fox fur with its tail in its mouth round her shoulders. I tried to imagine her having to put her gas mask on and what they would both look like. Needless to say she had left her mask in the cloakroom, as had Maurice presumably. Rhoda made a great song and dance about mine and Freddie's being in the way and when the waiter came for their drinks order, she told him to 'remove them hence', very Shakespearian. By this time she had the undivided attention of the restaurant.

'You don't see all these people here with their wretched gas masks under the table, do you, darling?' she said. 'What *is* that you're drinking, Freddie? Not a bloody beer, surely?'

'I asked for a large *Muscat de Beaume de Venise*,' said Freddie gravely, 'but the waiter said as it was running low it was only for officers and their ladies. Other ranks had to make do with a Worthington.'

'Don't be crass, Freddie,' said Rhoda. 'You'll only draw

attention to yourself. What've you got, Florence, white wine?'

'Yes,' I said.

'German, I expect,' said Maurice. 'These smart places bought it up like nobody's business when they saw which way the wind was blowing. Ironic when you think about it. We can't get a decent Chablis so we're all swilling Piesporter while the bastards who made it bomb seven bells out of us.'

Captain Gaillet made his entrance, lavishly apologising for the lateness of his arrival, underlining the fact that he alone was impeccably punctual. To my enormous relief for Freddie's sake, he was in civilian clothes. Rhoda's dismay at this was almost comic. Only one uniform on the table and it's my Freddie, the pay corps private.

Captain Gaillet kissed my hand and Rhoda's, shook the two men's and then settled himself next to Freddie. 'As a matter of fact, Maurice, they have some excellent Chablis here, don't you Henri?'

'*Oui monsieur,*' said the waiter who had been hovering. 'Will you have a glass, or your usual champagne, *monsieur*?'

'I think I'll start with a beer this evening, I have rather a thirst.'

'The Worthington's very good,' said Freddie.

Rhoda set about retrieving the situation. 'Why no uniform tonight, *mon Colonel*?' she asked, in her back-of-the-stalls delivery.

Captain Gaillet ignored his promotion. 'It is not obligatory for me. I still have my diplomatic passport if the police stop me. The Free French are not as insistent, as you British are. You know what we Frenchmen are like, don't you? Besides, I thought it would be more agreeable for Private Draper. Here we can just be ladies and gentlemen. Is that not so Madame Draper?' He turned to me.

'Rhoda's afraid they'll all think we're spivs on a night out and Freddie's a deserter,' I laughed. Wickedly, I hoped.

Of course that was just what she did think. I'd hit that one on the head.

'And I am so glad you could join us,' Gaillet said to Rhoda, coming to the rescue as Rhoda prepared to make an example of Freddie to humiliate me. 'You do not have a performance this evening, I think?'

'Not this evening, *mon Colonel*. I am between engagements for a few weeks.'

'Please, call me Raoul…everyone,' he said.

'And I am Rhoda, of course,' Rhoda purred happily, and the evening became almost delightful.

The menu was mouth wateringly wonderful, even by current

standards. If they were having to economise on the ingredients, they were still managing to come up with dishes that Freddie and I wouldn't be used to at the best of times. I ordered a chicken dish. Imagine, real chicken. And this was now. We only used to have it at Christmas, before the war. It said it was cold, but I didn't mind that, it was chicken, and served with a *sauce gribiche*.

'Gracious! *Sauce gribiche*,' said Rhoda, 'What on earth's that when it's at home, Florence? Good thing we've Raoul here to translate.'

I didn't need Raoul Gaillet's help, thank you. 'It's a mayonnaise made with hardboiled egg yolks and then chopped capers, parsley, chervil if they have any, and chopped *cornichons*. You're supposed to *julienne* the hardboiled egg whites and lay them on the top, but I expect they'll have had to use dried egg, don't you? Actually, I might try it that way at home with a bit of improvisation. It could cover a multitude of sins.'

Rhoda began to interrupt. 'Dear me, *cornichons*, what are...?'

'Gherkins,' said Freddie. 'Pickled hamptons to you.'

Rhoda was actually taken aback. 'I have to go and powder my nose, if you will excuse me,' she said.

We sipped our drinks and talked about the air raids, as one did, while we waited for her to return.

After a few minutes, Captain Gaillet said, 'You are *chef de cuisine* then, Madame Draper, I detect?'

'Florence,' I said, 'And Freddie, too, if it's not prejudicial to good order and discipline. And no, I'm not. But I was taught by a lady who studied under the great César Machin in Paris.' I watched to see if this was ringing any bells for Gaillet.

'Do you mean *maman*?' said Maurice, surprised. 'I've never heard of any César what d'you call 'im. Still she never spoke much about her past to us, if at all, really. I know she was a good cook though, but dad couldn't have rich food. Diabetes. It was what killed him in the end. Anyway, it put paid to anything fancy.'

'This is your mother, with the painting, Maurice?' Gaillet said casually.

'Yes,' said Maurice, equally casually, 'but no-one seems to know what happened to it, do they Florence?'

'You know a lot about art, Maurice says,' I said.

'A little,' Gaillet replied. 'My father, when he was alive, was something of an *amateur*, in English, that is to say an expert. He used to buy and sell at the auctions in Paris. He was one of the art advisers to the French government for the Paris exhibition in 1867.'

Rhoda re-entered, stage left. The men all rose.

'Goodness, 1867,' she said, completely revived, after Freddie's assault with the gherkins. 'Surely your father couldn't be that old?'

'My father's first wife died and he remarried my mother. He was sixty-three when I was born.'

'And that would be...?' Maurice began.

'1900,' Raoul Gaillet said. 'I am a child of the twentieth century, as you see.'

I was about to open my mouth and ask him if he had known of Adolphe de Marquise and Gaston Béranger and the others, but something held me back. I'm not really a believer in coincidence, I suppose. Rightly or wrongly I had already decided in my head that the appearance of Raoul Gaillet was no coincidence. If I asked him the question he might say he didn't know, or he didn't think so. Either way, I knew I wouldn't believe him. And if I asked the question he would know more about me than I knew about him. I had no doubt now that I was sitting opposite the man whose father had met Josephine Lucie in the house of assignation on her loveless afternoons off.

I kept my mouth shut.

None of us had really taken much notice of the raid. The sirens had gone of course, ages before, but the inner restaurant was in the bowels of the West End. Its thick hangings, and having no windows giving onto the street, must have deadened the noise to start with, that's all I can think. I heard the whistling of the stick of bombs. It sounded overhead. The restaurant fell instantly silent, save for the silvery rattle of a hundred sets of cutlery being laid down on their plates all at once. There were heavy explosions outside in the street, following one another in quick succession so that it seemed like a continuous roar.

In the restaurant there was a brilliant flash of blue and then darkness. Then crying and shouting, while underneath a steady murmuring, like the noise of a cinema audience spilling into the foyer at the end of the picture. Someone flicked a cigarette lighter.

'Put that bloody thing out, there may be gas.' It was my Freddie. Quite right, Freddie. You tell 'em.

There was a terrible smell. It wasn't town gas. I wanted to ask Freddie if it was the other kind of gas. The kind we had our masks for. But I couldn't make the words come. I tried to feel in the dark for ours under the table. Then I remembered Rhoda had had them removed to the cloakroom.

Rhoda. I tried to say her name but still no words came.

Then Freddie's voice in my ear, but somehow a long way off at the same time, as if he were speaking to me down a pipe. 'I think it's all right Florence Duck. Smells like a dud.'

Then there were wardens and lights, powerful lamps like one we have at the fire watch point, which is supposed not to ignite the gas if the mains have been broken. I could see that in the centre of the restaurant the ceiling had come down onto the tables and diners there. Some of them were hurt quite badly, one or two were still. People, blood and food, dust and plaster, table cloths and cutlery, all smeared and contorted like a horrible piece of stage scenery, while around them tables like ours, seemingly unscathed, save the diners and their food all covered in a fine white powder, as if we were all Pierrots and their Columbines watching like an audience.

We began to pick our way round towards the exit on the far side, ushered by the wardens' wavering beams of light. As we passed the mess in the middle Freddie said, 'I was right, a dud, and a bloody big one. Thank Christ for that.'

You could see the bomb, intact except where its casing had cracked open and a horrible yellowish muck oozing out of it. It was that causing the awful smell.

'Seen them like that in the City. Won't go off now,' said Freddie. You'd better get out though, Florrie Dee. I'll help some of these out.'

'We can all lend a hand, can't we?' said Rhoda. 'Tablecloths and napkins for bandages, that sort of thing.'

In the event and mercifully, as it happened, there were many more of us unhurt than wounded, too many for us to be anything other than in the way. Two men with ARP armbands were gathering up handbags and cigarette cases from the shattered tables while the dead and injured were being moved. That's a comfort, I thought, people will be missing those otherwise. But as we stood on the rubble and glass strewn pavement outside, gathering our wits and realising the danger had not passed, that the 'all clear' had yet to sound, I saw the same two men running off down Jermyn Street. Then the penny dropped. They'd been looting, probably weren't ARP at all, just had the armbands. You heard about it.

I went to say something to Freddie and the others, but then

we were being herded and shouted at by proper wardens, telling us to take cover. Our group set off at a smart trot towards Piccadilly Circus tube station. We reassembled in the ticket hall, by Swan and Edgar's basement display of winter coats.

'At least I didn't leave the fox in the cloakroom,' said Rhoda.

'We could try the Corner House again,' said Maurice doubtfully, 'The ballroom there is underground.'

'I think, if it's all the same to you, Florence and I will call it a night, if the tubes are still running. I've got a pass. What about you, Rhoda?'

'I've always got a pass, darling,' she said. 'Anyway look at us, we'd be lucky to be served at a pie and whelk stall in this state.'

'I'll see Rhoda home,' said Maurice. 'Might be lucky with a taxi. It's treble time in an alert.'

'I'm so sorry, Florence, Freddie,' said Raoul Gaillet. 'I had hoped to talk to you more about art and Paris, and to you, Rhoda, of course,' he added. 'You could give me a rest from my English, next time, Freddie. A little bird tells me your French is excellent.'

'I wouldn't say excellent,' said Freddie. 'Passable. I could get a cab to the Opera.'

'Only if you could find one first,' Gaillet laughed. 'But with such a rare talent for an Englishman, you must be wasted where you are. I had a proposal to make to you this evening, but for the moment, I suppose, it will have to wait.'

12

'What was it couldn't wait?' I asked.

It had seemed as if years had passed since Josephine Lucie and I had been safely closeted in the middle room. Even a lifetime, I suppose. Her fears about Mother's new treatment had been borne out. The attempt to collapse her lung with the hollow needle had not apparently been a success and then afterwards she contracted some kind of an infection, presumably as a result. In her already weak state of health this was, as I'd accidentally on purpose heard Grandmother saying to Pa in the best room, 'the last nail in my darling's coffin.'

'It's called artificial pneumothorax,' Leonard had told me, as if giving it a long winded scientific name would have made me feel better about it, 'I got my friend Mr Eggington at the library to find out about it for me. Apparently what they do is they get this long…'

'Yes thank you, Leonard,' Rhoda had come in late on his lesson. 'We already know how they do it, Grandmother told us. And anyway you shouldn't be discussing it with perfect strangers.'

I noticed the 'us' bit. Rhoda hadn't known whether to be angry with me for having found out about Mother's treatment, something even she might never have extracted from Pa, or angry with Grandmother for having told me. In the end she decided to act as if I had been merely the bearer of information intended for her all along. She'd even wanted it kept just between the two of us.

So I'd told Leonard.

But the upshot was that Pa and Grandmother actually went to the sanatorium together, frequently, several times in one week, in the early evening after Pa had finished teaching. That made it serious. After a brief interlude, Mother came home. Uncle Maurice fetched her in his car. We-who-should-not-be-told-anything, were encouraged by Pa to feel that this homecoming was a good thing and meant that she was getting better. Grandmother had said nothing as usual. She was spending all her time in Mother's room, even sleeping in the old wing chair at night. Pa had been evicted and was sharing with

Leonard, so that he started to smell of Players Weights too, although to Leonard's relief, he hadn't seemed to notice.

And then she died.

It was a ghastly anti-climax. Her illness had been there for as long as I could remember and I suppose I had always known that she would never get better, that she would die. That visit of mine to the sanatorium with Grandmother had sealed it as far as I was concerned. Mother was already dead there, they all were. The living weren't treated like that: those people working in the garden were ghosts. Collapsing her lung for it to heal and then plan to inflate it again had been a hopeless gesture of bodily resurrection. It was like Josephine Lucie's *Montgolfière*, doomed to fly once and never to come back.

I wondered what we were all supposed to do after the funeral tea was over. It was a quiet, short-lived affair. A couple of neighbours who had been at the church came in, so did one or two of Mother's old pupils. Maurice was there of course. Pa was barely civil to any of them, especially Maurice. I felt so sorry for both of them. I wanted Pa to squeeze my shoulder and say, 'All right, Florence, are you? All right?' I wanted him to offer poor Maurice his handkerchief and for Maurice to talk to him quietly in a corner and call him 'Charles, old man'. It would have been so nice. Instead Pa drank his tea down in one and disappeared upstairs and shut himself in his now lonely bedroom, leaving me to manage the neighbours, and Maurice to Rhoda. I don't know where Leonard was. Having a smoke down the bottom of the garden I shouldn't be surprised.

I wondered too where Grandmother had got to. She and Maurice were so close usually, I thought she would have been there for them to comfort one another. I had not seen her since the graveside. I'd come back with the others in Maurice's motor and assumed Grandmother had gone with Pa in the undertaker's limousine.

Needless to say nobody stayed long and when they'd gone I could see that if I didn't look slippy I'd be left to help Mrs Croucher, who had been brought in for the afternoon, with the clearing up. So when she wasn't looking I hopped upstairs to the middle room and tapped on the door, not really expecting Josephine Lucie to be there and surprised, therefore, to hear her say, 'Come in Florence.'

She still had her hat on and was holding the veil up with one hand so that she could sip from the small glass in her other.

'I was having a *Muscat de Beaume de Venise*, Florence. It is my last bottle I was keeping for an eventuality.'

She poured me a thimbleful. 'There are such eventualities when we have to choose the *Muscat*. You will know, Florence, when nothing else will do. When you have a great desire for it. Something of the rose, something of the flowers of orange, something of the evening sun. That's what Monsieur Adolphe used to say to me.'

'I thought we could only imagine this,' I said, sipping mine sparingly. 'Like the éclair fillings. I never knew you really had some.'

'After this, I think I shall not drink it again,' she said wistfully.

We were silent but not uncomfortable. Nothing more needed to be said out loud about Mother in the middle room. She had never belonged in it after Josephine Lucie had come to Coatwood. I couldn't recall ever having seen her there for more than a few minutes, after she and Pa had moved to the bedroom upstairs. I needed to come to terms with losing her, with the mundane emptiness left by tasks and chores that would never need doing again, the emptiness left by the final extinguishing of the family lie I had dutifully nurtured all my life: that one day she would get better. But I didn't need to deal with it in here, in the middle room. Neither did Josephine Lucie. In here she was a young woman with all her life and her children still to come . And so was I.

So I thought about the last time she and I had truly been together here. Before Pa had come brazening in and shut me out. I broke the silence.

'What was it couldn't wait?'

She looked at me, slightly quizzically at first and then with half a smile around her mouth, she said, 'What shall it be then, *ma chérie*? Shall we make the animal biscuits while we talk or shall we just finish the *Muscat*?'

'Mrs Croucher's in the kitchen,' I said. 'Wouldn't it look funny if we went down to use the range...now...today, I mean?'

'You are right, of course. And just for now I don't want to leave my middle room. Out there I will have to think about...everything. Where is Maurice? Has he gone, do you imagine? My poor Maurice.'

I said I thought Rhoda was looking after him.

'I suppose I should do that,' she said, not sounding as though she proposed to. 'Poor Maurice.'

'When the young man came running through the park with the message from the gallery, he said something couldn't wait. You told me that it was about a picture which wasn't one of the forgeries.'

'Ah yes, the man in the Cambrai lace.' She removed her hat and veil. 'Monsieur Adolphe went at once to the gallery by the Opera, as I said. When he came back he sent our own stable boy straight away to call the members of the *cabinet* and he told César and me to prepare for a dinner that evening, which we had not planned. César was very animated because it was unexpected. He had not been to meet the fish train from Boulogne, so the fish course would have to be from the fishmonger and it was already late in the day. He said the fish would not have a clear eye…'

'Yes, but what had happened about the picture?'

Josephine Lucie looked reprovingly at me. 'He had some quails, however, of which he removed the bones, stuffed with some foie gras and served with a sauce made with truffles and Madeira wine, *sauce perigueux*. It was an additional plate and made the tired fish more acceptable. They all came even though it was late to be asked. Monsieur Adolphe had said it was important and couldn't wait.'

I bit my tongue. There could be no short cuts. Like one of my Carnegie library heroines, the young, beautiful, carefree Josephine Lucie was there, a part of the private intimacy of that Paris dining room. If I spoke too soon its door might be closed against me. She was lighting the candles on the table, making the final tiny adjustments to the glasses and the cutlery. She was meeting their anxious murmured politenesses with a reassuring smile as they arrived in ones and twos, but no-one late, taking and giving the perfunctory embraces, trying to ignore the added affectionate squeeze from Louis Gaillet, his whiskery whisper in her ear. She was putting on the mailed glove and opening the oysters on the sideboard, carefully ladling the consommé, filleting the unhappy César Machin's fish with a spoon on the gently warming pewter platter, serving the quail reinforcements, two by two.

And as she did she was listening, soaking up the questions and their interrupted answers, the nervous laughter, the rising voices, Monsieur de Marquise's gestures of command bringing the swelling noise back under control.

The sudden appearance of the man in the Cambrai lace collar at the back door of the gallery by the Opera provided the *cabinet* diners with what, I now realise, was an intellectual problem of magnificently French proportions. The discussion at that dinner must, I imagine, have gone on far into the night. If Monsieur Adolphe had

had any doubts that it was truly the portrait of George Villiers, Duke of Buckingham, by Peter Paul Rubens, so long vanished from public sight that people said it may never have been painted at all, that was scarcely the point.

No, the point was that by one of those totally breathtaking coincidences that only happen in real life and in some of the books in the Carnegie Library, the *cabinet* diners now had two portraits of George Villiers: one almost certainly by Peter Paul Rubens and one by a man in a studio near the Luxembourg Gardens, which most people in the know would be prepared to swear was by Peter Paul Rubens. In point of fact, Monsieur Adolphe, it seems, had already sworn as much to several potential buyers individually, and to a very reputable auction house. True, the portraits were not identical to look at. But they were so nearly identical that to allow them onto the Paris art market side by side would have been, at the very least, to risk all the *cabinet's* carefully nurtured reputations, and quite likely to blow the lid off the whole enterprise.

'Monsieur Adolphe said it was a great shame that the two pictures were not more different,' Josephine Lucie said, 'because evidently they could have more easily been by the same painter. These old masters often produced more than one portrait for their *clients* but there were usually differences on purpose. Anyway, perhaps the forgery would be more apparent if it looked so much like the real one. There was a danger, as well, that they might both be declared to be false, that the sickness of the wrong one would infect the health of the true one, Monsieur Adolphe said.'

The *cabinet* members had gone over and over the ground, seeking for a solution to their dilemma. As she glided from diner to diner, replenishing their glasses, removing their plates, Josephine Lucie learned that the portrait painted by the man near the Luxembourg gardens had been based on two supposed copies of Rubens' missing original, a painting in oil and a chalk drawing, both of which had briefly passed through Paris as part of the wider artistic offerings surrounding the great exhibition in 1867. I could just hear the penny dropping as Monsieur de Marquise and his gallery owner saw them side by side, perhaps for the first time since they'd left Rubens' studio more than two hundred years earlier and realised no-one knew what had happened to the original. And how convenient for their forger to have them at his disposal for a whole month on public view. Who would have noticed him sketching away amongst the throng of Parisian art students all doing the same thing? And in any case, who would have remembered three years later?

'The big problem was the false one had already been shown to a number of possible buyers before it went to the auction, to make the competition stronger on the day. Otherwise it would have been possible to put the true painting in its place. But even then they had the problem of the *provenance*. Round and round they went, *chérie*, like true Frenchmen. If they had been certain that the true one was not true, I think they would have burned it there in the *cabinet* fireplace.'

'Why? Was it there? In the room?' I said, suddenly having to put another piece in my image of that evening.

'Both the pictures were, of course. It was normal at such dinners, I have told you. Monsieur Montel had brought them from the gallery.'

'The Opera gallery man?' I asked. 'I thought you couldn't remember his name.'

'I prefer not to recall his name,' she said, 'but it just came, when I wasn't thinking. It is probably the *Muscat*.'

This was so infuriating. Which way to go? Why didn't Josephine Lucie want to remember his name? Should I pursue that line or should we stick with the paintings? I knew what she could be like. If I encouraged her to go off on a sidetrack she could easily stay on it for ages and I'd probably get winkled out of the middle room by Pa before I'd heard the end of either story. I stayed with the paintings.

'Were they both good, then? Could you tell which one was which?'

'I know very little of such things, *ma chère*, but to me they both seemed sublime. And I would have said they had been painted by the same hand, yes.'

'They wouldn't have burned it really, would they?' I said. 'It was too beautiful to burn, surely.'

'Yes, Florence, I think you are right. For some of them, of course, it was a question of the money. I think Louis Gaillet and Papa Montel thought only of the money and for this reason they would not wish to destroy either of the paintings if there was another way. Gaston Béranger was not so much interested in the money. For him it was the danger of the auction room, pushing the price higher and higher like blowing in a balloon to see how big it will get before it explodes, *paf!* But for Monsieur Adolphe it was always, always, the beauty. For him it was something religious what they were doing, like a communion mass. To put the work of an *inconnu* from the *sixième arrondissement* in front of the elite of the Paris collectors and make them truly believe it was by a great master. Perhaps he thought that if they believed it hard enough, it would by a miracle become the thing it was not.'

'Like closing your eyes tight shut,' I said, 'and really wishing that something you know is impossible will have happened when you open them.'

'Exactly so, *chérie*, and as long as you keep your eyes shut that thing can still be possible. It is only when you open them that it fails. Monsieur Adolphe made them all keep their eyes shut forever and so the miracle could always be going to happen.

'So what became of the paintings in the end?' I asked.

Whoops! Josephine Lucie gave me a reproachful look.'There is no end yet, Florence. I have never told this story to anyone. Not to Maurice, not to Charlotte, not even to my husband, your grandfather, Edward Burnell. It must be told, course by course, like one of César Machin's great dinners, so that at the end you can remember every mouthful.'

This was all very well I thought, but even he had occasionally served up stale fish. Still, I could see that she was not to be hurried and I would have to bide my soul in patience, as Mother used to say.

Whatever Josephine Lucie might have liked to believe about Monsieur Adolphe's motives, there was no way the opportunity either painting provided for profit was going to be wasted, if the members of the *cabinet* had any kind of a choice. They had concocted a perfectly good provenance for the forgery, one which would enable it to be passed off as 'almost certainly Rubens' original portrait by his own hand'. The last purported public appearance of the painting had taken place in a sale in London nearly a hundred years before and it had not been heard of since. In fact, Josephine Lucie said, the description of the painting at that sale was so poor that it couldn't be identified for certain, even then. How easy for the *cabinet* to invent a home for it with a private family in Belgium, passed on with the estate several times after the death of the original purchaser, eventually fetching up a generation or two later as part of a job lot of household goods handed over to creditors, who had no idea of its worth until it came to the attention of Monsieur Adolphe de Marquise. No, passing up the opportunity to make so much money from two almost identical paintings was not an option.

'Gaston Béranger said it could be done. They would have to involve someone at the sale house, but for so much money he did not think this would be a problem. He would not have to know about the existence of the true painting and he would not have to know the painting he was selling was a forgery. Gaston's eyes were shining, he was so animated when he imagined himself already being in the sale room while it was happening and while it was so dangerous. He could hardly wait for the day to dawn.'

13

'I can hardly wait to begin, Florence Duck, I really can't.' I could almost reach out and touch Freddie down the phone, his excitement made him sound so alive.

'Well at least you won't be running around on the roof of the Bank of England during the air raids,' I said. 'And you're going to get a couple of stripes out of it, which will help pay the rent, won't it? It might even shut Rhoda up for two minutes.'

'What's Rhoda got to do with it?' said Freddie, 'Why do you have to bring Rhoda into it? No, for the first time in this damn war I feel I'm doing something useful, something that most of them couldn't do. He must have a lot of clout, that chap Gaillet. It's been hardly any time at all has it? He must have asked for me almost immediately. In fact, I wonder whether perhaps he'd already done it before we all met. It was very odd, wasn't it, the way the officer let me go that night and gave me an overnighter into the bargain.'

Yes, and nearly got us all killed, I thought. Still at least we'd had the main course. It would have been a shame if that bomb had fallen through the ceiling while we were still on the soup, even if it had been consommé. Maurice had asked for the devilled kidneys, but even his luck had run out there. All gone, if they'd ever been on in the first place. And then just a couple of days later Freddie gets marched in to see his commanding officer and asked, well told really, to transfer to the Free French headquarters in Carlton Gardens, as Captain Gaillet's clerical orderly and general interpreter. It was just off Pall Mall, very posh. Freddie was so taken aback it must have shown on his face, and the officer said they would throw in corporal's stripes into the bargain.

It was nearly two weeks before I saw Freddie in the flesh. The air raids seemed to have slackened a bit, although it might just have been our wishful thinking. People said it was because the evenings were drawing out. Whatever it was, Freddie managed to get home at a reasonably respectable hour and we sat down together at the kitchen table to a fairly awful meal involving the inevitable spam, a far cry from the last one we'd had in Jermyn Street, but a lot less eventful.

Freddie did his usual thing of carrying on the conversation he'd been having with himself, as if we hadn't been apart at all and I'd been participating in it all the time.

'Evidently they didn't just want any old interpreter – not that I'm not half bad, Florence Duck, and getting better all the time chatting to the French, especially the girls from the *Corps Féminin*.' He gave me a sideways look. 'They're like the ATS. They're all billeted over in Eaton Square, and they don't seem to get out much. I think it's a bit like boarding school for them. For one thing they've none of them got any money. Most of them came out of France just with the clothes they stood up in.'

I wasn't going to let him provoke me. He just wanted to make me a bit jealous so that I would pounce all over him and save him the effort. I can read Freddie like a book sometimes.

'What else do they want you for then?' I said, deliberately with a mouthful of spam so as to sound as least like I imagined a girl from the *Corps Féminin* would sound.

'I've to liaise with the French finance officer and our lot, government departments and so on, over the French's pay and rations basically. Well a bit more than that. Who pays their bills and where to. That sort of thing. Keep an eye on the procedures and the paperwork in French and English. Most of their correspondence is in French and nearly all of ours to them is in English, needless to say. Both lots being bloody minded I should think. Neither of them want to let themselves be hoodwinked by the other because they don't speak the lingo.'

'So the finance officer, that's Captain Gaillet is it?' I said.

'Well he's part of it although he's not the top man, but I have quite a lot to do with him and the girls who work for him.'

Bloody French ATS again.

'How is he now that you're actually serving under him? Is he as charming as ever?' I asked. 'Is he likely to take us all out to dinner again?'

'Well it's all very relaxed at Carlton Gardens, I must say. I wouldn't put it past him. He asked after you, by the way. Said "Had you had any more thoughts about your grandmother's picture?" What's that all about, Florence Duck? It keeps getting mentioned doesn't it? Wasn't Maurice on about it too?'

A very odd thought flitted across my mind.

'Have you seen anything of Maurice, Freddie? Isn't he helping the Free French with their office furniture and things? That's how he knows Gaillet isn't it? Do you think Maurice can have had anything to do with your getting this job?'

'Maurice? I shouldn't think so for one minute. He's not in the army or anything and he doesn't look much like a civil servant does he?' Freddie laughed.

'So do you see anything of him at…at Carlton Gardens?' I persisted.

'Yes, as a matter of fact. He's been in to see Gaillet once. It was about the typewriters.'

'What about the typewriters?'

'Well we haven't got enough of them and, of course, they're like gold dust just now. Firms like Remington and Imperial have all gone over to war work. Maurice said he thought he could get hold of some but they would have to come from somewhere by ship and would take a long time even assuming they made it at all. North Africa or Lisbon he said.'

'What on earth is he doing getting typewriters from places like that?' I said. 'It doesn't sound that important for the war effort, does it? Shouldn't the ships be bringing aeroplane parts or tins of spam or something?'

'The French want typewriters with accents.'

'French accents? Can't they just ignore the aitches? That'd make them sound a bit French.'

Freddie looked at me witheringly. 'You're so sharp you'll cut yourself one of these days. You know perfectly well what I mean: E acute, A grave and C cedilla. They hate having to put them in by hand in ink.'

'It was funny though, Freddie. French typewriters that drop their aitches. Anyway, what does all this make Maurice, then? Is he a crook, or is he official? Perhaps he's an official crook. Getting typewriters off the back of a lorry is one thing, but getting them off the back of a ship from Lisbon sounds a bit serious.'

Freddie looked thoughtful. 'I suppose you're right, Florence Duck, when you think about it. Perhaps he is a civil servant after all. Everyone is pussyfooting around the Free French, trying not to give them too much rope, especially while there's still a French government in France with an embassy here. That's why we're only lending them nonentities like me to help them out. We're even arguing about who should pay their gas, light and coke bills, or whether we should, and get the money back when the war's over. I've seen the letters.'

'So Maurice could be a nonentity too, you think? Helping out without making it too official.'

'Could be, Florrie Dee, could be,' Freddie said. 'He's very thick with Gaillet. Well we know that don't we? They're two of a kind. Smooth.'

'Well, Maurice always was adorable. But I'm not sure Gaillet is. And they're both after Josephine Lucie's picture,' I said. And wished I hadn't.

Freddie looked at me sharply. 'You said that as though there is a painting,' he said. 'When it's been mentioned before you've never even hinted that you know anything about it. Have you ever seen it, then?'

Do you know? I really hesitated then. This was the man I loved beyond anything, the man I feared for night and day during the raids, the man I secretly and guiltily thanked God for not having sent him to France before Dunkirk, thanked God for having sent Leonard and not him to Singapore, if anyone of mine had to go. Even so, I was really reluctant to share Josephine Lucie with him. It was as if he, too, had suddenly knocked on the door of the middle room, like Pa, and barged in without even waiting to be asked.

I felt awful. I knew I couldn't tell him a lie. I knew I shouldn't keep secrets from him when he asked me. But I just didn't want to be asked – not yet. Josephine Lucie and I had too much remembering to do, too much straightening out. Just the two of us and nobody else. Not Freddie, not Maurice, and not Raoul Gaillet. Especially not him.

'Well I've never seen it,' I said, and paused to see what would happen next.

'So…it exists but you've never seen it?'

'What is this, Freddie? The Gestapo?'

'I'm not pulling your finger nails out, Florrie Dee, but it could be arranged. Is there a blessed painting or not?'

'There might be.'

'That's it,' said Freddie. 'Finger nails first, then toes.'

'Grandmother told me about it, but I never saw it at Coatwood.'

Freddie ran his knife round his plate to pick up the last

vestiges of spam and cabbage, carefully scraped it on the back of his fork and put it in his mouth.

'Why are you being evasive, Florence? And don't say you're not.' he said.

This was getting serious.

'Look, my darling,' I said, 'it's just one of those family stories. If there ever was a painting, it's disappeared. So Raoul Gaillet and Maurice can eat their hearts out. They're not going to come up with it now, however hard they try.'

'So what's the family story? It was valuable was it, this picture that may or may not have existed?'

I actually wished for the sirens to go, I really did.

'She said it was a bloody Rubens,' I blurted, 'but it might have been a forgery.'

'A Rubens?' said Freddie 'Good grief!'

'Probably a forgery, though, Freddie.'

'Even so, Florrie Dee, even so. There's at least two chaps think it's worth finding. It's not just in the family, is it? Gaillet knows about it. I mean, where does he get in on the act?'

This couldn't go on.

'Stop it, Freddie,' I said. 'This is getting ridiculous. We're talking about something no-one has ever seen and probably doesn't even exist. You know what families are like, making things up and passing them on as gospel. It's just like Pa's story about the King and the cigar.'

'The King and the cigar? What cigar?'

'Aren't you supposed to say "What King"?'

'You're not going to tell me about this picture are you, Florrie Dee?'

'There's nothing to tell,' I said.

It was a blooming lie. I felt really, really dishonest. I stood up from the table and pulled my dress up to my waist. I reached for his hand and put it inside my knickers. 'Come on,' I said, 'don't you know there's a war on?'

14

'It felt like this when the war was on, in Paris you understand, when we called the Germans the Prussians, *chérie,* and I was a young woman. We were closed in like this.'

At last! At last! Josephine Lucie had arrived at the rat. And just as I was getting bound up with the man in the lace collar. I couldn't bear it. The merest mention of the rat now and we could be wandering off the point for days.

I'd been concentrating on peeling and slicing pears under her watchful eye. We were making *tarte aux poires* with fruit from the garden at Coatwood which were particularly good that year.

'Those that are a little too soft to slice, Florence, we will use for the *compote* to line the *flan.* If you separate them from the others we can take them to the kitchen to cook while we make the pastry.'

I'd told her Leonard was in the kitchen. 'He's doing his homework, and Rhoda's around somewhere.' It was automatic. Neither of us wanted to share the separateness nor the confidences of the middle room with anyone else. Mostly it was accepted that Grandmother and I spent more and more time here since Mother's death. Pa kept himself to himself as much as he could, too. It was the school holidays, so rather than be indoors he would take himself down to the bottom of the garden and 'do' his vegetable patch or if it was wet he would 'do' his little greenhouse or sharpen things in the shed. He had a grinding wheel he'd put together operated with the treadle of an old sewing machine. This all meant that Leonard had to go further afield with his Players Weights, and Rhoda spent as much time as she could being 'out' with her classy girlfriends. So all-in-all, apart from set mealtimes, we tended to wander round one another, never far away but hardly ever touching, like those magnets that push each other away when they get too close.

Of course, Leonard would be dismissive of my being closeted with Grandmother in the middle room. 'Going up for a cookery lesson?' he would say disparagingly, but you could tell by the way he always said it like that, he wanted to know if there was more going on, if he was missing something. After that time when he discovered we'd been on the wrong side at the Battle of Waterloo, Leonard was rather wary of his grandmother and tended to keep his distance in case she accidentally revealed some other alarming bits of family background. He once asked me what her name had been before it was Burnell.

'You don't think she might have been Jewish, do you Florence? I suppose the French do have Jewish people,' he said.

'Do you want me to ask her?' I inquired sweetly.

'Good heavens, no,' he said hastily.

So the mere possibility of the kitchen being occupied by one or other of the rest of the family when we two wanted to use it was enough to put Josephine Lucie out of countenance.

'Oh it is too bad!' she said testily. 'Go and listen over the banisters and see if they are still there. This pastry will spoil and so will the pears if we do not cook them at once.'

It didn't even cross our minds to go and use the range if Leonard and Rhoda were there. It just didn't work that way. Josephine Lucie and I were not to be shared at these times and nor was the *tarte aux poires*. It almost wasn't to be eaten at all. It was to be prepared. And its preparation, like all the other dishes Josephine Lucie showed me or simply described, was to transport her to Paris and Monsieur de Marquise's *grand hôtel* in the *dix-septième*, to a time when her life was still her own to shape.

I listened outside on the landing. The kitchen and breakfast room were still in enemy hands – there was nothing for it but to hide away in the middle room and watch the pears go brown. I didn't think it at all extraordinary that Josephine Lucie should be transported in her mind back to a Paris under siege, merely by the unwelcome presence of Leonard downstairs, nor that she should think of him as a Prussian.

'This is how it felt in Paris later, when we were closed in by them,' she said. 'But not at first when the war was far away, on the border at Metz and Sedan, a great adventure. It was a brilliant summer, very hot, and the boulevards full of beautiful uniforms which matched the blue sky. We could still leave the city, you know, on Sundays, for the country. Augustin and I went on the little local train to have lunch at the *Cabaret des Noctambules* even though it was more expensive on Sunday. They had a summer house there in the garden. They brought us everything to prepare our own *vinaigrette* for the salad, different oils, different vinegars, some of wine, some of fruits, raw eggs, cold boiled eggs to make a paste with the yolk, garlic, just to flavour the basin, you understand, and then to discard…'

'Augustin?' I interrupted her flow of ingredients, risking one of her disapproving looks, 'Who was Augustin?'

'He was my love, *chérie*. He was my love.'

'What about the other one…the older one? Wasn't he your…your love too?'

'Louis Gaillet? No, I told you Florence, he was not my sweetheart. He was too old, and he was married. He just wished to go to bed with me in the afternoon because his wife was sick.'

I wanted to ask her what the difference was between Augustin's love and Louis Gaillet's. But then, I only had a hazy idea about the whole thing myself. Bed did not feature at the Carnegie library. In any case, Josephine Lucie had a way of saying some things that meant they simply had to be accepted without further question because that was the answer.

'Then suddenly it all changed,' she said. 'The news from Metz and Sedan was terrible. Many, many Frenchmen killed or taken prisoner, even the Emperor. Soldiers returning to Paris, people we knew, with terrible wounds and so fatigued. The sights were too horrible and in our hearts, Florence, it was as if those beautiful summer skies had been filled with black clouds.'

The marble clock on her mantel piece struck the first quarter. All thoughts of love and lovers fled. It was as if Josephine Lucie had made it sound the single, deep chime, and into the silence left behind as the note faded away, memories had come flooding to fill it. Not half forgotten, hazy recollections, but fresh, harsh pictures full of smell and livid colours, still wet.

'After that we began to be closed in. Paris began to look very different. The *places* began to look like camps, full of tents and soldiers, everywhere trees were cut down. Why do they do that, I wonder, cut all the trees down? Later, of course, in the winter we needed them to burn because there was no coal. But we never saw them then, when we needed them. It was strange, you know, Florence, being a prisoner in a city when there is a war. In all that time in Paris I never saw a Prussian. I saw more Prussians in Paris at the Great Exhibition than I saw during the war. Still, they were all around us. Sometimes there were battles outside the city in the *environs*. Everyone is sure there is going to be a French victory and the war is going to be over. César Machin tells me there is going to be a battle outside the city at Châtillon because it is a high place and, of course, very important.' She paused for a moment. 'Do you understand, *ma chère?*'

I did. It was the kind of thing Leonard was always going on about. It was obvious then he was destined for the regular army.

'Was your…your sweetheart, was he a soldier, was he fighting?' I asked, nudging her in a more promising direction.

'Augustin? Not at that time, no I don't think so. He had to be registered for the *garde civile*, the National Guard, all the young men had to if they were not already in the army. But I know they did not send the guard to Châtillon because Augustin came to the *hôtel* that day in his uniform and said we should go up to Montparnasse to salute the soldiers back from their victory. Monsieur Adolphe said we should all go because now it was important to do something to encourage the soldiers. So we took a *fiacre* over the river to Montparnasse. Even César Machin came. It was a very strange party. A *folie* of war.'

'But the war did not end then?' This much I had grasped.

'No. There was no victory. On the contrary, the soldiers we saw this day in Montparnasse, many had run away. Frenchmen had run away, Florence. Imagine! We just could not understand it. And things became worse, much worse, for us all in Paris.'

'Couldn't you try to get away? Did people who weren't in the army have to stay? Mothers? Children?'

'Well yes, after a while everyone had to stay, even the women and children. The Prussians would not let anyone go after they had totally encircled the city. That was the problem about the painting, of course. Monsieur was fearful for it and it had to have an escape.'

What with the appearance of the obviously delicious Augustin on the scene, with his salad dressing in the cabaret garden, and his beautifully fitting blue and red uniform of the Paris National Guard, I had, for the moment, forgotten the man in the Cambrai lace. We were back on his track without too much effort, but now there was a sweetheart to think about, to say nothing of the rat.

Josephine Lucie alone had served at the private dinners which inevitably followed, as the *cabinet* argued and planned how to dispose of the paintings. Beyond the conspirators themselves, only she was privy to the discussions. Even César Machin remained apart from them, excluded in his kitchen by the need to practise his culinary skills as never before. It was as if, as the plot thickened, so did the sauces, and the dinners became more and more elaborate. I nearly despaired. For one moment I thought Josephine Lucie was going to go through each menu, course by course.

She told me that the auction in which the forged Rubens had been entered took place a few months before the outbreak of the war. Given its history it had excited a good deal of interest. Monsieur de Marquise became considerably excited and nervous, however, when it became apparent that the Louvre was thinking of bidding, and he began to wonder whether the *cabinet* had bitten off more than it could chew. It would have been very tempting to have one of their Luxembourg Gardens forgeries on permanent public display in the Louvre. I suppose Monsieur Adolphe would have thought it would soak up authenticity simply by hanging alongside genuine articles. However, Louis Gaillet and Papa Montel convinced him to be cautious.

They said it was too dangerous to have the Louvre buying the picture. Their professors would be meticulous in making sure the *provenance* was verified even though the *cabinet* were all convinced the quality of the work in the painting itself would easily stand examination. No, they said, the painting had to be sold to a private individual and the auction had to be fixed to ensure this happened.

Moreover, they needed to be able to sell the second painting, the genuine Rubens, without causing alarm bells to ring in the Paris art world. What they really wanted to do was sell the forgery, not at auction, but privately through the gallery. But it was getting very late to withdraw it without provoking difficult questions.

'One evening, just as time was beginning to run out, Papa Montel announced to the others that he had been approached by a new collector, a wealthy mine owner, with more money than knowledge, and who was desperate to have the painting. "He is so determined, I think it has affected his mind – so much that I think he would buy the painting even if he thought it was stolen," he said. "Then," said Monsieur, suddenly very animated, "he is just the man we need."

I had no doubt Josephine Lucie was back at that table and the years had slipped away again for her. As she recalled it, I could see the effect of Monsieur de Marquise's lightning bolt on his fellow diners: César Machin's *cordon bleu* offering growing cold on their temporarily forgotten plates, the burgundy untasted in their neglected glasses.

Monsieur Adolphe proposed they should put it about that the owner was unaware of the painting's worth, and had almost forgotten of its existence. Perhaps it was in a room where no-one went very often, perhaps this owner was an invalid and confined to bed. Now, said Monsieur, let us suppose he has a nephew who is in need of money. He has been quietly selling his uncle's things, a few spoons here, some porcelain there, which he takes when he visits. It is easy. So one day he becomes more ambitious. He takes the painting. He may even replace it with some daub from the cellar to cover the patch where the wallpaper has not faded. He sells it to a country dealer. Of course, Monsieur Adolphe says, when eventually the painting's true character has been realised by our *cabinet* in Paris, we are obliged to reconstruct its history. We work back and discover that the nephew who sold it was not the true owner.

'What are we to do?' he asks. 'If the painting becomes famous, if it is purchased by the Louvre, no less, the original theft must become apparent. The painting will have to be returned, and we all stand to lose a great deal of money as well as our reputations. All this we tell to Emile Montel's desperate client.'

'So,' says Gaston Béranger, who loves the danger of the sale room, 'he pleads to buy the painting from us now, knowing that he must keep quiet about it afterwards except perhaps to close friends, at least until the invalid uncle drops off his perch, and then we "ghost" it at the auction and the Louvre goes away empty handed.'

Josephine Lucie didn't actually say 'ghost it'. She called them *acheteurs imaginaires*, imaginary buyers, but I can just see Gaston Béranger calling it ghosting. I always had a soft spot for Gaston Béranger in Josephine Lucie's plot. For me he had nerves of steel and a twinkle in his eye. His hair would be dark and beautifully cut, he would wear black silk brocade to the sale rooms and carry a silver topped cane with hidden steel inside it, like his nerves. I asked her once what he had been like but she just said, 'Béranger? He was quite ordinary, a small man. He had a poor moustache, but he had pretty hands. He could not drink champagne, I remember that. It was not good for his digestion.' I didn't believe a word of it. She must have been confusing him with someone else.

Anyway, that's how it was done. Josephine Lucie was hazy about the detail because, of course, she didn't actually go to the sale.

'But Augustin went and he told me. His father must have paid the *commissaire priseur*, you know Florence, the one who calls out the money and bangs a hammer when it is enough.'

'Auctioneer, I think,'

'Yes, that one. He pretended there were people making the money go higher and higher…'

'Bidding?'

'…exactly so, but they were imaginary. He pretends he can see them bidding, but they are not. I don't know how. When I sold some of your Grandfather Edward Burnell's furniture, everybody had to shout out or wave their *catalogue*, so I don't know how it could be done with imaginary people, but Augustin said it was incredible. The men from the Louvre had no chance. Augustin had been told to sit behind them. He could tell by their distracted air that they did not have the authority to bid higher. Perhaps if there had been the telephone then, it would have been different, I don't know.'

'What did Augustin's father have to do with it? You said he must have paid the auctioneer?'

'But of course, *ma chère,* Augustin's father was Emile Montel, Papa Montel who had the gallery.'

A huge penny dropped.

I never did ask Josephine Lucie whether Augustin Montel or his father knew about her afternoons with Louis Gaillet. I preferred to tell myself that all that had finished when the delicious Augustin had come into her life.

I took the pears down and shared them with Leonard. 'Do you know anything about auctions, Leonard?' I asked.

'Auctions? What are you and the old girl up to up there?'

'Nothing. Do you have to shout out your bids, or put your hand up, or what?'

'Not at somewhere like Christie's you don't. You have to be jolly careful you don't scratch your nose if it's itching in case you find you've bought an old master for hundreds of thousands. The auctioneers are trained not to let on whose bidding against whom.'

'So as far as everyone else is concerned, they might not exist at all if you can't see them doing it…bidding.'

'Yes…no,' said Leonard puzzled. 'Bidders who don't exist? What would be the point of that?'

15

'What would be the point of that, Freddie?' I said.

'I don't want to think about it,' Freddie said. 'There's a bloody war on and these Free French are supposed to be heroes and all that, and all I can think about Gaillet is that he may be a bastard. He seemed such a nice chap: they all are at Carlton Gardens. Even Seedy Gee gives me a kind of grimace when I salute.'

I was seeing a fair bit of Freddie in the evenings now, provided the tubes were running, which you couldn't always guarantee of course. The air raids were still a worry but there was no doubt they had tailed off compared with what they'd been like last year and through the winter. The Blitz, people were calling it, although now they tended to talk about those raids that came night after night after night as if that was a thing of the past. It didn't stop me worrying myself sick about Freddie until I had him safe home indoors. The worst thing was if I was expecting him home and he got stuck down in the tube and couldn't get to a phone that was working, or get to one at all, come to that. On my birthday there was a heavy raid on and he actually managed to find a taxi prepared to bring him up to north London. I heard it draw up and opened the front door to see who it was, hoping it would be Freddie and not some bearer of bad tidings. He and the taxi driver were having a right old set to. Shouting, not fisticuffs, although I thought it might come to that. Eventually the taxi drove off and when Freddie came in he said, 'Would you believe it? He agreed to bring me home for ten bob which is all I've got until pay day, and when I gave it to him he called me all kinds of bits of your anatomy and mine because I hadn't given him a tip as well.'

I said I supposed it was because he'd driven Freddie through an air raid at considerable risk to both their lives and limbs, but he just said, 'that's not the point.'

So while I couldn't actually say he was getting home from the office every evening at six o'clock, it did sometimes feel like that. And I suppose I had a happier time than the girls whose chaps were away in the desert. Except I had to worry about him every time he didn't come home, and they only had to worry in general. Freddie had made it safely this evening. As usual he was halfway through telling me all about it hardly before he'd taken his key out of the door.

'Gaillet wants me to stop notifying the Red Cross about the French who are dying out at White City... shush... You're not supposed to know about that. Them dying I mean, not White City. Everyone in Shepherds Bush and miles around must know about the French camp at White City by now. And the one at Crystal Palace. Anyway...' he paused just long enough to give me a kiss and a squeeze, 'I'm to stop their money, obviously, but Gaillet has told me not to put all the dockets through to the Red Cross anymore.'

'What would be the point of that?' I asked him again when I'd recovered my breath. 'Why does that make him a bastard?'

'Well it means their next of kin in France won't get to know that they've died, which I think is heartless. Gaillet says it's for security reasons. They don't send relatives messages when they're alive, so why should they when they're dead? Might let the enemy do a head count. Quite a lot are dying of wounds they got on the beaches before the evacuation, I know. But even so...'

'Isn't that the sort of thing they worry about, though? Not giving things like that away,' I said.

'Yes, but Gaillet isn't doing it for all of them who die, just some of them.'

'Some of them?'

'To cause confusion about the numbers, apparently. Obviously you'd expect some to die, so the Red Cross would have to be told something. I have a funny feeling about it that's all.'

'Well are you going to talk to him... someone about it?' I said.

'I don't know, Floss. I'm not there to rock the boat. Maybe he's right about the security thing. And anyway, who would I tell?'

'Who's this Seedy Gee chap? Perhaps you could tell him, unless he's too seedy that is.'

Freddie hooted. 'Seedy Gee is the General, Cheer-up Charlie, Charles de Gaulle. I call him that just to myself. It's because he initials everything "CdeG", you see.'

He became thoughtful again. 'No, I can't tell anyone, but I *am* going to have another good look at the ones Gaillet's said "No further action". Why's he picking them and not others, I wonder?'

'Have the typewriters arrived from Lisbon?' I asked. 'You know, the ones with the French accents.'

As far as Freddie knew they were still on their way. 'But they could be at the bottom of the Bay of Biscay, of course. Torpedoed. We wouldn't get to know about that, would we?'

'I bet Maurice would get to know. How is my adorable uncle? Have you seen him lately?'

As soon as I mentioned Maurice's name I knew I shouldn't have done. Too late: Freddie remembered the painting.

'Good old Maurice,' he said. 'I haven't seen him lately. Haven't had a chance to mention the Rubens to him. Haven't mentioned it to Gaillet either, come to that.'

I was aghast. 'Freddie you haven't…you wouldn't, would you?'

He laughed. 'Of course not, Florence Duck. Especially not Gaillet, now that I think he might be a bit of a shit. They're a right pair, Gaillet and your uncle Maurice. Telling them where they might lay their hands on a valuable Rubens would be like asking a couple of foxes to keep an eye on the hen house.'

'You don't know that. You've really got a down on them both all of a sudden. You've no reason to suppose that Louis Gaillet is anything other than a thoroughly charming French officer and gentleman. There's probably a perfectly sound reason why he doesn't need to talk to the Red Cross.'

'I thought his name was Raoul,' said Freddie. 'Why did you call him Louis?'

I know I blushed. I could feel it all the way down to my waist. I muttered something about all Frenchmen being Louis like all Germans are Fritz. It wasn't very convincing, because I wouldn't normally call foreigners names anyway.

Freddie looked at me thoughtfully. 'Stop prevaricating, Florence. You were really panicking just then when you thought I might have mentioned it to them. You know where it is, this painting, don't you? And Gaillet, what does he know? Does he really know anything? I've only heard him mention your grandmother's painting in passing, but as usual, Florence, you change the subject very skillfully whenever the conversation gets round to it.'

This couldn't go on. I was going to have to share at least some of Josephine Lucie's story with him. I couldn't believe I didn't want to tell him the whole thing from start to finish. Well, that's not strictly true. To be honest, I knew that Freddie would want to take the bones out of it, like a kipper. It would be like a Dorothy Sayers whodunit to him and Freddie always has to work out who did do it by the beginning of chapter two. It's the same with crosswords. He'll worry away at an obstinate clue off and on all day if necessary. Sometimes when he hasn't managed to get it at all he won't even let me look up the answer when the paper comes the next morning, until he's had another worry at it. He just can't bear to have me know the answer before he's solved it himself. It's as if it's his personal property. Mind you, I have enormous fun snatching the paper from the letter box first and making him think I know the answer. As I never do the difficult crossword, I wouldn't have the faintest idea which clue was which anyway, but Freddie can never be sure.

'As far as I know,' I said, picking a path that might prove to be the shortest way out of the wood, 'the painting never came to England. It's still in France. So however much Messrs Burnell and Gaillet ferret around for it, in the circumstances that would seem to be that. Not much chance of either of them going to look for it.'

'Whoa, hang on!' said Freddie. 'What do you mean, still in France? This Rubens is from your Grandmother's dim and distant past then, is it?'

'Yes,' I said. 'Apparently it was in a house in Paris where she worked when she was a young woman. It was all mixed up with the siege and the Prussians and had to be hidden somewhere.'

I know what I really wanted to say to him next. There, now leave it alone Freddie, I'm not ready to tell you any more, especially with a Gaillet on the loose. Just accept that it's an old story and we may never get to the bottom of it, please.

'So, your grandmother. Did she ever say where it was hidden? Somewhere in Paris? In this house where she worked?'

Not my grandmother, silly, I wanted to shout. Josephine Lucie. My grandmother was a tired old lady who made vegetable soup and braised lamb's liver for my mother and toiled across Middlesex on two buses and a tram to visit her at the dreadful sanatorium, with its army of dying gardeners. Not her. Josephine Lucie — a ravishing *demi-mondaine*, who made love in the afternoon and once served rat prepared by the great César Machin.

16

'I served rat to them in the *cabinet,* you know Florence. César Machin prepared it of course, so that none of them would really tell what it was. But I think they all suspected something: it was so good, too good, and by then there was very little meat left in Paris of *qualité.*'

It had finally come then. Leonard's suspected rat, the biscuit rat of my imagination, my long awaited rat, Josephine Lucie's tantalising rat. *The* rat.

I don't know what suddenly prompted her to give it life. I hadn't spoken of it for a long time. Not since she had decided to stop being Grandmother during our afternoons together and had chosen to become Josephine Lucie again. She had never spoken of a rat and for all I knew it might never have existed outside Leonard's fervent wish, the time he first told me about the siege of Paris. It had become a bit of a superstition with me, like holding my breath until I reached the end of our road, so that something I wanted to happen, might. I had decided very early on that if I raised the rat before Josephine Lucie did, it would risk getting in the way of her telling the rest of her story. But after a while when neither of us had mentioned it I began almost to wish the rat, if there was one, might never be broached, in case its arrival revealed our bond in the middle room to be too fragile and doomed to die.

I think we'd been talking about truffles – *truffes* Josephine Lucie called them. She was telling me the difference between white ones which should only be eaten raw and the black ones, which were far superior, would never ever be obtainable in the Broadway, and should be cooked with pork fat even if they were to be served with chicken. Maybe it was the truffles or the chicken that put her in mind of the rat, I don't know, but here it was at long last and I could safely let my breath out again, as she had spoken of it first.

'Did you have some yourself?'

Josephine Lucie nodded briefly.

'What must it have been like?' I asked, and then, I don't know what possessed me, 'Did Mother know you'd eaten rat?'

She looked at me, startled, almost panic stricken. 'That is just what foolish old *paysans* like my family in Orgelets believe. I have never heard anyone say it here. Who has said it to you? That Rhoda? No, Leonard, I make sure it is Leonard. Anyway Maurice has nothing. He is in good health.'

I was flabbergasted at her outburst. For the first time in the middle room since that time Pa had barged in on us she had let Josephine Lucie be put aside by Grandmother. I think she, too, realised the enormity of what she had done. The look on my face must have instantly shown that whatever it was she thought I was saying was entirely unintentional. I naturally thought my worst fears about the arrival of the rat had come true.

But she softened. Josephine Lucie returned. 'It is an old *canard*, Florence. How could you know of it, of course? They believe that eating the rat can bring *malaises* into the family. Not just to those who do it, but somehow it will come down to the children and their children.'

'You mean things like TB that mother had?'

'Especially that, but other things as well. Things that babies have wrong with them when they are born. They used to say in Orgelets that these things happened to the families who travelled on the *chalands* along the Oise and the Sambre, the long boats, you know, with horses to pull them. People said they suffered from the consumption because they used to eat the rats who lived on the boats with them. The *chalands* carried grain and often wine in barrels to the port at Anvers, so I have no doubt the rats were well fattened and with a good taste. The *malaises*, I am certain, came because there were too many in the families on those *chalands*, so many children in such a small space, and the babies who died or became sick in the head, I think that was because the *chaland* families all married themselves, you know, *ma chère*. Farmers know better. They bring the bull from over the hill for their cows.'

She fell silent. I didn't say anything either. Josephine Lucie had never strayed back to her roots along the rivers and canals between Cambrai and the Belgian border. It was the place of her girlhood she had turned her back on when she had parted for Paris. She had left behind a time and a place where her life had been at the beck and call of others, I suppose. A situation which must not have recurred until she met Edward Burnell. I was just taken aback at the mention of it. It felt like an intrusion that had been my fault but which nevertherless had been waiting just below the surface to come out.

'Come, Florence,' she said at last, 'we must not be miserable at the thought of Charlotte. Not here in our room.'

We both knew that was not it at all, but it broke the tension and put us back firmly in the middle room for which we were both grateful.

'So what was it like? Horrid I should imagine.'

'*Au contraire, ma chérie*, it was very delicate. The best thing, perhaps, I had tasted for some weeks, not since we had one of Monsieur Adolphe's horses.'

'A *chose de qualité* then? Not something you could get in the Broadway.'

She smiled. 'I wonder what they would say at Stringers if I should ask for some rat? Even so César Machin turned them into a work of art in his kitchen. I think perhaps he did not have to produce rat. Horse was perfectly acceptable and for people like Monsieur Adolphe with money some *choses de qualité* were possible even after we had endured many weeks of the siege. No, I think César Machin was a formidable chef who wanted to demonstrate to himself that if the normal food became impossible to obtain and too expensive even for Monsieur, we could eat well.'

'But aren't they dreadfully dirty, rats?'

'Well, *chérie,* it depends what they have been eating and where they have been living. It is like the rats on the *chalands*, isn't it? Monsieur Machin trapped the rats from the wine cellar alive and imprisoned them. Then he fed them on a kind of pastry we made from the stale flour he could no longer use in the kitchen, some duck fat which there was always in jars. He said the fat was no good without the meat to baste with it, so why not baste the rats while they were still alive? And some red wine. We had plenty of wine, at least, and Monsieur Adolphe always said he would not want the Prussians to drink it when they came. He never had any doubt they would come, of course, poor man. That is why the painting had to have an escape…'

This was no time for the painting, I thought. 'So he fed them on this pastry stuff…'

'Yes and the peel of oranges and lemons which had also gone dry in the cellar and they drank nothing but wine.'

'They must have got awfully tiddly.'

'They were…all the time. They became very sleepy and when

they were like this Monsieur Machin would hold their heads so they would not bite me and I would brush their coats over and over. He said this was to encourage good oil to come from their skin and clean them, but I don't know.'

'And so after a while they became what they had eaten?'

'Yes, like *escargots*. If you feed them on parsley and garlic for long enough that is how they will taste.'

So in a way I had been right all the time when I'd suggested to her that the Noah's Ark animal cutout could have been a biscuit rat. The great Machin's rats must have been very biscuity indeed after all that fatty pastry he'd fed them.

'Did the rats taste of duck pie and red wine, then?' I asked. 'After he'd fed them?'

'Certainly of red wine, that I remember. And the meat was greasy, a little like *confit*. He thought a long time about how to prepare them. First he thought he might make a *saucisson* but he was afraid to serve it hardly warm, in the fashion of the *saucisson de Lyon*, just in case. We also lacked skins by then because he had used the last of the pigs' intestines to make a sausage from Monsieur Adolphe's horse.'

I knew then that the rat really had been worth waiting for. 'His horse? What all of it?'

'But of course not all of it, Florence. Just what was left of its insides when we had served the meat in the *Hôtel*. Yes he was very generous, Monsieur Adolphe, even when Paris was encircled by the Prussians. He told César Machin to make soup with the horse bones to take up to the poor people in Belleville. Our *garçon* was too afraid to go there, so was the groom, so in the end César gave it to the Americans for their hospital.'

'So how did he decide to do them? Not sausages.'

'He decided that the rats should be treated like *gibier*…'

'*Gibier*?'

'I think Stringers in the Broadway say "game" although they never have anything better than rabbit. Because César reasoned it was wild and he had hunted it, although with a trap not with a gun.

'So how do you do that – like a rabbit stew or in a pie? Ah, but he couldn't make pastry because the flour was stale.'

'He made what we call a *salmis*. First he cut off their tails…'

'With a carving knife?' Rats, mice, I couldn't resist it.

'No, with my manicure scissors, *Coquine*! Of course, with a big kitchen knife, Florence. If you really want to know, he left a little piece on each one, to hold when he peeled off their fur coats. It was like taking the skin off a flat fish, holding the flesh down with an old towel. Everything came off in one piece, even their whiskers and ears.'

'And what did you do with their skins? You had brushed them so carefully, hadn't you?'

'You are joking with me now, Florence, I don't remember. Perhaps we made *pantouffles* with them for presents at Christmas that year. There was nothing else to buy in the Rue Rivoli because of the Prussians.'

'So he made this salami with the rats. But isn't that a kind of sausage? I've seen that in the Broadway. Leonard says it's donkey, that's why Pa won't buy it.'

'Your father actually says it is French donkey. That is why he won't buy it. Anyway, a *salmis* has nothing to do with a salami, which is Italian, in any case, but I don't imagine that would change Charles's opinion of it. For the *salmis* César roasted the rats in the oven with a little duck fat, which he still had plenty of, until they were nearly cooked. Then he took them out and took the meat off their little bones and kept it hot over boiling water with a little *demi-glace* sauce which every grand kitchen has even when it is encircled by Prussians, César said, although he did smell it carefully. It was rather old and had been made from the horse. Then he made the sauce *salmis* with the rat bones, the duck fat where their meat had been roasted, some bay leaf and a very good bottle of Bordeaux wine. He chose red. He said it would be better than champagne with rat. There was some onion, too, because we did not have any *echalottes* left by then. You have to cook it and cook it until it is half the quantity. Then I had to press it through a muslin bag for him. When the *cabinet* were ready for their dinner, César poured the *salmis* sauce over the rat meat on a metal dish and I carried it in behind him. "*Messieurs!*" he announced in a big voice, "I propose to you, *Gibier Parisien de saison, sauce salmis à la façon César Machin*. Then he finished it on a hot flame on the buffet and I served everyone in their place. It was his little joke, you see, because everyone knows there is no game in Paris, no matter what the season.'

'And you had some, you said. What did it taste like?'

'The sauce was magnificent, but I don't remember the taste of the meat, except it was like a *confit*. It is often like that with such a sauce.'

I broke my golden rule never to say anything to Leonard or Rhoda or Pa, especially Pa, about what Josephine Lucie and I talked about in the middle room. They were all in the kitchen when I came down. We were having tongue, mashed potatoes and beetroot for tea. I didn't mind it, but I knew Leonard loathed tongue. Still he had to eat it. Pa would not abide 'faddiness or waste'.

'You were right about Grandmother, Leonard,' I said.

'What about her?' said Leonard, his mouth full of as much of the tongue as he could cram in at once to shorten his agony.

'She did eat a rat in Paris during that war.'

Pa frowned at me down the table but for once Rhoda showed a glimmer of interest in something I had to say. 'Really, what was it like?'

'She couldn't properly remember. Tongue, she thought.'

17

I put some more coppers in and pressed button A.. 'A little bit of tongue,' I repeated.

'That's what I thought you said,' said Freddie at the other end. 'What with?'

'I thought mashed potatoes and I've got a bit of beetroot.'

'Just the job, Florence Duck. That's me you can hear already, coming up the path.'

Freddie and I were quite lucky, well very lucky, that he was billeted at home then. It meant I got the army rations instead of the normal civilian ones. That's where the tin of tongue came from. Make the most of it, Freddie said, it will all come to an end one day soon, as sure as powdered eggs are powdered eggs.

Naturally I didn't let on to the girls at the post office about the rations. They thought it was jammy enough my having Freddie at home more often than not, without rubbing it in. Their chaps were away, so it didn't arise.

'I got into awful trouble at home once over some tongue,' I said as we were finishing.

'How was that?' Freddie said.

'I made Leonard so sick at the dinner table, it went all over Rhoda and Pa, the cloth, everything. It got in Rhoda's hair, although I still think Leonard made sure of that. We'd had beetroot too, so it was bright red sick which made matters a million times worse.'

'What'd the tongue to do with it?'

So I told him about the rats. I'd made up my mind by this time to tell Freddie a little, at any rate, about my grandmother, if not yet about Josephine Lucie. It had been nagging away at me that I wasn't sharing anything with him about her story, especially as it had started to preoccupy me so much lately. Since the war had started, I suppose. Something about France giving in to the Germans, perhaps – being bombed – short commons, I don't know. Then once I had started thinking about it, Maurice turns up, out of the blue really. And this man Gaillet. Then the picture kept being mentioned all the time it seemed, when nobody'd given it a thought for how long – forty years? Something like that, because how old was Maurice now – nearly fifty? More, probably. The thing was, because of Maurice and Gaillet, and the job at Carlton Gardens, I felt Freddie was involved. I didn't know what in exactly, but it just felt as though something was waiting to reveal itself and when it did, if it did, I would turn out to be the one who knew everything. Fingers would point and I really didn't want one of the fingers to be Freddie's. But there again the middle room still belonged to Josephine Lucie and me. And she was dead, so I still stopped short of telling him the whole story. Something told me to leave it at the rats for the time being and see what happened.

When we'd finished and I was clearing the dishes away, Freddie said, 'Maurice Burnell was in today.' It's uncanny isn't it how people who are close seem to be thinking about the same things at the same time.

'The adorable Maurice?' I said.

'Yes, the typewriters have arrived and he came to see them in. He said hello and asked after you.'

'That's nice, the typewriters, I mean, and Maurice of course.'

'Thing is, they'll all have to go over to Eaton Square to the *Corps Féminin*, because, do you know what they've done? Gaillet and co have turned the top floor, that was meant for their new typing pool, into a French Officers club. They say they can't get decent food in London, can you believe it? And I think your adorable uncle is stocking it with booze for them. There's hell to pay with the Office of Works. They say it's all been done under false pretences. Apparently Carlton Gardens was requisitioned from a very respectable firm of accountants who were none too pleased to be thrown out, I can tell you. They're really steaming now, according to the man from Works. Lots of references to the *Folles Bergères* and that sort of thing. He's asked me out to lunch tomorrow, if I can squeeze half an hour.'

'The man from the Office of Works?'

'No, Floss, Maurice Burnell.'

I phoned Freddie from the box, as usual, on my way home from work. 'How did lunch go with the adorable Maurice?' I asked him.

'Tell you later, not on the phone,' Freddie said briefly and abruptly hung up.

I had a huge attack of butterflies as I walked the short distance to the maisonette. It felt like I was a child back in Coatwood again and someone had just passed me and said 'you're for it when you get home, my girl' and I wouldn't have the faintest idea what it was I was supposed to have done. But you always knew it would be something. As far as I was concerned, now it was going to be about Augustin Montel and Maurice. Maurice must have known something after all. Freddie would worm everything out of me. The middle room would be thrown open for anyone and everyone to poke around in and turn upside down. It was only a few hundred yards from the phone box to the front door, but in that short space of time my guilt over not having told Freddie everything from the word go was really making my tummy churn. I kept telling myself it was ridiculous. Why read so much into a piddling little exchange of words on the telephone? It could be anything, anything at all. Perhaps they were sending him back to his unit. Yes that was it. That would account for Freddie's curt tone. But then, that couldn't be anything to do with Maurice and lunch, could it? God! It couldn't be about Rhoda and me, surely to goodness.

'That you, Freddie?' I called from the kitchen when I heard him wiping his feet.

'Who else has got a key? Anton Walbrook?'

'And the milkman.' I began to relax, just a little. This was so stupid, all this guilt and anxiety.

'Which one do you prefer?' Freddie said, coming in and giving me a big, hairy battledress squeeze.

'Well,' I said, almost entirely back to normal, 'the milkman's a better kisser than Anton Walbrook, but his gold top's not so good as Anton's. Do you want a drink?'

'Have we got anything to drink, Funnycuts? Not milk though.'

'It so happens that there was some gin doing the rounds in the sorting office, so I took advantage.'

'I didn't think the civil service girls fraternised with the sorting office. I'm sure Mr Webber would have something to say about that.'

'Actually, I think Mr Webber is probably not averse to a little black market hooch himself. I know he was making overtures about some stockings for the Masonic ladies night.'

'Good Lord, I didn't think old Webber was like that.'

'For Mrs Webber, Fathead.'

After a couple of sips of neat, warm gin I had totally convinced myself that all my fears were groundless. 'So how was Maurice?' I said. 'Adorable as usual? What did you have for lunch?'

'God, how could I forget? It must be the gin,' said Freddie. My butterflies came bobbing back.

'He took me completely unawares, I can tell you. No beating about the bush. Came straight out with it in the cake house, you know, in the Park. I only had twenty minutes. Asked me if our friend Capitaine Gaillet had tried to put me up to anything.'

'Put you up to anything? What sort of "anything"?'

'You know – something iffy he meant.'

'What did you say? You didn't tell Maurice about the Red Cross, did you?'

'Well not as such, Florence Duck, but the thing is, I've a funny feeling I might have to.'

'Why? Not long ago you said Maurice wasn't to be trusted. Something about a fox and the hen house. We think he's the one who's a bit iffy, don't we? You know, car with petrol, biscuits…'

'…brisket and bad, bad booze. Yes I know all that, but he was different somehow today, he had… I don't know… authority. To tell you the truth, I thought I was having a cup of tea and a liver paste sandwich with a rozzer.'

'Maurice? A policeman? You have to be joking. He's much too shady.'

'Well that doesn't always signify. No, I don't mean he necessarily *is* a policeman. He just felt like one.'

'Look, Freddie, I know a thing or two about Uncle Maurice, believe me, he's shady,' I said, and wished I hadn't.

'What do you know about him? The black market stuff? God's sake, I mean everyone's at it, your sorting office, His Majesty's civil service, Mrs Webber. Doesn't make your uncle Maurice the devil incarnate, a bit of contraband, Florence.'

He was serious. He was 'Florencing' me. What should I say? Whatever it was, it didn't sound like the painting. The middle room seemed safe from imminent violation at any rate. 'It was just something he did for Rhoda a few years ago,' I said. 'It wasn't the sort of thing you'd expect a policeman to do, that's all. Much more likely from a crook.'

Freddie wasn't really interested in my sister at the best of times. 'Rhoda? She'd get the Archbishop of Canterbury to show his bum on a bus for a couple of matinee comps if it suited her purpose. No, Florence, Maurice introduced the subject of Captain Gaillet almost as soon as we'd found a place to sit down, and right from the word go he made it sound…you know…businesslike. As good as told me he thought Gaillet needed watching and I was perfectly placed. If I thought he might be up to anything untoward I could count on Maurice to see that it reached the right ears.'

'Yes, but that could just as easily be about dodgy typewriters and booze for this illegal den of iniquity they've set up for the officers at Carlton Gardens, couldn't it? Maurice is just covering his back, surely. He's hardly likely to want our authorities to know what he's doing under the counter for the Free French, so he wants you to keep a lookout for him.'

Freddie was not convinced, I could see, but he didn't look quite so sure of himself. 'You might be right, I suppose, old girl. It's just that it didn't come across that way in the Cake House. Anyway, we don't particularly want Maurice getting into deep water with the powers that be, do we? So I might just tip him off if something looks as though it's getting close to home, so to speak.'

'So is he up to something, then, Louis Gaillet?' I said. 'What about the French soldiers who've died? What's become of that?'

'That's the second time you've done that,' said Freddie. 'Called him "Louis". His name's Raoul. Who's this Louis? And don't give me the "all Frenchmen are Louis" routine.'

I could have kicked myself. 'I think there may have been a Louis Gaillet my Grandmother talked about sometimes,' I said. 'I expect that's the reason. It's probably a common enough name.'

'Where did she know him? In Paris? Why don't I ask Gaillet if there's a connection?'

'I shouldn't bother. It would have been a very long time ago, if there was a connection. Don't expect it would mean anything to him, if there were. What about the Red Cross business, though?'

'I think I may have been barking up the wrong tree there. Turns out it's only about nine or ten of the dozens who have died here since Dunkirk. I looked at the pay files but I couldn't see any particular reason Gaillet picked these. A couple of them weren't actually sick or wounded when they arrived here. They were killed in an air raid. Just bad luck. They were in a pub somewhere and didn't make it to the shelter. Pissed I expect, although it didn't sound as though they had enough money to get pissed.'

'Why do you say that?'

'They'd both made a request through the White City people, to see if they could draw on their bank accounts in France.'

'How on earth did they expect to do that? There's a war on. France is occupied by the Nazis. That was a ludicrous request, surely?'

'I would have thought so, Florrie Dee. It looked as though they were asking for tick from the Bank of England until the war was over. Nice try. It got turned down of course. Lots of the French service people don't want to be here you know. They're not all volunteers. Some just had to come out with their units whether they wanted to or not, if they were ordered to evacuate rather than surrender. I expect these two didn't want to be here and thought that if they were still back in France they'd be able to have access to their money in the bank. Sod's law really.'

'So their families won't be able to get at the money in their bank accounts either, if they haven't been told they're dead.'

Freddie poured us both another gin. 'Ice and a slice would be nice,' he said. 'I suppose you're right. I wonder if Gaillet's thought of that. If he has, and doesn't care, then he's a double bastard, isn't he? Perhaps I should mention it to him.'

'Would that be a good idea?'

'I don't know. What do you think? After all, the fact that a couple of families in France can't get at their loved ones' bank accounts can't possibly be of any purpose to Gaillet or anyone else here, can it? They're no use to him over here, either, are they? I mean he couldn't get at them, either, could he, even if he wanted to steal their money somehow?'

'Yes, but he might get the idea you're poking your nose in. Do be careful what you say, Freddie love.'

'Well maybe I'll just say something in passing when I take him the daily pay book returns. If he hasn't spotted the problem with these two perhaps we can substitute some other names to give the Red Cross instead. I mean if it's just a matter of keeping the head count down. Dead count more like. I say Florrie Dee, I'm famished. Where's this tongue and mash? Any afters?'

I had some cooking apples as it happened. They were windfalls from Mr Webber's garden that he'd brought in for the civil service girls to share. He had loads, too many for his wife to keep. 'I put them in the attic in boxes so they aren't touching, like the Ministry says we're to do, but, I don't know, Mrs Draper,' he sighed, 'they have a worm in, a lot of them, and they go brown whether they're touching or not. I can't get grease bands for the trees. Essential for the war effort, the nurseryman says. A few grease bands will hardly slow Hitler down, now, will they? Mrs Webber's tried drying them in rings, but it takes a lot of gas and I feel a bit guilty about that, what with the coal situation and everything. And then they've not to be touching in the oven, apparently, so you can only do a few at a time in our "New World".'

Ruby got the giggles of course. 'Not a lot of touching at the Webber's then,' she said when he'd gone back to his office, 'in case they go brown or run out of gas.'

There wasn't enough sugar left from the ration to do stewed, so I'd cooked them slowly with barely any water, just enough to stop them catching on the bottom of the saucepan, and a couple of sprigs of mint from our little patch of garden. Mint seems to be about the only thing that thrives in it. It was a Josephine Lucie tip, another one of César Machin's ways of dealing with the privations of Paris under siege. The apples just turned to a gorgeous minty froth.

'A few blackberries in this wouldn't come amiss,' said Freddie as he made short work of his pudding. 'Wrong time of year, though, I suppose, is it? No, that can't be right, we wouldn't have the apples either if it were the wrong time of the year, would we? We should go blackberrying, Florrie Dee. We could take a picnic.'

When? I thought. You're in the army, Freddie. There's a war on.

18

We made jam from the blackberries we had all picked that Sunday afternoon. Pa had proposed walking up to Bushey through the fields and taking a picnic. It had been lovely, particularly as it was the first time Pa had suggested we should all do something together since Mother's death. Because I found it difficult to feel anything about my mother dying, especially sadness, however hard I tried, I felt a huge surge of elation at that seemingly small thing, a Sunday afternoon walk to Bushey and a picnic. I knew it meant Pa was capable of thinking about something other than his grief and about being somewhere with the rest of us, instead of somewhere else with Mother's presence. He usually managed to hide away on his own, apart from mealtimes. When he wasn't at school he'd be in the garden working, if it was anywhere near nice enough, or else sitting up in his and Mother's bedroom, reading his Robert Louis Stevenson.

A year or two before Mother's death he had started buying one of Stevenson's books each month as they were published. They were really pretty little matching dark blue books with a golden palm tree on the spine. I assumed Robert Louis Stevenson must be still writing them and made the mistake of saying to Leonard that he really must be a very quick writer to have a new one ready every month for Pa to buy. Leonard, of course, took great delight in putting me right. Robert Louis Stevenson it seemed had been dead for thirty years and so one by one this set of little books was being brought out to commemorate the fact.

'He wrote about pirates in *Treasure Island* and died young on an island himself, in the South Seas,' Leonard concluded.

'I would have thought you would have known about that, too,' said Pa, 'He was one of our greatest writers since Dickens. Well, I say "our", actually he was Scottish.'

Grandmother – we were all in the kitchen together, so she must have been there preparing a meal for Mother – came to my rescue as I sat feeling totally demolished because, yet again, I knew I had only myself to blame for being at the receiving end of Leonard's superior ridicule, and because, in a way, Pa had sided with him.

'He was a Frenchman *honoraire*, this Louis Stevenson, you know, Leonard.' She laid stress on the "Louis". 'He wrote about the countryside where I was born and a man I was going to marry, before I knew your grandfather Burnell, met him and spoke with him. He was with a friend in a *canot* on our canal, this Louis Stevenson. My *fiancé* told me he spoke beautiful French. He loved France. I thought you would have known that too, Charles,' and she swept out with Mother's tray.

'He pronounced it "Lewis", *Madame*, not "Louis",' Pa said to the kitchen door as she closed it behind her, and then added 'Honorary Frenchman, my hat.' But Grandmother had yet again managed to vanquish him and Leonard with her irritating nationality and the subject was dropped.

Pa did continue to read Stevenson despite Grandmother successfully annexing him as a fellow countryman, although I have sometimes wondered if he skipped *An Inland Voyage* and *Travels with a Donkey* which I borrowed from his collection later out of curiosity, particularly the first one, which, as she had said, described the countryside of Josephine Lucie's girlhood, even though she must have been married to Grandfather Edward Burnell and living in Essex by the time Stevenson was canoeing down the Oise. It didn't occur to me, then, to ask her about the man she might have married from Orgelets.

So the walk to Bushey had been a rite of passage for Pa, I suspect, and for me too, because I felt that the gulf between his grieving and my inability to do so had been bridged. Surprisingly, Grandmother put on her black button boots and joined the expedition. I am not sure why. She hadn't been there when Pa had proposed it, she just came down into the hall as we were all about to set out, without a word, as if it was the most natural thing in the world. Pa just said, 'Good. Are we all set then?' and held the front door as we filed out. I wonder if she, like Pa, needed to create something that no longer involved his beloved wife and her beloved daughter. Something, moreover, outside her middle room, where her Charlotte had rarely been before her death and was not permitted after it.

The blackberrying had been shared too. The ebony jewels

were an offering to that afternoon, a rare moment of family togetherness freely entered into, where before it had only ever been something forced as a result of Mother's health. The moment did not last. As soon as we were home Leonard and Rhoda disappeared their separate ways and Pa went to mow the grass. It was left to Josephine Lucie and me to make jam together.

We had boiled the fruit and the sugar up in the kitchen and then carefully carried the preserving pan up to the middle room. It would have been simpler to have carried on in the kitchen, but it seemed natural to conclude the ritual in our sanctuary, especially as Pa and the others had lost interest in being a part of it. Josephine Lucie stretched a large piece of muslin loosely between the backs of two upright chairs and tied its corners to them so that it formed an open bag.

'Now, if we are clever, Florence, we shall do this with only one pan,' she said. She placed an empty jar on the floor below the muslin and spooned a largish amount of the jam into the bottom of the bag just above it so that the weight of it shaped the muslin into a narrow cone. The still hot liquid from the jam began to drip through into the jar, leaving the pips and bits behind in the muslin. Between us we lifted the pan and began to pour the rest of jam into it. It was a race between our emptying the contents of the pan into the muslin before the first of the strained liquid filled the jar so that the empty pan could be put in its place. The jar began to fill too quickly.

'This is not going to work, Florence, I should have doubled the muslin to make it slower. Run down to the scullery and fetch another big pan quickly, quickly, before it flows onto my carpet.'

I galloped down the stairs, through the kitchen and into the scullery. It was a good thing I had, too. There was a strong smell of gas. We had left the tap on the stove on. I turned it off, seized the first large saucepan I could see and rushed back to the stairs. Josephine Lucie was standing at the top.

'I can smell gas. It smells like the Gare d'Orleans, but be quick with the pan first,' she called.

'It's all right, I've seen to it. It was the stove.'

We just about rescued the situation, substituting the saucepan for the nearly overflowing jam jar in the nick of time. Then we opened some windows to let the smell of the gas out. When it had virtually disappeared, Josephine Lucie told me how the smell always brought back the memory of the Paris balloon factory at the Gare d'Orleans during the siege.

'There was a smell of gas everywhere, *ma chérie,* as soon as you got within a few streets of the *gare*. Of course there were no trains running out of Paris because it was completely encircled, so the station with its huge glass roof became a factory for making *Montgolfières*. Under the roof there was enough room to inflate the balloons inside so that they could not be seen by the Prussians until they were ready to fly away.'

'Did they use gas like we have in the house, then? The gas we've just been boiling this on? Gas from the gasworks?'

'But of course. I think it is normal. What else do you use to fill a *Montgolfière*? It has to fly after all. They had to carry the post out of Paris, and sometimes other things. One took Gambetta to rally the army in the north, Augustin told me.'

'And did he rally the army? Were you saved? Is that how it all ended? What happened to Augustin?'

'You always want to know how my story ends before I have hardly told you the beginning. Perhaps it has not ended yet. After all, I am still alive. But that is no thanks to the *Montgolfière*.' Josephine Lucie pursed her lips and frowned at me with exaggerated reproof. Once again I had tried to push her along too fast. Her look said she would let everything unravel in its own way, for her benefit, hardly for mine at all.

After her pause she went on. 'The gas was always escaping because the balloons were very old some of them and had to be darned like an old shirt, you know. One of them had been at the Great Exhibition, some years before, fixed on a long rope. I ascended in it, I remember, for one franc, which Monsieur Adolphe paid. So it was already quite ancient for a balloon, I imagine. I don't know whether it had been kept very carefully after the exhibition. Perhaps not. Perhaps before the people began to eat them, the rats and mice had been lunching on the *Montgolfières*. When Augustin took me, there were many women sewing up the old balloons as well as making new ones, from cotton of course. I had to cover my face because of the gas and because of the varnish they painted on the cotton afterwards. Augustin told me that sometimes the old balloons burst in the station because the darning was not very good. He said he would make sure he had a new one when the time came.'

I couldn't bear it. 'When what time came?' I asked. 'And why was it no thanks to the balloon that you are still alive?'

'Did I not tell you? The painting had to have an escape from Paris.'

This was just infuriating. She had no difficulty recalling the events of more than fifty years earlier to me in minute detail, but even so she seemed determined to play her past like a game of patience, and even though she knew it would all come out in the end, she had to surprise herself no less than me, with the turn of every card.

It seemed the Prussians had encircled Paris at a very inconvenient moment for Monsieur Adolphe de Marquise and the members of his *cabinet*. The forged version of the man in the lace collar should have left for the relative obscurity of a château on the outskirts of Béthune, belonging to the mine owner who had paid over the considerable sum of money he had agreed, and gone on ahead to await delivery. The speed with which the armies of France were encircled by the Prussians or forced back on Paris was greeted with mixed emotion by Monsieur Adolphe and his colleagues, still eating relatively well in the *cabinet*.

'The portrait had not left for Béthune, but already the roads and railway in that direction were closed. They even spoke of destroying the painting and pretending it had already been sent. Then they could say it had been a casualty of the war. But Monsieur could not, of course,' said Josephine Lucie.

'Why couldn't he? That would have solved his problem about the two paintings, wouldn't it?' I said.

'Well because it was a thing of beauty, as I have told you before. He could not destroy it.'

'Then he could have kept it and just said it had been lost in the fighting. Anyhow, the man who'd bought it wouldn't have known either way, would he? Because there wasn't any word getting out of Paris.'

'Monsieur Adolphe could not do this, simply because he was not a thief, Florence. None of them in the *cabinet* was a thief. They played tricks, yes, but the man from Béthune had paid for his painting and so it was his. The problem was he was in Béthune and the painting was in Paris and the Prussians were between.'

At first the siege had not been total. People who had money were able to buy their way through the Prussian lines, Josephine Lucie said. Monsieur de Marquise had considered trying to get the true portrait out of Paris this way until he learned that the Prussians were not only taxing those who were leaving, they were also confiscating their valuables.

'In any case, said Josephine Lucie, none of his *cabinet* friends wanted to leave our city and neither did he. In the beginning hundreds of people were coming into Paris, not leaving, even from quite a long way off. Everybody wanted to be there. That was why the food was finished so quickly. We did not know, I suppose, how terrible it would be. Everyone thought the Prussians would be stopped by the great forts that protected us all around the city, but the Prussian guns were too great for them and nearly all were lost in one day. Poor Monsieur! He should have gone while he could, with or without his painting. But very soon it was, in any case, too late. The Prussians were close enough to bombard the city and they stopped anyone leaving. They wanted to make it worse for us, I imagine, so that we would ask for peace.'

So Monsieur de Marquise and his friends now had two paintings in Paris that they very much wished to be elsewhere. Any optimism they felt about the siege being lifted and the Prussians being pushed back rapidly evaporated as the city's streets became filled with demoralised troops whose efforts to break out had come to nothing. For them it was only a matter of time before Paris must fall. Monsieur not only feared that the Prussians might seize his property, but if they did not, the Paris mob from the slums of Belleville and Montmartre would set about destroying it. The mob always took its revenge for political failure on the bourgeoisie. Monsieur had seen it before. 'Look what they did to poor Machin's restaurant in 1848,' he told Josephine Lucie after one particularly fruitless and gloomy evening.

'It was Papa Montel announcing suddenly that Augustin had been accepted as a balloon pilot and was being given leave of absence from the National Guard that gave them the idea to make the pictures escape from Paris that way,' said Josephine Lucie. 'I was at first horrified that Augustin had not told me himself he was to be a pilot. It was very dangerous because of the gas and the Prussians shooting at them, and in any case the pilots could not come back once they had gone, so I would not see my darling Augustin until after the war was finished. That was when he took me to the Gare d'Orleans to try to put me at my ease, which, of course, it did not. But then, Monsieur called me into the *cabinet* on my own one evening and said they wanted the paintings to go to London to be safe until the end of the war. I said it was unknown for a *Montgolfière* to go all that way and besides, he would have to tell Augustin about the paintings.'

I was rather surprised. 'Didn't Augustin know about the paintings, then? Hadn't you told him? Hadn't his father told him?'

'He did not need to know. It was better that he did not know.

Monsieur's rule was that only people who had a responsibility for something to do with the pictures should know.'

'What about you?'

'I had to serve the dinners.'

'César Machin then? He must have known. He announced the rat dinner, you said.'

'Yes and then he left me alone when he had finished flaming them on the buffet.' She paused though, and thought a moment. 'César Machin was one of the wisest men I have ever met. Perhaps he guessed, *chérie*, but he never asked me anything and he never told me anything. He just cooked and cooked and cooked.'

Monsieur de Marquise, however, did not intend even then to let Augustin Montel in on the whole story.

'He asked me to go in the *Montgolfière* with Augustin and take the paintings to London. He did not expect it to float all the way to England. He said he would give me plenty of money to buy a ticket for the train and for the packet boat when we had descended on the other side of the Prussians.'

'Take the train?'

'Yes. This was what the aeronauts had to do when they landed with letters. They had to make their way to somewhere which was not occupied that had a big post office. And anyway, most of France was free from the Prussians. I think they were mostly around Paris. Monsieur Adolphe said I should post a letter to the man from Béthune to say his painting was safely in London for him to collect or wait for better times.'

'Wait a minute,' I said, 'what were you supposed to do if you didn't reach the other side of the Prussians? They might have shot you down. Anything might have happened.'

'Monsieur de Marquise did not discuss such an event. I was not interested, in any case, because all I could see was that I would be with my dearest Augustin. He could come to London with me and then we could return to France. The war would be over. Suddenly, for me, it was not dangerous any more.'

I was speechless at the torrent of information Josephine Lucie had let rip, the unanswered questions, the loose ends. Where should I start to pick it all up and piece it together?

'I suppose now you are going to ask me what happened,' she said.

19

'Has anything happened, Florence? Is Freddie here?'
'Good Lord, Uncle Maurice,' I said, first amazed to see him totally unexpectedly on the doorstep during the blackout and then immediately frozen with fear. 'Happened? What do you mean, "happened"? Is it Freddie? He's not due home tonight. He's on firewatch at Carlton Gardens. So am I in about half an hour.'

'Sorry, Florence, sorry. Nothing like that's happened to him, as far as I know. Can I come in?'

I stepped aside to let him in and then led the way through to the front room.

'God, you frightened me, Uncle Maurice. I really thought you meant something had happened to Freddie.' As I said it, though, I sensed that whatever the reason was for the adorable Maurice being here did concern Freddie. Everything Freddie had said about him, that I had pooh-poohed, came flooding into my mind in an instant. Isn't it funny how your imagination can slot so many pieces of information into place in a twinkling? Things you'd take minutes to say out loud.

'Not so much of the "uncle", I keep telling you Florence. We're both a bit grown up for that, aren't we? No, I wondered if he'd mentioned anything out of the ordinary happening at Carlton Gardens. Freddie doesn't seem to have been there for the last week or so. I just wondered if something had happened and he'd been moved.'

'He's been over at Eaton Square with the French floozies, training them up on some paperwork or other,' I said. 'It's only for a few days, Freddie assures me.' So why didn't Maurice know that. It would hardly count as classified information, surely.

'Ah, the delectable *Corps féminin,* that explains it.'

'I'm surprised they didn't tell you that at Carlton Gardens,' I said, 'It would have saved you a journey. Anyway, what did you think he might have done to get him moved?' I wasn't going to let Maurice off the hook, that lightly. It was ridiculous for him to drive all the way out here in the blackout to ask a question he could have had answered on the spot by the French in a trice. No, he wanted to talk to Freddie without the French spotting him at it. It had to be about Raoul Gaillet.

Maurice looked at me shrewdly. Well it might have been shrewdly. There again, it could have been more of a cunning glance.

'I had a chat with Freddie a little while ago. Did he mention it?'

I was blowed if I was going to be buggered about, as Ruby would say. Maurice was the one who'd turned up on my doorstep out of the blue, twice now, come to think of it, and he was still the one asking all the questions.

I thought about saying, 'I think you and that French captain are up to something. You've fallen out with him over some shady deal, and you want Freddie to keep *cave* for you. That's why you've somehow engineered this job for him at Carlton Gardens.' But there was a sudden thunderous knocking at the front door.

It had to be ARP or police or both, a noise like that. I did a quick check of the blackout in the front room and glanced into the kitchen on the way to answer the summons, but the light was out there anyway. I made sure I turned the hall light off before opening the front door. I was right. It was a Special with his tin hat and his armband on.

'Is this motor vehicle anything to do with you?' He indicated Maurice's big Austin at the end of the path.

Maurice had followed me to the door. 'It's mine, constable. Anything wrong?'

'You've left the lights on. That's against regulation…'

'It's all right, they're properly shaded,' Maurice interrupted.

'…And I have reason to believe it may not have been correctly immobilised.'

'Oh come on,' Maurice said. 'I'm only going to be five minutes, I don't live here. I'm just visiting…'

Go on, I thought, say it, get me a bad name. Say 'visiting your niece'.

'…Mrs Draper,' he concluded.

'I'll need to see your identity and I'll take a look in the boot as well, while we're at it, sir. And have you brought your gas mask in with you for your short visit? Or is that left in the vehicle.'

'Just pop back indoors a moment, Florence, while I sort this out,' Maurice said.

I pushed the door to without closing it and listened in the hall. I couldn't hear what Maurice was saying, he was speaking very softly. I saw him reach inside his coat pocket, presumably for his identity papers. The special constable took them round to the dim light of the shaded headlamps and examined them. Then he straightened up, handed them back and I heard him say, 'All right, thank you, sir, sorry to have disturbed you, but if you wouldn't mind just seeing to the lights.' I swear he was going to salute, too, but Maurice had already walked round to the other side of the motor to open the driver's door, and he let his arm fall back.

'Where were we, before we were so rudely interrupted?' Maurice said, when we were back in the front room.

'You were just about to tell me why you didn't want the Carlton Gardens people to know you were asking where Freddie was,' I said sweetly.

'Is that what Freddie says?'

'It's what I think. Freddie says you're some kind of policeman.'

'Well I hope he doesn't say it too loudly, it could get me a bad reputation in some quarters.'

'Why do you want him to keep an eye on Captain Gaillet?'

'Did he say that?'

'Oh come on, Maurice. Why are you here? Why don't you just talk to Freddie when you deliver your typewriters to Carlton Gardens. Freddie's convinced you've asked him to snoop on Gaillet. How come you got rid of that Special so easily?'

'If I tell you, Florence, not a word to a soul.'

'Oh God, you *are* a policeman.'

'Not as such, which is why I would prefer you said nothing to anyone.'

'What have you got Freddie mixed up in? You *did* wangle him this job, didn't you?'

Maurice was silent for a moment. I wondered what he was going to say next and whether I could believe a word of it when he did.

'Yes,' he said after a moment, 'I suggested Freddie for the job. I'm close to Gaillet but not close enough. I don't have a reason to be at Carlton Gardens all the time. Anyway Gaillet wanted someone who could handle the pay and rations administration for them on a day-to-day basis. Freddie's Pay Corps, and his French passes muster, so he was ideal all round.'

'Ideal?'

'Yes, because he's virtually family as well. It's so neat, I wouldn't be surprised if Captain Gaillet thinks he engineered the whole thing himself. He couldn't wait to bump into Freddie at the Corner House.'

'I thought he was there by chance.'

'He made it look that way didn't he? I should think he followed us from the theatre. I'd mentioned we were all going to see Rhoda.'

Maurice still wasn't really telling me anything. He was just waiting for my questions and answering them without any further explanation. I'd forgotten that shifty side to him when he was really under pressure. I'd only seen it once and that was a fair while ago now. For all I could tell he was making it all up as he went along without any real idea where it might all lead. Any minute now, I thought, he's going to plead the Official Secrets Act and ask me to trust him. Well I'm a blooming civil servant and I've signed it, so he can trust me instead.

He began to backtrack. 'Look, Florence, all Freddie's got to do is let me know if Gaillet seems to be up to anything peculiar. Come to think of it, it might be easier if he tells you and then I can pop round here and talk to you. That way Freddie and I won't look too cosy at Carlton Gardens, especially as I have fewer reasons for going there now that they are more settled.'

'Not good enough, Uncle Maurice. If you want to rope me in as well as Freddie we want to know what it's all about before we get involved any further. Why was it "so neat"? What has Freddie being family got to do with anything? Come on, give. It's not too late for Freddie to ask to go back to his unit, you know.'

Maurice sighed and reached in his jacket pocket for his cigarette packet. He offered one to me but I don't. 'All right Florence, I suppose you're right, but I really don't want Freddie knowing too much. He might get caught out if he does, might say something out of place, that sort of thing.' He tapped his cigarette on his thumbnail and put it in his mouth. Then he patted around his pockets and located his lighter. When he had lit it, he took a deep breath of smoke, held it for an age, then tilting his head back, blew it out of the corner of his mouth into the top left hand corner of the room. I felt like screaming, 'Get on with it, get on with it' and all the while wondering if he was just playing for time to think of a yarn to spin me.

'A whisky would be nice,' he said, 'I don't suppose…'

'There's warm gin,' I said. I opened the sideboard and poured him one and then thought 'why not' and poured myself one too. If I was going to be told a fairy story I might as well make myself comfortable.

'I'm not a policeman, Florence. I'm a businessman. Until this war started I did a lot of business in Europe, buying and selling, putting people in touch. I still do around the edges, but it's a lot more difficult now. Germany and Italy are out of the question, France is difficult although there are still ways and means through Portugal and Switzerland. Can't deal directly of course, it's called trading with the enemy, but I've been encouraged to keep links with my former business agents in the neutral countries.'

'What do you mean "encouraged?' I asked. I knew I shouldn't have interrupted his flow but I couldn't help myself. I can't bear loose ends. I knew if I didn't ask then it would niggle away at me long after Maurice had gone.

'Well, leaned on rather heavily by the authorities, if you prefer. I'm coming to that anyway. If it hadn't been for the appearance of our friend Gaillet I might not have got caught up in all this myself. He gave them the opportunity to go through my books with a fine tooth comb, including my little black book of business contacts, I may say. But there again, if they hadn't, I suppose I would have just shut up shop in 1939. They have made it easier for me to stay in business, although I wonder if it is *my* business any more.'

'Sorry, I interrupted you, Maurice,' I said. 'You were going to tell me about Gaillet and Freddie.'

'Yes, I was. It must have been in about March 1939. I know it was a few months before war was actually declared. You know, when Hitler took over the whole of Czechoslovakia and we knew the balloon was about to go up. I got a telephone call, out of the blue. It was Gaillet, but I didn't know him. He said he was sorry to bother me at home, blah, blah, blah, but was I by any chance related to Edward Burnell of Billericay. He had difficulty saying "Billericay" I remember. Seems he'd been going through the Burnells in the telephone book trying to track the right one down. Well, of course, I didn't know him from Adam, so I was a bit cagey. I wasn't about to come straight out and say Edward Burnell was my late father, your grandfather, Florence. I asked him what it was all about. Anyway, he knew that Edward Burnell was dead and he said that there was a possibility that there was some property of his that had once belonged to his own father, who was also dead, which he would be happy to buy back for sentimental reasons. I started to ask him what sort of property, but of course he wasn't having any of that unless I told him whether or not I was connected to Edward Burnell. I couldn't think what the old man might have had that could have belonged to Gaillet senior, other than my mother's furniture, which of course she had kept after he died. I don't think Gaillet realised at that point that my mother had outlived my father. I smelt a deal, the minute he said "sentimental reasons". That usually means something they want really badly but don't want you to know how badly.'

I was curling up inside myself with anticipation and excitement, bottling an almost unbearable desire to say, 'I know, I know'. But I held myself back. I still couldn't entirely trust Maurice even though he seemed to be genuinely unburdening himself. I thought, if I even give you a hint that I know something you don't know, you'll use it somehow to trap Freddie even deeper into whatever it is you've already got him into.

Maurice went on, 'So I decided to take a chance and I told him Edward Burnell was indeed my father. Do you know, Florence, Gaillet had looked him up in Somerset House. He knew when he had died. He got the date out of me to double check my bona fides. I had to rack my brains I can tell you, for the date, I mean. Then he said he was attached to the French embassy in London in Belgravia and could we meet somewhere nearby. I suggested the Star behind Belgrave Square. So we met up and he told me about this painting that had once belonged to his father but had somehow been acquired by my father, 'at an auction,' he thought. He was very vague about this. He described it, you know, man with a pointy beard and a lace collar. I knew I'd never laid eyes on anything like that at home. But it was the kind of thing the old man would have gone in for. He was a bit of a dealer, you know. It's probably where I got it from. In any case I could smell money. Man with a lace collar? That says to me, old master and it says valuable. My guess was, unless Gaillet was barking entirely up the wrong tree, it was something to do with my mother, not my father at all. I had another look at the stuff she had in store when she died. I'd sold most of it, heavy French furniture, not to my taste. What was left I'd put into a place I keep myself for the business, but there was no picture matching Gaillet's description. I even checked the auctioneer's catalogue from the sale of my mother's effects, but no luck there either. So that was that. Gaillet was not being very forthcoming, still playing the whole thing down in case I should think he was too interested.'

He took another drag on his cigarette and held it for a few seconds before letting the smoke trickle out of his nose. 'Did you ever see it, Florence? This painting? Seriously?'

'No. Didn't you, then? I thought you said it had been at home when you were a boy.'

'Well if it was, it wasn't hung on a wall. Not that I can remember. If Mother had it she must have had it stored away somewhere. Or got rid of it.'

'So is the painting the reason you and the police are interested in Captain Gaillet?' I was a bit confused now.

'I keep telling you, it's not the police. And no, it's not the painting, that's just something Gaillet is keen to find. But our meeting at the Star to talk about it was what got me into this other business.'

They must have been watching Raoul Gaillet, of course. Two of them at the pub, because presumably one must have followed him afterwards to see him back to the embassy which was only round the corner.

Maurice had walked the other way to the corner of Halkin Street at the end of the mews, and whistled up a solitary taxi from the rank.

'Are you going my way at all? This seems to be the only one. I'll gladly pay the fare.' It gave him a bit of a start. The man suddenly at his elbow must have followed him down the cobbled alleyway from the pub, but Maurice hadn't been aware of anybody. He was surprised and taken off guard. He'd already told the cabby his address, which had probably been overheard, so it wouldn't have been difficult for it to appear they were both headed in the same general direction. Still, the chap didn't look too tough, not the sort to be carrying a set of knuckle dusters in his crombie pocket, and it didn't look as though he might be in league with the cabby.

It didn't occur to him until they were both settled in the back of the cab that he had been picked up. *Are you going my way?* God, what a fool!

'I'm Gerald, by the by. I say are you in a rush? We could have a drink at this club I know in Goodge Street if you fancy going on. Share another cab home afterwards.'

Gerald put his hand on Maurice's knee in an unassuming way, but then left it there a little too long. Maurice waited for him to remove it and when he didn't, lifted it up by his coat sleeve and placed it carefully back in Gerald's lap.

'Doesn't sound like my kind of place,' he said, 'if you get my drift.'

'No, no, don't get me wrong. Each to his own as they say. Club's got some rather nice honeys, actually. Come on, my treat.'

Maurice leaned forward and tapped on the glass. The cabby turned round. 'Yes guv?'

'This gentleman has changed his mind. Can you drop him here?'

It was too late, of course. Maurice's address had been noted, although when they came looking for him it was at the office, not at home. His heart sank when he saw 'Gerald' with another man who was clearly a superior of the official kind. 'But evidently not police,' he thought. 'Tax inspectors?' The thought must have stamped itself visibly on his forehead.

'No Mr Burnell. Not the Revenue. But we could always pass something on, if that would be helpful. We are very well connected at quite senior levels.' Gerald's superior opened a file of cablegrams Maurice had left on the cabinet and closed it again.

Maurice retrieved it and put it away, deliberately making a point of locking the drawer, while making a mental note to take it with him when he went home.

'So I assume you are not here to ask for my subscription to your friend's after hours club in Goodge Street,' he said.

The superior laughed gently. 'No Mr Burnell, I'm very pleased to say you passed that little test with flying colours. We civil servants so much prefer to do business with volunteers for King and country rather than men placed under duress. But we always like to know if you're a nancy. It can be both a strength and a weakness in our line and as ever, knowledge is power.'

'Gerald offered me girls as well, I recall. Must be a very accommodating kind of club.'

'There are several clubs in and around Goodge Street, Mr Burnell, catering for a variety of tastes. We know people in them all. What we don't know and are very much interested in, is how you know Raoul Gaillet and what business you have with him.'

'I realised "bugger off" was probably not the right thing to say at this point in the conversation. Anyhow, Florence, I'd only met Gaillet on that one occasion, so I hardly wanted it to look as though I was hand in glove with some diplomat our government was watching, especially with my business interests.'

'So you told them about the painting?' I said.

'Did I hell! No, I told them that his father had apparently had some dealings with my father and he thought we should talk so that he could fill in some more pieces in his family history. General rubbish of that kind. No fibs exactly. After all Gaillet has hardly been straight with me over the painting, if it exists at all, has he?'

'They're not interested in the painting at all then, these civil servants?'

Maurice looked at me with ill-concealed irritation. I know I was being deliberately stupid, but even so I do wish men wouldn't do that. Still it did the trick. I'm sure he hadn't been intending to tell me as much as he did.

'Florence, the painting is just a sideshow, strictly between Gaillet and me…well and you as well, I suppose…'

'And Freddie…'

'They're pretty sure Gaillet is a Nazi stooge.'

'A spy do you mean?'

'It probably amounts to the same thing. When they came to see me they were worried that Gaillet was seeing stuff from us at the French embassy and might be passing it on to Berlin.'

'They told you that? You could have been anybody. Doesn't sound very "careless talk" to me.'

'No, they didn't come straight out with it then. I've had the details filled in since, after I joined up, so to speak. When they came to the office that time they just showed me the old carrot and stick. They said that Czechoslovakia was just the beginning, Poland would be next and then we would be at war. Munich had given us a bit of breathing space to get ready for the inevitable. It shook me I can tell you, to hear it that way from chaps in the know. I thought Munich was a shambles but that Chamberlain would just go on keeping it all away from our doorstep. I suppose it was mainly wishful thinking on my part because I had quite a lot of business in Europe. But that day at the office the scales fell from my eyes. We were actually preparing for war. I realised it would perhaps be a year away at the most and I could see ruin staring me in the face, so to speak.'

It's funny isn't it, just when you think you've got a man worked out he throws a spanner in the works and you think 'Oh well, perhaps I was wrong about him' and you're just trying to see him in a new light when he says something else to make you think you were right the first time. But the trouble is, you've already let a doubt creep in and you can't get rid of it. So you end up trying to work him out all over again from the beginning. I was quite convinced Maurice and Gaillet were up to no good together, but now I was being convinced that he was actually doing his bit for the war effort on something really quite important. Just when I was coming to terms with that, I realised that the reason he was doing it was probably because Gerald and his superior had shown him a way to stay in business in Europe if he allowed himself to be cultivated by Captain Gaillet and reported back on him.

'If they thought Gaillet was a spy back then in 1939, why didn't they just tell the French embassy?' I said.

'That's just what I said, but it doesn't work that way apparently. We didn't trust the French embassy that much anyway, so if they were wrong about Gaillet he would have got it in the neck and someone else there would have been tipped off. As it turns out we were probably right. Most of the French embassy couldn't wait to pack up and throw their lot in with Vichy after Dunkirk.'

'Not Captain Gaillet though.'

'That's right. So is he friend or foe? We don't know for sure and now, because he's in with the Free French at Carlton Gardens, the name of the game has changed. When he was still at the embassy we wanted to smoke him out and then see if he could be more use to us where he was, rather than denouncing him to his own government. Now it's different. There's nothing going backwards and forwards between our government and Carlton Gardens that we're particularly worried about getting into the wrong hands. There's a bit of to-ing and fro-ing on getting a few important French people out of the clutches of the Gestapo, trade unionists and so on. That's where my business agents in Spain and Portugal and Switzerland come into the picture. But even if Carlton Gardens have asked us to see about getting someone out and we agree, we make damn sure they don't know how it's done. De Gaulle is a nobody when all's said and done and when the war's over he'll probably disappear without trace. The government of France is Marshall Pétain in Vichy and that's the way it'll be in the long run.'

You had to hand it to Maurice. If this was a piece of hokum he'd really put a lot of thought into it. I hadn't even begun to think about the end of the war except as a distant longing. Freddie said we were in for the long haul. But you had to believe we'd win in the end. We always do, don't we? I certainly hadn't thought what would become of France. You just assumed victory meant everything would be put back the way it was before, and Freddie and I could get on with our lives.

'Why do you want Freddie to keep an eye on Gaillet? You still haven't told me. If he can't do any harm…'

Maurice began to search for another cigarette. 'I didn't say he was harmless, Florence. He didn't go back to France when he had the chance, so if they… we're right and he is a Nazi agent or even a Vichy placeman, he's stayed for a reason.'

20

'I had no reason to stay in Paris and a few big reasons to go, Florence. It was not difficult in the end to persuade Augustin to take me. He was only worried about getting past the men from the post office.'

'Men from the post office?'

'Yes, they controlled the balloon departures. Augustin said they would be more difficult to evade than the Prussians.'

Josephine Lucie knew this was true. She had read in César Machin's copy of the weekly siege newspaper, *Almanach des Remparts*, which the great man said was better than listening to rumour and gossip, that a wealthy Parisian had brought ridicule and shame on himself by trying bribe the post office authorities to let his wife escape by balloon. He was informed stiffly that the balloons were for important letters and despatches and could not possibly take the extra weight of passengers in addition to the aeronaught.

'He told them that if they met his wife, they would realise how light she was,' Josephine Lucie said. 'But we were all becoming thin, after all, so it was not an argument.'

I had hardly been able to contain myself for the week that had passed since Josephine Lucie had dropped the bombshell about her planned escape from Paris by balloon. On the day of the jam making, just as I thought I was getting somewhere with her story, Pa had come in from mowing the back grass and had smelled the gas in the kitchen. It mattered not that I had been and turned the stove off already. There had to be an inquest. He stood at the bottom of the stairs and shouted up to the middle room, where he knew we would be.

'Why does the whole house reek of gas, *Madame*?'

Josephine Lucie frowned and pursed her lips as she concentrated on ladling the jam pulp into the muslin, ignoring him, but I knew there was no point in ignoring the insistence of Pa. I opened the door and went out onto the landing. My grandmother brushed past me and leaned over the banisters, glaring at him.

'Why do you roar to me from the bottom of the stairs, Charles? I am not a housemaid to be abused so.'

'The house smells of gas,' Pa said, in slightly more measured tones. 'And I want to know why. I don't know why we had to have the stove. What's wrong with the range? At least the range won't kill us all in our sleep.'

'We are making jam, *confiture de mûres*, and you are not the one who has to clean the range.'

'Florence cleans the range, it's her task,' said Pa.

'*Exactement*,' said Grandmother. 'Leonard should have to do it sometimes.'

'Leonard? What's anything got to do with Leonard? He has his own tasks. Why should he clean the range?'

'*Ainsi qu'il ne devienne pas à l'image totale de son père*,' said Grandmother, as she had shut the door to the middle room firmly behind her.

'What did your grandmother say, Florence?'

'It was French, Pa'

'Are you being saucy, my girl? I know it was French.' His voice had risen again, so I decided to burst into tears. I felt like it anyway, I felt so disheartened that Pa had completely forgotten how the day had been. A hymn to our family, at last free of mother's health. I could never have eaten the blackberry jam now, it would have choked me.

'What's happening?' said Leonard appearing just then through the front door, confronted with a red-faced Pa at the foot of the stairs and his younger sister bawling on the landing.

'That's enough,' roared Pa. 'This is probably all your fault. Or mine.' And seizing his hat from the hallstand he pushed past Leonard and out into the evening sunshine.

Leonard looked up at me, helplessly.

I turned off the tears. 'There was a smell of gas,' I said. 'And we were having such a lovely day.'

Grandmother kept herself even more to herself for a week, punishing Pa by inflicting her presence on him by deliberately removing it, apparently not even emerging to use the outside lavatory beside the scullery, which she generally preferred to the nearer one next to the bathroom. Rhoda who had missed the moment of altercation Grandmother had engineered, did have the grace to wonder, after a couple of days had passed, 'whether she was all right.'

I knew she was because I had tapped on the door once or twice when no-one else was within earshot to ask if she wanted anything, to be rewarded with a 'no-thank you, Florence'. However, I didn't volunteer this information, rather hoping that Rhoda might make the mistake of going up to the middle room to see for herself. Leonard remarked that as she did not appear to have been out for days 'the old lady's pot must be pretty full by now' which caused Pa to look up from his *News Chronicle* and say a little severely, 'She may be old, and she may be a lady, but to you Leonard she's always *Grandmother*.' Then he said to me, 'Still, Florence, you'd better go up and see if she needs anything from the Broadway, when you come back from school.' Yet again, I felt both irritated and gratified that Pa had acknowledged my overriding responsibility for my mother's mother.

Josephine Lucie beckoned me into the middle room as if nothing had transpired, as I knew she would when she felt she had unsettled everyone sufficiently. She made no reference to the rest of the family and looked as though she would take up her story as if time had not passed.

'Weren't you worried about leaving Monsieur Adolphe and César and everyone?' I said, when her story appeared about to climb into the balloon beside Augustin with hardly a backward look.

'You know, Florence,' she said, after what seemed an age made slower by the ticking of the clock on her mantelpiece, 'what made César Machin weep in the end wasn't because there was no food. He usually managed to find something he could transform almost into a *chose de qualité*, with his great skill. Gentlemen still dined at the *hôtel*, you know, and never questioned what I put in front of them. Cheese was difficult, of course. Very difficult. I believe the Americans had some for a while. Monsieur Adolphe had some of it after César had given them the horse soup for their hospital.'

No, what had made Machin weep in the end was the cold. While fuel lasted he could still fire up his ranges, but as coal became non-existent and wood became scarcer and scarcer, his dishes had to become doubly ingenious, so that they not only tasted good, but needed the minimum of cooking time. The battle with the rest of the household for spare firewood was one he could not win as Paris faced Christmas under siege and the cold deepened. Nevertheless he fiercely resisted Monsieur Adolphe's half-hearted suggestion that some of the *hôtel*'s habitués might be prepared to take their meals in the kitchen rather than use precious fuel for the dining rooms.

Machin produced more and more over a few handfuls of charcoal, which the *garçon* made in the courtyard from the kitchen's allowance of old furniture legs and other lumber from the attics. He would have it glowing in the two iron crucibles sunk into the top of the range over which he had a clever arrangement of tripods at varying heights, to increase or reduce the heat and so avoid having to light the whole range for the different-sized hot plates. He told Josephine Lucie proudly that this was the way it had been done in the old days when meat was cooked on spits in front of an open fire and soup boiled in cauldrons suspended above it. The sauces, needing a lightness of touch, were stirred over such tripods. When he really had to have an oven, Machin had recourse to the old fashioned hay box, the hay no longer being required, as the horses had been eaten. Anything to save fuel. Nevertheless, as the stored warmth of generations of cooking slowly ebbed from the walls, unreplenished by the daily business of a great kitchen, so too the chef's veins began to run cold and his spirits to flag.

'You see *ma chérie,* I knew if I went it would mean one less mouth to feed.' Josephine Lucie paused again, looking into her lap. Then she said, 'No, that was not the case, *en effet.*'

Louis Gaillet's wife died during the early weeks of the siege, she said. Like my mother, Madame Gaillet, too, had a consumption and should have gone to Thonon-les-bains for the winter, as she usually did. But the war made it impossible that year. Thonon-les-bains sounded a good deal more promising than Harefield in Middlesex. I didn't suppose that Madame Gaillet would have gone there on two buses and a tram. I saw her as the Lady of the Camellias, delicately fading away as the Prussian armies squeezed Paris tighter and tighter. She would probably have died anyway, I knew, whether or not she had reached the lakes and mountains of Haute Savoie, although it wouldn't have been as a result of septicemia brought about by having a hollow needle inserted in her back.

After her funeral Louis Gaillet returned enthusiastically to the pursuit of Josephine Lucie, which she claimed she had quietly been avoiding, as her love for Augustin had deepened. Gaillet would not take no for an answer and, she said, she feared that he might in some way make life difficult for Augustin if he realized that her coolness was due to her feelings for the younger man.

Quite what Gaillet would have been able to do to make life difficult for the dashing National Guardsman who was, moreover, the son of one of his close colleagues and influential partners in crime, Josephine Lucie failed to make clear. For a moment I glimpsed her slipping away, not unwillingly, to the house of assignation on her Wednesdays off, to meet with the whiskery and braced Gaillet, knowing full well that if Augustin called for her at the *hôtel*, he would be fobbed off by the *garçon*, whose loyalty would have been bought with a succulent portion of *salmis de rat*.

I shut my mind to such an image and replaced it with one of Josephine Lucie soothing Louis Gaillet's brow as he sobbed quietly over the passing of his wife whom he now realized he had deeply adored, and with an understanding Augustin looking on, touched by his sweetheart's compassion for the broken, older man.

'Louis Gaillet became engaged to be married in a matter of weeks. It was the war, I suppose. The conventions were put aside. A woman who was no older than me. Imagine. And I knew when his wedding day was over, he would still go to the house of assignation afterwards,' said Josephine Lucie. 'Certainly, Florence, I had nothing to keep me in Paris. Augustin had to go in his *montgolfière* and he could not come back. The trees had all gone in the Bois de Boulogne, everywhere were soldiers sitting in the streets, dirty, silent and drunk. And there was such a cold, *ma petite,* such a cold.'

I'd had enough of Louis Gaillet. His presence in Josephine Lucie's story seemed always to give it a hard, disturbing quality when I wanted it only to be exciting and romantic, I suppose. It never occurred to me then to wonder if she was making the whole thing up. But when the thought used to cross my mind later that it might all have been an old lady's fabrication, an elaborate bedtime story, I only had to recall the unpleasant image of Louis Gaillet and tell myself that he at least was real. And if he was real, why not the rest?

'So how did Augustin manage to get you into the balloon?' I asked.

She passed me a half empty jar of blackberry jelly with her silver jam spoon sticking out of it. I took a large mouthful and it didn't choke me. Then I noticed several other jars on the chiffonier, all empty.

'There's no bread left,' she said. 'It lasted until yesterday. I am used to a siege, *n'est-ce pas?*'

I waited.

'It was quite easy in the end,' she said. 'Although not for César Machin, I should say. He did not wish me to go, but he did not wish me to stay either. He said if the Prussians took the city no young women would be safe. "And," he said, "afterwards there will be a revolution in Paris. There always is. And there will be trouble for Monsieur Adolphe and this house." I told him that it would be very difficult for Augustin to get me past the post officers and so perhaps I would not be able to go in any case.'

'But you did go. After all, you're here now. You must have gone.'

'When Augustin came next to the *hôtel*, César asked him when his *montgolfière* would go and he said it was to be in less than two weeks. César asked him if he had a plan to get me into it. Augustin said it would leave at night time from Montmartre and he hoped the post officers would not see me.'

'That wasn't very likely, was it?'

'César thought the same. He asked, who was the *Directeur des Postes* at Montmartre? And when Augustin had gone, he asked Monsieur de Marquise to invite this gentleman to dinner in Augustin's honour, before the night of the *montgolfière*. It was normal, *n'est-ce pas?*'

At first Monsieur de Marquise had been naturally dubious about squandering his dwindling food on a not very grand official from the post office, but when César said it was so that Josephine Lucie could leave Paris and be with Augustin he appeared, reluctantly, to agree. He was, of course, secretly delighted to know that the pictures could be on their way.

'He said he would give me a letter to a man in London who would know what to do with the true painting, but I was absolutely not to show him the false one or even to mention it. He said I had to post another letter to the man from Béthune from France or from London, whenever I could.'

'And what were you to do with his painting, the forgery?'

'It had to go to Monsieur's bank in London to wait.'

'Golly, you didn't need to get them muddled up did you?'

Josephine Lucie looked at me, thoughtfully. I remember wondering what I'd said.

'There was no question,' she said, 'They were in separate boxes, flat because they hadn't their frames, and Monsieur wrote some poetry on them so that it would be easy for me to tell them one from the other.'

'What poetry?'

'I don't remember now. It is not important. Shall I tell you about the post officer, or not?'

She was really quite short with me. Almost Grandmother. I

had a sudden premonition that the story was coming to a climax. Perhaps it was coming to that point in her life where the path she should have taken became a secret kept from her, as she had told me at the very beginning.

'Yes, tell me about him. What did César Machin cook for him? Rat?'

'No. After the soup we served *pigeonneaux á la Mazarin.*'

'Pigeon? Well that was proper meat, then, was it? You can get them at Stringers sometimes. I've seen them hanging in the window, poor things.'

'Well, Florence, I think César's pigeons did not sing "coo, coo". I think it was more "miaow, miaow".'

I refused to rise to this. Anyway I'm not very keen on cats. I should think they're all right to eat. Depends what they've eaten themselves I suppose. Milk would be all right, fish at a pinch. I'm not so sure about mice. That would depend on what the mice had been eating. Goodness knows what they would have been eating then in Paris.

'It can't have looked very pigeony, can it? What was it like?'

'Ah well, César planned *pigeonneaux á la Mazarin* because he had seen a case of stuffed *perroquets* in the flea market which he sent the *garçon* to buy for him. People were selling anything then, because if you had no money you did not eat.'

'I thought you said cats, though. Not parrots. You couldn't eat stuffed parrots surely. They'd be done with…I don't know…sawdust and glue.'

'No, *ma chérie*, but *pigeonneaux á la Mazarin* are served on the dish with the bones taken out and the feet of the birds left on and glazed. So if you see pigeons' feet, you are eating pigeons, *n'est-ce pas?*'

Looking back at it now I can't imagine why I didn't wonder whether Josephine Lucie was having me on.

'You must have been able to see where they joined on.'

'No because this *recette* has a sauce of tomatoes and purée of dried peas around it. And he had these, the *chef*. He had dried tomatoes in the early days of the war and the peas were already dried, of course. It was a perfect dish to serve, a perfect *trompe l'oeil.*'

'And he could save the parrots' feet for another day and another cat.'

'But of course, *mon ange*'

'And afterwards?'

'Afterwards there was, I think, some of the last of the

Americans' cheese. Yes I think so, because Monsieur Adolphe said before that he would decline it and he hoped Augustin would do the same, especially as he was soon to leave Paris and could eat cheese until he blew up. And yes, I remember Papa Montel had some anyway even though Monsieur Adolphe blew his nose on his handkerchief very loudly to try to stop him. And after the cheese I think there was saffron rice with some *confiture*. Monsieur whispered to me when I brought in the jam that I should not let the post officer or the others serve themselves. I should put a small spoonful on each plate and then take it back to the kitchen at once.

"I didn't know we still had *confiture*," he said to me, so the others could not hear. "What else have you and the old so-and-so been hiding, Josephine Lucie?"

'So the man from the post office enjoyed his dinner so much he agreed to let you go with Augustin in the balloon?'

'No, it was not so easy as that. When it was over, the post officer said he wished to visit the kitchen to thank the *chef* personally for the best dinner he had tasted since before the war. Everyone stood up, too, to accompany him, but I said the *chef* wouldn't wish a crowd in his kitchen.'

'Didn't want them all to see the pigeons' fur, I suppose.'

'On the contrary, he had told me to make sure the post officer came to the kitchen alone.'

'What was he going to do, chop him up and steal his uniform for you to get past the others?'

'Perhaps, Florence, that would have been a good idea and finally not so expensive.'

'He didn't give him money, surely? After all that effort with the food. Monsieur Adolphe could've done that in the first place and saved his cheese. Anyway, you said they wouldn't take money from that man who wanted his skinny wife to go in the balloon.'

Josephine Lucie ate a large spoonful of blackberry jam from the jar and then dabbed the corners of her mouth with the edge of her apron.

'You do not understand, *ma chérie*, the total power of food when you are hungry, I mean absolutely hungry. This poor man had just been eating the things his dreams were made of.'

'Cat and parrot's feet?'

'It is not amusing, Florence, to be so hungry, and cold as well, that you can believe cats with parrots' feet are not just something to eat when you are encircled by your country's enemies, but believe it is a truly great dish of *pigeonneaux á la Mazarin* put before you by the legend, César Machin.'

'Sorry,' I said. 'So it was the dinner, then?'

'The dinner was only the beginning, *l'amuse bouche* to awaken ideas of food in the post officer's mind. To make him suppose that he had stumbled into an Aladdin's cave of *alimentation* in Monsieur Adolphe's *hôtel*, while the rest of Paris starved. Money? He didn't want money. He wanted meat.'

'But there wasn't any. Not proper meat, was there? Only cats and rats.'

'This, too, is what I thought at first. But then I had forgotten the great chimney. César took the post officer to the great chimney where the spits had been in the old days. And when he reached up inside it with the long hook, I thought, "Surely there can be none left" and I held my breath, you know, waiting to see.'

'See what? None of what was left?'

'*Jambon fumé*. Smoked ham.'

'Ham? In the chimney?'

'Yes, *ma chérie*, ham. But not as you think, pale ham from Stringers in the Broadway, already just four slices and resting on a damp piece of paper. This was a whole *jambon* on the bone, the skin almost black from the smoke. And if you would eat it, it would be cut so thin you can see through it to the pattern on the plate. But as you would chew it, it would last and last, filling your mouth with the flavour of…of…'

'Soot?'

'You see, Florence, you see what your father and Leonard would try to do to you. That is exactly what Charles would say, "*soot*". *Jambon fumé, ma chère*, will never be served in Coatwood, I can tell you. *Soot*! It has the taste of the smoke from ancient forest trees burning on a frosty night. Then you add to it, the taste of fresh, ripe figs from the south and a fine red Bordeaux wine. Ham? From Stringers? I bite my thumb at such ham.'

'So there was one left, then? In the chimney?'

'No Florence. Not one. There were *two*! Two *jambons*, dressed in fine muslin. They looked like two great babies going to their christening.'

'And you had forgotten them? While you were starving and eating horrid things?'

'César Machin had not forgotten them, of course. He was keeping them for Christmas Eve as a surprise for Monsieur Adolphe and his guests. I think he wanted to become famous for having *jambon fumé* under the noses of the Prussians.'

'So he gave one of them to the man from the post office so that he would let you escape in the balloon?'

'In effect. Yes. And he said there would be the other one waiting for him when I was safely away. Then he put them both back in the chimney.

'He didn't give him the first one then and there? I suppose he didn't entirely trust him to keep his end of the bargain?'

'No it was not that. It was not safe for the post officer to carry a whole *jambon* home that night. Anyone carrying anything that looked as if it might be food might never see his family again. He agreed to send his wife the next day to collect it in a *voiture d'enfant*.'

'A what?'

'A baby carriage. I said the *jambons* resembled babies. The post officer's wife evidently had a baby which she could bring, together with another shawl and a bonnet for the *jambon*.'

There was a tap on the middle room door. I couldn't believe it. It was Leonard.

'Pa wants to know if Grandmother needs anything, Florence.'

I opened the door a crack.

'You're to come down if she's all right,' said Leonard, so that she would hear. 'Pot need emptying?' he hissed for my benefit, but not quietly enough.

'As a matter of fact it does, Leonard,' said Grandmother. 'If you would be so kind.'

21

'My office, Mrs Draper. If you would be so kind.'
My heart sank. It sounded like some kind of a bombshell had dropped. I didn't know the day would bring two.

Mr Webber had been calling me Florence recently, I suppose as a concession to the fact that we might all be blown to smithereens while we were on fire watch. One of the old chaps in the sorting office who was in the ARP had been killed when he accidentally set off an unexploded bomb which had fallen on the Rising Sun in the High Street. The roof had caved in and he was the first in looking for survivors. Or whisky, the others in the sorting office said. I heard them talking about it at tea. The ambulance men could only find one of his arms, apparently, and then someone who knew him told them he'd already lost the other one in 1916, on the Somme. The thing is, we all laughed, at the whisky and then the arm. You had to. It got like that. We were frightened if we stopped to think about it. It's why Mr Webber started calling me Florence.

'There's a hysterical woman on the telephone demanding to speak to you, claiming to be your sister. I think she may be drunk. I really cannot have this, Mrs Draper. The post office does not permit this kind of thing in peacetime and now we are at war…well, the lines must be kept clear. I haven't forgotten that call from that other fellow.'

'What other fellow, Mr Webber?'

'Smooth talking type you said was from the War Office.'

'I'm sorry, Mr Webber, but it might be important. Especially if she's hysterical.'

Pompous ass. Just let him try and 'Florence' me, next time there was a heavy night. Still, he was right. Rhoda was hysterical and somewhat the worse for wear.

'What is it, Rhoda, for God's sake?' I said. 'Telephoning me at the post office. I'm in serious trouble. Is it Pa?'

'Is it Pa? *Is it Pa?* Is it fuck, Pa! No, it's your fucking Freddie.'

'Freddie?' I put my hand over the receiver and turned my back as much as could on Mr Webber so he would not hear her. I assume she hadn't spoken to him like that or he would have passed out.

'Your precious Private in the Pay Corps…'

'He's been made a corporal and he's with the…not exactly in the Pay Corps…'

'I don't care if he's been made a bloody air vice marshal. He knows about Switzerland. What d'you have to go and tell him that for?'

'Knows about Switzerland? I didn't tell him. I wouldn't. Why would I?'

'Came round during rehearsals. Left a note at the stage door. Presumed it was some Johnny and turns out to be your fucking Freddie, wanting to know if it was true. Anyone could have heard, Florence, anyone.'

'What did you tell him? And stop using that word,' I said, acutely aware of Mr Webber's mixture of deep disapproval and burning curiosity. 'No don't tell me, not now. I can't talk. I'll talk to Freddie when I see him. He may be home tonight with any luck.'

I hung up.

'I'm so sorry Mr Webber. My sister, Rhoda. She's had a very bad shock. She's an actress, I'm afraid. I thought it might have been my father.' In case he wasn't sufficiently confused, I choked back a sob and fled from his office with a trembling lip.

Needless to say, Freddie didn't materialise by the time I had to go on fire watch. I tried to telephone him from the box by the shelters where we mustered, but I just got number unobtainable. This was the worst of all possible worlds. You could tell yourself until you were blue in the face that there were a hundred and one reasons why the telephone wasn't working. It could be the exchange at my end or the one at his, or lines disrupted anywhere in between. That was the most likely explanation, especially as I couldn't raise the operator when I dialled O to see what the problem might be. But no, as far as I was concerned Carlton Gardens had taken a direct hit and Freddie was buried under the rubble along with General de Gaulle.

Helpless with irrational worry, I was concentrating even less than usual on my stirrup pump drill and removing fag ends from the sand buckets, which the warden insisted on for some reason that escaped us all. He wanted to smoke them later, Ruby always said. The warden made some oily comment to me about me not being my usual happy, blooming self this evening. It was his usual tactic with the girls, smarm round us first to see if he would get the brush off or not, and then when he did, he'd start being officious and bullying. Ruby blamed the blackout, 'Thinks we won't mind whose hand is in our knickers'. Anyway, I made the big mistake of blurting out that I was worried sick because Freddie hadn't come home and I couldn't get hold of him on the telephone.

Well of course, Hilda Dworkin burst into tears and Ruby went for me. The usual stuff, 'At least your old man gets home most nights. Hilda's bloke is in Singapore and she doesn't know if he's dead or alive.'

I know I shouldn't rise to it and I've only got myself to blame. 'My brother Leonard's in Singapore, too. And in any case, there's no fighting out there, is there? So 'dead or alive' hardly comes into it, does it? Talk about cushy numbers, the middle of London in the blitz is a lot worse,' and so on. Fortunately the warden started saying "Ladies, ladies…" so we were all able to turn on him instead.

There were at least two of them. Heavy bombers. You could tell by the engines. We all stopped talking and listened. Hilda said, 'Are they ours?' But as Ruby pointed out, if they were they were home early and very lost. The searchlight at the back of the allotments was trying to pick them out, without any luck. I knew the sirens had gone earlier than usual but it had been pretty quiet, certainly where we were to the north of London.

Suddenly the warden said, 'Take cover, quick!' and we all piled into the shelter where by rights we should have been anyway, only it's so damp and smelly in there, and you mostly have to sit with your feet in a puddle, we prefer to hang about outside. We were so rarely getting anything this far out lately, very few people who didn't have to do fire watch were bothering with the public shelter at all. They preferred to take their chances in the cupboard under the stairs if they had one. We didn't, being a maisonette. I suppose we should have at least got one of those cage things, a Morrison shelter, but it would have taken up so much space in the sitting room, we hadn't bothered. Freddie said, 'under the kitchen table is as good as anything, because if your number's on it, your number's on it.'

We heard the whistle of the bomb. It seemed to last for hours, filling your head. Louder and louder. I knew this was it. It couldn't be anywhere else except on top of the shelter. Nobody said anything, not even 'Oh God!' Not even swear words. The first bombshell of the day was totally driven out of my mind by the real thing.

Out of my head went Switzerland and Rhoda. Instead it was full of me, silently screaming, 'I love you Freddie, my darling, I love you,' over and over and over. I was so angry with myself that he wasn't there to hear me, so desolate not to have kissed him goodbye. And I know later I had Ruby's finger marks on the top of my leg, and she had mine on hers. The bruises lasted for weeks.

Then the earth shook and the noise came up through the soles of my feet and my bottom where we were sitting on the shelf thing, right into my stomach. My ears went like they do on the tube because of the air pressure, only much, much worse.

For just a moment everything was quiet, then Ruby said, 'You were right, Hilda. That was definitely one of ours.'

The throb of the aeroplanes' engines was already fading away. There were no more whistling bombs. We jostled our way out of the shelter and I bashed my shin on one of the stirrup pumps which had been left outside the doorway. Contrary to instructions, I have no doubt.

The bomb had fallen on one of the semi-detached houses on the other side of the road, right opposite the little ornamental green where the shelter and the telephone box were. I remember looking and thinking, 'It's demolished number fifteen and left number thirteen next door standing. So will they have to pull them both down, or will they be able to shore the good one up?' And then I thought, 'Would I want to live in a house that was shored up, or would it be better to lose it altogether?' Ridiculous, I know, to be thinking about things like that when, if the bomb had fallen on our side of the road, I probably wouldn't have been able to think at all, I'd have likely been dead. And if it had fallen a few yards further up it would have just made a big hole in the allotments and we'd have been listening to Ruby making jokes about cabbage having a similar effect on her too. It's the shock, I suppose, makes you think of commonplace things to get through it.

The warden was asking if we knew whose house it was. Someone said it was a Mrs Baird.

'Mrs Baird. Mrs Baird here?' the warden called to the few local people who had come to the shelter. But I knew she was not. I knew her by sight and to say 'good morning' to. Her husband was an officer so she didn't get too chatty. Not that she was snotty or anything like that. It was just the way it fell out when the men were called up. Hers had been in the reserves, so that's why he was an officer I suppose.

'She may still be in there then, or is there an Anderson?' said the warden.

'Or she might have gone to see her sister in Wolverhampton,' Ruby offered.

'Has she got a sister in Wolverhampton?' Hilda asked.

'I dunno,' said Ruby. 'She might have.'

I don't know why Hilda falls for it.

'Or she might be lying badly hurt under that lot,' said the warden. 'You just don't know when to cut it out, do you Ruby?'

I have to say we trailed rather hesitantly across the road to the wrecked house, clutching our stirrup pumps to our chests, although there was no sign of fire. The warden was doing his best to look as if he was in command, but this wasn't an instruction exercise. This was the real thing and he had no experience of the real thing. I suppose, of our little squad, I was the only one who'd actually had any experience of the real thing. That unexploded one in the restaurant in Jermyn Street. I tried to remember what that had been like.

'Don't light anything,' I said, 'There might be gas.'

'Oh dear!' said the warden. 'Where's the bloody brigade? They must have heard this one. What do they expect me to do with a lot of girls from the post office?'

'You could ask us to stamp your...'

'Shut up, Ruby,' we chorused.

We picked our way up what had been the front garden path. Curiously the front door was still standing in its frame in the porch although everything behind was a jagged outline of collapsed bricks, splintered wood and broken glass. I thought, it's as if the house has been blown down at the back and then been swept up towards the front by an enormous broom. All we needed was a giant dustpan to neaten it all up.

The warden tried the front door. I couldn't believe it. Stupid pillock, Freddie would have called him.

'It's still locked,' he said with some surprise.

'Try ringing the bell,' I said, just beating Ruby to it.

The warden clambered round the side of the door, flashing his lantern. 'Mrs Baird, Mrs Baird,' he called.

'Ssshh, I thought I heard something,' I said. 'Why don't we try round the back? There's bound to be a gate through from the allotments.'

'You go and see,' said the warden. 'We'll work through from the front here.'

It was a good deal easier said than done. The warden was the only one with a light. Well, he was the only one allowed in the blackout. They don't really think these things through, do they? I suppose they think there'll be moonlight and everything will always be on fire. And a lot of the time it is, I suppose. There was a bit of a moon, as it happened. I picked out the pathway leading into the allotments at the side of the house. The fence was all over the place, though. I worked my way down it until I had come level with what had been the end of the side wall of the house. I thought I would clamber over the fence here and into the back garden. I still hadn't come across a side gate. Anyway, I thought, I expect it will still be locked even if it's standing.

I found a panel of the fence that had fallen inwards at an angle of about forty-five degrees and I crawled up it almost on all fours, making it sway and bounce. When I reached its top edge, I half stood up ready to jump down the few feet into the garden.

It was pitch black. The moon had decided to disappear completely behind the clouds just when I needed it. It was too late to change my mind. The fence had a mind of its own and as I began to stand upright it catapulted me forward into the blackness.

I suppose it was a good job I had my tin hat on. It saved me from a worse crack than the one I got anyway. The bomb had actually fallen into the garden immediately behind the house. God, it must have been a big one! No wonder Jerry didn't want to take it home. Well we'd heard it, hadn't we? Shrieking like some monstrous whistling kettle. It must have detonated as soon as it hit the ground, blowing the back of the house in and making a crater seven or more feet deep for me to launch myself into. The fence decided to follow me in for good measure.

How long is it before you sort your head out after a thump like that? I don't know. You see people knocked unconscious apparently for minutes on the films, just by being punched on the jaw a couple of times, but I'm not convinced. I always think it must take a lot more than that to lay someone out cold. Still, I must have been winded or something, for quite some time, because it took me a while to work out where I was and what had happened to me. And the first things that occur to you are quite stupid. I thought I must have ruined my stockings. Stockings! When had I last worn decent stockings? I knew it was a ridiculous thought to have. We girls all wore trousers for fire watch anyway.

I was face down with the fence panel on top of me and

wedged into the sides of the hole. I could move, but not very easily in my coat, but I didn't feel too trapped or too helpless. I'd hurt my hands and face, I knew, but not seriously. I thought about calling out for help, but decided that might be a bit unnecessary, especially if they were all trying to dig out Mrs Baird from what was left of her cupboard under the stairs.

The fence was proving quite troublesome to shift. I couldn't turn over properly to get a purchase to lift it off me and arching my back had little effect because it was well and truly stuck in the earth and whatnot in the crater.

And then, just when I was thinking perhaps I would have to shout for help after all and not looking forward to either the prospect of being manhandled by the warden or living with Ruby's accounts of my indignity forever and a day, I heard my name being called from the direction of the allotment path.

It was Freddie.

I shouted back, but being face down in the dirt, it must have sounded a bit feeble.

'Where are you, Florrie Dee?' Freddie sounded very anxious. 'Are you all right?'

'I'm in a hole in the garden. I can't get out, but I'm all right.'

The moon decided to reappear.

'I still can't see you,' said Freddie.

'Can you see the fence?'

'I think so, yes.'

'I'm under it. Look I'm moving it with my bum.'

'I see you now. Nothing wrong with your bum, then?'

I felt the fence lift up on one side, dislodging more dirt and filling my mouth in the process. I emerged spitting and coughing and wormed my way to the top of the crater where Freddie was lying on his stomach, heels in the air, holding the edge of the fence.

'Have they found Mrs Baird?' I asked

'Who's she?'

'It's her house.'

'I don't know about that. I came haring down from the station when I heard the bomb. I thought…I don't know…it was bloody close wasn't it? Too bloody close. I didn't know where…just knew it was close. I saw that warden and your lot. Couldn't see you though. That Ruby Whatsaname said you'd gone round the back.'

I clung on to Freddie and together we stumbled back to the road. The fire watch party were standing in front of the house. I let go of Freddie and straightened my coat and tin hat.

'Have you found her? Mrs Baird?'

'No,' said Hilda Dworkin. 'Was she round the back?'

You despair sometimes, don't you?

'I didn't get that far. It's all come down.'

'The brigade's on its way,' said the warden briskly, as if he were making a report, and taking in Freddie's stripes. 'They'll be able to make a proper search.'

The siren on the police station began to sound the 'all clear'

'I'd better get Florence home,' said Freddie. 'She's been in a bomb crater all night.'

I must say it felt like it.

We shared a bath and I have to say it was well above the red line. I needed it. Anyway, two can have it deeper.

The frightful panic of the bomb had gone but I still had something that seemed just as bad gnawing in the pit of my stomach.

'You were late,' I said, remembering. 'I tried to get you, but it was unobtainable.'

'I expect the exchange was out. Was there something or did you just miss me?'

'Rhoda phoned me at work. She was squiffy. Old Webber was fairly bloody about it. You've been to see her.'

'Christ, yes! Switzerland! I had to know. Is it true? She wouldn't tell me, needless to say. But then, I suppose you can't blame her.'

'Who's told you about Switzerland?'

'It is true then?'

'Depends. Who's said what?'

'Rhoda had an abortion in Switzerland and you were there.'

'Christ, Freddie. I wasn't actually there…Who said that? Don't say it was Pa. Not Pa!'

Suddenly that possibility rose up inside me, like my worst nightmare that had been lurking, deep down. Pa had wormed it out of me after his chum from the Co-op Holidays had asked him, over one of their chess games, why Rhoda and I had ducked out of the last bit of our trip. Pa took me off-guard. I'd forgotten about the connection through his pal. I tried to fib my way out of it, not very convincingly, but Pa said, if I wouldn't tell him the truth, he'd put his hat on, then and there, and go up to the theatre, to have it out with Rhoda.

So I made a huge scene. Pa was stunned when I told him,

although, I think, not entirely surprised. Then, having got it out of me, he swore me to secrecy, which wasn't difficult, and it wasn't mentioned again.

'Your father?' Freddie sounded just as flabbergasted as I felt, at the idea. 'No, it was Captain Gaillet.'

22

'Louis Gaillet. Just like him.' Josephine Lucie said, shortly after our first, very strained Christmas since mother's death. Neither Pa nor his mother-in-law had really put in more than token appearances. Rhoda had made sure she was invited to friends and Leonard had obtained a very large cigar in a silver tube, which occupied his attention in the shed, until well into the new year.

Grandmother had come back from the Broadway with, of all things, a large cock crab. It was a cooked one, which was a blessing.

Pa had been very iffy about my spending so much time in the middle room since her locking herself away for a week. It had confirmed his view that the French were all mad and likely to get madder. To have found a crab boiling away on the range, I just knew, would have been seen as a deliberate act of provocation on her part. Crabs were not the kind of thing Pa had any truck with, outside the Isle of Wight.

'What are you wasting money on now, *Madame*? A crab? What good is a crab? The place for a crab is the seaside or in a jar of Shipham's paste. Dead men's fingers, that's what crabs have. We might as well eat a toadstool or two.' I could just hear him.

So being cooked, we were able to deal with it out of sight in the middle room, and I only had to worry about being summoned away peremptorily, if Pa thought I had been there too long.

'What was just like Louis Gaillet?' I said.

'This crab. *Monsieur le Torteau.*'

'What do you mean? Old?'

Josephine Lucie picked the crab up and sniffed it.

'It is not so fresh, it is true. But you cannot get *choses de qualité* in the Broadway. But it is not yet *putride*. Monsieur Machin would have had better from the Gare du Nord at midday than we have here. No, I did not mean old, but I suppose he was that, too.'

'What then?'

'Louis Gaillet became like a crab when he realised I might leave Paris. He moved sideways, you understand what I am saying? Not honest anymore with me or with Monsieur Adolphe. Monsieur Adolphe who was like a brother to him, as I have told you. More than Béranger. More than Papa Montel. And the crab's claws. Always a little sinister, *n'est-ce pas*? Holding on and not letting go.'

'Was it because he…?' I hesitated, '…because of your Wednesday afternoons off?'

'It might have been, I suppose, although I don't think they were so important to him. It was the paintings he was more concerned about. I think he had a suspicion Monsieur Adolphe would let me take them. Louis demanded to know, in front of me, if this was the plan. But Monsieur said it was not possible and did not mention it again.'

Then I realised what she had just said. The penny dropped.

'You hadn't stopped being with him on Wednesdays, then? I thought you had because of Augustin.'

She looked at me, unblinking, her lips pursed. Weighing something up.

I floundered on, not wanting to resurrect my imaginings of the House of Assignation and the smell of cabbage. I wanted her to tell me I'd got hold of the wrong end of the stick.

'You told me Monsieur Adolphe wouldn't have let him…' I waited.

'Say it, *chérie*. "Wouldn't have let him go to bed with me." No, and it was a secret well kept between us, for that reason. And the fact that I found the whole thing a little *ennuyant*.'

I looked at her.

'Boring, *chérie*. I found it boring.'

Of course, I was still struggling with the whole bed business, anyway. Left to the tender offerings of the Carnegie Library, I was all right with falling into one another's arms and long lingering kisses. Pa, rather surprisingly, had once or twice recently allowed me to accompany Rhoda to the new cinema in the Broadway too. Much to her disgust, I may add. It was after Mother's death. I suppose, looking back on it. I bet the old fox thought it was preferable to my spending even more time in the middle room with Grandmother, now that there was no longer need for me to attend to Mother. So I was exposed to languorous looks and even more lingering kisses there, which I could savour and squirm at in the privacy of the darkness.

But bed was still a mystery. Nothing at the library or the

Broadway Cinema, ever took place in bed. And yet I knew, full well, there was a veil to be drawn aside there. Everything Josephine Lucie said told me that. Rhoda's dark teasing of Leonard told me that. And I was utterly certain I wasn't going to give Rhoda the satisfaction of asking what it would reveal.

Inside myself I wanted it to reveal Josephine Lucie and her Augustin doing something deeply delicious involving – I didn't know – chocolate perhaps.

I fervently hoped Josephine Lucie herself would finally draw that veil aside for me so that I could confound Rhoda when the time came for her to start on me. But bed had only been mentioned in the same breath as Louis Gaillet, not the beloved Augustin. And mentioned in a way as to suggest that I must already know the mystery.

So what was it she found boring? I didn't want to know. My disappointment and, I expect, my disapproval, must have shown.

Josephine Lucie took my hand, a thing she only did as Grandmother if we were out, to make a point to Rhoda and Leonard. Not that Leonard would have noticed.

'You are wondering about Augustin, *ma chère*. You feel for him a little as I did. It is normal.'

'You were…' I struggled for the Carnegie phrase, '…being untrue to him.'

She sighed. 'Is it impossible, Florence, for you to be a little French? I was never unfaithful to Augustin until I met your Grandfather Burnell. And not even then, perhaps. Not even then.'

I waited.

'I had not slept with Augustin, *tu comprends*? I would have married him. *Voilà*. This was not a question with Louis Gaillet. Oh, you English!'

Yes, yes. But it wasn't about sleeping, was it? No, I did not *comprend*.

'What shall we do with him, Florence?'

'Louis Gaillet or Augustin?'

'I was thinking of *Monsieur le Torteau*, here'

'Brown bread sandwiches?' I had a memory of Seaview, on the Isle of Wight.

'So English, Florence, so English you are. Is there no hope?'

'What would César Machin have done with him?'

'A bisque perhaps, with cream and cognac. But we have neither. Does Charles have cognac? I don't suppose. Whisky for a visitor at Christmas, but no cognac. So what else? A *gratin*? With a *sauce mornay*. But just a little. And cheese over it, of course. Not too strong for the crab. What would you say? A light *comté*? Perhaps not. And *maroilles* would cover him too much.'

She took her cook's knife and with the point carefully prised off the top shell.

'Which are the dead men's fingers?' I said.

'These. They are the lungs. They come away, so. Not difficult.'

'Pa worried about them. At Seaview.'

Josephine Lucie sniffed the crab again.

'He is not fresh. I don't suppose we can take the meat from his claws without breaking it. We can try. It would be good for you to do.'

She rummaged in one of the drawers in her chiffonier and produced what looked like nut crackers, but smaller and thicker. Neatly twisting one of the claws from the shell at the joint she then separated the pincer joint from the leg and placed it in the crackers.

'One must remove this shell completely without damaging the meat inside…so.' She squeezed gently in several places so as to craze the shell all over and then began to peel it like a hardboiled egg.

'You are right, Florence. I was still seeing Louis. Not every Wednesday, it is true, but frequently. But that is not why he did not want me to go. As I told you, I think he still had a suspicion that Monsieur Adolphe meant me to take the paintings and he did not want them to make such a perilous journey. If I did not go, there was no chance they would go too. That was the reason. Not me.'

She picked off the last piece of crab shell, leaving just the pincer jaws intact.

'Now then *Monsieur*, let us see…' She gently teased the slenderest meat out of the jaws leaving none behind, keeping their shape whole.

'Perfect, but a little stale even so. Not so big and strong now.'

I attempted the other claw, as she had done, but only managed to extract the meat in several pieces and had to arrange it artfully, to disguise my bungled effort.

But there! It was Louis Gaillet, laid out soft and helpless on the plate.

'So would Monsieur de Marquise ever have told him about the balloon plan? Or would he have kept it a secret.'

'No, because I think he had a *prémonition*.'

'A premonition?'

'Yes. He had been walking by the Luxembourg,' she broke off. Something dawned on her. 'Yes, of course, the Luxembourg. He must have been visiting the painter. Even so, it was dangerous because the Prussian guns could reach the Luxembourg. He saw an old lady and her little dog killed in the street by a – what is it *un obus*? A *bombe*?'

'A shell do you mean? Like Leonard's got in his bedroom?'

'He has?' Is it alive?

'No, it's just the outside, Leonard says.'

'Yes, I expect like that. Anyway, Monsieur Adolphe was very upset by it and kept saying how near he had been to the old lady and her dog. I think it was after that, he decided Louis and the others should know of the plan, and what was to become of the paintings, in case anything should happen to him.'

'When, though?'

'He was going to do it when we had landed safely.'

Josephine Lucie was beginning to sound a bit flummoxed. I had the feeling her story was taking a direction she had not fully intended. I began to have my doubts again.

'He wouldn't have known you'd landed safely. You said they couldn't come back, the balloons.'

'Yes, but there was a pigeon. Augustin had to release it when we were safe. It was normal. To say the post had been delivered.'

A carrier pigeon. I was surprised to hear there were any left. Not one of César Machin's pigeons, at any rate. And again I wondered if it was all a big leg-pull. Time to move on, even at the risk of a disapproving look for jumping the gun.

'The man from the post office, with the ham babies, must have kept his end of the bargain, then?'

He had apparently.

On the night the balloon was to ascend, Augustin had brought Josephine Lucie a sheepskin waistcoat, leggings and voluminous trousers issued by the Head Postmaster for her in addition to his own. It was then she realised that she was truly going. Monsieur de Marquise furnished her with a pair of his leather riding boots, which were sufficiently large for her to pull on over the leggings, and a pair of knitted bed socks into the bargain.

There was no provision for personal luggage, but *Monsieur* had given her a considerable sum of money to provide for her onward journey, supposing that she would eventually be able to buy herself more suitable clothes. It was sewn into a bag with a tape to go round her waist under the trousers.

The paintings, minus their frames and carefully wrapped, did not, fortunately, look like very much. Josephine Lucie was able to pass them off to Augustin as 'some private post of Monsieur Adolphe's he would like to see safely out of Paris'. Which indeed was true.

Augustin did not enquire further, and said it had better go with her in the sack.

So Josephine Lucie was to be loaded into the balloon gondola in a mail bag in front of the crowd of spectators, including Monsieur Adolphe de Marquise. It must have seemed an appropriate solution to the postmaster's dilemma

'But surely you must have looked just like a body in a bag,' I said.

'Not so. We went first to the post officer's *bureau*, where I stood up in the sack, and Augustin put letters and packets, including the parcel of the paintings, all round me to disguise my shape. And don't forget it was very dark.'

Augustin made sure it was he who pulled the sack with Josephine Lucie in off the hand cart and bundled her over the edge of the balloon's basket, before climbing in himself. The Postmaster told him which of the sacks of mail should be jettisoned first in case of an emergency, and which, under no circumstances, were to be allowed to fall into Prussian hands, if he had the misfortune to come down in occupied territory.

'I heard Augustin say, not this one either, *Monsieur le Directeur*, and he gave me a push in the sack, of which I was very glad.'

She stopped and I waited. Did the niggling signs of disbelief show on my face, I wonder?

'No questions for me? Not so much "What happened next?" but more "How can this be true?" Sometimes you begin to doubt my history, I think. It becomes more difficult when you see this old lady in her middle room. I know. I hear the doubt in your voice this evening.'

This could be a disaster. She'd spotted me checking her story for holes. But she must realise how much more there was to swallow now than there had been at first. Far from disbelieving her, I really wanted it all to be true. But I could just hear Leonard scoffing at the idea of old ladies escaping in balloons at the dead of night, wrapped up in the postman's sack. No matter that he called her Josephine Lucie behind her back, she was still his grandmother and couldn't be anything else. Not like her and me in the middle room.

I needed to retrieve the situation. Or did I? True or false, it was the history she'd said she wanted me one day to pass on, perhaps to my own granddaughter, so that… what had she said at the very beginning…? So that we could recognize when men were about to change the directions of our lives? Something like that. So the story had better be a good one, hadn't it? I wondered if I shouldn't let her off lightly.

I suppose I must have mumbled something unconvincing, at any rate, because she redirected her thoughts to the crab. Deliberately to punish me, I should think.

'Probably brown bread is all he is good for. You had better go down to the kitchen, Florence and cut some.'

'But Pa will say I must go back down and help with tea if I go now.'

'If you must,' she said, not seeming to care one way or the other, 'Or you can tell him you are having tea with me. Crab with brown bread and butter. Oh, I forget. Brown bread and margarine. Charles does not permit butter in the evening.'

Do you know? For once, I felt sorry for Pa. He was, I knew, still paying off the doctor's bills and the sanatorium, even though Mother had been dead for months, and, as far as I was concerned, paying the ones who had killed her.

23

I'd felt so sorry for Pa. Very sorry that he should think so much the worse of me, and very angry too. He took so much convincing that I hadn't known what Rhoda was planning when she persuaded him to let me go with her on that tour with the Co-op Holidays, I gave up trying.

So all that anger and pity all came welling up when Freddie said what he'd been told. My first thought was that for some extraordinary reason Pa had told him. As far as I could see, Pa was the only person who could have told him. Other than Rhoda, and she obviously hadn't, or I wouldn't have had the call in the office.

When Freddie said it was Captain Gaillet I almost laughed with relief. Except it was so bloody awful. My next horror was that somehow it had become common knowledge and was being gossiped about all over the West End. Well, up-and-coming young actress going places. They would, wouldn't they?

'How on earth does Captain Gaillet know? Who else knows? Poor Rhoda. Did you tell her she's the talk of Carlton Gardens?'

'As far as I know she isn't and I didn't.' Freddie levered himself out of the bath after me and started gently rubbing me down with the towel.

'Are you all right, Florence Duck?'

'No, of course I'm not all right. This is terrible. Why does Gaillet know? I'm speechless. Why does he feel he's got to mention it to you, either? Was he gloating, or what?'

'I meant,' said Freddie, kissing my shoulder, 'are you all right after having been buried in somebody's garden half the night by Hermann Göring?'

'Good God, Freddie! This is far more important than Hermann Göring. I've forgotten all about that.'

Which was true. Freddie's bombshell had driven the other one clean out of my head.

'So what? Gaillet just came out with it did he?' I said, 'By the way, I hear your sister had an abortion in Switzerland a few years ago while she was on holiday with your wife.'

Freddie turned me round and started towelling my breasts in that way where one thing usually leads to another. But it wasn't going to tonight.

'He's making his move. Your Uncle Maurice is right. He's up to something fishy.'

'Yes, yes Freddie. But what's being fishy got to do with Rhoda and me in Switzerland?'

'He's using what he knows to lean on me. He wants me to turn a blind eye to things I would have to see going across the desk. That's why I had to go straight away and ask Rhoda if it was true. I didn't want to use the phones at Carlton Gardens. People listen to them I'm sure. I was going to use a phone box, but then I thought, she's only just up the road rehearsing for her next opening. I thought it might be better face to face.'

'Better? How could it possibly be better?'

'I didn't think it could be true. As you say, how could he possibly know a thing like that?'

'Why didn't you ask me? If Gaillet said he knows I was with her, I mean?'

Freddie looked shifty. But I know what that means. It means he realises there was an easier way of doing something but it didn't occur to him until afterwards. He can go off at half cock sometimes.

'I told you, Florence Duck. I didn't want to believe him. And I especially didn't want to believe that you had any part in it, if it was true.'

'So what's made you believe it *is* true?'

'Rhoda's reaction at the stage door. I think she'd already had a couple. Made me a bit mad with her usual old nonsense. You know. "Oh I thought it was at least a Colonel in the *wegiment* of guards coming to call for me, but it's only a *wanker* from the Pay Corps. Have you brought our wage packets?" All that rubbish. And at the top of her Sybil Thorndike voice, so she could turn heads all down the street. So I'm afraid I lost my rag a bit and came straight out with it.'

'How?'

'I must have said something like "How'd you like me to shout your bit of Swiss business all down the Haymarket at the top of my voice.".'

'Something like?'

'Well, those words, actually'

'Oh Freddie!'

'Don't "Oh Freddie". Rhoda really gets up my nose sometimes. I don't know why she has to say all those things. Trying to make me feel small when I've never given her cause.'

I know why, of course. It's because he refused to be impressed by her theatrical ways when they very first met. Just once would have been enough to cement their relationship ever after. But no, Freddie had to make some smart alec remark about wearing her Persian lamb hat and appearing in operating theatres. It wasn't even funny. I think she had him marked down as a communist from that moment. I know Rhoda gets up my nose too, half the time, but that's a bit different. We're sisters.

'So what are you going to do? About Gaillet, I mean. What's he leaning on you to do? You'll have to tell Maurice, won't you? We can't have him saying things about Rhoda. Who would he tell? The police? The *News of the World*? God, Freddie, I feel sick.'

'Whoa, hang on Florrie Dee! I shouldn't think for one moment it's a police matter. I don't know, but I shouldn't think it's a crime if it happened abroad. I mean how could they prove it, especially now? No, it's more likely a nasty whispering campaign. I shouldn't think even the *News of the World* would use her name if they couldn't prove it. Still, you know what they're like. They just give hints about someone's identity without actually saying who they are. Even then…'

'Even then, what?'

'Well, I should think Rhoda could handle it, don't you? Provided she kept her mouth shut. You know, never explain, never apologise, kind of thing. Publish and be damned. Mightn't do her reputation any harm at all in her business.'

'Oh come on Freddie. Don't be bloody ridiculous. She's not in provincial rep now. She's West End. From what she says, the managers are a lot of stuffy martinets and it's dog eat dog with the other actresses when it comes to getting parts. No Rhoda won't want it even hinted at, let alone out in the open. And anyway, what about me?'

'Oh, I should think you're safe from the *News of the World*, Florrie Dee. I mean you're not famous or anything.'

I could clout Freddie sometimes. It's a good job he has some special endearing qualities.

'I'm a civil servant, Freddie. They wouldn't put up with it. Old

Webber makes it quite clear it's only thanks to Hitler that I've got a job at all. My feet wouldn't touch. It'd be the sorting room for me, if I was lucky.'

'Well, I don't see how they'd get to know. It isn't as if Gaillet's going to pick up the phone to the Postmaster General, is it?'

'Isn't it? I don't know, Freddie. You tell me. If some blooming inspector from the Ministry came and said, "Is it true your sister had an abortion and you helped her?" I don't know what I'd say.'

'You could lie about it. Barefaced. Damn their eyes.'

'Yes. And I'd be going bright red all the way down to my bum. Freddie, this is just blooming ridiculous. And you still haven't told me what Gaillet wants out of all this. It must be something terrible if he's already trying to blackmail you…us. You must tell Maurice.'

'That mightn't stop Gaillet blabbing, though.'

'Maurice could have him shot or something.'

'Maurice could? What do you mean? That's at least twice you've called on Maurice tonight. I thought you said he was a crook. I was the one who thought he was a copper. You've changed your tune, Florence.'

'He is a crook. Well not exactly a crook. A dodgy businessman, that kind of crook. The government are leaning on him to work for them.'

'How do you know?'

'He told me. He came to see me.'

'Bloody hell, Florence. Now you tell me. Why all the secrets all of a sudden? Christ! Am I your husband or what?'

'It's not secrets all of a sudden. It isn't like that, Freddie darling. It isn't really.'

'Yes it is. There's this abortion business in Switzerland. There's this bloody Rubens everyone wants to know about. And now you tell me Maurice is some kind of a secret agent. What is it with you sisters and your adorable Uncle Maurice?'

He had a point. I could see how it must seem to poor Freddie. I suppose they were secrets in a way. But they were all different and not meant to deceive him. Apart from what Maurice had told me. I supposed I could tell him about Maurice now. Now that Gaillet had declared his hand. Well, I assumed he must have.

I shivered. We were still naked from the bath and it was past two in the morning. My bruises were beginning to ache.

'I'm cold, Freddie. Look at the time. Come to bed and talk.'

It seemed that Captain Gaillet had been very clever. Either that or Maurice and his cloak and dagger civil servants were barking up the wrong tree after all. The blind eye he wanted my husband to turn to things going across his desk at Carlton Gardens was, he had assured Freddie, a patriotic undertaking, albeit a surreptitious one.

'We have to have some means of channelling money outside this country, Corporal Draper, which your Treasury does not need to know about. Money that, because of your function here with us, you will necessarily have to transfer and record.'

Freddie, who was more than a bit suspicious of being 'Corporal Drapered' all of a sudden by the normally affable Gaillet, was not disposed to swallow his Gallic rhetoric either. He naturally wanted to know why the Treasury had to be kept in the dark.

Captain Gaillet closed his office door.

'Your government gives us some money, but there is a strict agreement with the General on how it can be used. This, I regret to say, is because your government does not recognise the Free French and our General as the future government of France. It is politics, my friend. Even during war, when we are fighting and dying on the same side, there is always politics. Our agreement with your Treasury says that we can use the sterling they permit us, to finance Free French representatives in neutral countries. To try and gain support there, for our part in the war.'

'It's so that they can try and recruit people in places like South America and Africa, Florrie Dee. People who used to work for French companies and are still there, engineers, Air France pilots, people like that and then pay their fares to somewhere where they can join the Free French. Canada and places. It's pretty small beer, really. But what Gaillet says they want to do is to create dummy offices as well, so the money paid to them can be used for other things. Things the Treasury wouldn't sanction because they wouldn't be for the war effort.'

I asked him what sort of things.

'He didn't really say. But he hinted it was all about setting up Seedy Gee around the world as the official French Government in exile. Apparently the General is already planning on being the next President of France.'

'Maurice says he's a nobody, who'll disappear without trace when the war's over,' I said.

'Is there nothing you and your Uncle Maurice don't chat about when I'm not around? Still, he's probably right. It's certainly the way the government is hedging its bets.'

We still hadn't got round to the Rhoda business, or why Gaillet had seen fit to mention it.

'So I presume you refused to play ball, Freddie. Is that why he's turned nasty? God! It's all a bit dangerous isn't it? I mean they wouldn't push you under a bus would they? I mean, if it goes all the way up to de Gaulle and the only thing in the way of him becoming King of France is Corporal Draper?'

Give Freddie his due, he had thought that through, too.

'I didn't say yes, and I didn't say no. I just said something about it sounded a bit too much over my head for me to get involved one way or the other.'

Evidently this hadn't been enough for the *Capitaine*.

'Corporal Draper... Freddie... we need to know that we can at least rely on your discretion. We would not expect you to do anything other than turn a blind eye to the documents you see crossing the desk and not to create a reason for questions to be asked.'

'I said, I supposed so, and if it went wrong it would have to be for the General and the government to sort out, wouldn't it?'

Then, as Freddie was about to open the door to go back to the main office, Gaillet said, 'By the way, Freddie, I think I can be of some help to your family. It is the least I can do in return for your assistance in the future of France. As you know, I have to be in touch with the Red Cross in London and Switzerland over the repatriation of some Frenchmen here who do not wish to fight with the Free French and wish to go home.'

Freddie said he knew. But wasn't it very difficult for them? Gaillet said it was, especially as the Germans had refused to allow a ship under flag of truce to cross the Channel.

'One of these renegades, for that is what I think they are, Freddie, is an army doctor who was tending the French wounded during the evacuation and did not have the opportunity to surrender to the Germans. He asked to see me when I was last at the White City camp. He tried to put pressure on me to get him back to France through Lisbon. I said I could not. It was a matter for the British. I could not intervene with the Red Cross, as he was not wounded, so as to be *hors de combat*. Then he told me that before the war he was a partner in two clinics in France and Switzerland. They performed abortions on many foreigners including English, some of whom were quite well-known and members of the *beau monde*. He has a list, Freddie. He showed it to me. He wanted me to make use of it to put pressure on the British government. It would be a *grande scandale* here if the names became public. I told him I would see what I could do. I shall not, of course, and I shall not return the list of names to him. Your wife's sister, the actress Rhoda Denning, is one of those on the list, but I will make sure it remains a secret.'

'I told him straight, Florrie Dee, "With all due respect, Sir, is that meant to be a favour or a threat? Because I could take it either way. I'm frankly not too bothered about Rhoda Denning. So why don't I just ask to go back to my unit, even if it means dropping the stripes, and you and the General can get on with your plans to your hearts' content and I won't be in your way."'

'What did he say to that?'

'Well that was when he mentioned you. He said it wasn't quite so simple as that, because your name was next to hers. Companion or next of kin or something. In case anything went wrong, I suppose.'

It sounded to me as though this French doctor – I couldn't remember his name, but I could see his face – had brought his entire medical records with him out of France. Still, as it was all pretty much the truth, as far as Rhoda was concerned, I mean, Gaillet had obviously got hold of something.

'Sounds like a pretty weighty list to be carrying around on the beach at Dunkirk or Caen or wherever he came across from, doesn't it Freddie? Did you ask to see it?'

'It's hardly the point, is it? If it's true, it's true. I just considered myself well and truly done over and dismissed myself. Of course, when I saw Rhoda at the theatre about an hour later, her reaction said it all. And you haven't exactly denied it, have you?'

'Well, I could deny it. Suppose there is no silly old list.'

'Yes, but that just goes round the circle again. So how does he know, if there's no list? And there's still the option of getting pushed under a bus. Anyway, you can't deny it to me, Florence.'

'Why can't I?'

'You're the one who said it happened when you were on holiday with Rhoda in Switzerland. Gaillet didn't.'

'So, we need to talk to Maurice. We simply must. You said he wanted you to keep an eye on Gaillet.'

24

'I whispered to Augustin through the sack, "Tell Monsieur Adolphe to keep an eye on Monsieur Gaillet. And tell him he will have to forgive César Machin", because Monsieur had come to the edge of the pannier to say goodbye. He asked if the post sack had any last wishes. He was laughing,' said Josephine Lucie, when I returned with the cut bread. There was brown and white, because we were low on both. But brooking no denial from Pa, I *had* contrived butter.

'Did you have to stay in the sack all the time?'

'No, only as we rose in the air above Montmartre. It was strange, you could hear everything on the ground below so clearly. More clearly, I think, than if you were on the ground and the same distance away from the people. Perhaps the sound goes up more easily. I could still hear Monsieur calling up to Augustin.'

'What?'

'Oh, you know. *Bon voyage. Bon courage.* Florence, is this butter? *Vraiement.* So, *ma chère*, you begin to speak as a woman to your Father now.'

'What did you mean, forgive César Machin? Oh, I know. About the ham.'

'Yes, of course, about the ham. César would not be able to keep it from Monsieur that he had two great *jambons* for Christmas but now they were no more. I knew he would weep on Christmas Eve and confess what he had done.'

'And why did you ask him to keep an eye on that Gaillet man?'

'Well, it didn't mean anything in particular. It was just one of those things we women say sometimes to keep the men thinking, "What did she mean?" Besides, I knew Louis Gaillet would be very angry with Monsieur when he learned the paintings had truly departed with me in the *montgolfière*.'

'And you still hadn't told him you were really going?'

'No. I thought he would find a way to stop me.'

'So what about no-one knowing what was to become of the paintings?'

'So… if we had a fortunate voyage, Augustin and I, we would send the pigeon to the post office and in this way Monsieur de Marquise would know where the paintings were. And if we had an accident and disappeared no-one would know about the paintings. Or worse, if we fell into the hands of the Prussians and were shot – because, *chérie,* this is what we believed they would do to aeronauts to discourage them – then what might they think of two such similar paintings by Rubens being smuggled out of Paris?'

Josephine Lucie scooped the remaining brown and orange meat from the inside of the crab shell and laid it beside the white meat we had taken from the pincers.

'What do you think, Florence?'

'Well, you mean the Prussians might have said they were forgeries to make Monsieur look like a criminal?'

'No, Florence. I mean, do you think we must mix the white meat with the brown for our sandwich, or shall we make white and then brown meat, and white and brown bread one on top of the other? Stripes. That would be elegant, *n'est-ce pas?*'

We settled for elegance, of course. Josephine Lucie may have turned up her nose at the quality of the crustacean from the Broadway, but in the middle room she would never allow the ingredients to be false to the memory of the great Machin's *gibier Parisien de saison, sauce salmis* or his *pigeonneaux de Mazarin*. The little towers of crab sandwiches, daintily cubed, their crusts ruthlessly sacrificed for art, in a way that would have made Pa's eyes water, looked for all the world like stacks of oversized liquorice allsorts or the coloured layers mother and I had scraped into glass phials from the cliffs at Alum Bay that year we'd gone to the Isle of Wight.

'It is still a sadness to me, you know, Florence,' Josephine Lucie said, with her mouth still slightly full, 'after all these years.'

I waited, knowing only too well by now how to recognise when she was about to deliver a bombshell.

'Yes,' she went on, after waiting a moment for my question which did not come, 'A great sadness that those were the last words I ever said to Monsieur, but I did not say them myself, Augustin did, because I was in a sack. I realised when it was too late I had not even embraced him.'

'But didn't you ever go back to Paris? Didn't Monsieur

Adolphe come to London after the siege was over? For the real painting you put in the bank?'

'Alas, *ma chère*, he did not. You see, his premonition was right.'

'Was right?'

'He was killed by a Prussian *obus* near *Les Invalides*. I think it was the very next day after our parting.'

Josephine Lucie's eyes filled with tears and she reached into her pocket for a scrap of hankie. I went and sat on the floor in front of her and put my head in her lap.

'Oh, Grandmother! I'm so sorry. You were so very fond of him, weren't you?'

Her grief had entered the middle room, an intrusion that had not been allowed to the death of my mother. I think we both realised it as soon as I called her 'Grandmother'.

'He was like a father to me and a big brother too. Both together. But, Florence *chérie*, when I remember it now, I imagine it was the moment when I lost my path. I told you. Men make it happen to women.'

I think she must have deliberately kept the sudden death of Monsieur from me until that moment, simply to see it take my breath away. As with most of the twists and turns of her history, she delighted in saving them up, in allowing my expectations to run on, and then to bring them to a juddering halt without prior warning.

But this time I saw it was she who had been taken by surprise, she who had been brought crashing down by her own recollections. I had seen before, her ability to remove herself from the present into her past as if she were still there, recalling in minute detail the *cabinet* dinners, the laying of the table, and César Machin's offerings, course by course.

This was different. Instead of allowing herself to go back in an orderly way, just for the time being, she had let her forgotten grief come flooding into the here and now, into the middle room. And I guess it stayed there for a long time.

I boiled her little copper kettle on the gas ring in the fireplace and made her a cup of camomile tea. I didn't want to go back down to the kitchen. I wouldn't have been allowed to make a second return journey to the middle room that evening, and I didn't want to have to say to Leonard, who would be doing his homework, that Grandmother needed me because she was upset.

There, thinking of her as Grandmother again. And I was still in the middle room.

'This *infusion* is full of comfort,' she said, clasping the cup to her bosom with both hands. 'I used to pick the little flower heads of camomile for my mother in the garden at Orgelets. We used to dry them in the *grenier,* you know, at the top of the house under the roof, where it is warm and dry in summer and the air comes under the tiles. *Maman* always said, when she made the *camomile* in the winter time, she could smell the summer hay being cut. That is why it is such a comfort. In the dark and the cold.'

She was a little girl on the farm again, a place she had only taken me to once in the middle room and never taken me back. I wondered if this was the place she had chosen, in her grief, to give a new lease of life to Josephine Lucie. I realised I had banished all thoughts that she might have been pulling my leg.

'Did you ever go back to your home? To Orgelets?'

She was silent for a moment and then she nodded in a way that made me see that, in my attempt to put things back together the way they had been before, I had stumbled over another hidden unhappiness. I went to squeeze her hand but couldn't because of the teacup.

'You know, Florence, I thought at first it would be amusing to tell you my history, little by little. Just enough to keep us going until the next time and then the next time. Like my magazine. The one I buy in the Broadway every week.'

'The Home Companion?'

'No. The other one. With the stories. It doesn't matter.'

'I like it too. The way you tell it to me.'

'Yes but now, *ma chère*, I remember things I should prefer to forget. No, not forget, but to say them all at once because they are painful to me.'

She sighed a gusty sigh. 'Some pain perhaps but mostly *déception.* Do you know what this is?'

'Deception? Yes, but I don't understand. What deception?'

'No, it is not that. It is when you expect something nice and then it is not nice.'

'Disappointed?'

'*Voilà*. I am disappointed.'

'What with? What were you…are you disappointed with?'

'Almost everything.'

'You don't want to stop, do you? Telling me.' I was suddenly really alarmed.

'I don't know, Florence. Do you want me to go on, even if

there is sadness and disappointment?'

This was totally unfair. Putting it on me to decide, when I'd put up with her tantalising me and refusing to be rushed along all this time. Well all right, if Josephine Lucie was having a crisis, she needed a firm hand.

'You must carry on, of course,' I said, adding in a stately, grown-up way, 'I shall have my own grand-daughter to tell it all to one day. You said, remember? If you stop now, then I shall feel a deception too, and so will she.'

She put her teacup down and fumbled again for her handkerchief. Then she gave her nose a good, loud blow.

'So, we shall begin again. You must ask me something.'

'I did. I asked you if you ever went back home…to Orgelets.'

I did feel a bit brutal. But she was the one who'd mentioned Orgelets again, first. And hadn't she once said something about a man there she might have married. The one who'd met Robert Louis Stevenson on the canal? Who was that? Where did he fit in?

'Yes, *ma chère,* I did go back to Orgelets.'

The balloon had made a good ascent above Montmartre and had headed off in a slightly east of north direction, which was as intended. Josephine Lucie had carefully manoeuvred herself out of the post bag, fearful lest she should rock the basket and upset them, while Augustin busied himself with his barometer and notebook and pencil, calculating their height and rate of ascent.

'We have to rise high enough to avoid the Prussians shooting at us from the ground if they see us,' he explained. 'But not so high that there is too much pressure in the envelope and it starts to split at the seams.'

Josephine Lucie, if she had given it any thought at all, had assumed that the balloon would just go on getting higher and higher. The idea was new to her that, left to itself, it would reach a height where its weight, the surrounding air pressure and the amount of gas in the envelope would all balance, so that it couldn't go any higher, or lower for that matter, without Augustin making some adjustment to those elements that he had some control over. It took some explaining.

'So, my darling, I may have to throw one of us out, if we need to go higher. The dispatches must get through at all costs, you know.'

'Be serious, Augustin.'

'I am being perfectly serious.'

'No you're not. How do we get down, then? Just let all the gas out? What happens if we have to let a lot out before we arrive anywhere we want to be? To stop it splitting, if we are too high? I don't want it to split Augustin. Promise me it won't split.'

'That depends on how good the girls at the Gare du Nord have been with their needles and thread. But in any case, I have a small pump here, so we can pump some of the gas into this reservoir. The envelope gets heavier with less gas in it, but the metal of the tank does not have the same reaction to the air pressure. So we still have the gas to pump back into the envelope if we want to make it lighter. At least, my darling, that's the general idea, I think.'

'What do you mean? You think? Haven't you done this before?'

'Yes but only on the end of a rope at the Gare du Nord. It's not quite the same. And they can't make enough illuminating gas to waste on practising. There isn't enough coal left in Paris.'

It had begun to dawn on Josephine Lucie that ballooning carried with it a certain amount of risk. She had up to that point been concerned with getting herself into the balloon unopposed. Getting out again safely had not really featured very prominently in the exercise. She had, when all was said and done, put her trust in the man she loved.

'So, you've only been up and down inside the Gare du Nord?'

'In effect.'

'On a rope? No balloon?'

'Well, a small one, to play with the pump. But not enough to lift the basket by itself. We had some sailors pulling on the rope to do that.'

Josephine Lucie digested this. She didn't know whether to believe him or not. But of course, nearly all the experienced *montgolfière* pilots had left Paris already, and were unable to return. It did only leave enthusiastic volunteers like Augustin. Still, silently drifting a hundred feet above the northern *faubourgs* of Paris, it hardly mattered any more.

Soon they could see the lights of the Prussian lines and bivouacs. Augustin said he could wish that they were higher by now and that the breeze would pick up to speed them out of harm's way. They were climbing, it was true, but only slowly.

'Are we high enough?' said Josephine Lucie, seeing Augustin peering anxiously over the lip of the basket.

He shook his head, at the same time putting his hand to his

mouth to indicate that she should keep her voice to a whisper while they were floating immediately above the enemy lines. They could hear the sound of voices carrying up to them from below, the noise of animals, horses and mules, metal scraping and being struck. A dog barked and was answered by another, a sound no longer heard inside of the hungry city for some time now. It seemed to Josephine Lucie impossible that they should pass over so much activity unseen or unheard. The slight rush of air around the balloon, the intermittent creak of the basket and its ropes, sounded positively deafening to her. How could the soldiers on the ground below not be aware of their presence?

'Should we throw something out?' she hissed.

But Augustin shook his head again and mimed a startled Prussian being hit on the head. He put his hands together as if in prayer, and, as if in answer to it, the balloon suddenly began to rise rather more rapidly into the icy darkness. The lights from the lines became smaller and soon began to thin out, visible now as twinkling clusters here and there in an otherwise inky void.

Augustin shone a lamp on his barometer. He had to wipe away the condensation beginning to congeal into frost on its mercury tubes. After a little calculation he decided to pump some gas from the envelope to the metal reservoir.

'It's a little tricky to calculate,' he said. 'With the cold, I think the air pressure drops more rapidly even though we are not so high, but I am not sure.'

Josephine Lucie was quite cold enough as it was and asked him not to go higher than he had to if they were safe from the Prussian bullets now. She was still nervous about the seams of the envelope holding out under the pressure from within.

Now there were no lights of any consequence below them, just the occasional glimmer from a hamlet or a farmhouse. Without any other fixed point of reference in the darkness it was almost impossible to judge how fast they might be travelling or what distance they might have covered. She settled down in one corner of the basket as best she could for the sacks of mail and the pigeon's cage, trying to ignore the chattering of her teeth.

'I suppose you didn't manage to get anything for us to eat out of old César Machin, did you?' Augustin said.

Josephine Lucie had in fact declined the precious potatoes and exorbitantly priced bread the *chef* had tried to press on her, saying that she would be breakfasting on chocolate and rolls somewhere in

France far away from the Prussian blockade, while the inhabitants of the *hôtel* would still be having to make do with the products of his ingenuity. 'He gave me this,' she said. 'It's cognac. It'll keep out the cold, at any rate.'

'And did you? Have chocolate and rolls for breakfast? That sounds lovely. Better than porridge and a shared egg. Although I don't mind porridge. Or the egg, come to that. Still, chocolate for breakfast...'

'No, I did not, Florence. I think it was a very long time before I had anything good to eat.'

'Why? What happened?'

'We came down with a very big bump.'

'Crashed? Heavens! Were you hurt? Augustin...he didn't...?'

'No. He had some broken bones. His ribs and his arm. His leg'

Josephine Lucie's fears about the seamstresses' handiwork had been fulfilled. Some time before dawn, when they had been travelling for nearly five hours, but latterly only with a very light breeze, the envelope had sprung a leak.

Augustin had pumped some of the gas into the reservoir to reduce the pressure, but of course they started to come down quite fast. It was still very dark and they had no way to tell how near to the ground they were. Only the barometer. But that showed them their height above Montmartre. They could not tell how close to the ground below they were, compared with Paris.'

The first inkling they had that their time was up was the sight of tree tops coming up at them out of the dark. Augustin pumped like a man possessed, but could not by then re-inflate the balloon faster than the gas was escaping from the torn seam. They struggled to lift one of the mail sacks to jettison it, but it was too late. Dragging through the branches reaching out to grasp them like splintering fingers, they finally collapsed to the ground in a field on the other side. They were thrown out of the wreck of the basket, engulfed in the shredded remains of the balloon envelope, cruelly battered and bruised.

'I was not so hurt as Augustin. He had broken bones. His arm was broken and it had come out of his shoulder as well, you know?'

'Dislocated? Like Leonard did at football. Pa did something to make it go back. Leonard didn't half yell.'

'I did not know how to do this. And besides, his arm was broken. I did not dare to move it.'

Josephine Lucie fell silent and I could see the tears welling up in her eyes again. It was touch and go in the middle room still, I could tell.

'You're a bit tired. All this chatting,' I said as breezily as I could. 'Perhaps I should go down now.'

'That would be best, *ma chérie*. But we must talk. It becomes more important to me than I imagined. Come up and see me soon. Tomorrow.'

25

'This is more important than you can imagine, Florence. You must come up and see me – soon – tomorrow.'

'I can't. Not tomorrow, Uncle Maurice. I'm working. You'll have to come here in the evening or wait until the weekend. You said you would if Freddie told me anything.'

'I don't particularly want Freddie there, that's all.'

I'd telephoned Maurice in my dinner break from one of the booths out in the main post office, taking care to shut the folding door firmly behind me, as Ruby was hovering and would certainly have listened in if I'd left it ajar. I'd rather have gone to a box outside, but she'd only have smelt a rat if I had. It would have looked too furtive. Maurice took a while to pick up the phone, which made me wonder where it was I was calling him. I'd assumed it was his office. It was a number on the Primrose exchange, St John's Wood, somewhere round there. But it was a switchboard, quite a big one by the sound, so I was a bit cagey when I eventually spoke to him. I told him it probably wasn't important, but 'the captain' had said something to Freddie.

That was when he cut across, partly to shut me up on the phone I supposed, and said we had to meet. From his manner I got the distinct impression Maurice was already one jump ahead and my call had almost been expected.

'But Freddie knows all about it. It's silly to exclude him. I can't pretend I haven't spoken to you. I told him I was going to.'

That threw him, though.

'You haven't told Freddie about our conversation, have you? I thought we agreed…'

'Not everything, no. But it's not what Freddie knows. It's what Gaillet knows, I need to talk to you about.'

'What Gaillet knows? Just give me a rough idea what we're talking about, Florence.' He sounded almost – I don't know –

panicky.

'Isn't this phone…?'

'Well, if it isn't, none of them are, but that wouldn't surprise me. Just give me the top line, so to speak.'

'He knows about something that happened to Rhoda and me in 1936 in Switzerland, well France actually, but it started in Switzerland. Well, the holiday started in Germany to be precise…'

'Good God!' said Maurice at the other end of the phone. 'Are you talking about what I think you're talking about?'

'You can't possibly know what I'm talking about…'

'Can't I, though, Florence? Hang up. Go back to your typing pool, or wherever it is you work, now. I'll get you out this afternoon.'

'How?'

'I'll think of something. When I do, wait at a bus stop. Where is the nearest?'

'By the church in the High Street.'

I hung up and after the usual brief struggle emerged from the folding door of the booth. Ruby was still there. I guess she'd been waiting till I'd finished.

'You going out the back for your dinner?' she said. There was a bit of a recreation ground on the other side of the post office yard where we girls shinned over the fence, Ruby making sure she showed everything to the men in the sorting office when she did, to eat our sandwiches if the sun was shining. Mine were cheese and onion, mostly minus the cheese, so I didn't really fancy them anyway.

'No, I think I'll go back in, Ruby. I've got a lot to finish today for Mr Webber.'

'Got to take your break, Doll. Anyone would think there's a war on. Who was that you were on the phone to, so how's-your-father? Not your Freddy, by the looks.'

I could crown her sometimes. She was just threatening she'd spread some gossip about me if I didn't give something.

'It was my new boss, Ruby. I've joined the secret service. But it's only three afternoons a week. Mum's the word, eh?' I said. How I was going to regret that in the next twenty minutes.

'That's your story and you're sticking to it,' said Ruby. 'So, three afternoons a week, eh? That's some fancy man. Poor old Freddie. Shame he's not further away, really.'

There was nothing for it. I went with her to the field and wolfed my sandwiches down in double quick time. Anything to keep her nose in joint.

When I got back to my desk, Mr Webber was hovering, looking extremely put out.

'Really Mrs Draper, where have you been?' No 'Florence' today, then.

'It was my dinner time, Mr Webber. I didn't go far. I've only been out a short while, really. Is something wrong?'

'Golders Green Sorting have been on. Apparently they have a sensitive package for us that should have come by special messenger, but it's been overlooked. It has to be collected and they've asked for you by name. I don't know, Mrs Draper, really I don't. Why should they ask for you? I sometimes think there's something you should be telling me. That business with the War Office? Hitler has a great deal to answer for. Yes indeed.'

'Golders Green? How am I to get there, Mr Webber?'

'You'll just have to take the trolley bus.'

'But if it's a sensitive package, I shouldn't bring it back on the bus, surely?'

'That's their problem. You're obviously so important, Mrs Draper, they'll probably put you in a cab.' His unaccustomed nastiness was upsetting. Fussy, yes. But not normally spiteful.

'Well, why can't they find another messenger…tomorrow? I'll have to get there and back by six, won't I? I have my husband to think about, if I'm going to be late…'

'I've been through all that with them myself. They're insisting on you. You'll have to go.'

It was only then it crossed my mind that perhaps all this was a ruse by Maurice to get me out of the office. But how could I be sure?

'Well, may I call my husband, and warn him?'

'You can perfectly well use the public booth in the post office, Mrs Draper, if you have to.'

I gave up. He was quite unbelievable sometimes, about his wretched telephone. I put my hat and coat on, picked up my gas mask, and went back out to the public area. I dialled Maurice's number again.

'Mr Burnell is not available,' said the woman on the switchboard.

So what did that mean?

The motor car pulled up beside me as I was beginning to think about giving up waiting at the trolley bus stop by the church.

The uniformed ATS girl who was driving wound the window down. Even then I assumed she was going to ask me for directions or something.

'Mrs Draper?'

'Yes?'

'Mr Burnell's compliments. And can I give you a lift to Golders Green?'

So it was Maurice after all. Mr Webber had better not check whether I'd arrived or not. He'd have apoplexy. That Hitler's got a lot to answer for.

'Yes please,' I said, climbing in beside her, but instinctively glancing back to make sure Ruby was nowhere in sight.

We didn't head down the main London road, but instead turned west towards Elstree. In about twenty minutes we pulled into the forecourt of a big roadhouse near the reservoir.

'What now?' I asked the driver.

'You go in. I'm to wait.'

Maurice was sitting in the hall. He waved me over.

'ATS driver?' I said. 'You really are something official, aren't you, Uncle Maurice?'

'Enough, Florence,' he said, propelling me into the lounge and over towards a far corner. There was no-one else around. No guests.

'It's very quiet here,' I said. 'I'm surprised it's open at all. I came in with Freddie once. Before the war.' It's funny how we were all saying that now, "before the war", as if it had been going on already for years and years.

Freddie and I were walking, you know, with knapsacks. We were just engaged. We thought we might get a pot of tea and some scones, but decided we wouldn't be able to afford it, and were just about to leave, when a rather snotty head waiter type told us, very disapprovingly, we should have left our knapsacks in the hall luggage place. So of course, Freddie had to stay, rather than be put down. We were right, too. We couldn't afford it.

'It's not open,' said Maurice. 'We're using it.'

'What for?'

'This sort of thing.'

'What sort of thing?'

'Quiet chats. And it's quite close to the airfield.'

'So what happens if someone ordinary comes in looking for a pot of tea and some scones?'

'You are quite extraordinary sometimes, Florence. The way

162

you want to know about the B picture and don't seem to give a damn about the main feature. If anyone comes in on the off-chance, they're simply told the place is closed to non-residents for the duration. It's all very low key.'

'Yes, but what if they want a room?'

'Oh do shut up, Florence. You made it quite clear you didn't want to trail up to town…'

'I'm working. I can't just drop everything.'

'…And I don't want to have to talk to Freddie at Carlton Gardens. It's much better if you act as our go-between.'

Tea appeared. And scones and jam and butter. I stared at the tray and then back at Maurice.

'Is all that butter for us?'

'I think it's a special service ration. We get some rather important people going through here. I told you. It's close to the airfield.'

'And all that jam?'

'Ah now, that was already here. Tins and tins of it. I've seen it. They must have been expecting a contract to paint the Forth Bridge with it. And then came the war.'

I loaded a scone with the delicious contraband. My mouth full, I could almost believe there was no war, and that Freddie and I had wandered in again for tea on a Sunday afternoon, and that this time we could afford it.

Maurice brought me back to reality with a bump.

'So friend Gaillet knows about Rhoda's spot of bother. That's very interesting, very interesting indeed. And I suppose he's using it to lean on Freddie.'

'What's really interesting, Uncle Maurice, is how on earth you know about Rhoda's "spot of bother" as you put it. You haven't told me that. You wouldn't have called it that if you'd been there.'

Maurice put his tea cup down and started to pat his pockets for his cigarettes. Here we go, I thought. Needs time to think what to say next. Still, when he had finally gone through his little ritual and aimed his first drag up to the corner of the ceiling, what he did say shook me rigid.

'I know about it, Florence, because I was the one who made all the arrangements.'

I'd been really taken aback. Rhoda asked me out of the blue one day. Had I got any holiday coming? Well I hadn't made any plans.

It was still early. I said I thought I might go with the Co-op Holidays again, group walking and staying at one of their hostels. Hindhead perhaps. The fares wouldn't be too much. I could even get there on the Greenline bus.

Pa was all right about the Co-op. They were a bit Methodist, like him, and he was pally with some high-up in it, whom he played chess with. He had let me go on my own the previous year, 1935, with only a token show of fuss. Well I was nearly twenty-one when all's said and done.

'They go abroad too, don't they, the Co-op?' Rhoda asked.

I said they went to Switzerland and Germany, as far as I knew, but I couldn't afford that.

'I'll pay,' said Rhoda.

'What? To go to Switzerland? Why?'

Then I twigged that she meant for both of us to go, not just me.

'We don't do enough together.'

Yes, I thought, but that's because we don't like one another all that much.

'I'm getting more parts now and I'll be off touring and things, and I expect you'll be getting engaged to some chap in the Civil Service and settling down. We'll never have done anything, just the two of us.'

'Well…' I said hesitantly. It was all so unexpected and so unlike Rhoda. I couldn't for the life of me see what might have brought on such late flowering sisterliness and I was still looking for the catch. But that didn't manifest itself until later.

'Only thing is, we'll have to go soon. I've probably got some rep coming up shortly and I'd like to get some holiday in first. It could be a longish run with any luck.'

'How soon?'

'Well in a couple of weeks. Three at the latest.'

I said, I didn't know if the office would wear it. But Rhoda said, 'Try. It's early still. You'll be leaving the best of the summer for the others.'

That wasn't the point, as far as the Civil Service was concerned. Mr Webber didn't like to be taken unawares. I could already hear him. 'You should wait for the rota to come round, Miss Denning. We cannot have junior staff stealing a march, when others more senior have quite probably not made their plans.'

'What about Pa? Who'll look after him if we're both away?'

Not that Rhoda was ever around that much to concern herself about shopping and cooking for Pa.

'You leave Pa to me. Anyway Florence, you shouldn't let him take you for granted. You'll end up an old maid at that rate. You know…youngest daughter, widowed father. Do him good to have to do without you. Might realise he could really be doing with a wife. Can't cramp his style if we're not around, darling. What's the Co-op's number? I'll give them a ring and do the necessary.'

I wasn't at all sure you could make arrangements with the Co-op on the telephone. They were in Manchester somewhere. You had to get their brochure and fill in the form. Send them a postal order for the deposit. Rhoda brushed it all aside.

'I'm sure we can find a few strings to pull, darling.'

The only strings I could think of to pull with the Co-op were the ones that sent the money whizzing across the wires to the cash desk. Rhoda actually laughed at that. I should have smelt a rat then.

But I had to hand it to her at the time. She had it all sorted out in about ten days. Of course, I didn't have any idea then that the adorable Maurice must have had a hand in it. I suppose he must have suggested a ready-made tour would be a better bet than fixing railway tickets and hotels independently given the urgency of the situation. Of which, of course, I was blissfully unaware. I have to say, I could have done with him pulling a few of Mr Webber's strings. I had to plead an ailing Pa who was in urgent need of a seaside holiday.

It was as the ferry was coming into the harbour at Ostend that Rhoda told me. We were sticking with the Co-op for the couple of days and nights it was taking to travel down through Germany to the Swiss border and then she had to see a doctor in Basle. I was totally horrified and I remember feeling very, very used. When I finally got some of my breath back, I asked her, through gritted teeth, why she hadn't seen fit to let me in on her secret a bit sooner.

'Because you wouldn't have come, darling, would you?'

'I probably would. I wouldn't have had much option, would I, if you're in trouble?'

'Well then. What's the difference, darling?'

That's always been Rhoda all over. She just can't see the other people. We're all just an audience out there in the dark, beyond the footlights.

I did ask her where the man was, but she said it was 'best you don't know.' So I said I hoped he was paying the doctor and she said,

'Yes, and your holiday.' I seriously felt like pushing her overboard.

It was a bit tricky persuading the Co-op group leader that we would be spending a day or two in Basle, and would catch them up in Lucerne. Not that it was that simple, either. We turned up at the doctor's surgery, if that's what it was. It was more like a large private suburban house. I don't know what I was expecting. I had absolutely no idea how this sort of thing worked. All I knew about abortions were that they happened in backstreets and were very, very shaming, to say nothing about them being illegal. I had sometimes read court reports in Pa's paper, which were always couched in a mixture of legal jargon and coy euphemism that somehow seemed to emphasise the disgrace and reinforce the awful taboo.

However, I let myself be carried along on Rhoda's unshakeable confidence. I had no alternative, and anyway this surgery in a respectable district of Basle seemed a million miles from being a backstreet. I had been imagining a cross between Josephine Lucie's Wednesday afternoon Hotel of Assignation and the ghastly sanatorium where I had taken her on the bus to see Mother.

A starched receptionist had taken Rhoda away, leaving me sitting on a banquette in the spacious hallway. Not that it was spacious enough for me. I assumed anyone seeing me there would take it for granted that I was waiting for an abortion. I felt I had a placard round my neck saying, 'In trouble. Bad girl.' Nobody came, but that didn't make me feel any the less conspicuous. Then Rhoda reappeared with a man I assumed was the doctor. I remember thinking, 'God, have they done it already? Do I have to meet him?' But that was clearly nonsense, I knew.

Rhoda was not quite so full of herself. Rather subdued. I saw, for perhaps the first time, her bravado had sagged, showing it for what it was – a pose. She was really rather frightened, after all, I thought. I felt suddenly sorrier for her, than for myself. So that will show you how serious it was.

'We have to go somewhere else, apparently. It's going to be a bit of a bore,' she said.

'Somewhere else? Why? It's not…you know…'

'Not what?'

'You know…the police or something,' I hissed.

The doctor looked rather haughty. I supposed he'd heard me. 'There has merely been a misunderstanding, Mademoiselle. You should have gone to our clinic in Luxeuil-les-Bains. I thought this had been made clear. We do not carry out these procedures here.'

'It's in France,' Rhoda said. 'Apparently.'

'Do not be alarmed, Mademoiselle, it is only about eighty kilometres from here by road. It is in the Vosges.'

'By road? We have no motor car. Are you proposing to take us there?' Rhoda demanded, beginning to recover herself.

'I, Mademoiselle? I am not travelling to Luxeuil.'

'But aren't you going to…?' I left the words in the air. I suppose I must have gone red to the soles of my feet.

'My partner, Mademoiselle. In Luxeuil. This should have been explained. I am desolated.'

So was I. All I could think about was, what would we tell the Co-op? Come to that, how would we tell them? But these were the least of our problems, since it was clear we would have to abandon the Co-op. Really, I hadn't the foggiest idea what was going to be involved in Rhoda's 'procedure' and I don't think she can have done, either. Any thought of rejoining our walking party in Lucerne for a hike in the mountains, afterwards, was always going to be a ridiculous notion.

We took the train to Belfort where we changed. At the border, the customs official asked what the purpose of our visit to France was, I remember.

I told Maurice about Freddie's run-in with Captain Gaillet.

'So did you get a look at the other doctor, as well?' He lit another cigarette.

'Yes, I suppose so. Why?'

'Well, one or other of them must be our friend at White City, if he exists at all.'

I suppose I hadn't really made the connection until he said that. One or two other things were beginning to connect up, too.

'Don't you know him, too, if you made all the arrangements for Rhoda?'

'No. I never met anyone. It was done through one of my business associates in Basle. I assumed he was Swiss. Not French. Were they both French?'

I hadn't thought about it. They both spoke French. I mean, how are you supposed to tell? I had a vague feeling he might have been German, for some reason I couldn't quite remember, so I suppose he could have been Swiss. They're a bit of everything, aren't they?

'Perhaps we should pop over to White City and have a peek at him,' said Maurice. 'If we knew who he was,' he added. 'I don't suppose you remember his name?'

'Would that be safe?'

'Why wouldn't it be? They're Free French. Not German paratroops.'

'No, I meant he might recognise me, or something.'

Maurice looked at me. 'Hardly likely, surely?'

'Except, he's supposed to be trying to use Rhoda, so we might be on his mind.'

Maurice drew on his cigarette. 'Perhaps I can ask to have a few inquiries made about his background. No need to go in person.'

'Yes,' I said. 'After all, it all comes back to Gaillet knowing about Rhoda's problems. How he knows is rather immaterial, isn't it?'

'Unless the White City doctor is a fiction. In which case, who else might have fed him the information? And why?'

'The point is, what is Freddie supposed to do? As far as I'm concerned I'd rather he just packed it in and asked to go back to his unit. I mean, you can tell your lot Gaillet's up to no good and put a stop to him, can't you?'

'Well no, Florence. My lot, as you call them, will want to let Gaillet run. See where he leads them. He could turn out to be more useful doing whatever it is he's doing than being locked up in Pentonville for the rest of the war. And we don't know, either, whether he's working for the Free French with De Gaulle's blessing. If he is, as he claims, then the whole thing gets really tricky – politically I mean.'

'But why wouldn't it be with De Gaulle's blessing? That's what he's told Freddie. Who else could he be setting up these fictitious agents for? I can't see what use they'd be to anyone else. I just don't want him threatening Freddie to tell the world about Rhoda and me.'

'Well he won't, will he, if he thinks Freddie's playing ball? You see, Florence, the thing is, Gaillet doesn't know about me, you know, working for my lot. He just thinks I'm a useful fixer of typewriters. As far as he's concerned Freddie has no-one to tell except his superior officers in his unit and that would risk the whole Rhoda business coming out. Baby and bathwater, so to speak.'

I wasn't at all happy. I'd wanted Maurice to wave a magic wand and make everything all right. But instead he'd just drawn Freddie and me deeper into something neither of us really understood or wanted to.

'Do you want this last scone?' Maurice asked.

'Uncle Maurice, why did you have to make all the arrangements for Rhoda in France? Didn't the baby's father want to know? Was that it? She never did tell me who he was.'

'Last chance,' said Maurice, holding the scone, loaded with jam and butter, to his mouth.

'No, you have it.'

He took his time. When he'd finished it he said, 'I had all the right contacts, through my business associates in Switzerland.'

'So you know who the father was?'

'Yes.'

'But you're not going to say.'

'No.'

We walked through the hotel lobby to the front door. The motor car and driver were waiting on the forecourt.

'What happens now?' I asked.

Maurice opened the car door for me. 'Freddy plays ball and I'll be in touch.'

Then, as if it were an afterthought, he said, 'Has Gaillet asked about the painting again?'

26

'Now you want to ask me about the paintings, I imagine,' said Josephine Lucie.

I'd gone up to the middle room when I arrived home from school, not knowing how I might find her after her anguish of the day before. When I asked Mrs Croucher, who was just finishing up as I got in, she said 'the old lady hasn't come out all day.'

'I came to see if you were all right. I haven't been thinking about the paintings.' This was in part true. It was Augustin I'd been thinking about all day at school and getting my knuckles wrapped for daydreaming. I kept seeing him in a thick coat with a huge fur collar and a leather flying helmet like I'd seen the men wearing in the biplanes taking off from Hendon. Sometimes they were quite low over the garden at Coatwood, and they'd lean over the side and wave at me. They'd make the wings waggle for Rhoda.

But I couldn't get out of my head what Josephine Lucie had said about Augustin's broken bones and his dislocated shoulder. How badly hurt had he been? Did the bone show through his arm or his leg, and could he feel it? Or was he mercifully unconscious? All day I had worried about Josephine Lucie not knowing how to put his shoulder back or deal with his fractured limbs, trying to move him probably, wrenching him back from oblivion and making him cry out in the darkness, the two of them alone.

'I, however, have been thinking about the paintings today, *ma chérie*. I think the man in the Cambrai lace has always brought nothing but misfortune. Perhaps he couldn't stand to be copied and was punishing everyone who had taken a part in it. After all Monsieur Adolphe was killed by a Prussian *bombe*. I told you. But of course I didn't know this until much later.'

'So did Augustin…was he…?'

'No, *ma chère* Florence. Not then. But later. For me, he died later.'

I didn't understand what she meant. Had the gallant Augustin laid down his life for Josephine Lucie? What did 'for me' signify? But I knew better than to interrupt. I could tell that Josephine Lucie was back to her old self. She had spent her solitary day exorcising the disorderly grief she had carelessly allowed to invade the middle room. She had reorganised her past into her present again. All would be revealed at the right time and in the right way, I knew.

'Have you had your tea, Florence?' she asked me.

I said I had not. I was the first one in from school, as Leonard had further to go now to the County Grammar, and Rhoda was now at her private academy in Mornington Crescent, where they did speech and drama, as well as the usual things. So she had to come as far as Edgware on the steam train and then get the bus. Leonard had a scholarship to the County, but where the money came from for Rhoda's acting lessons was not something I really gave any thought to at the time. She told me later that Mother had paid into something as a music teacher, which meant that when she died, there was a bursary or something for dependent children to pursue music and the performing arts. I did wonder, then, whether there mightn't have been some left over for me, but Pa never mentioned it and it was always accepted without any real discussion that I would stay at the elementary until fifteen and then do shorthand and typing. The Civil Service exams came later. They were my idea. Pa never thought I'd pass.

'That *Madame Crouchaire* – I never let her in here – she will, I imagine, have left something cold for you all under a plate?'

This was the usual arrangement on the days Mrs Croucher came in. On the days she did not, it was increasingly falling to my lot to get something ready for the rest of the family. They all had something provided at midday anyway, and in any case I was frequently supplementing my rations with the things Josephine Lucie prepared with me, as comestible props for her recollections.

'Come, then *ma chérie*, we shall occupy ourselves in the kitchen before they return. Because of my beloved Augustin and his poor broken bones, I propose *omelette aux confitures*.'

I didn't like the sound of this. Pa didn't approve of omelettes. They took too many eggs. He much preferred us to have scrambled which could be watered down with milk and made to go further, even if they were inclined to separate rather unpleasantly when he did. That was when he wasn't slicing boiled eggs in half, although he didn't insist on that so much since Mother's death.

'What sort of omelette?'

'Omelette with jam.' Josephine Lucie bustled about the kitchen, liberating eggs and butter, in a way that filled me with horrific elation.

'And that was a favourite of Augustin's, was it?'

'I don't know. But it is a favourite of mine and he loved me, so…besides I still have the blackberry *confiture*. It is perfect for omelette.'

'I never heard of jam in an omelette.'

'Now, I suppose it is too much to hope that there is a pan which is only for omelettes. This is the secret, Florence. A pan which has never had anything cooked in it but omelettes.'

She made me run back up to the middle room and bring down the copper frying pan she had on her chiffonier. There was a pencil end in it, an old piece of sealing wax and the husk of a small spider. I mentioned this to Josephine Lucie.

'It is of no matter. Nothing has been cooked in this pan but omelettes. It was a *grave* rule of César Machin's.' She wiped it carefully on my pinafore.

I was confused and curious. More equipment from Machin's kitchen. I'd never questioned it before. The Noah's Ark, biscuit cutters. Now this. And what else besides? When had she come by it? Had she returned to Paris after all?

'When did you get it? The omelette pan?' I said.

'First, you must have the flame very, very hot,' she said, turning up the gas on the stove almost as far as it would go. 'Then you must be generous with the butter. A little is not enough. But not so much as to drown the eggs.'

I don't know what she meant by 'drown'. I watched her put a great wedge of butter in the pan. About enough for a week's breakfasts with Pa and a couple of suppers besides. Josephine Lucie's *omelette aux confitures* was evidently designed especially to drive him insane.

'You have to beat the eggs…Eggs! Eggs, Florence, quickly, before the butter blackens too much. Yes, all of them. We should really have eight, but a half dozen will have to do. Beat them. Beat them, but not to a froth. Not too many bubbles. So…and…' She whooshed them, hissing and foaming into the hot butter.

'The second thing after the special pan…' she said, 'the second thing is to be brave. You will only make a fine omelette if you have courage, otherwise the omelette will sense your fear and defeat you.' She stirred the mixture roughly with a fork and as the omelette began to set, lifted it up and shook it fiercely so that it spread evenly in the pan. Then, as it began to turn from runny to just soft, she added a large dollop of her blackberry jelly and spread it slightly with the back of the spoon.

'Knife! Knife, Florence!' Josephine Lucie slapped her hand on the kitchen board beside the stove without taking her eyes off the emerging omelette.

I rummaged in the drawer. 'What kind?'

'A big dinner knife.'

I fished one out and placed it in her outstretched fingers, like the nurse handing the retractor to the surgeon while he continues to stare into his incision. I'd seen this scene played out recently in a film at the Broadway Cinema with Rhoda.

Josephine Lucie neatly folded one side of the omelette into the middle of the pan and then folded the other side over the top. As she did she let out a triumphant *Hup! Hup!*

'You see. Here we have six eggs, Florence, so it is important that the omelette does not become too hard before you *hup, hup*. Otherwise it will crack, here, and the *confiture* will escape itself into the pan.'

'So it wouldn't taste nice?'

'No, because then you have a big problem with the washing up. Is there a *brochette* in the drawer, *chérie?*'

'A what?'

She moved me aside and peered into the drawer herself, while removing the omelette pan from the heat.

'That is another thing, Florence, César Machin learned to me, over and over. In a kitchen always look with your eyes, never with your hands. Here is one!' She produced a long skewer and proceeded to heat it in the gas burner recently vacated by the omelette pan. When it was thinking about becoming red hot, Josephine Lucie laid it deftly and briefly in a criss-cross movement on the folded *omelette de confiture,* leaving a darker pattern on its plump, golden flesh.

'*Et voilà.* Plate, Florence, plate! No, no, a big one.'

She held the handle of the copper pan with her palm underneath it, tilted it at an angle to the proffered dinner plate, and slid the omelette out without turning it over and obscuring the pattern she had given it. A little melted blackberry jelly oozed expectantly from each end.

In the hall beyond the breakfast room we heard the front door being opened.

'Tooty, toot toot!' It was Leonard.

Josephine Lucie and I looked at one another with the same aghast expression and then looked down simultaneously at the guilty omelette. For a moment I thought Josephine Lucie was going to run out into the garden with it.

'Anyone in?' Leonard erupted into the breakfast room and flowed into the kitchen. 'Oh hello, Florence…Grandmother. Everything all right? What are you…? I mean is anything…? Grandmother. I mean, hello. What's that thing?' He gazed on the omelette, seizing thankfully on the unfamiliar object Grandmother and I were still holding on the plate between us, as a means of escaping from his mortification at having discovered the two of us 'up to something'. He must have felt, as I did then, that he had somehow lost his way and, by mistake, had found himself appallingly in the middle room, rather than the kitchen. Then I realised what a forbidden place it had become to all of them but me. For a fleeting, triumphant moment I smelt his discomfort and savoured it.

Grandmother placed the plate with the omelette at the opposite end of the kitchen table to Leonard.

'You are just in time, Leonard. In the nick of it. Your sister and I were just going to celebrate the Emperor's birthday. We have made one of his favourite things.'

'What is it?' said Leonard suspiciously, 'A cake of some sort?' And then he added, 'What Emperor, anyway?'

'Napoleon, of course. The French Emperor.'

'Which one? There've been three.'

'Leonard, it does not matter which one. They all had a birthday. I was thinking of the one my grandfather fought for, perhaps. Or perhaps that poor, fat man I saw at the *Grande Exposition*…'

'The one in 1867? Did you go to that, Grandmother? Napoleon who capitulated at Sedan during the…'

I wasn't having this.

'It's an omelette, Leonard,' I said. 'But it's made with jam and…' I paused for effect, '…six eggs. No, eight.'

'Jam? In an omelette? Sounds disgusting. Anyway, eight eggs. Pa'll have a blue fit, won't he? I mean, eight eggs.'

'He let me have butter the other day.'

'What for?'

'Crab sandwiches.'

'*Crab! Pa?*'

Our grandmother pressed home our advantage before things deteriorated into a brawl.

'There are some things, Leonard, it is best your father does not know, *n'est-ce pas?* Such as…' She cut a piece of the *omelette de confiture*, walked it, balanced on the dinner knife to Leonard's end of the table and held it under his nose, '…such as your secret amusement with cigarettes, for example, which because I am French does not trouble me at all. Here, try it. Wish the Emperor a *bonne anniversaire.*'

Leonard's mouth opened automatically, despite the look of blind panic on his face. He received the omelette on the blade like one who knows he has a choice between cold poison and cold steel.

'Come, Florence.' Josephine Lucie moved to the door. 'We will resume our conversation in my middle room.'

'You aren't going to leave the rest of that there, are you?' mumbled Leonard through his omelette which he seemed to be having difficulty getting down.

'I thought perhaps your father would also like to wish Bonaparte a happy birthday when he comes in. Propose it to him, Leonard.'

Leonard looked at me, pathetically.

'I'd rather take it up,' I said. 'I haven't had any yet, anyway. Leonard, would you mind washing the pan?' Well, it was worth a try.

'There is no need, Florence,' Josephine Lucie interrupted. 'As the jam did not burn, we have only to wipe it with brown paper until the next time.'

Leonard handed the copper pan to me gratefully and as Josephine Lucie closed the door of the middle room behind us, she said, 'The eggs and cigarettes were enough, *ma chérie*. And the Emperor of France. Washing-up would have added humiliation. Too much.'

I had been given a lesson in men.

'*Eh bien*, the paintings, the unfortunate paintings.' Josephine Lucie arranged herself methodically in her chair, as if nothing had happened downstairs and no time had passed. I divided the rest of the omelette on the plate and offered it to her first, but she waved it aside. 'Eat what you want, *ma chère,* it is probably cold now.'

I wolfed it down. The melted jam inside was still piping hot even though the egg was beginning to cool. No wonder Leonard had mumbled through it.

Josephine Lucie had made Augustin as comfortable as she could, considering his injuries. She dared not try to move him and had shed her own sheepskin to cover him as he drifted in and out of consciousness. The balloon canopy had almost entirely deflated, leaving only a faint odour of coal gas lingering on the frosty early morning air. Josephine Lucie made up her mind that it would probably not drag the basket out of the hedgerow it had mostly demolished and that it was safe enough to leave Augustin while she went to see what help might be at hand.

Instinctively she followed the slope of the field downhill, thankful that it was rough pasture and not ploughed. At the bottom she encountered another hedgerow with trees and an embankment on the other side. She skirted along it until she found a less dense part, free from brambles, she might push through. It was a struggle, nevertheless, and as her arms in front of her face to protect it were scratched and torn, she wished heartily she had gone in the other direction to look for a gate. Breaking through eventually, she crossed a narrow ditch and mounted the embankment towards the line of trees at the top.

'Imagine my happiness, Florence, when I discovered I had reached the *halage* of a canal. What do you call that? You know, the path for the horses to pull the boats.'

'A towpath?'

'Perhaps. I was happy because I knew it would eventually lead to an *écluse* – I don't know – where they have gates to hold the water for the boats to go up and down. There might even be a village first. You know, Florence, because I had grown up beside a canal. But which way to walk? I had no idea where the balloon had descended, you see. Perhaps I was still in France. I hoped so. César Machin had told me he read in his *Journal des Remparts* that one of the *montgolfières* had flown all the way to Norway. How did they know that in Paris? Perhaps the pigeon told them. Perhaps it was a fabrication. I did not think I was in Norway, however.'

After walking for about half an hour and with a wintry sun getting higher in the sky, Josephine Lucie did indeed come across a lock with its keeper's cottage emitting a homely smell of wood smoke from the chimney. The lock keeper was busy winding the paddles to raise a barge which had already entered, while several others queued on the far side, waiting their turn. His wife watched from the cottage door exchanging words and laughter with the barge captain's wife, while her youngest children played on the lock side. They all paused to look at the strange figure of Josephine Lucie approaching along the towpath in her assortment of men's and women's woollen garments and Monsieur de Marquise's oversize riding boots.

'They were all French, anyway, which made me happy. But they did not really understand about the balloon. I don't think they had ever seen one. They did know about the war, of course. The keeper told me his son had gone to be a soldier at the *grand* fort at Péronne. I knew about this place. It wasn't that far from St Quentin, which wasn't very far from Orgelets. "Is this the Sambre-Oise, then?" I asked them. "But of course," they replied. "Then which way is Orgelets?" I asked the *chaland* wife. She pointed the way I had come.'

'So did you get your breakfast? You know. The chocolate?'

'I don't think so, *chérie*. I think it was bread and *saucisson*. The people of the *chalands* don't have enough for rolls and chocolate.' Josephine Lucie chuckled. 'I suppose, *ma chère*, you are thinking, "Perhaps the *saucisson* was made of rats," because I told you that about the *chalands*. But I think it was just ordinary old donkey, as usual.'

'So they took you to your home, to Orgelets? What about Augustin? Was he all right? Did the canal people help him?'

'Yes, of course. They were very patriotic. At first I offered some of Monsieur's money to the *chaland* captain to help Augustin, but he refused absolutely. He told me he was a French sailor who had been to the war in Russia, the *Crimée*. He was very elevated about it. Very proud.'

The captain of the barge, the *Nénuphar,* had harnessed his horse to a cart belonging to the lock keeper and, together with the keeper's wife and Josephine Lucie, set off round by the road in the general direction Josephine Lucie indicated she had left Augustin and the wrecked balloon.

'He knew how to put Augustin's poor shoulder back in place. But my darling was very cold and blue, you know? I thought he would die. His leg was very bad. but he was very, very brave. When we came back to the *écluse*, I said we must leave him there and send for a doctor. But evidently there was not a good one anywhere near, only a horse doctor. I asked how long it would take to get to Orgelets on the *chaland*, because I knew there was a good doctor near there, a friend of my father. The *chaland* captain said that it would not take more than the next day to reach Orgelets, but perhaps Augustin's leg would be turning *putride* by then.'

'What's that?' I asked.

'It would become black and the doctor is forced to cut it off. But I thought, if he stays here, the horse doctor will probably try to cut it off anyway. And Augustin would certainly die of that.'

'So?'

'So, I said we had to take him to Orgelets.'

'And what about the paintings? And the post? Did you have to leave it all behind with the balloon?'

'Absolutely not. We used the post sacks to make Augustin comfortable in the cart, and I made sure I had the paintings. I told you they were not very big without their frames. We had to leave the *Montgolfière*, however – and the basket. The captain said he would consider it an honour to take the Paris post and the pigeon, of course, to the *bureau* in St Quentin. I told him he might have a medal from the Emperor, like my grandfather.'

'And he was all right, was he? Augustin. You said something about him not dying then, but later.'

Josephine Lucie looked at me, saying nothing for a moment or two, and I know there were tears in her eyes.

'There is so much about this, Florence. So much pain I had forgotten. And afterwards. After a long time, there was more pain. You must have patience, *ma chèrie,* my little dove. I cannot tell all the pain at once. My heart would break with the weight of it.'

I actually felt physically sick. I realised Josephine Lucie was remembering things she had long ago forgotten or hidden away. Things she had not known would have to be told when she had embarked on this voyage into her past with me. I felt, too, her tears were my fault.

'I don't feel very well,' I said. 'I think it was the omelette. All that jam and butter.'

27

'How are you?' said Maurice.

'Better than when I got home last week. Too much jam and butter on those scones. I threw it all up when I got in. That ATS girl was lucky I didn't do it all over the back seat of the car. I expect that was the Ministry paying me back for being a pig. It's amazing how we've all forgotten how to manage out-of-the-ordinary food.'

'You speak for yourself.'

Maurice and I had agreed that I would telephone him after our meeting at Elstree. Even he accepted that he couldn't go on calling me on Mr Webber's telephone, much as he enjoyed provoking him. It would cause far too much unwelcome speculation.

'I'll come round on Saturday. Will Freddie be at home or at Carlton Gardens?'

I didn't know.

'It would probably be a good idea if he was at home. There have been a few developments.'

'Yes, and I won't have the neighbours tittle-tattling so much about the man with the big Austin if you come when Freddie's here. But I won't know until he appears on the doorstep. Still, I wouldn't be surprised. Most of the French seem to clear off for the weekend now, from what I can make out. All the nobs seem to invite them. What developments?'

'Not on the phone, Florence. May I come for dinner?'

'Do you mean midday dinner? Or six o'clock dinner? Not that it makes much difference. You'd better bring your ration book.'

'I can probably do better than that.'

Freddie arrived home early on the Saturday afternoon, calling out from the door that he didn't have to be back at Carlton Gardens until Monday morning.

'Your Uncle Maurice here yet?'

'That looks like him now.' The Austin slid to a halt outside and Maurice got out.

'I've brought my dinner,' he announced as I shut the door behind them both. 'I think there's enough for us all.'

He opened his attaché case and pulled out something wrapped in brown paper. I unfolded it to reveal a piece of steak the size of a house brick.

'It's not fillet I'm afraid. It's porterhouse, I believe,' Maurice said.

Freddie and I gazed at the offering.

'Good Lord!' said Freddie.

'No need to apologise, Uncle Maurice,' I said. 'Porterhouse is fillet. It's chateaubriand.'

My grandmother had told me that one day when she had been eyeing a piece on Stringer's slab.

'Fancy a nice bit of porterhouse, do you, Mrs Burnell?' Mr Stringer ran his steel tentatively along the blade of his butcher's knife. He was wary of my grandmother. She made a habit of saying disparaging things in French to his display of cuts, on her occasional visits to attempt to buy something special for Mother.

'*C'est un chateaubriand, Monsieur Stringaire.* I am amazed to see one here in the Broadway. However,' she had sniffed, 'it will not be old enough to eat for many days.'

'Good Lord!' Freddie said again. 'I expect we could get six months just for looking at it.'

'Better dispose of the evidence quick, then,' said Maurice. 'Got any chips?'

'I'll go and liberate a few spuds from the garden,' Freddie said.

'Digging for Victory, are we?' said Maurice.

'Ah, but my way it's twice the return and half the work,' said Freddie gleefully.

'It's his patent spud bin,' I said.

He'd been growing some in an old dustbin with its bottom removed, barely covering the leaves with earth every time they showed through, so that by the time they reached the top, the rest of the bin was full of potatoes. By lifting the bin slightly off the ground he could get at the bigger ones furthest down. César Machin would have been proud of him.

'There's a problem with chips, though,' I said. 'I haven't

enough lard for the deep fryer. It'll have to be sauté with a little onion.'

'Better and better,' said Maurice.

I tackled him while Freddie was out in the back garden.

'You've changed your tune, then?'

'What about?'

'About Freddie knowing.'

'I told you. There've been some developments. We need Freddie on-side. I can't have him going freelance and going off at half cock. He just might, now that he's worried about your welfare in all this.'

After the episode with the scones and jam, I refused all entreaties to cook the entire piece of steak. I cut three small slices from the porterhouse to fry and put the rest in the larder.

'It'll go bad,' said Freddie. 'That would be a dreadful waste.'

'My grandmother would tell you that steak will only really be ready in about two weeks' time. It'll give you something to look forward to.'

As we ate, Maurice told Freddie how important it was that he should appear to be conniving with Captain Gaillet.

'You said there'd been some developments. What developments?' I asked.

'My lot have discovered that Gaillet probably had access to some quite secret stuff when he was still a military attaché at the French embassy, and we were still sharing things. Now they don't know whether he's working with de Gaulle or against him. If he's against him, and heaven knows, most of the French over here are against him, then who's he working for? Vichy? Or worse, the Germans directly. It's bad enough having to have Vichy diplomats over here. But at least we know who they are and more or less what they're up to. And even if he isn't exactly a spy, we know Carlton Gardens is as leaky as a sieve. Even if he touts this stuff around there just to impress de Gaulle, it's bound to end up either in Vichy or, worse still, on the Avenue Kléber.

'I didn't know that,' I said. 'About the French diplomats, I mean.'

'Oh yes,' Freddie chipped in, 'Carlton Gardens are really pissed off with them.'

'But aren't they the enemy. No, I suppose not. They're the French, aren't they?'

'It's totally bizarre,' said Maurice. 'We've had to sink their fleet because we don't trust them, but we still have their consulate service all over the country.'

It all seemed very odd to me. Especially when Maurice said that most of the French military over here after the fall of France actually wanted to go home. I'd assumed they'd all be itching to join the Free French.

'They won't be allowed to, will they?'

'Can't keep them all under lock and key, can we?' said Maurice. 'No, my bet is they'll all be put on a boat in Liverpool and shipped off to Marseilles. If the Germans sink them on the way, well too bad.'

'Which still leaves me with *Capitaine Gaillet*,' said Freddie. 'What am I supposed to do? Just play along with him?'

'And tell Florence anything you see going on,' said Maurice. 'And I'll keep in touch with her. What I really need to know is the name of this doctor before he gets repatriated. That could be how Gaillet intends to get his information out of the country, if that's what he's up to. I assume this doctor's an officer, but you never know. If he is, he's probably left White City. They're putting the officers up in a hotel somewhere. Bloomsbury I think.'

'What about your famous contacts in Switzerland?' I said. 'Wouldn't they remember?'

Maurice pushed his plate away and felt through his pockets for his cigarettes. When he had lit one and taken a long drag, he said, 'It's not that easy, talking to the Swiss these days. It'd be quicker if Freddie could find out.'

'How, do you suggest?' asked Freddie.

'You'll think of something, I'm sure, Freddie. Keep an eye to the main chance.'

'That's all very well,' Freddie grumbled. 'I'm not exactly an expert in cloak and dagger. I thought that was your department.'

About a week later, however, he came bursting through the front door, almost giggling with glee.

'You've been given a weekend pass,' I hazarded.

'Better than that, Florrie Dee.'

'A weekend pass and a set of French silk lingerie in my size?'

'I've got the name of the doctor. He *is* real.'

'I'd have settled for the undies.'

It transpired that Freddie had taken some papers in to Gaillet and had omitted to knock. The captain was just finishing a telephone call and at Freddie's sudden appearance, looked and sounded rather put out at being interrupted.

'I could tell he was wondering if I'd been listening outside. Something made me think, this could be it. He's up to something fishy.'

Gaillet had no sooner got rid of Freddie than he left the building abruptly, taking the lift. On an impulse, Freddie snatched up his forage cap from the outer office, hurtled down the back stairs and out through the side entrance into Carlton Gardens. He was in time to see Gaillet, still in a tearing hurry, it seemed, heading off in the direction of Pall Mall. Freddie followed him at a discreet distance, up Lower Regent Street, across Piccadilly and then up Shaftsbury Avenue. Turning a little way up Dean Street, Gaillet stopped at the pub, known as the French House, and went inside.

Freddie hovered about on the other side of the road, uncertain what to do next. The pub had virtually been colonised by French and Belgian exiles in London and Freddie knew that he could stick out like a sore thumb if he went in. It was very much 'officers only' as far as he could tell, especially as the French other ranks would have difficulty leaving their camps at White City and Crystal Palace.

There were two entrances to the pub. Freddie crossed the road and peered into the one Gaillet had not used. It opened into the tiny snug. There was no-one in the bar and no-one serving either, although Freddie could hear there were people in the larger front bar beside it. He stepped inside and stood where he could see into the other bar. There was no sign of Gaillet.

'I thought he must have gone to the back bar. I couldn't see, so I was a bit stumped. The only thing I could think of was to hang around outside waiting for him to leave to see if he was with someone. But time was running out. I wasn't even meant to be out of the office, although with Gaillet out too, no-one would bother to wonder where I was for a while. Still, I knew it wouldn't do not to be there when he got back. I'd have been buggered if he came out the pub and took a cab. I was just about to call it a day, when the barmaid came through from the other bar and asked me what I would have.'

Freddie had to think quickly. Making it up as he went along he said he had a message for one of the Free French Officers, but he couldn't see him. Perhaps he was in one of the other bars?

The barmaid said, 'I know most of them. Who is it?'

'Well, Florrie Dee, I thought, if he's in one of the other bars, I'll tell her I'm just going round to the other door and then bunk off instead. I couldn't see what else to do, really. But when I say, "It's Captain Gaillet," she says, "Oh, he's upstairs in the dining room with Captain Guttmann. You'll have to go through the saloon bar on the other side." So I thought I'd push my luck and said, "Captain Guttmann sounds a bit German, ha ha. Are you sure?" And she laughs and says, "No, he's French all right. He's one of their army doctors. I know all the French uniforms and that, in here. I expect he's a Jewboy. A lot of them are, aren't they? Doctors." That was enough for me, Florrie Dee. I thanked her kindly, nipped out into the street and scarpered off down Dean Street. She went back to the other bar and I don't suppose she would have noticed I hadn't gone round.'

It did come back to me, then.
I remembered the brass plate beside the gate of the place Rhoda and I had eventually found in Luxeuil-les-Bains, that summer's evening, late, in 1936. Doctor something-or-other Guttmann. That's why I thought he might have been German, or Swiss. It hadn't occurred to me that Maurice could have asked Rhoda what his name was. She'd probably have remembered, in the circumstances. She had made a half-hearted joke about it as we rang the bell. Something about it being a good job tomorrow wasn't Saturday. But neither of us were laughing. We were very, very tired, very frightened, and a long way from home. A long way from the Co-op Holidays party, come to that. I remember the sinking feeling I had when it began to dawn on me what an awful thing we were doing and how I was supposed to be back at my desk in just over a week, and what would I…we do if it all went wrong?

The doctor wouldn't see Rhoda then, of course. We were too late. Come back in the morning. He was a bit distant. But a nice woman I took to be his wife, took pity on us. She got someone, a nurse, or the maid, I can't remember, to bring us a cup of something, and she telephoned a *pension* in the next street to the clinic to arrange a room for the night. I remember she asked them if we were too late for something to eat. Her husband, who had reappeared, interrupted, and said that it would be better if Rhoda had nothing.

She came to the door with us and asked if we were all right carrying our cases. I said we were, but Rhoda gave a bit of a sob. Madame Guttmann put her arm round Rhoda's shoulders and said to her, kindly, 'Be content, my dear. You are in good hands. He is a good doctor.'

28

'So you found the good doctor for Augustin, did you? In time I mean. For his leg?'

It had been quite some time since Josephine Lucie had called me up to the middle room again. She had been to stay with a sick friend in Billericay and when she got back, I had begun almost to suppose that perhaps our business was to be left unfinished after all.

But a little voice told me we had come too far and that if I were patient with her, she would finish her story. Then I wondered what would happen when that day came. Would Josephine Lucie simply cease to be and leave me once again with just my grandmother?

'Ask me something, *ma chérie*. This is how we must begin again, mustn't we?'

My question was born of hope rather than expectation. I thought if I tried to suggest everything had turned out for the best, then perhaps it would have done.

Josephine Lucie took an apple from the fruit bowl on her chiffonnier and started to peel it.

'Why did I choose this apple and not that one? There is nothing between them. They are the same. But now we will eat this one and that one will remain in the bowl. It is a small choice and life will not be very different afterwards. Unless, of course, you are the apple. But sometimes, Florence, sometimes even a very small choice will make the world a different place for you and you do not know it. And if you are forced to look back, you might not even remember what was this small thing.'

I expect I looked puzzled.

'I left the boat.'

'You left the boat? Why?'

'I thought I began to recognize the canal again, where it comes near to Orgelets. I thought I could walk quicker by the road because it cut across a long, long bend. I thought I would arrive in Orgelets perhaps an hour or more before the boat. I wanted to find the doctor, perhaps to bring him back with me. I wanted to do something for Augustin, not just sit there, I suppose. And now I think if I had remained, everything would have been different. I could just have stayed with him. Like the other apple.

'Why, what happened?'

'I had not remembered properly, the distance to Orgelets. It took me a long time.'

Not until she was finally on the outskirts of the village, towards midday, did it begin to occur to Josephine Lucie what a strange and difficult homecoming this would be. Arriving out of the blue and as far as her family was concerned, back from the dead or a fate worse than death. After all, they had heard nothing of her since she had absconded from her relatives in Lille. Arriving, too, dressed in an assortment of clothes, some her own and others borrowed from the barge captain's wife to replace the masculine items from her balloon voyage.

She began to rehearse what she would say to her father or her mother, whoever would answer her knock at the door. The more she repeated it in her mind, the more improbable it sounded. Like in a bad dream, she imagined, no matter what she said, she would be unable to make them understand who on earth Augustin might be and that he needed the doctor. Worse still, she imagined herself being rebuffed, unwelcomed by a family that had hardly cared what might have become of her, nor she of them. Perhaps they would be just as uncaring about the plight of poor Augustin.

More and more convinced of the futility of her journey, Josephine Lucie came to the conclusion she should find the doctor herself and put off confronting her family for as long as possible. Augustin would need to be taken somewhere to have his injuries treated and, she reasoned, she would have to persuade her family to take them both in. But it would be easier if she and Augustin had the doctor with them when that time came.

So ignoring the familiar turning to her old home, Josephine Lucie carried on into the centre of Orgelets and up to the doctor's front door, where, after a moment's hesitation she tugged at the bell pull. A young woman she did not know answered, and, after sizing up Josephine Lucie's clothes, left her waiting on the step while she went to fetch the doctor.

Josephine Lucie could tell at once that he did not recall her.

'Why should he? I was changed after five or six years. A young girl changes much between fifteen and twenty-one. On an instant I decided not to tell him who I was. It was easier just to say I was from the canal and a young man on a barge had broken his leg seriously. He frowned a little and hesitated for a moment.

'I could see the problem, of course. Don't worry, Monsieur, I said. We have enough money.'

The doctor had blustered a little and said that the matter of his fee had not crossed his mind. What concerned him was the prospect of dealing with a serious injury in the confines of a canal barge.

'You must return and get them to bring him here to me, Mademoiselle. We are only a few hundred metres from the canal bridge. I can ask some village boys to show you the way, and bring a hurdle if necessary. Go, and I will prepare the surgery.'

'I told him I knew the way perfectly well, because I had been here many times before, at which he began to observe me more curiously. By now I had decided not to reveal my identity unless it was absolutely necessary.'

'Not even to your parents?' I asked.

'I don't know. Perhaps I thought I would wait and see what happened, since Augustin would have to be brought to the doctor's house and need not go at once to my parents'. Perhaps I thought he would be well enough to go back to the barge and we could continue together to St Quentin. I wasn't thinking sensibly. All I knew was, I wanted less and less to see my parents again. However, it was of no consequence in the end.'

'What do you mean? Of no consequence?'

'He was not there.'

'Who wasn't where?'

'Augustin wasn't on the boat, *ma chère*.'

Deciding she could enlist the aid of someone to help carry Augustin down on the towpath if necessary, Josephine Lucie chose not to wait for assistance to be summoned to the doctor's house. She hurried off along the main street, past the church and the mairie opposite it. She wondered if her father was still the mayor and lowered her head as she passed, in case he might be looking out of the window.

When she reached the canal bridge she was rather surprised and slightly alarmed not to find the barge already moored there, since it had taken her much longer to reach Orgelets than she had supposed it would. She crossed to the middle of the bridge and looked along the canal in both directions. There were a couple of barges approaching from the right direction, but as they drew slowly nearer, Josephine Lucie could see neither of them was the *Nénuphar*. She hurried down onto the towpath, and walked briskly to meet the first barge.

As its horse and driver drew close, she called out, 'Have you seen the *Nénuphar*?'

The bargee replied that he had.

'How far back?' Josephine Lucie asked him.

'About an hour, Mademoiselle. The captain has been taken by the Prussians.'

Josephine Lucie's heart jumped into her mouth. She had not given Prussians a thought. She assumed that the balloon had left them far behind to the south.

Evidently it had been some kind of mounted patrol, according to the bargee, about six men and an officer. They were searching the barges, 'probably to see if we are carrying horse shoes from Mauberge.'

His was only carrying tiles, so had been allowed to go on his way.

'I don't know what the *Nénuphar* was carrying,' he said. 'But I looked back and saw them taking the captain along the towpath. He must have had something their army needs. They don't need roof tiles, thanks to God.'

Josephine Lucie didn't know what the *Nénuphar* was carrying either in the way of cargo, but she knew full well it was carrying her injured Augustin, unmistakably dressed as a balloon pilot, to say nothing of the sacks of mail from Paris.

'I didn't think the Prussians were this far north,' she said.

The bargee shrugged. 'Neither did I. I have not seen them before. I thought they were at Metz and Sedan, but not here. Perhaps the war is lost. Who knows?'

Josephine Lucie did not reply, but set off as fast as she could, along the towpath in the direction she knew the *Nénuphar* to be.

'I was already very tired and hungry, Florence. I had walked and walked all the day and had eaten nothing since some *saucisson* when I woke. But I was so worried for Augustin, I gave little thought to myself.'

'Still no rolls and chocolate, then, for breakfast?' I couldn't help myself, I was getting a bit peckish myself and I made the mistake of mentioning it.

Josephine Lucie took the other apple from her bowl and began to peel it for me.

'We will have chocolate for breakfast one morning, if you wish, *ma chère*. Do you wish to go down for your tea? I imagine my Augustin can wait, even if you cannot.'

I must have gone very red at the rebuke. Josephine Lucie gave me the peeled apple neatly cut into four quarters with the core taken out and chuckled, easing the tension.

'It is unusual, *n'est-ce pas*, Florence, for us not to have made some éclairs or some biscuits, or something, to have in my middle room. You see, I worry for Augustin, even after nearly sixty years. It has quite 'put me off my grub', as Leonard would say.'

The last thing I wanted just then was for my brother to be introduced into the proceedings. Josephine Lucie's thread was in danger of breaking altogether, just when we had managed to rescue her narration from the disturbances of over-emotional recollection. Now she had not only used a horrible Leonardism in the middle room, she had put her story into her own grandmotherly past. After sixty years, indeed! Whatever next? We both knew perfectly well that past, present, and possibly the future, too, were as one in the middle room. Nothing ever elapsed. It only persisted.

It was my fault for having mentioned the chocolate at just the wrong moment. But she was right. It was odd that both our hands and minds weren't occupied with food at this point in the history. Only with our hunger. Hers from the past and mine present and real. One and the same hunger in the middle room.

I ate a piece of the apple.

'Was it bad? When you found the boat?'

'Madame, the wife of the *chaland* captain, was, you know, what do you say?'

'I don't know. What?'

'*Éperdue*. Beside something, you say, Florence.'

'Beside the canal?'

'No, of course not the canal... Beside herself.'

The Prussian patrol had come upon the Sambre canal from the east. Partly they seemed to have been scouting further and further from their own main lines to see how far the French army of the North might have ventured from Lille. And partly they were foraging for food and military supplies, as the bargee had suspected.

It was unfortunate that the *Nénuphar* had been the first of the three barges they surprised. Otherwise the captain might have had time to dump the incriminating balloon dispatches overboard. Even so, they would probably have floated and alerted the Prussians. But at least a soaking might have made them illegible. Nothing could make poor Augustin disappear, however. He lay in a state of semi-consciousness on a bunk, still wearing his Paris militia uniform and covered with his own unmistakable aeronaut's sheepskin.

When Josephine Lucie arrived only the *chaland* captain's wife was on board with her youngest children. Beside herself indeed, she told Josephine Lucie how the Prussians had found Augustin and the sacks of dispatches.

'They shouted at my man, in German, and manhandled him and struck him with the butts of their *fusils* and when my eldest boy left the horse and came to try and help his father, they beat him too. Then they marched my man away...that way, away from the canal. I could not leave the children. I could not go with him. What will become of him, mademoiselle?'

'Did they take Augustin? Where is he, madame? They could not surely make him march. He could not even stand.'

It seemed that Augustin had been carried off the barge and more or less strapped to a horse.

'He must have been in terrible pain, madame.'

'I don't know. Probably. But what will become of my man, mademoiselle, for pity's sake? Will they shoot him for carrying the sacks?'

With a sinking heart Josephine Lucie set off along the towpath in the direction the *chaland* had come from. She reasoned that, as she had not encountered the patrol herself, coming from Orgelets, it must have gone north, towards Mauberge. Towards four o'clock, she saw the bridge over the canal at Landrecies and quickened her pace.

'When I reached the bridge, Florence, there were little groups of people, just standing, talking quietly. It was not normal for this time in the afternoon, I could see. At once I asked what had happened. They told me the Prussians were there, searching the *chalands*. I crossed onto the bridge to see for myself.'

There was a detachment of soldiers along the canal on the other side side, considerably more than the number who had taken

Augustin and the captain of the *Nénuphar*. Josephine Lucie strained to look, but could see neither of them.

'There were several officers. One, a young man, was standing apart. Arming myself with my courage, I approached and asked if he spoke French. He said he did, a little. I looked at him with my best eyes. You understand, *chérie?* I asked him if he knew what had become of the men from the *Nénuphar*. He asked me why it interested me? Suddenly he was mistrustful. I told him I knew the captain's wife a little, because I lived by the canal, and had come to find what had happened to her man, because she was so frightened. I didn't mention Augustin.'

The young officer had seemed satisfied with this explanation. Perhaps it had something to do with Josephine Lucie's beauty.

'If you are a friend of this man, *Fraülein*, then I am sorry for you. This morning a court martial found him guilty of harbouring a spy. His wife is fortunate we did not arrest her too.

'A court martial? But he is not a soldier.'

'No matter. We are at war, *Fraülein*. The man he was sheltering on his boat was a soldier. It is a military matter.'

'A soldier? What soldier?' Josephine Lucie pressed him recklessly.

'A balloonist, *Fraülein*. From Paris.

'What will happen to them? What shall I tell the captain's poor wife?'

The young Prussian glanced up and down the towpath, as if he was worried about being overheard. The other officers and soldiers in the vicinity must have merely thought he was chatting to a pretty young girl.

'The boat captain will be taken to Sedan. Tell her that.'

'What will happen there?'

The officer shrugged. 'Perhaps he will be shot. Perhaps not. As you say, he is not a soldier and we are not uncivilized, even in time of war.'

Josephine Lucie wanted to strike him, thinking of the starving, bombarded civilians in her beloved Paris, but she controlled herself.

'And the other one? The soldier? What of him?' She could barely keep her voice steady.

'You are very curious, *Fraülein*. I have perhaps answered enough questions.'

Josephine Lucie looked at him in a way she hoped looked both proud and beseeching.

'He may be an enemy to you, monsieur, but to me he is a loyal Frenchman, as you are a loyal Prussian, and perhaps far from his home and family, as you are, too. Who will tell them what has become of him?'

The young Prussian looked taken aback for a moment. Then he drew himself to attention, clicked his heels and bowed his head curtly to Josephine Lucie.

'I will make it my business to do so, *Fraülein*. He will undoubtedly suffer the fate of all spies. He will be shot. As a brave Frenchman, I have no doubt he will understand and accept it.'

Josephine Lucie had felt her knees beginning to buckle. She controlled the tremor in her voice as best she could.

'Then is he here? Still alive?'

There was a call from further up the towpath. The officer glanced back. It was evidently for him.

'I must go, *Fraülein*. You will excuse me.' He clicked his heels again, turned, and strode off.

'Can I see him?' Josephine Lucie called out. But in her abject misery her voice had barely carried. If the officer had heard her, he did not look back.

I heard Rhoda at the bottom of the stairs, calling crossly to Leonard and to me that our tea was getting cold. Rhoda hated being Pa's messenger for tasks like that. She felt it was beneath her. Too much of Mother's function being put upon her, I suppose, although I shouldn't think it crossed Pa's mind one way or the other. It had been a long time since Mother had called us for tea, anyway, even when she was alive.

I pretended I hadn't heard.

'Was he still alive?'

'Augustin? I told you, Florence. For me, he died then.'

'I don't understand. Did you see him again at this place?'

'No, *ma chère*, I did not. Now you must go for this bizarre meal Charles calls tea. It is not right to keep food waiting on the table, whatever its name.'

I could have crowned her.

'Are you coming down?'

'No, but you can bring me something up here before I go to bed. That would be kind. I am very tired, very tired.'

29

'God, I'm tired, Florrie Dee. I haven't slept in three days. It's like…I don't know what it's like. Like we've been bombed, I suppose. Why would that have to be *like* anything else? All the windows out. Glass everywhere. It's like walking on…It's like walking on broken glass. God, I'm talking gibberish. I'm so tired.'

'When will you get a pass, Freddie? I miss you so much. I want you home. We could all hear the pasting you were getting. It was as if it was never going to end. Just one long roar all night long. Every night. I was so scared, thinking about you. Not supposed to say that sort of thing, are we? Keep the boys' spirits up, girls. Don't tell 'em you're worried. Well I am worried, Freddie. I *am!*'

'The girls over at Hill Street were hit. Half the building gone. One of them was killed. It seems most of them were out on the razz and missed it.'

'What girls at Hill Street?'

'The *Corps Féminin* girls. They're not called that any more. People kept taking the rise. FFL they are, now. *Forces Françaises Libres*.'

'You know, I don't really care, Freddie. Just so long as I can have you home safe and sound.'

I did care though. Just a bit. 'Anyway, I thought they were in Belgravia, not Mayfair, these French floozies. Mayfair sounds more appropriate, I must say.'

'Some were to start with. The Hill Street lot are in the Turkish baths at the Dorchester now. I've been up there helping out. Sifting through the rubble to retrieve the paperwork.'

'What do you mean, Turkish Baths? Couldn't they have ordinary ones like the rest of us?'

'No Florence Duck. Not *having* one. Somewhere to sleep till they're found something permanent.'

'Perhaps we could stay at the Dorchester then, if you got a pass.'

'Fat chance to either of those, Florrie Dee. Still, I should be home for the night if the tubes are running. I'm not on guard duty for a while after all this. I've just seen your adorable uncle, by the way. I think he was having his dinner with Gaillet. They were both heading out together at midday, anyway.'

'Did he say anything?'

'No, he didn't see me.'

I put the telephone down just in the nick of time. Old Webber came back from his dinner a bit early and nearly caught me at it. I didn't really care any more. I was so worried about Freddie, I couldn't be bothered with all that copper for the phones in the post office. Hanging on and not getting through before the money ran out. I just wanted to talk to him.

Mr Webber looked at me sharply as I was coming out of his office.

'Was there something, Florence…Mrs Draper?'

Make up your mind. Don't know whether to tick me off or not, in the circumstances.

'I thought I heard the telephone, Mr Webber. But if it was, they must have rung off before I got there.'

He relaxed. 'How's that young husband of yours getting on, Florence? It must be hard on him up there in the thick of all these air raids. Hard for you too, I expect. Not knowing.'

That was it. I burst into tears. Real ones. How dare Old Webber be nice to me! He stood awkwardly in front of me, not quite sure what he had done and still less sure what to do about it. He pulled out his slightly off-white handkerchief from his top pocket, clumsily bringing his pocket watch out with it so that it hung comically on its leather strap from his lapel button hole. He handed the hankie to me.

'I'm sorry, Mrs Draper…Florence. That Hitler's got a lot to answer for, when the time comes,' he said.

His hankie smelt slightly of Players Weights. A picture of Leonard came flooding into my head. I wondered how he was in Singapore. He wrote to Rhoda occasionally, but everything took so long. I suppose he assumed Rhoda would pass on the news, such as it was in army letters. I expect she told Pa more than she told me. When she had a chance. Pa had been evacuated with the school. To Liverpool of all places. Talk about out of the frying pan. Not the centre of the city though. Singapore didn't look all that cushy any more, either. Not with all the talk about the Japanese.

I blew hard on Mr Webber's handkerchief. I'd have to wash and iron it now and he would have to go home to Mrs Webber and explain where it was, and she would worry privately that perhaps it hadn't been a clean one that morning. That Hitler certainly did have a lot to answer for.

'You don't have to be sorry, Mr Webber,' I said through my tears. 'We all have to grin and bear it, don't we? Keep smiling through. I'm sorry to make a fuss. There's plenty worse off. And anyhow, my Freddie will be home this evening, with a little luck, though what I shall get for him, I don't know. I haven't been to see what's in the high street today. I couldn't face the queues.' It was a lie. I'd spent my dinner time on his telephone.

'Just a minute, my dear.'

'*My dear*'? Whatever was coming?

I stood aside to let him go through into his office. He put the string bag he'd been carrying in his non-hankie hand on his desk, took out a newspaper wrapped packet from it and proceeded to unfold it.

'I purchased some salt cod, myself. I'd like you to have some of it. There's plenty.'

'Oh Mr Webber, I couldn't possibly take your dinner.'

'Nonsense. I said there's plenty. It's not on ration, you know. Mrs Webber makes up some dried milk and water and soaks it for about an hour and then makes them into fish rissoles. It really is quite palatable. You can use the salty milk and water for a soup stock.' He looked rather embarrassed at his giving me cookery hints.

'So I believe, anyway,' he added quickly. 'It was on the wireless, *The Kitchen Front*. Freddie Grisewood on the Home Service. Do you listen in? Mrs Webber and I are very partial.'

My Freddie struggled home about eight-thirty.

'Two buses and a tube. We had to go miles out of our way, my darling duck.' As usual he was talking before I had fully opened the door, as if we had been in conversation all the way home.

'Stroke of luck. Managed to liberate some bacon and eggs. Real eggs not powdered. The mess at Hill Street got hit. It was a *real mess*. And would you believe it, these eggs were intact? Extraordinary! One poor girl dead. Staircase gone. Ceilings down. Whole front gone, really. And these blooming eggs, not a scratch, not a crack. Quite extraordinary! Bit of dust on the bacon. Nothing serious.'

He caught my look. 'What, Florrie Dee? Why are you looking

like that? We were told to take the files and leave anything else alone. So it was just so much rubbish. Shame to leave it.'

I told Freddie in no uncertain terms he was having salt cod rissoles for his dinner, like it or lump it. It was the least I could do. His loot would have to wait.

As we were finishing, I said rather peevishly that the BBC was wrong. The salt cod needed soaking for about a fortnight, if it was going to be anything like palatable. Not an hour. And we'd just missed ITMA on the wireless.

Freddie said, 'Talking of *It's That Man Again* reminds me, I saw Maurice today.'

'Yes, you told me. On the telephone. You said he didn't see you.'

'No. Later. I saw him later. He stuck his head round the door after he'd come back with Gaillet. Or rather, not with Gaillet. *Mon Capitaine* didn't return until later. Come to think of it, that's probably why Maurice came to see me.'

'What do you mean?'

'Well, he's always a bit wary about Gaillet seeing me with him now, isn't he?'

'What did he want? Has he found out something about that doctor?'

'I don't know. He was very brief. As I say, just stuck his head round. Said he wants a family conference though. You're right about that cod, Florrie Dee. It's given me a raging thirst.'

'Both of us?'

'And Rhoda, apparently.'

'Rhoda? Are you sure? It must be about the doctor then. I don't know when we'll manage that. Rhoda's in something at the moment. I forget what. I saw it in the paper.'

'Maurice said he'd arrange something.'

I didn't see Freddie for several nights after that and I was on fire watch over on the little green by the shelters anyway. I sneaked off to the phone box when the warden's back was turned and on the second night, after about two or three goes, I managed to get through to Freddie in the guard room at Carlton Gardens. After I'd finished biting his head off for making me so anxious, he said Maurice had fixed for us all to meet on Sunday.

'Sunday? Oh Freddie, we'll never get a bus or anything on

Sunday.'

'No, my darling duck. He's coming for us in the motor.'

'How does he know you'll be able to get away?'

'Says he's fixed it. I'm being summoned back to the unit at Finsbury Circus for something. Only I'm not, apparently.'

Maurice's big Austin drew up outside the house at about eleven o'clock on the Sunday and hooted. That's right, I thought, let the neighbours all know we're off gallivanting, probably on black market petrol. Oh no. I forgot – special service ration. Rhoda was already settled in the back, so I got in next to her and Freddie sat next to Maurice.

'Where are we off to then, old man?' Freddie asked him.

'We're all going to the zoo,' Rhoda said.

'Isn't it shut for the duration?' said Freddie. 'Hey, that's a thought! What happens if Göring drops one on the lion house and they all get out?'

'The fierce ones have all gone to Whipsnade,' said Maurice. 'That's where we're going. I've got a special pass for us.'

'Whipsnade?' I said. 'Isn't that rather a long way to go for a chat?'

'I've something a bit special in the boot. Don't want the whole world gawping at us, do we? Whipsnade's out of bounds to the hoi polloi, so we can find a nice quiet spot up there on the downs.

Needless to say, when the Austin was parked under some trees just at the back of the ridge running along the Dunstable Downs, and its boot was opened up, it looked like a miniature version of the Home and Colonial circa 1938. There was cheese, blue cheese, for goodness sake! In a piece you needed a big knife to cut. Corned beef in proper slices in greaseproof, and, wonder of wonders, a slab of dark chocolate.

'What's this?' said Freddie, unwrapping another paper parcel 'Liver paste?'

'It's chicken liver pâté, more like,' said Rhoda. She scooped some on her little finger and put it in her mouth. 'And it's got brandy in it. Must be out of a tin then, Maurice. Nobody's making stuff like this, fresh. Not in London, surely? Well, the Savoy probably, I grant you. Been raiding the kitchens, Darling?'

'And the wine cellar,' Maurice laughed. 'A half decent Beaune. 1936. We shall not see its like again. Well, not for a while at any rate. What do you think, Florence? A glass of Burgundy with your corned beef?'

'That Hitler's got a lot to answer for, Mr Webber always says.' The silence I felt seemed somehow inappropriate. What were we all here for?

While everyone tucked in, I went through the motions, memories of the scones and cream at Elstree still lingering. The late summer sun was warm and the war seemed a long, long way away. Grasshoppers rasped away to one another, competing for our attention with Rhoda, name dropping with her mouth full. To listen to her you would have supposed she had completely forgotten her run-in with Freddie in the Haymarket.

Then, almost at our level where we sat on the top of the ridge looking down on the countryside far below, a single fighter came from behind us with a sudden roar of its engine, dropped down and veered away to the east. I ducked instinctively, it seemed so low.

'Hurricane,' Freddie shouted, jumping to his feet to watch it go. 'I could see the pilot, he came so close.

'No-one you would know, though, Freddie. RAF, not Pay Corps,' said Rhoda, 'so I shouldn't go running after him.'

Out of sight behind us somewhere an elephant trumpeted, no doubt alarmed by the noise of the aeroplane.

I needed to defuse Freddie before he started in on Rhoda.

'Old Jumbo needs to thank his lucky stars he can sit the war out here. The elephants in the Paris siege were eaten, you know. I wonder if the Ministry would put him on or off the ration, if it came to it,' I said.

'My mother obviously talked to you girls about her Paris days a great deal more than she ever did to me,' said Maurice. 'Don't tell me she ate an elephant, Rhoda.'

'Don't ask me.' said Rhoda, 'I was never let into that room of hers. That was strictly for Florence. Closeted day after day.'

Maurice looked at me.

'Well, Florence. And what did you and my mother find to talk about, day after day?'

I wasn't having this. It was my fault for having mentioned Paris.

'Look Uncle Maurice,' I said 'Oughtn't we really to be talking about Captain Gaillet and what he knows about Rhoda?'

'Yes,' said Freddie, a little bit nastily, I thought. 'Doctor Guttman's famous list. What's to be done about that?'

'So that's his name is it, Freddie? Guttman?' said Maurice.

'How long have you known this?'

'Who's Doctor Guttman?' asked Rhoda.

'It's Captain Guttman, actually,' said Freddie, 'Free French medic.'

'You remember, Rhoda.' I lent forward and clasped my knees, resting my chin on them, and gazing down the steep escarpment, suddenly afraid to raise it all again with her, now that the moment had come. 'You remember. He was that doctor in France. In Luxeuil. Wasn't he?'

'No, he wasn't.' said Rhoda. 'If we have to talk about this. His name was Schiffmann.'

'Are you sure?'

'Yes. He had the nerve to give me his card. As if I'd need him again!'

'Are you sure?' said Maurice.

Rhoda stared at him in blank amazement.

'Of course I'm bloody sure. I wouldn't go through all that again!'

'No, no,' Maurice said hastily, 'I didn't mean that. Of course I didn't. I mean are you sure of the name?'

Rhoda was certain. Maurice asked Freddie if he might have made a mistake.

'Well that's what the landlady at the French House said. I suppose she might have got it wrong. Some of these Jewish names sound the same, don't they?'

I was on the point of saying to Maurice, well if he's a Jew he surely won't have been talking to Gaillet about being repatriated, will he? But something stopped me. I looked to see if Freddie had registered the point and our eyes met. It was one of those husband and wife looks, completely telepathic. Both thinking precisely the same thing at the same time, often when nothing at all has been said out loud to provoke it. 'Telepathetic' Freddie calls it.

'Well, it shouldn't be too difficult to find out, now that we've narrowed it down to two possibles,' said Maurice.

'You'll ask your people, will you?' I said. It was wicked, I know, but I couldn't help myself.

'What people?' said Rhoda, bang on cue. 'What does she mean, *your people,* Maurice?'

Maurice sat forward on the grassy slope and patted his jacket pockets methodically. Looking for his cigarette case. When he had tried them all, he eventually found it in the one he'd tried first. He took it out and offered it first to Rhoda. She took one. He half offered it to me.

'No, you don't, do you Florence? Freddie?'

'Pipe thanks, old man,' said Freddie, fishing around for it in his battledress.

Maurice went through the same ritual to find his lighter and then offered Rhoda a light. Then he took a cigarette for himself, tapped it slowly and deliberately on his thumb nail, put it to his lips and lit it. Taking a really deep drag and holding it, he lay back on the turf before slowly exhaling the blue smoke to the heavens above.

Really got you thinking, haven't I, Uncle Maurice? I thought.

We all waited for Maurice to say something, but it was Rhoda who broke the silence.

'What the hell's going on here? What list? What's this Doctor Guttman got to do with us? Why did you think he was the one who…you know…in Switzerland or France, or wherever we bloody were, Florence? Is this about Freddie coming round to the theatre, whenever it was and being so bloody rude? I thought that was just between you and him, Florence.'

'*Rude*? You can talk, Rhoda,' said Freddie.

I glanced at Maurice. 'Well?' I said.

He sat up.

'Captain Gaillet claims the doctor from the clinic is here with the Free French and has a list of his prominent…patients. Your name is on it, apparently. He's trying to bargain…'

'But it isn't him, is it? Not the creep from Luxeuil. We've just said,' Rhoda interrupted him.

'Well, perhaps there's more than one doctor. Didn't he have a partner? I'll try and find out,' said Maurice, not very convincingly, I must say.

'That's not very likely, is it, old man,' said Freddie, unhelpfully. I could see he was enjoying seeing Maurice on the back foot for once.

'You still haven't explained.' Rhoda said. 'What did she mean, *your people*? Who're they when they're at home?'

Maurice put his cigarette out and took another one from the case.

'Well?' said Rhoda.

'It's difficult,' he said. 'I'm…I'm in the…'

'In the soup, old man. He's a spy,' said Freddie. 'One of ours, of course. You are one of ours, aren't you, old man?'

'We think Gaillet may be up to something. He says he can

prevent it becoming public that you're on a list of this doctor's patients, Rhoda. I'm trying to catch him out.'

'I've really had enough of this,' said Rhoda. 'Why am I being used, Maurice? What for? You of all people should be looking after me.'

'I do, Rhoda. I always do.'

The penny dropped. I stared in disbelief at Rhoda and then at Maurice.

'Don't, Florence. Don't say it. Let's just think,' he said quickly.

'Don't say what?' said Freddie.

'Oh shut up, Freddie,' said Rhoda, 'I'm going home. Take me home, Maurice.'

'Hang on,' I said. 'We haven't come all this way just to eat liver pate. I don't think Uncle Maurice should get away with it so easily. You've brought us out here to a remote spot. There has to be more to it than a picnic.

Rhoda actually began to cry. I hadn't seen that for a few years.

'Just let it drop, Florence, for goodness sake, why don't you? It was all over and done with a long time ago.'

'It's not about you and Maurice,' I said. 'It's something else, isn't it, Uncle Maurice. You don't want anyone to see us all together. Why's that? Is someone watching us? Or are they watching you?'

Maurice patted his pockets for his cigarette case and then must have realised he still had one going. Our eyes met, briefly. He saw I had seen it, too, and grimaced.

'Oh well.' he said. 'What the hell! Yes, I think I am being watched. My people, as you keep calling them, don't entirely trust me. They never have. They know I've still got contacts in Europe. Business contacts. They're very happy to make use of them, of course. But it still doesn't exactly make me one of the chaps. Not the right school. No military service. A few brushes with the law.'

'So what, then?' said Freddie. 'They think you're a double agent or something?'

'Trading with the enemy, Freddie, trading with the enemy. They think I'm still in business and stashing away a fortune in some Swiss bank.'

'And are you?' said Freddie.

'If only. No, seriously, I may not always have been entirely legitimate, but I'm not a bastard, either.'

'And Captain Gaillet,' I said. 'Where does he fit in? What about this list with Rhoda's name on it, and mine?'

'I'm not sure yet. But what I do know is that "my people" think he and I are in business together. That's why I desperately need Freddie on the inside to get to the bottom of his financial fiddles. If he thinks you and Freddie are cooperating with him because of Rhoda, we may be able to flush him out.'

You haven't really answered my question, though, have you? I thought.

'I don't see how,' said Freddie. 'Gaillet already thinks I'm going along with his subterfuge for the sake of General de Gaulle's pipe dreams of being in charge of France after the war. On a flying pig, I should think. But he hasn't actually threatened me, if you see what I mean. I can't see what more I can do to flush him out.'

It was as much as I could do not to giggle. 'Flush him out'. What on earth did they think they sounded like? Something on the wireless or *The Thirty-nine Steps*. I still couldn't bring myself to believe it could be like that.

Maurice stubbed out his cigarette and felt for another. 'What we need to do is see if he has access to money, himself. I mean *a lot* of money. Especially if he's still moving it around Europe somehow. Spain, Switzerland, Portugal. Best of all would be Vichy. That would be enough to blow the whistle on him and pack him off to Pentonville.'

'And how do you propose to do that?' asked Freddie.

'Florence could offer to sell him the painting.'

Ah, the painting! So that's it, I thought. And you used to be so adorable.

'What painting?' said Rhoda.

'That one he was asking about that belonged to my mother. The man in the lace collar.'

'I don't remember him asking about it,' said Rhoda. 'When did he?'

'Didn't he mention it when we all had dinner? You know, the unexploded bomb?'

'Well I don't remember. But I suppose that's not surprising really. We all thought our number was up that night. I can't even remember what we had.'

'I think you had a Worthington,' said Freddie. 'They were out of absinthe.'

Rhoda, to her credit, ignored him. 'And do you have it, Florence? This painting?'

Everyone's eyes were on me.

'That doesn't matter, does it Maurice. It's enough if Captain Gaillet thinks I have. Isn't that right?'

Maurice inclined his head in agreement, but I thought his eyes looked rather irritated. Perhaps it was my imagination. It was turning into a very odd day, indeed. Full of unanswered questions, which nobody seemed interested in pursuing. It was as if we were all locked together, but prowling round separately, in our own space, just like those big cats in the parkland behind us.

'Well, you obviously haven't found this valuable painting,' said Rhoda, 'otherwise you'd have sold it and bought a few new frocks.'

That more or less finished the proceedings. Maurice drove us home in virtual silence. I could see the day had not gone according to plan as far as he was concerned. But I was blessed if I could see what that plan was.

We dropped Rhoda off at her flat in Highgate first, which I thought odd because it meant Maurice had to double back with Freddie and me.

'Why didn't you go straight down the Great North Road, old man?' said Freddie. 'Much quicker.'

'I needed to talk to you two alone.'

'About this infernal list of Guttman's or is it Schiffman's?' said Freddie. 'I must say that's looking very rum, isn't it. Do you think there is one at all? Still that's not the point is it, I suppose. Gaillet knows about Rhoda and it doesn't matter how.'

I dug Freddie in the ribs. I hoped Maurice wasn't looking in his driving mirror.

'No,' said Maurice. 'Not the list. Forget the bloody list. We need to talk about offering him the Rubens. You need to get him somewhere where my people can listen in. But it'll have to be somewhere he won't be suspicious of going. What about your flat?'

'Maisonette.' I said. 'I don't know, Maurice. This is all turning very peculiar, if you don't mind my saying.'

'Well, I can't help that. You'll have to think of something.'

As the big Austin drove off down the close, I shut the front door and pulled the blackout over it instinctively, even though it wasn't yet time.

'Nice cuppa?' said Freddie.

'Did you tell Maurice it was a Rubens?'

'No. I haven't spoken to him about it until today. Good grub, wasn't it. I liberated some of that chocolate, by the way. Couldn't have Rhoda scoffing it all.'

30

'*Voilà* Florence. *Chocolat chaud.* I promised you. And we will have hot rolls from the Broadway if you run down now.'

It was a Saturday morning, early. Josephine Lucie had been listening out for me as I went downstairs to see to the range. It was my turn. It was always my turn, as Leonard had started giving me thruppence a week to take his. Despite Pa's feared gas stove, the range still needed lighting for the hot water.

I protested weakly that I had my chore to do, but Josephine Lucie was oblivious. 'Hurry, hurry, otherwise they will be cold from the baker.'

The front door was still locked and bolted from the night. Not wanting to make a noise opening it up, I went out of the back door in the scullery and through the passage to the front. I ran all the way to the baker's and all the way back, hoping to make the sanctuary of the middle room before the rest of the house was stirring. Of course, I had to go round the back, the way I had gone out. And of course, Pa was already in the kitchen.

'Have you been out, Florence? The range isn't lit yet. Where have you been?'

'I've been down to the baker's for Grandmother.'

'Well hurry up and get the range lit. There's no hot water. You'll have to boil a kettle on the wretched gas for my shave.'

Pa still did not trust the gas stove and would not operate it himself if he could possibly avoid it.

'What did your grandmother want, anyway, that was so urgent the range couldn't be lit?'

I felt the warmth of the rolls in the paper bag. At first they had been almost too hot to hold, but already they were beginning to lose their heat.

'Hot rolls for her…our breakfast, Pa. They're getting cold already.'

'Hot rolls? Whatever next? What's wrong with good old-fashioned toast, then? Still, seeing as you've run all the way, by the colour of your cheeks, you'd better call her down before they spoil. I must say, I could just fancy a hot roll. I wonder what put that into her head? She gets some funny ideas sometimes, your grandmother. It's being French. They do that, you know – hot rolls. No, on second thoughts I'll call her. You put a match to the range and put the kettle on the gas for my shave. And some tea. Have we any marmalade, I wonder? Do you know, Florence? What's the marmalade situation in this house?'

This was not going at all well. But somehow I didn't want him to be disappointed either. He so seldom passed any comment on his mother-in-law at all, that remarking that she sometimes had some funny ideas and assuming, too, that she had included him in her continental breakfast plans seemed positively indulgent.

'Not tea, Pa. We were meant to be having *chocolat chaud*. With the rolls.'

He'd walked out into the hallway to the bottom of the stairs. 'Having what?'

'Hot chocolate, Pa.' I applied a match to one of the newspaper battleships we made to light the kindling and clinker he had laid the night before in the bottom of the range.

'Good heavens, Florence. Cocoa? For breakfast? What on earth for? Ah, there you are, *Madame*. Cocoa and hot rolls, I gather. Special occasion, I suppose. Something French?'

My grandmother had come to the door of the middle room. Wondering what was keeping me, I expect.

'But certainly not your disgusting cocoa, Charles.' She didn't pronounce the 's' of his name. It was another way of irritating him with her Frenchness when he called her '*Madame*'. But this morning neither seemed to take exception to the other's slight. '*Chocolat chaud*. And are the rolls still hot, Florence?' She came into the kitchen.

'Just about, Grandmother. Well, they're not quite cold, anyway.'

'Good. Observe. And you, Charles.'

She took down one of the copper saucepans that hung over the range. I couldn't remember them ever being used. Rhoda maintained they had come with the house, like the range itself.

'This will need to be washed.' She handed it to Pa who took it without a murmur to the scullery tap.

'Make this cloth a little damp, Florence, from the kettle. Wrap the rolls in it and put them in the oven. This will keep them warm without they become hard.' She took my arm, conspiratorially. 'Do we have enough for your father, Florence?' she whispered, while he was still out attending to the saucepan.

'I got six. They come joined up in six and I thought, as you'd given me thruppence, I should spend it all. I got white ones. Was that right?'

'Perfect. And we shall have enough if Leonard and Rhoda come down, too. But we shall not call to them, however.'

Pa returned with the copper saucepan.

'Needs a bit of brasso on the outside. But it's respectable enough inside. It had a bit of a cobweb with something nameless in it. Shows how long since these have been down. Good pan. Solid bottom. Perhaps we should use them more.'

Grandmother took it from him, poured a little milk from the larder jug into it and set it on the lighted gas to warm gently. Then she reached inside her voluminous satin dressing gown, which fell to the ground like a triangular tent and had slit plackets like a mackintosh instead of patch pockets on the outside. From one of these she produced a huge wrapped slab of what proved to be very dark chocolate indeed.

Pa and I were both mesmerised. The size of it. And all in a piece. Not broken squares from a jar on the sweet shop counter.

'This is a *chose de qualité,* Charles. I had to command it in the Broadway, Florence. They do not have it normally at Williams Brothers. I am sad to say it is not French, but Swiss. But never mind, it is very good, even so.'

She broke it, piece, by piece, into the warm milk and chivvied it gently with a wooden spoon. Imperceptibly almost, the lumps of chocolate in the saucepan began to soften, losing shape, flowing into the milk in liquid coils. A heavy, bittersweet smell began slowly to fill the room and, as it did, I prayed fervently that it would not reach to Leonard's room, or Rhoda's and mine. Pa was still silently transfixed, as if the alchemy in the saucepan and its magical incense had cast a spell over him.

Grandmother, sensing the moment, whispered reverently, 'It is important not to let the *chocolat* boil. Now…'

She drew the saucepan off the heat and poured in a little more milk, beating it into the molten chocolate with a fork, then returning it to the heat, beating it all the while, then off the heat again, more milk, a little at a time, more beating, back to the heat, until there was a good pint at least.

'*Voilà, chocolat chaud.* Truly we should have some cream to put in. But I know, Charles, that you do not regard cream as important. So we will have none, I know.'

Pa was still staring fixedly at the copper saucepan, at its dark, barely moving contents, only gradually losing the pattern of the whisking, like the final chime of a bell, fading on the wind.

Without taking his eyes off it, he said: 'There's a tin of condensed milk in the larder. I've seen it.'

Most of the breakfast was spent in the kind of silence you find in church. Pa did watch, horrified, as Grandmother dipped her roll into the chocolate and after a moment's hesitation I had followed suit. He said nothing, however, merely going over to the larder and fetching out butter and marmalade.

Grandmother could not resist this. 'Both, Charles? It is, as you say, truly a special occasion.'

'So what were we all celebrating, then, in the end?' he said a little later.

'An anniversary, Charles. Of a kind.'

I listened with mounting alarm. She wasn't going to tell Pa anything about anything, was she?

'Not your wedding anniversary, surely, *Madame*...Mother-in-law.'

His small courtesy wasn't lost on her. The *chocolat chaud* had evidently worked a magic for Anglo-French relations. For the time being, at any rate.

'Not my wedding, no, Charles. But it was the first *repas* I ever took with my husband, except he was not yet my husband. I had not had *chocolat chaud* for a very long time before. Not since I left Paris.'

Enough, enough. In panic, I dived in without thinking first.

'But you said he'd died. Didn't he, then? *Did* you marry him after all?'

Josephine Lucie looked across at me coolly. I blushed right down to my feet. It was *I* who had said too much.

'Edward Burnell?' Pa sounded puzzled. 'He died only a only a year or two back, I remember. Of course I remember. Twenty-two or three, was it? Well after the war. He was too old for that. Went to the funeral, didn't I.'

'Yes Charles. You did. Florence is confused by the *chocolat chaud*...'

'Well, it was very rich, I must say. Perhaps we shouldn't have added the condensed…'

'No, Charles. Florence is mistaking the occasion. She thinks I had hot rolls and chocolate another time, don't you, *ma chérie*? But I did not. Not for a long time. Not until I met your Grandfather Burnell.'

The kettle, which had been quietly hissing to itself on the stove decided to rattle its lid to attract someone's attention before it boiled quite dry.

'Good heavens, I'm not shaved yet.' Pa stood up. 'Look at the time. Florence, that gas is still on under the kettle. The range should have been lit by now!'

'I did light it, Pa.'

'Yes, but not soon enough. That's what comes of cocoa for breakfast.'

Grandmother stood up too. 'And I must get dressed. Come and talk to me in my room in a little while, Florence.'

I thought, 'Yes, Josephine Lucie'.

I'd barely got through the door to the middle room before she was scolding me

'You must not think I would tell your father my *histoire*, Florence.'

I tried to protest that no such thought had crossed my mind, but we both knew it had.

'I told you at the beginning, *chérie*. My story is for you. One day, perhaps, you will pass it to your own granddaughter. I chose you because you are the youngest, you know. If you do the same, my story will endure for a long time without change, because there are not many people to tell it.'

'You mean like telling Leonard your grandfather had fought at Waterloo? It's more than a hundred years ago, but you knew him. And if Leonard tells his grandchildren, it'll probably be two hundred years ago.'

'*Voilà* Florence. You have it. And it needs only be two people in the middle to make the chain of time. To hold hands between the living and the dead.'

'Only Leonard might not tell his grandchildren because…you know.'

'Because my grandfather was French?'

'Yes.'

'Leonard will not be able to stop himself. He loves to show off.'

'And is it true, that you didn't have hot chocolate and rolls for ages and ages?'

'Yes. It was not the *petit déjeuner* one found in the homes of country people. I had been spoiled by Paris and César Machin.'

'Oh,' I said, and we fell silent for a moment, each knowing, I suppose, that the memory of that breakfast not taken, was the memory of much besides which had not come to pass.

After the Prussian officer had left her so abruptly, Josephine Lucie could think of nothing save the fact that Augustin was likely to be shot, if indeed he had not already been so. The detachment of soldiers had already mounted up and was moving off, its business in Landrecies clearly completed. Josephine Lucie hurried up onto the bridge to watch them go by until they passed out of sight, straining to see any sign of a prisoner. But Augustin wasn't with them, and her heart sank at the thought that he might already be dead.

A woman who had seen her watching the Prussian column go past, spat contemptuously. She assumed Josephine Lucie had been admiring the uniforms and the moustachioed men wearing them. She had probably seen her talking to the officer, too.

'Oh no, indeed, Madame, I am looking for the boy. The wounded boy they took from the *chaland* this morning. And its captain.'

But the woman had seen nothing. But she didn't think they had executed anyone in the town, either. 'We would have known that, *Mademoiselle.*'

When Josephine Lucie mentioned that they may have been taken to Sedan the woman looked very vague. It was obvious she had barely ever considered the existence of the city perhaps sixty or seventy kilometres distant and had no idea which road might take Josephine Lucie in the right direction.

'And what would I do when I got there, in any case? Even supposing I could get there.' Josephine Lucie's experience of Paris under siege had left her under no illusions about the likely state of affairs in a city which had already fallen to Prussian force. But the thought shamed her, when she remembered how she had left Augustin. Was it only that morning? It seemed a lifetime ago.

She had still eaten nothing since daybreak and not much then. Suddenly her hunger, shame, and despair hung on her like lead weights. She had resumed the canal towpath without really thinking, mooching abjectly in the direction she had last seen the *Nénuphar*. Now as the wintry sun began to set behind the trees, Josephine Lucie's legs buckled under her and she subsided in a sobbing heap on the damp canal bank.

As the darkness became virtually complete, she was roused from her misery by a hand on her shoulder.

'Was it him? Was it your Augustin?' I didn't want this story to be so horribly real any more. I wanted happy endings.

'No, *ma chérie,* it was not Augustin. It was the captain of the *chaland,* the *Nénuphar*. My heart jumped when I realised. "Is Augustin with you?" I cried. But he shook his head. He helped me to my feet and we began to walk along the towpath again.'

It seemed that the Prussians had not worked out what was to happen to the captain and Augustin. From what the captain was able to piece together, some wanted to shoot them both out of hand as spies, but the senior officer wasn't prepared to take the decision without either a court martial or specific orders.

'And your friend was unconscious, mercifully for him, most of the time. You could see they didn't like the idea of shooting a man in that condition. They were still arguing when the order came to move out. I thought they might shoot me anyway for being a nuisance, so I hid in a cupboard.'

'In a cupboard, *M'sieur?* Didn't they look for you?'

'Yes, but they didn't look in the cupboard.'

'Why not?'

'I don't know, *Mademoiselle*. I think they were going to and I was beginning to feel very stupid about being found hiding in a cupboard. It is not a very brave place for a loyal Frenchman, you know. But then, your friend…'

'Augustin?'

'…Yes. He gave out a cry and fell off the table where they had put him…'

'Table? Why was he on a table?'

'Because a doctor had been to see him.'

'A French doctor?'

'Yes. He said your friend should go to the hospital. That was why they were arguing about what was to happen to him.'

'What happened to this doctor?'

'I don't know, *Mademoiselle*. He was shouting at the Prussians and that's when I got in the cupboard when they were shouting back at him.'

'So Augustin fell off the table…'

'Yes, I could see through a crack. They carried him outside and left the door open. When they came back for me, I thought they must look in the cupboard, but they must have thought I had already gone out of the door. I think your friend must have known I was in the cupboard. He did his best to create a diversion. He is a brave young man. It was a long way to fall in his condition, you know. The journey on horseback had not been easy for him, you understand *Mademoiselle*.'

'When I heard this, Florence, I said we must go back to Landrecies at once and find the doctor. He would surely know what had become of Augustin. Perhaps he had been sent to the hospital after all. I knew Augustin hadn't been taken with the Prussian column because I had watched them leave. It hurt me to think that while I was watching them, Augustin must have been still close by.'

By now it was pitch dark on the canal path. The moon, if there was one, had not risen. They had left the town well behind them. The captain was anxious to get back to his wife and children on the *Nénuphar*.

'My wife doesn't know whether I am alive or dead, *Mademoiselle*. We have no light and there are perhaps several doctors in Landrecies. It is a big enough place. Come back to the *chaland* with me now and you can return with us tomorrow when it is light.'

Josephine Lucie protested that she could not bear the thought of Augustin lying somewhere, in pain and without her by his side, but the captain was not to be moved.

'You are starving, my girl and as like to fall in the canal in the dark. Dead or alive, your friend will keep until daylight.'

'Do you think Augustin might be dead, then?'

The captain was silent for a moment before replying.

'To be honest, I think he was dying when he fell off the table. I reckon that was why they were all shouting at one another and not paying any attention to me in the cupboard. He was a brave man, your friend.'

Josephine Lucie stopped. I wasn't sure what to do. So I said nothing.

'You know, *ma chère* Florence, it is a moment of profound regret to me that I listened to that *chaland capitaine*. If I had followed my heart everything would be different now. I probably should not be here.'

I thought for a moment. 'But then neither would I. At least not here, in the middle room, would I?'

'That is perhaps *plus sage* than you understand. A second of hesitation, just enough to change your mind and your children and your grandchildren may cease to be.'

'You mean Mother and all of us…and Uncle Maurice might just not have happened. Or been someone else?'

'Yes, all of you…Maurice. Especially Maurice.'

31

'Why Maurice especially?' said Freddie. 'Why don't you trust him all of a sudden again?'

'What do you mean, *all of a sudden again*?'

'Well I can't fathom whether you do trust him or you don't. One minute he's adorable and the next you're giving me looks in the motor car and digs in the ribs in case I give the game away. Only I don't know what the game is, half the time. Well, not at all, really.'

'All right then. Who told Maurice the painting was a Rubens, if it wasn't you?'

'I didn't. Are you sure you didn't?'

'I certainly didn't. I've been very careful not to mention it. I only let it out to you because you were giving me the third degree.'

'Why don't you want him to know? It's obviously valuable, so surely it doesn't matter if it's a Rubens or a Rembrandt or...or Whistler's Mother, does it?'

'No Freddie. But the point is...' I hesitated. Hesitated for that second that might mean my future granddaughter might be somebody different.

'The point is what?'

I decided.

'Apart from my grandmother, who is dead, and me, only one other person alive knows that painting could have been a Rubens.'

'Who?'

'Captain Raoul Gaillet.'

'He might be guessing. Anyway, how would he know?'

'He's not guessing, Freddie. That's just ridiculous. He knows because his father told him.'

'His *father*?'

'Yes. He knew my grandmother when she was young.'

The vision of the man in braces came flooding into my head, bringing with it a smell of over-boiled cabbage. Whatever else I might tell Freddie, some things would go with me to the grave.

'That's right. He told us his father was sixty-something when he was born. He was an art expert. So, all right, Florrie Dee, Gaillet knows it's a Rubens and he told Maurice. Oh Good Grief! *He* told Maurice!

'Exactly, Freddie. He told Maurice, who, throughout everything, has not seen fit to tell us. He only let it slip by accident the day we went to Whipsnade. So now do you see why I don't entirely trust him?'

'Not so adorable after all. So, my duck, what else haven't we been told? Do you think all this cloak and dagger stuff is a lot of hooey and they're both in it for the painting?'

That was bothering me too. I didn't know the answer to that one. Maurice was obviously in some kind of hush-hush bunch, because of Elstree, and the scones, and the ATS driver. And he had influence with the army because he was able to make sure Freddie got weekend leave and late passes. But that still didn't mean we should take him at face value, did it? He could still be a crook. He clearly thought Gaillet was one. Or did he?

'Freddie, do you think Gaillet could be telling the truth when he says these financial subterfuges he wants you to turn a blind eye to are all for the sake of the Free French war effort?'

'Could be, Florrie Dee, could be. Perhaps he genuinely meant it as a favour when he said he would keep Rhoda's and your names a secret if this doctor started to cut up rough with his list.'

That was it, of course. The apple at the bottom of the pile which brought all the others tumbling down.

'Yes, but hang on, Freddie. The man Gaillet's been meeting, this doctor, he's not the one…you know…Rhoda's one.'

'That really threw Maurice, didn't it? Did you believe that codswallop about there being another doctor at the White City and he'd try and find out? And then after we'd dropped Rhoda off, suddenly he wants us to forget all about "the list" and start dangling this non-existent old master in front of Gaillet's nose to see if he can afford one. Buggered if I can make sense of it. Can you Florence Duck?'

I couldn't. I do know I just wanted the whole thing to go away, but I had no idea how to make that happen. After all, the whole tangled mess went back a good deal further than Freddie's involvement with Raoul Gaillet and my Uncle Maurice. It felt as if Josephine Lucie had somehow engineered the whole thing, even though she'd been dead for years. Being entrusted with her story meant that, like it or lump it, I had no option but to see it through. It was ridiculous, I know. But I couldn't get it out of my head that she'd known something like this would happen.

'We can't put the clock back, Freddie. What's happening is happening. Gaillet's going to make you an accomplice to whatever financial jiggery pokery he's up to. I'm really worried that if you don't appear to be going along with him something awful will happen.'

'I know, Florrie Dee. And that means we have to go along with your adorable uncle's plan, such as it is, and see what happens. There's no-one else. The way things are, there's no-one else. I couldn't go to anyone else at Carlton Gardens, could I? If Gaillet's telling the truth about the money, then they're all in it, including Seedy Gee, as far as I can see. And I can't see myself turning up at Finsbury Circus and telling the Major all about it. What would I say about Maurice, for goodness' sake? And then there's still the list and you and Rhoda to think about before we start casting around like that.'

It always came back to that damn list. We were going to have to find out the truth about it, one way or another. I was about to say to Freddie he should have it out with Gaillet and make him produce the doctor and the list, but he beat me to it.

'You know, Florence Duck. I think we need to know for certain that this Doctor Schiffman is nothing to do with any of it. After all, I'm the only one who's seen him. He could be Dr Crippen for all I know.'

'Because if he is nothing to do with it, and doesn't have a little list, then we'll know…'

'…that Gaillet's telling fibs and must have got to know about Rhoda and you from…'

'…my adorable Uncle Maurice.'

'*From Maurice*? Good grief! I never thought of that. Why on earth would he do a thing like that, for heaven's sake?'

I couldn't begin to answer that. All I could think about was that Gaillet had told Maurice about the picture being a Rubens, when Maurice right from the very start had said that Gaillet had played down its value. So perhaps they were both in cahoots about the list as well.

So, instead, I asked Freddie how he proposed to get this Doctor Schiffman to agree to an identity parade for me to eliminate him from our enquiries, or not, as the case might be.

'Easy, Florrie Dee. I shall invite him out to dinner.'

32

'So, *ma chère*, I was invited to dinner on the *Nénuphar*. I went back to the *chaland*, when in my heart I wanted to find my Augustin. I even remember, you know, what we had to eat. Of all the things to remember at such a time.'

'Was it something nice, then?'

'The captain's wife was happy beyond anything to see him. She made something she called *zewelewaï*.'

'Doesn't sound very French.'

'She was from Alsace.'

'And Lorraine? That's what the war was about. Leonard told me.'

'Yes, sometimes French and sometimes German. Leonard would have great difficulty eating *zewelewaï*, *n'est-ce pas*?'

'Yes, he would, wouldn't he? Only I wouldn't tell him until afterwards. Like the beetroot.'

'What beetroot, *chérie*?'

'Well, it was the tongue really. But the beetroot was the crowning glory.'

'I don't understand you, Florence, sometimes. I think I shall not try. But perhaps we should give Leonard a piece of Alsace to digest. He is, as you say, interested in history. Perhaps we should go to the kitchen, however. We have to make pastry. Oh, and I have just thought. We need some cream. There will be none in the larder. Your father does not consider cream to be important. In fact, Florence, we shall buy everything, including the eggs.'

I was enormously relieved to hear that Josephine Lucie was going to buy her own eggs. Although my poor mother no longer needed to have first call on them, eggs had become no more plentiful in the house since her death. I was less pleased about the prospect of her preparing one of her story delicacies in the kitchen. It would mean me running up and downstairs trying not to bump into the others.

In the beginning when Mother was still alive, everyone tended to assume, if they thought about it at all, that these culinary treats were intended for her. Some of them would indeed find their way up to Mother's sickbed, alongside the meal Grandmother prepared separately for her.

I would carry this up to the bedroom on a plate under an oval warmer of silver plate, which Grandmother referred to as her *couvercle*. Discovering this to be a holy relic from César Machin's kitchen, perhaps even a survivor of the wrath of the Paris mob who had set his restaurant ablaze in 1847, always gave me a feeling of solemn mystery when I lifted it for Mother to reveal whatever secret lay beneath. On the way up to her I would stop off at the middle room and ceremonially place beside it, as my own offering, the sacred remains of what we may have made that day. Mother had been rather fond of my Noah's Ark biscuits, but less overwhelmed by the éclairs with the imaginary fillings.

Since her death, and, I suppose, as I rapidly entered that time of my life when I became more awkward and ready to imagine myself being silently mocked, I was less and less inclined to run between the kitchen and the middle room on food errands. Each one meant switching in my head between Grandmother and Josephine Lucie, a split I found to be more and more irksome as I increasingly identified with the latter and recognising the role of the former much less.

Nevertheless my heart leapt at the prospect of my accompanying her in her grandmother role on an expedition to the Broadway. Usually I would go alone to fetch her bits and pieces and then have to put up with her tut-tutting at the poor quality purchases on my return.

Though her own visits to the shops were infrequent, they were always memorable. She turned heads with her Parisian-style hats from an earlier time. I always thought they gave an air of superior gentility which would rub off on me and the rest of the family and in a small way made up for the social burden of Mother's TB. It was a brave acquaintance who attempted to pass the time of day with Grandmother. If I was with her they would generally catch my eye first with a 'good morning, Florence' and then wait to be acknowledged in turn, by her. Often she would greet them simply with a slight inclination of her head and a *'bonjour Madame'* and that would be that.

If she did choose to prolong the conversation, it would probably be to invite a neighbour to agree with her about the lack of *choses de qualité* on offer, in front of whichever unfortunate shopkeeper was within earshot. The greengrocer had long since ceased remonstrating with her for squeezing the fruit and Mr Stringer did not try a second time to palm her off with mince from the tray. If she asked for mince he would, without a word, take up one of his choicest cuts of beef, trim it of all fat before even weighing it, and put it through the mincer specially. Grandmother would be charged the price for mince from the tray and be asked if she would 'like the suet packaged separately?'

This particular day's excursion passed relatively easily for the local tradesmen, although I did think the young assistant in Williams Brothers was about to give some backchat to Grandmother when she pointed out in no uncertain terms that the cream in the churn on display was 'tired' and was beginning to form a skin. However, in the nick of time, Mr Williams senior called sharply from the far end, by the bacon, that the lad should 'fetch Mrs Burnell some cream from the cold press and look sharp about it.'

Two women, further down the queue, whom I knew by sight, raised their eyebrows questioningly at one another and one mouthed silently, 'Mrs Burnell?"

On the way out I heard one say, 'Not French, then?' to the other. Grandmother affected not to hear. But it was as much as I could do not to turn round and retort proudly, 'Yes, she is, and what's more her grandfather fought at Waterloo. And she came here in a balloon.' Well almost.

Then joy of joys! There was a French onion Johnny standing with his bicycle hung with strings of red gold by the new war memorial. I bet Grandmother knew somehow he was going to be there. I'd seen him before at this time of the year. He'd started calling at the house when he realised that French was spoken there, although if Pa answered he got short shrift. That's why she decided to go shopping herself instead of sending me. It's probably what had brought the memory of the *zewelewaï* to the front of her mind in the first place, too. She bore down on him, addressing him in her nineteen-to-the-dozen *Lilleoise*, mostly unintelligible to my schoolgirl ears, while she felt every onion on every string before settling on one. And even then she made him divide it, not wanting to keep them '*pour l'hiver.*'

There was no sign of the others when we returned. Pa's hat and coat were missing from the hall stand, so I supposed he had gone out for one of the long, solitary walks he had taken up doing since

Mother's death. Leonard, too, had probably been and gone without any breakfast. Off with his chums on their bicycles to one village or another in rural Middlesex. Far enough away to smoke in comfort, drink half pints of mild and eat a pork pie outside a pub where no-one knew their fathers.

It was a good guess Rhoda was still in bed. The pile of dirty breakfast things we had left had not been added to.

Grandmother took possession of the kitchen with an air of satisfaction. She set about laying things out for the preparation of the *zewelewaï*. I found myself in a state of anxiety at the thought of the entire operation being conducted downstairs and not in the middle room. Would she continue her history while we cooked here? She had been about to embark on the next bit, hadn't she, and then we'd gone down to the Broadway. Would she be Grandmother, Josephine Lucie, or both? What would we say or do if anyone came in? Pa and Leonard were probably safe for a couple of hours at least, but what about Rhoda? I comforted myself with the thought that even if she was awake, she would have her nose deep in a book, soaking up the silence of the house on Saturday. I made sure the kitchen door was firmly closed before we began.

Grandmother must have sensed my nervousness. Without looking up from her preparation, she said, 'We will make this now and then we can talk upstairs afterwards while we eat it. We can take our dinner in my middle room. Now first you must peel the onions and slice them very, very thin. With the big knife. As I have shown you.'

'What? All of them?' We must have bought three or four pounds, even though the onion seller had split them.

'No, perhaps not all. But a good *livre* nevertheless. They become less when they are cooked like this.'

While I sniffed wetly over the onions, Grandmother took down a heavy copper frying pan from the pans above the range, which she now regarded as her own set, and removed it to the scullery to wash. Returning, she melted a very large spoonful of butter in it. Although she had purchased it herself at Williams Brothers, I still felt a stab of guilt at the size of it and prayed silently that Pa would not walk in on us at that very moment.

'Now, *chérie*, cut some greasy paper to cover over this *poêle*. Only inside it.'

I rummaged in the kitchen drawer for the packet of greaseproof paper, which I knew had been there since I was only a little girl. It mostly got used for tracing paper by Leonard, if his homework said 'first draw a map of India'. I cut a piece out round one of our large dinner plates and then buttered it, as I was bid, making sure enough of the butter went on fingers to need a good licking.

In the frying pan the melted butter was just beginning to turn brown. I added the onions.

'We should have a bay leaf. Do we have a bay leaf, Florence? Quick, have a look.'

At the back of the larder I found the battered and slightly rusting tin box which had once contained Jacobs Cream Crackers and then been pressed into service for little-used herbs and spices, gravy browning and the mysterious arrowroot.

'These?'

'Yes. But they are so old. Put in two. And salt and pepper…so.'

I laid the buttered greaseproof paper over the onions and then the plate I had cut round, for a lid. Grandmother moved the pan off the centre of the hotplate on the range so that it would cook nice and slowly. She put more coke on the range fire.

'Now, Florence. Do you remember your pastry?'

'Short crust or flaky?'

'But certainly, *brisée*…short. It is flan not pie.'

'I wasn't sure. You didn't say what it was going to be. How much should I do?'

'Enough, I imagine.'

This wasn't at all helpful. But I spooned away with the flour into the pastry bowl, until I saw Grandmother purse her lips slightly and knew that was enough. I mixed in enough butter, chopping it with a knife, and adding a little water to make the dough 'not too dry and not too wet' as she had shown me many times before. And I ran my hands under the cold tap until they were in danger of going blue before putting them in the bowl, not needing to be told for the umpteenth time how the great César Machin had always insisted on 'very cold hands for very good pastry.'

When the pastry had been rolled, I lined a flan case with it. The large one with the crinkly edge. I didn't recall that coming out since Mother used occasionally to make a treacle tart for us, when she was still able. That was a long time ago. Treacle tart with porridge oats was a favourite of Pa's, I seemed to remember. Perhaps after this, I should have a go at one for him.

'In a *rêverie*, Florence? What are you thinking? Come now, beat the eggs. Two…so. And the cream and a little milk because the cream is so thick otherwise. And now, Florence, look in Jacobs Crackers again and see...do we have a *muscade*?'

'I don't know. What is it?'

'It is a nut. Very hard. You have to rub it on this...'

'The cheese grater?'

'Yes. Just to make a few crumbs. But very scented.'

Grandmother rummaged in the tin herself.

'*Voilà.*'

She held up a small pot whose label said 'nutmegs' but when opened proved to contain only half a one, deeply grooved with previous grating. Grandmother tutted, first over its size and staleness and then again when she rubbed it on the grater and managed to scrape her knuckle as well. She dipped the smarting finger in the liquid mixture and tasted it.

'A little salt and some pepper...Now, Florence, how are the onions?'

Under the greaseproof the onions were beautifully soft and golden, having absorbed all the butter they had been cooked in. I took out the bay leaves and eased the onions into the pastry case, spreading them out evenly with a spoon. I went to pour in the beaten eggs and cream from the bowl, but Grandmother stayed my hand. She handed me the sieve.

'If you do it through this it will spread all over and you won't have to disturb the onions again. Now...is the oven hot enough? It should be very hot to cook the pastry and the eggs.'

Grandmother said the *zewelewaï* would take about forty minutes to bake, but I should look at it after about half an hour, because you couldn't be certain of the range oven. She said she would go back upstairs to make her bed. I was left with the washing up, the breakfast things as well as the cooking things.

I kept an anxious eye on the clock, not wanting the flan to spoil and equally not wanting Rhoda or Pa or Leonard to appear while it was still doing. It was my *zewelewaï*. I wanted it to be perfectly cooked and up in the middle room before anyone else could start putting their oar in.

After twenty-five minutes its delicious baking smell was beginning to fill the kitchen, resurrecting and rejuvenating the smell of the onions from earlier and adding a richness to it from the setting cream and eggs. I couldn't bear it. I opened the oven door a crack and peeped in. It looked done to me. The top was beginning to form a darkening skin, like a rice pudding does. I reached for the oven cloth, took a deep breath and drew the *zewelewaï* out of the oven. *My zewelewaï*. It only remained for me to get it up the stairs to the middle room without interruption and the chain would be unbroken. The chain that stretched back to a barge on a canal in France nearly sixty years ago.

'Isn't it wonderful? Look at it! Smell the onions! And the cream! All that cream.'

Josephine Lucie smiled at my bubbling enthusiasm. 'But of course, *chérie*. You have done very well. Shall we taste it hot? Or shall we wait until it has become just warm? The onions will be sweeter if it is not too hot. Put it by the window to cool a little.'

I could hardly contain myself, but I knew better than to rush a dish Josephine Lucie said would be better for the waiting. So we waited. Then, at a nod from her, I proudly cut the first slice and handed it to her on one of her own Dèvres plates she had fetched out from the back of the chiffonier. One of them even had a canal scene on it, with a barge being drawn by a comic-looking horse and a man with fat legs in knee breeches waving a switch over it.

Then I saw the tears trickling down her cheeks. It was a trick of the light, but the lines on her old lady's face seemed to have melted away and I caught my breath as I saw a girl, as if sideways in a mirror – myself in a very short while.

'What is it?'

'I haven't tasted this since that evening on the *chaland*.'

'But surely...you told me how to make it and everything.'

'I watched the captain's wife make it. But I have never made it. It is not difficult to imagine the recipe...I thought perhaps if you made it for me, *ma chère*, it would make it better, what happened.' And she began to sob quietly.

'Now that I taste it again for the first time, I remember it is the first thing I had to eat after I abandoned Augustin.'

'Abandoned? So you didn't find him, then? Did you go back to the town in the morning and wasn't he there?'

'I asked for him, of course, in the morning. But no-one knew where he was, or if he was alive or dead. He had just disappeared. It was as if Augustin had never existed, you know.'

The barge captain waited while Josephine Lucie asked in vain for Augustin in Landrecies, and offered to take her on to St Quentin which was journey's end for the *Nénuphar*. But on an impulse she decided to leave the barge when it eventually came within sight of her old home town of Orgelets.

She and Augustin had talked about Orgelets. Someone, she began to persuade herself, might be hiding him, nursing him back to health somewhere in the neighbourhood of Landrecies, frightened in case the Prussians came back looking for him. She convinced herself that would explain why she, a stranger who had been spat on for talking to the Prussian officer, had been unable to come by any word of him. If she waited for him in Orgelets, he would eventually find her.

'It was a hopeless idea, Florence. But I had to do something to make up for losing him. All I could think was I should have gone back to Landrecies on the first night, instead of eating this *zewelewaï* and I would have found him. I felt so guilty then and I remember the feeling now.'

'So did you go back to your family, then? To your father?'

'At first I imagined I would be obliged to. But then I thought, nobody recognises me. Perhaps I will just find a room and stay in the village. I still had Monsieur Adolphe's money.'

'The Prussians hadn't taken it?'

'No, it was sewn into a bag to go under my clothes, the things I had worn in the *montgolfière*. The captain's wife had given me some of her clothes to wear, of course, but I had kept the bag safe.'

There was a café in the village. Josephine Lucie decided that would be the most likely place to find a room to stay, or to inquire for one in the neighbourhood, if they didn't have one. She recognised the owner vaguely, but to her relief he showed no sign of knowing her.

'I have a room, Mademoiselle, but I have to tell you that I have lost my wife and I have no cook. All I can offer you, or come to that any of my customers, to eat is what the baker can provide. I would not give anyone what I manage to prepare for myself.' He laughed.

Josephine Lucie felt her heart lift for the first time since the balloon had fallen out of the sky.

'Monsieur, I am a cook. Perhaps we could come to an arrangement about the room in return for you giving me a job.'

'A cook? Truly, Ma'mselle?'

'But of course. I have studied under the great César Machin.

In Paris.'

'The name means nothing, Ma'mselle. But a cook from Paris. You might have been sent from heaven. Why would you want to stay here, in this out of the way place?'

Why indeed? Josephine Lucie thought fast. She needed a plausible story to preserve her anonymity.

'I have escaped from Paris, Monsieur. I was among the last civilians to be allowed to leave before the Prussians closed the city entirely. It was because I was cook for an English family and we all left. Now the Prussians do not even let the foreigners leave.'

'And have the English left you behind? Typical.'

'I didn't want to return to England with them. So I went to find my only relative, an elderly aunt, in…' Josephine Lucie struggled to think of somewhere near enough to explain her presence in Orgelets and still far enough away for her story be unverifiable. Where had the *Nénuphar* come from?

'…in Mauberge, Monsieur. Do you know it?'

He had heard of it, of course, but he had never been there.

'So how did you fetch up in Orgelets, ma'mselle?'

'My aunt had died, Monsieur. There was nothing for me in Mauberge. So I reasoned the war cannot last forever. One way or another Paris will be open again. I am making my way slowly back there to wait. I came on the canal.' She wondered if she should have put that bit in. 'But, not to put too fine a point on it, Monsieur, the bargee was becoming over familiar. So I got off here.'

'Over familiar, Ma'mselle? Those canal folk are no better than they ought to be. They gave you rat to eat and pretended it was beef, I wouldn't be surprised. You need have no such fears here, Ma'mselle, I can assure you, you will be quite safe.'

'So, Florence, I became the cook at the Café de la Mairie and had a little room in the attic and my food for my wages. And my story went round the village and everyone came to look at me when I was behind the bar or serving the tables. Even my father. Imagine, Florence, even my father, the mayor. And he did not know me. So then I did not care. I just called him *"M'sieur le maire"*, if I had to speak to him, which was not often, I can assure you.'

'So did no-one suspect?'

'Not one person thought I was anything but a *Parisienne* through and through. I spoke like a *Parisienne* and I cooked like a *Parisienne*. Who would suggest I might be little Josephine Lucie from

Orgelets, the daughter of the mayor who did not know me himself?'

'So what did you call yourself?'

'Lucie Marquise, of course. I left the "*de*" out. Too *comme il faut* for Orgelets.'

'And the paintings? What happened to them? Tell me about the paintings.'

33

'Do you suppose this painting still exists, Florrie Dee? I mean, do you think it ever existed? You've never really said, have you? All you've ever said is that your grandmother said it might have been a forgery. So did she ever actually have it in her possession, I wonder? Or was it just some family tale, one of those stories that tends to get rather lost in translation? I mean, if we're actually going to stick our necks out with Gaillet over it, I would at least like to know it existed, even if it was a forgery.'

'Paintings, Freddie. Paintings plural. There were two of them.'

I'd waited for Freddie at the foot of the steps to the Mall below Carlton Gardens, still feeling extremely ashamed of having pleaded the curse to Mr Webber and sending him into a state of red-faced confusion. I felt bad. There was a war on. Menstruation was meant to be part of the effort.

Freddie'd wanted to meet me outside Leicester Square tube station but I was curious to see where he worked. Needless to say, he didn't want me to wait outside. He'd had to make up some yarn about needing to report over to Finsbury Circus in his dinner break, to explain why he might be absent for a bit longer than the usual half hour.

'There's a grain of truth in that if they check,' Freddie had said, 'They've been nagging at me about missing the hand grenade training. It's all very well being on loan to the French, but they still want me to be a British soldier, too. Ridiculous. Most of us are only in the Pay Corps because we're short sighted. I 'spect I can throw a grenade. The question would be what at?'

One way or another, his unit at Finsbury Circus was beginning to miss him. Perhaps his secondment was going on longer than anticipated. 'And I know the sergeant-major just thinks I'm on a skive,' said Freddie. 'He's got it in for me because the officer won't tell him why I'm to be left alone. Keeps checking up on me.'

I said, 'You'd better report him to Maurice then. He seems to have sorted out your officer. A sergeant major shouldn't give him too much trouble.'

But Freddie just said, 'Don't you believe it, old girl.'

I'd been waiting at the steps for about five minutes, when he appeared at the top with two girls in Free French uniforms. He shook his head briefly, when he saw me, and I realised he didn't want me to speak to him. He walked on past with the girls, who were extremely pretty *and* wearing decent stockings. They went to cross into the park and he went as if to turn down the Mall towards Trafalgar Square. There was some laughter as they parted and I heard Freddie say something to them in French. When the girls were safely over the road and into the park, Freddie doubled back to me.

'Sorry, Florrie Dee. They caught me up as I was leaving the building. I had to tell them I was on my way to Finsbury Circus or they'd have asked me to share their sandwiches in the park. If they'd cottoned on I was meeting a girl, even if she is my wife, it would have been all over the typing pool in an hour.'

'You didn't tell me your French was *that* good.'

'What French?'

'That French you were making up to those girls in, just then.'

'Oh come on, Florence! Hardly making up to them. Still it's come on a treat, hasn't it, the French?' '

'So this is the famous *Corps Féminin*.'

'*Les Françaises libres*, they are now. Because of the jokes.'

'A sight too *libres*, if you ask me. Did you see their stockings? They weren't ATS issue. They looked like those nylons to me.'

'You needn't worry about those two.'

'Who said anything about worried?'

'They're not interested in chaps. There's a lot like that over at the *caserne*.'

'What?'

'You know, Florence Dee. Ladies from Lesbos. Followers of Sappho. *Well of Loneliness*. You know…'

'No Freddie. I meant what's the *caserne*?'

'Oh I see. That's the French for the barracks. They're over at Ennismore Gardens since they were bombed out of Hill Street.'

'Sounds rather posh for a barracks. Anyway, are you sure?'

'Sure about Ennismore Gardens? 'Course I'm sure.'

'No, you chump. Sure about them being lesbians. What about

the nylons?'

'I expect they like nylons just as much as you do. More, I shouldn't wonder.'

We bickered on at one another as we walked across Trafalgar Square where the fountains were all boxed up, as if they were expecting the removal men to arrive.

I wondered why they hadn't put something round the lions, as well.

Freddie said they were 'waiting to go out to Whipsnade with the real ones.'

We crunched over the previous night's broken glass towards Charing Cross Road. People were crowding into the National Gallery for the lunchtime recital. More were already queuing down into Leicester Square tube station, laden with bedding and blankets to secure a good place.

'There's kids down there all day, by the look of it,' I told Freddie, 'keeping their places warm 'til mum and Grandma arrive for the night. And when I was coming up the escalator this morning, some youngster asked me if I wanted a place kept for half a crown. East Enders. They think Hitler won't drop so many bombs on the West End, I suppose.'

We had to negotiate the temporary bailey bridge that had been put across an enormous crater just before Cambridge Circus, where we turned off to Dean Street. That was when he'd asked me about the painting again and I'd finally decided I could no longer keep Adolphe de Marquise's dilemma locked away inside myself.

'Two paintings? What do you mean, *two paintings*? Freddie tugged my sleeve, almost bringing me to a halt in the middle of Old Compton Street as we were crossing over. A taxi had to slow down for us and hooted impatiently. I skipped to the other side and by then we were almost outside the French House.

'Later,' I said. 'Later. Let's concentrate on getting through the next hour.'

When we reached the top of the stairs to the pub's dining room, the nervousness we'd obviously both been suppressing ever since we'd met came to the fore with a rush of butterflies. Freddie gripped my hand. His was clammy.

'Do you have a reservation?' The woman with the open book was slightly taken aback at his corporal's stripes. Not only was Freddie's the only non-commission there, most of the other diners were Free French, with a sprinkling of Polish airmen.

'It's Captain Gaillet's table,' Freddie said. 'But he can't make it, unfortunately. We're his guests and he was expecting another...Captain Guttman. Has he arrived yet?'

The *maîtresse de* looked even more perplexed at this.

'Yes, Captain Guttman is already here...but...'

I sensed she was going to make some allusion to Freddie's rank. I had no idea what subterfuges he'd gone to, but we were beginning to attract a small amount of attention.

'It's all right,' I blurted out. 'They were all railway enthusiasts before the war. It takes all sorts, doesn't it? Funny how the war throws the most unlikely people together in uniform.'

'Railway enthusiasts?' Unfortunately I appeared to have kindled a spark of interest in her. Her father was about to turn out to be an engine driver.

'Yes, that's right,' said Freddie. 'In the alps. Funicular funiculi. Which table is it?'

She pointed to one further along the back beside the dumb waiter. It was set for four and a Free French officer was sitting in one of the places. He had not noticed us arriving, seeming partly distracted by the label on the half bottle of wine in front of him and half-heartedly chewing one of his thumb nails.

'Well?' Freddie hissed. 'D'you recognise him, or not?'

'Give us a chance, Freddie. I can't possibly be sure. I only saw them for a few minutes. I wasn't exactly concentrating on committing their faces to memory. But I think it could be. Yes.'

'Them? All of a sudden there's more than one of everything.'

'You're forgetting the one in Basle...'

We arrived at the table. Its occupant looked up, uncertainly.

'Do I have the wrong table, perhaps? This is for four...'

'Captain Guttmann?' Freddie asked.

'Yes. But...Excuse me, Madame.' the captain half rose awkwardly, scraping his chair in the slightly confined space. 'I am only two, I think. They have given me the wrong table.'

'I'm sorry, Sir,' said Freddie. 'Captain Gaillet won't be able to make it today, after all. He's sent us to hold the fort...'

'Hold the fort? What fort?'

'It's a bit of a long story,' said Freddie. 'May we join you?'

If I was feeling nervous, it was nothing to the anxiety clearly being felt by Captain Guttman. He was positively quaking. Freddie, however, began to relax, which was more than I could say for myself.

Not only had he got this man here under false pretences, I'd been so preoccupied with scoring points over the Free French floozies from the typing pool, I had no idea what part I was supposed to be playing in it all.

Freddie said later that up to that moment he hadn't the faintest notion how we were going to handle the situation. He'd simply waited until Gaillet was out of the office for some time and told the *Corps Féminin* girl, who acted as a collective secretary, that Gaillet had forgotten to ask her to book lunch with Guttman at the usual place. When she'd done that, Freddie waited until she'd gone to powder her nose and on her return said Guttman had phoned to cry off and that he'd said he would phone again with a new date.

'So as she'd only pencilled it in, it got rubbed out again and no-one the wiser. Clever, eh?'

I wondered what would have happened if Guttman had phoned Gaillet back later, anyway. But Freddie had been so pleased with his stratagem, I didn't like to spoil his ship for a ha'porth of tar, as Pa would have said. Anyhow, Guttman didn't phone back, so that was that. In any case, Freddie'd said that as soon as we'd sat down with Guttman and he'd seen the state he was in, he realised the best thing to do was get straight to the point.

'Poor chap was terrified of something or someone. My money was on the someone being Captain Gaillet.'

In fact I did wonder about the 'poor chap' bit. As far as I was concerned, he was a blackmailing abortionist.

So to my horror, Freddie had let him have it, right on the chin, so to speak.

'Actually, it's not Guttman, is it? It's Schiffman. Dr Schiffman of Luxeuil les Bains. I assume you're not the doctor from Basle. You'd hardly have left Switzerland to join the Free French, would you?'

The captain looked ashen. He relapsed into French, which was all right by Freddie, who did the same. I managed to keep up, just. He didn't reply to Freddie's questions. Instead he wanted to know if Freddie had been 'sent' by Gaillet. Freddie asked him if that was important.

'Yes of course it is important. How do I know I can trust you? Why is an English soldier…a corporal… interesting himself in my affairs?'

'I work for Captain Gaillet. At Carlton Gardens.'

'And who is this lady?'

'She's my...she's Rhoda Denning's sister.

'Rhoda Denning? The actress?'

'Yes. Rhoda Denning, the actress. She's on your little list, I believe.'

My heart stopped. Talk about all your eggs in one basket, Freddie.

But the captain looked genuinely confused. 'What list?'

I could see in his face he had no idea what Freddie was talking about. I took a deep breath and stepped in. In English.

'Dr Schiffman... you performed a service for my sister a few years ago...'

'Don't call me that. I am Guttman here.' He whispered, glancing round at the other tables. But no-one seemed any longer interested in us.

The waitress came to take our order. I asked what the soup was and was told it was *potage bonne femme*. I said I'd have it and the dish of the day. Freddie and Guttman, or whoever he was now, had the same. I don't think any of us was really interested in the food at that stage. The soup appeared almost at once. Of course, it didn't have any egg yolks in it, or cream, come to that, so it wasn't so much *bonne femme* as a thin vegetable *old maid*. I hadn't really expected it to be anything else.

'You were saying, Madame? Something about a service. I understand you perfectly. It will be difficult here, but not impossible. I would have to come to your home, perhaps.'

I was speechless. Freddie had twigged too.

'Steady on. This is my wife you're talking to.'

'Then, I don't understand. Is it perhaps someone else's?'

'Look. Get it into your head, she's not expecting.'

I laughed – well, sort of snorted into the *bonne femme*.

'You don't remember me, do you? I came to Luxeuil with my sister in 1936. You're supposed to have a list of them and her name's on it. Only there isn't one, is there, Captain? Your business with Captain Gaillet doesn't have anything to do with a list, does it?'

The waitress came and cleared the soup dishes. 'You're all having the *blanquette*?'

'And a bottle of the *cuvée maison*,' said Guttman. He'd finished the half bottle he'd ordered first. Clearly in need of a stiffener, I thought.

'A list of my patients? Is that what you are saying? No, that is in Luxeuil, I imagine. It has nothing to do with Captain Gaillet.'

Freddie and I looked at one another in a 'plot thickens' kind of way.

Guttman was beginning to look nervous again.

'I thought you had news of my family, perhaps. From Captain Gaillet. And the money.'

A little light began to dawn on me. I could have been wrong of course. I played for time.

'I think I met your wife. In Luxeuil. She said something very kind to Rhoda, I remember. Rhoda was rather frightened, and we'd come a long way. In fact we went to Basle by mistake and had to get the train.'

'You know, Madame, I believe I remember you both. My partner telephoned ahead and told me what had happened. It was unusual.'

'Three *blanquettes de veau*?'

It was too. Real veal. Not half bad. I could see why the French liked the place if they could lay stuff on like this, with a war on.

'Hang on a minute,' said Freddie, with his mouth full, it has to be said. 'Let me get this straight. So you aren't using your list of illustrious establishment clients as your ticket back to France.'

'No, certainly not. I told you, it is in Luxeuil. And why would I want to go back to occupied France? I'm a Jew.'

'What are you doing with Captain Gaillet, then?' I said.

'I think I have said enough. If he has not sent you, then I don't know why you are here asking me all these questions. You cannot touch me about my practice in Luxeuil. I have done nothing wrong here. More probably you have, Madame.'

Freddie polished off the last of his veal. 'So what're you afraid of, old man? It must be something, else you wouldn't have changed your name. What's this message about money you thought I might have brought from Captain Gaillet?'

The light began to dawn on me

'You aren't trying to get yourself back, are you? You're trying to get your wife out of France to come here. That's it, isn't it?'

Guttmann's shoulders drooped miserably. I could see he was having an enormous struggle with himself. About us, presumably. He didn't know who we were or where we'd come from, but we knew all about him. For two pins, I think he would have stood up and run down the stairs, only Freddie's chair was in the way. He looked round.

The tables nearest to us were occupied by Poles. The nearest Free French were over by the taped up windows.

'*Pas ici.*' He relapsed back into French again. 'We must go somewhere less conspicuous. They know me here.'

He called the waitress over and, declining her offer of rice pudding to follow, asked for the bill, which was good of him, in the circumstances, especially as the veal wasn't on ration and must have cost the earth.

Freddie suggested we walk round to the church in Wardour Street and sit in the garden, but as it was coming on to rain and finding the door unlocked we went inside and took a pew. Perhaps it was the comfort and quiet of the surroundings that made up his mind, because Captain Guttman, despite his own faith, unburdened himself as if at confession.

Being in the reserves as a medical officer, he had reported for duty in late 1939. He had been involved in the French last stand on the Aisne before France fell. The prospect of ending up a prisoner of war as a Jew had not filled him with much enthusiasm. His position as a military doctor had given him access to dead men's papers. So when he came across one from Alsace, like him, and with a similar name to his own, Captain Schiffman quietly pocketed the late Captain Guttman's identity along with his Catholicism, as a precaution, in the likely event that he would fall into German hands, if he were not killed first.

However, he found himself in charge of a withdrawal of severely wounded, first to Amiens and then, as the German advance continued, to the Normandy coast near Dieppe, where remnants of the French army had linked up with the British last ditch attempt at a bridgehead.

This was all news to me, by the way, and, I think, to Freddie. As far as I was concerned, the last year had been all about Dunkirk. Apparently though, there had been an almighty cock-up in Normandy which ended in a second British evacuation, not to mention the surrender of the Highland Division. Some of the French who chose not to stay, managed to get themselves evacuated with us, including Captain Guttman, newly resurrected into the medical service and whose skills were, therefore, much in demand. Captain Schiffman had quietly been torn up and burnt some little while before when surrender to the Germans had once again seemed unavoidable.

'And your wife and children?' I said. 'You've had to leave

them, haven't you?'

'I told my wife before I left, that if the worst happened and the Boche came, they should go to my partner in Basle.'

'So they're safe then?'

Captain Guttman sank forward on the pew. I thought for one moment he was going to say a prayer.

'They were prevented from crossing into Switzerland by the Swiss border authorities and sent back.'

'Because they were French? Won't the Swiss let the French in, then?'

'No, not because they were French. Because they were Jews.'

Freddie sat up straight. 'Oh come on. Not the Swiss. They're neutral. Perhaps they just wouldn't be able to cope with the rush. That's more likely.'

'It's what Gaillet tells me. He says now they will have been forbidden to move from Luxueil under pain of arrest. He thinks arrest may be inevitable anyway. He has a way to get money to them. He says there is a network of imaginary people. He says it is a device to channel money from this country for the Free French war effort. The French banks are still operating outside France apparently. That's why I thought you had some news for me.'

34

'I have some news for you.'

We all looked up from the breakfast table.

'News? What news Pa?' said Rhoda.

'I'm going to take you all away in the school holidays. It's been long enough since your Mother…and I thought we would go to Seaview again.'

None of us said anything.

Pa looked irritated. 'Well?'

'I was hoping to go to St Mawes with the Taylors,' said Rhoda. 'They're renting a house. I meant to say. Oh don't look so disapproving, Pa! It's my last holiday before I go to RADA.'

Marion Taylor was one of Rhoda's posh friends from her posh school. The one Pa 'mightn't be able to afford' for me when the time came.

'I should have thought that was all the more reason.' Mention of RADA only made Pa grumpier. Rhoda's place there was very much over his dead body. But Mother had given it her approval at the sanatorium in front of him. And evidently there was a little bit of money from her music teachers' benevolent fund 'for artistic development'. So it was set in stone.

'I suppose I'll just have to settle for Leonard and Florence, then. I hope the Taylors are paying your fare, by the way.'

'They're taking their motor car.'

Pa ground his teeth visibly.

'Will I have to miss cadet camp, Pa?' Leonard had recently joined up with his chums. I think he thought the uniform went well with the Players Weights.

'I *don't* know. When is it?'

'August some time, I think, Pa.'

'Oh for pity's sake! What about you Florence? Have you got any plans I don't know about? Running away to sea?'

'Is Grandmother coming?' I said.

Everyone went quiet at that.

Eventually Pa cleared his throat. 'Your grandmother probably has other plans…'

Even Leonard couldn't let that go. 'Plans, Pa? Grandmother doesn't have plans. She just sits up in her room nattering to Florence.'

'Didn't she go somewhere with your Uncle Maurice Burnell? I distinctly remember…'

'That wasn't plans,' I said. 'He used to take her over to Billericay sometimes to see an old friend. But I think the friend died. Uncle Maurice hasn't been for ages. Not since Mother…'

'All right. All right. *All right*,' said Pa. 'I'll go to Seaview with just you and my mother-in-law.'

'What if she has plans, though?'

'You're not too big to go over my knee, Florence. Go and ask her now.'

I thought about saying the invitation would come better from him. But I knew it wouldn't. Grandmother would probably decline if Pa asked her. If I did, I might at least get to go to Seaview with Josephine Lucie and the middle room.

She pursed her lips at first, but when I made a point of telling her that neither Rhoda nor Leonard would be going she smiled and said, 'Perhaps we can persuade Charles to stay at home also and you and I can go alone.' Oh how I wished we had thought of that sooner. If only I had mentioned a holiday to her, I'm sure she would have taken the two of us somewhere. Pa wouldn't have wanted to go with her. He was only offering now because he had to in front of us all.

So in the end Rhoda went off to Cornwall with the Taylors, Leonard went to stay with one of his cadet friends before they both went off to smoking camp the following week, and Pa, Grandmother and I took the train and ferry to the Isle of Wight and *Ferndown*, a private hotel owned by 'Mrs Browne-with-an-ee', at Seaview.

Grandmother and I shared. I'm not sure whether this was because Pa was paying or not. Nothing was said by either of them in front of me. But when we arrived at *Ferndown* and were shown to our rooms, Grandmother had a bedroom with its own sitting room with a put-you-up for me. Pa made no show of surprise at this, so perhaps he can't have been paying. I was delighted. It was indeed as if the middle room had come on holiday with us.

There was a brief show of holiday togetherness at breakfast

time on the second day. Pa asked what we were all going to do, in the kind of way that implied we might even do whatever it was as a group. It was plain none of us wanted that.

'I was going to propose we might all go to Carisbrook on the bus,' said Pa. 'The weather doesn't look very settled, does it? The bus might be a good idea if it comes on to rain…'

'I do not want the bus, Charles. I find them too smoky, you know. You go. Florence and I will take a promenade with our parasols, which can be our umbrellas if it rains.'

So Pa stumped off to the bus stop, trying not to look too relieved and Grandmother and I walked along the shore path towards Ryde, she having agreed both parties meet up over high tea, 'whatever that can be'. The sun did shine on us for a while and I wondered whether the middle room was allowed out with us too. I decided to try anyway. I put my middle room voice on and addressed Josephine Lucie in the open air.

'Did you ever go to the seaside in France? Is there seaside in France or is it just Paris people go to?'

'You know *ma chère*, I was just thinking as we promenade, this is the first time I have been to the seaside since I came to England. Because, you know, after I left Orgelets I lived for a while at the seaside.'

'In France?'

'Yes. In France, near Boulogne.'

'But I thought after Orgelets you went back to Paris.'

'Yes, I did go back to Paris. Did I say that before?'

Josephine Lucie had remained for nearly a year in Orgelets, cooking and serving at the Café de la Mairie. At first she lived in hope that Augustin would appear. When he did not, her dread began to be that she would hear somehow that he had perished by firing squad or under the knife of some Prussian surgeon, though how such news might be brought to her was another mystery to which she could find no answer. So as the time passed and one or two of the farmers in the vicinity began to cast their eyes in her direction, to say nothing of the proprietor of the café, who thought he might as well try and save himself the money side of her upkeep, paltry though it was, Josephine Lucie found the time had come to move on. In Paris, she reasoned, Papa Montel might at least have had some word of the fate of his son.

I still wanted to know, of course, what she had done with the paintings. Josephine Lucie was rather cagey, I thought, about them.

And not for the first time, I found myself wondering how much of her story might be fantasy, or imperfect memories cobbled together with fantasy. As we strolled along the path towards Ryde, with the wide blue sky reflecting in the Solent beside us and the sun shining brightly on Southsea on the far side, the holy confines of the middle room were loosened and the truths it usually managed to contain, freer to be questioned.

'So did you take the paintings back to Paris? After all that hardship and sadness, surely you didn't just take them back?'

'I hid one in Orgelets. I thought it would be better to separate them. Together, they had always been bad luck. I thought perhaps I could make some of the bad luck go away and that Monsieur Adolphe could still sell the other one. The news from Paris was not good. I wrote a letter to Monsieur, but there came no reply. I did not know what state the *Hôtel* would be in. People said there had been fighting in the streets. After the Prussians had gone home. That it was another revolution. I remembered what had happened to César Machin's restaurant when this had happened before in Paris.'

'Which one did you hide? The real one or the fake?'

'Do you think it will rain, *chérie*? I think perhaps we will need to take the bus back to Seaview after all. I hope it is not the one with your father on it. That would be a pity...'

I certainly wasn't standing for this. 'Real one or fake one?'

Josephine Lucie came to an abrupt halt. She stared across at Southsea and muttered something I didn't catch.

'Pardon?'

'Oh you heard me, Florence!'

'No I didn't.'

'I said, I don't know.'

'You *don't know*? But you said you couldn't get them muddled up. There was a different poem on each one, or something like that, you said.'

'*Alors, j'ai oublié, quand même...*'

'I can't believe it...after all this...you forgot.'

I was incensed. I wanted to give her a good shake. This is what came of trying to bring the middle room out into the open air. I thought that things from the past were somehow going wrong now, in the present. Things that hadn't gone wrong at the time. And I realised I had fallen into a trap of my own making. Because half the time, deep down, I'd always thought Josephine Lucie might be making it all up, I was actually getting angry with her when the story didn't go the way I wanted it to go. Because of what she'd just told me, I'd caught myself out, not knowing whether I wanted it to be real or not. I wanted a Carnegie library ending, and now, perhaps, that was not to be.

To be fair, though, Josephine Lucie said she hadn't worried too much about which painting was which. She knew they were each worth a great deal of money separately, but not together. If she took one back to Paris and hid the other one, that might be for the best. She had long since put the mine owner from Béthune out of her mind. Too much had happened to her to worry about him now.

Very occasionally she helped out with the cleaning in the church, on the opposite side of the square to the café and the mairie. It was not particularly a labour of love. Josephine Lucie was not a regular church-goer. After she had been in Orgelets for a few months, the priest began to drop hints that she would be welcome to attend and reminding her of the hours of confession. Josephine Lucie had not been to confession since she had last lived in Orgelets and was not about to resume going now, taking the view that she could hardly not mention her deception as to her true identity if she did. As far as she was concerned, the Almighty already knew who she was and needed no intervention by a priest who drank regularly in the Café de la Mairie. The cleaning, therefore, was a self-imposed penance.

It was in the course of this that she came across a deep cupboard behind the paneling in the sacristy. It wasn't a secret place or anything like. It contained bits of forgotten church lumber and a great deal of dust and cobwebs, indicating to Josephine Lucie that noone had cleared it out for a very long time. Nor by the look would they be likely to in the future. When the time came for her to leave Orgelets it seemed an ideal place to deposit one man in a lace collar, carefully wrapped in a piece of discarded oilcloth from the café and tied with string. The other one, similarly wrapped, went with her on the train from Orgelets to St Quentin and thence to the Gare du Nord for the second time in her life.

The Paris to which Josephine Lucie returned was almost unrecognizable as the city she had left barely a year earlier. At first she supposed the burnt out ruins of many buildings and streets were the result of the Prussian bombardment. It had been gathering strength in the weeks before her departure. But more of the destruction, she came to learn, happened during the bitter street fighting, Frenchman against Frenchman, in the days of the Commune which followed the withdrawal of the victorious Prussians.

Monsieur Adolphe's hôtel in the seventeenth was untouched, but strangely shuttered and dark. After strenuous ringing at the doors to the courtyard, the *guichet* in the left-hand one finally opened. There stood the great César Machin, a man who had never answered the door to anyone in his life. He was looking gaunt and thin.

Josephine Lucie was appalled. '*Chef*, what has happened? Why do you come to the gate yourself? Where is everyone?'

She stepped into the courtyard. César Machin kissed her gravely on both cheeks, seemingly unsurprised by her sudden appearance.

'Not dead then, Josephine Lucie?'

'No, not dead, *Chef*.'

He led the way across the courtyard and into the kitchen by the outside door.

'Coffee, *ma petite*?' His voice was weary and thin, just like his appearance.

'I'll make it, *Chef*. Are there croissants today?'

'Not today, nor any other day.'

'No croissants for the gentlemen?' But Josephine Lucie already knew there would be none. The kitchen was cold. Colder than it had ever been in the depth of the siege. Then it had still been a kitchen, exalted as a kitchen, in spite of everything. Now it had become a place that had once been a kitchen, and the great César Machin a man who had once been a chef.

'They do not come now, the gentlemen.'

His voice had that flatness that comes from tears that have dried inside, unshed. Josephine Lucie let him take his time. She could already feel the tears welling up inside her, too.

The green coffee beans were in the cupboard where they always lived. That was something they had never run out of in the weeks and months of the siege. César Machin bought large quantities of coffee beans at tasting sales. He had prided himself on his nose, despite the fact that the green beans were almost odourless. Nor did they go stale with keeping. In fact, he maintained they improved, and only when roasted and ground did they begin to deteriorate almost at once.

Josephine Lucie put a handful on to roast.

'Shall I filter it or use the Italian percolator, *Chef*?'

He waved his hand in a 'you decide' way. She opened the drawer where the muslin filters were kept, but there were none.

'They are not clean. Use the Italian.'

He watched Josephine Lucie grind the roasted beans and empty the ground coffee into the percolator.

'Monsieur Adolphe…?' But she already knew he would not be taking a cup.

She had known of the premonition Monsieur had had, seeing the old lady and her dog by the Luxembourg Gardens. He had been more shocked by seeing their random, individual deaths from a Prussian shell than at the mass slaughter he had heard of from the defeated soldiers fleeing back from the battlefields outside the city. Still ashen faced that evening, he had impressed on César Machin that his mother must not be allowed to see him, when he, too, was blown apart by a shell.

'Nor you, *ma petite*,' he had added to Josephine Lucie, who had come into the room at the tail end of their conversation. 'They were in pieces together, you know. Mixed up. The old lady and her dog.'

And back in the kitchen, César Machin had tried to make light of it to her, in case she had been upset.

'She should have eaten the dog weeks ago. What a waste!'

But there was no doubt he had been shocked to see the effect it had all had on Monsieur.

'And Madame…?' Josephine Lucie meant Monsieur's mother, the other old lady. The hidden chaperone upstairs who was rarely seen.

Monsieur Machin shrugged. 'Yes, Madame as well. She had a terrible toothache and he had pushed her in her wheel chair all the way to *les Invalides* to her dentist, because, of course, the horses were all eaten and the carriage was already firewood.'

The sun disappeared behind the thickening clouds, although it was still shining on Southsea across the water.

'It will rain. We shall have to take the bus.'

'Yes, but what happened? What did you and César Machin do? And the painting…you still had the painting.'

'The *hôtel* was left to us, you know. Everything. Because his mother was killed too, he had no other family. After her he had left it to us.'

'So you must have been rich. But you're not rich now.'

'No. There were just debts. It was all an illusion, after all. We sold what we could, but of course it was a very bad time. I have some of the furniture you know. It is at Pickfords. And some of the things from the kitchen I was fond of, you know. César found an Englishman, a dealer. He was looking for bargains in Paris. After the war. There are always people who come after wars to see what they can pick up. He was very nice. His name was Edward Burnell. He picked me up too.'

35

'I can pick you up from your work in half an hour. You'll have to square it somehow with that boss of yours. Do you want me to phone him? I could try the War Office routine again.'

'No Uncle Maurice! Don't you dare!'

'Well you'll have to plead your time of the month. That'll bring a blush to his post masterly cheek. It's important we get there before Rhoda blows the whole thing sky high. Anyway, I'm on my way.'

I told Mr Webber I would have to go home early. Something to do with the doctor, I said. He was very grumpy about it, of course, but I didn't lie to him and he drew his own conclusions. In a way it was about a doctor...the one we'd met at the French House. Things had come to a head very shortly after that. Freddie had been in a dither about how to use the information we'd gleaned, and I hadn't been much use.

But in the event it was Gaillet who started it.

'I want to thank you, by the way, Corporal Draper...Freddie. I know you are being discreet.'

'Discreet, Sir?'

'What we talked about...the bank accounts. France will not forget you.'

It was the *France will not forget you* claptrap that got up Freddie's nose. He just sounded off without thinking, as he can from time to time.

'We all have to hope that England will. Forget to ask me what I know about it all, *Sir*. It's not just Free France or the General who's found ways of getting money out in wartime. Not officially, at any rate. If you can call it that.'

Gaillet glanced at the door. It was shut. 'What are you talking about? Perhaps you have misunderstood something...'

Freddie began to cool down. But he realised the cat was a good halfway out of the bag. He decided to press on, but adopted what he hoped was a more disarming tone

'Look, Sir. I've seen more than just the monthly bank transfers you told me to forget about. A blind eye, you said. I've seen the stuff going backwards and forwards to the Treasury. About getting money out of the country to your chaps' wives in France and so on. And about the money going to your propaganda people in South America to help the war effort...'

'How can you have seen this? It is secret. Under lock and key. Or do you have the key? Are you here to spy on us, Draper?'

'I see it, Sir, when the *françaises* in the typing pool, to say nothing of some of the officers, ask me to help with the translations. Discreet? I should say I'm discreet. Place is like a sieve.'

'And so...?'

Freddie thought carefully, for a change. He took his time. According to the French doctor there was no patients' list. So Gaillet had no way of backing up his threat to reveal Rhoda's and Florence's dubious trip before the war. Freddie on the other hand was pretty sure he'd worked out what Gaillet was up to. It was Guttman who'd clinched it when he said Gaillet had ways of getting money to his family. Freddie saw the lists of those Free French who were managing to have money transferred regularly in francs to their families in unoccupied France and the French colonies. It was a risky business, in more ways than one. Getting money into occupied France was even riskier.

Freddie wasn't sure how the people at Carlton Gardens were operating the transfers. He'd seen a copy of a Treasury letter which talked about the Free French having 'devious' routes. One of the French officers had shown it to him and asked whether 'devious' was meant to be insulting. Freddie told him it meant *'malin'*, smart, although he knew that wasn't quite the same thing. From the tone of the letter we British clearly didn't want to know what the devious routes were and Freddie had never seen anything which revealed them to him.

What he did know was that the French francs came, in part, from a huge stock held at the Bank of England. He'd been part of the Pay Corps detail which had shifted them there after Dunkirk. Needless to say the Bank wasn't giving them away. Carlton Gardens had to buy them. With sterling. Of course, no hard cash changed hands. It was all done on balance sheets. Money moved from one account to another at the Bank as soon as Freddie sent across the return to say the transfers had reached their final destinations.

What puzzled Freddie was where were the Free French in London getting hold of the sterling to pay the Bank of England? Mostly they were as poor as church mice. Not even enough money for typewriters with accents. Well, not without a little help from Maurice Burnell, of course.

'I know all about the money that goes out every three months. The money that's legit. I'm the one sends the chitty over to the Bank. That's what you asked me to turn a blind eye to...that and the dummy Free French offices.'

'Correct, Draper. And I shall, of course, overlook the fact that you have been shown other documents which do not, at any rate, concern you...'

'Good of you, Sir. And I, in turn, shall overlook the payments going into the dead men's accounts.'

'Dead men?'

'I've checked the list of those people whose families we're sending money to. A lot of them are dead...'

'...so we want their families to get some help, even so. A little *ruse de guerre* which does no harm, Draper. And if they find out, the *Boche* will think they are still alive, and we are more numerous. No harm in that either.'

'That shook me, when he put it that way, Florence. Shook me rigid.'

'Oh *Freddie*! Has it all been a big mistake, then?'

'I really thought for a moment I'd been barking up the wrong tree. But then I thought about Guttman or Schiffman, whatever his name is. If he was telling the truth, then Gaillet still had something to hide. Or why would he have made up all that stuff about Rhoda and you. *And* I was damn sure Guttman wasn't on our family payment list. So then I thought "Why isn't he? If his family needs money? Is it something to do with their being Jews? Then I remembered what he'd said to us. He mentioned the network of Free French in neutral countries..."

'Yes, he did. So...?'

'Guttman called them imaginary. I didn't think about it at the time, because that's what Gaillet had told me Carlton Gardens were doing. But then, why would Gaillet tell Guttman about them? And in any case, I couldn't see the powers that be at Carlton Gardens letting their secret network be used to dish out a bit of bunce to the family of a French Jew who may or may not already be under arrest. These imaginary offices are supposed to be channelling money to further de Gaulle's ambitions after the war. It's big stuff.

'So why *did* he tell Guttman about them?'

'He didn't, Florence Duck! Gaillet told him about something else imaginary. I just didn't twig at the time. It's quite clever, you know. Not making it all up. Mostly the truth and only one or two fibs. So when he says "imaginary" to Guttman, there's me thinking I already know what he's talking about. About the dummy offices. But he wasn't, Florence. He'd told Guttman about the dead men, I wasn't supposed to know about. Although I don't suppose he called them that.'

So then it was Freddie's turn to check if Gaillet's door was still closed.

'And I thought you had a nice nest egg salted away in Switzerland, sir. Thought you might be able to afford an old master, if it suddenly became available. A man in a lace collar…'

'And you thought this…because?'

'Why, because the dead men on the family payment list are all those you told me not to inform the Red Cross about. All the ones with bank accounts in France. That's what singled them out from the other dead men we did tell the Red Cross about, didn't it? Their families don't know they're dead, so I suppose they're not able to get at their bank accounts…'

'No, Draper. Wrong. You didn't look far enough. But then, of course, you don't see *all* the files, do you? It is much more simple. They are dead men who *do* have bank accounts and *no* close families at all. A surprisingly gratifying number, wouldn't you say? Not informing the Red Cross was to make sure the banks themselves do not suspect anything when money keeps coming in. As far as Crédit Lyonnais in Berne or Buenos Aires, or Lisbon are concerned their customers are alive and well somewhere in the world. The money is transferred into their accounts in Béziers, Biarritz, or Boulogne-sur-Mer and there it remains untouched. Perhaps even on deposit, who knows?'

So that was it. Gaillet made it sound so simple, but Freddie knew there must be more to it than that. He also began to feel quite apprehensive. Why had Gaillet unburdened himself so readily? Why would he want Freddie to understand how his swindle worked?

'Don't look so frightened. I'm sure my secret is safe with you, Freddie.'

'Why?'

'Well, I look at it this way. On the one hand I could have you arrested for fraud and you could spend the rest of the war in a military prison. Or, on the other hand I could make you quite rich when the war is over. Enough to move to Switzerland, when the Germans win. As, of course, they will.'

'Arrested for fraud? You're the one who'd be arrested for fraud.'

'Yes, but you are overlooking the fact that you are apparently working as a representative of the Free French. Somewhere in our African colonies, I believe. You are the one making a nice little nest egg, Freddie, Not huge, of course, not yet. About a hundred thousand francs. But, naturally, when the gold payments start…'

'Gold payments? What gold payments?'

'You see Freddie? That was your first question. I would have asked the same question, too. But I might have expected you to ask if I was making it all up. Do you want to know that, Freddie? Or do you want it all to be true? Are you already feeling greedy for more? Your government is secretly buying French gold from our colonies. There is a difference between the sterling rate and the market rate, but we have no option but to sell to you if we want some of the profit to be paid to us here in England, to use to further the Free French cause. Fortunately or unfortunately for you, Freddie, I have designated you one of the agents in West Africa to receive the transfer of money. A little extra insurance policy for me. Most of it will go into the official account. But some of it will find its way into the account of one of my dead comrades-in-arms. Keeping them usefully alive, wouldn't you say?'

Freddie had a horrible feeling it was all true. That Raoul Gaillet had well and truly stitched him up. He struggled to regain some control.

'I can't be one of the phoney representatives. There must be other people at Carlton Gardens who know who they are. They can't all be crooks.'

Gaillet frowned briefly. 'As far as my living comrades-in-arms at Carlton Gardens are concerned, all the Free French representatives exist. I'm afraid I lied to you, Freddie about the phoney ones. They are known only to me. And to you, of course. I made sure you see the returns. But I add their payments afterwards. It is you and I who send the requests for payment to the Bank of England, although you only see the totals, not the names.'

'I could go and tell someone. Right now...'

'Don't be ridiculous, Freddie. I have implicated you too closely. And besides I still have this...'

He unlocked a drawer in his desk and took out a sheaf of paper. He riffled through it. 'Here they are, Freddie. Look. June 1936...Mademoiselle Rhoda Denning. Accompanied by her sister, Mademoiselle Florence Denning...'

'But that doctor said there *was* no list, Freddie. Not here, anyway. How...?'

'I don't know, Florrie Dee. I really don't know. I can only think Guttman was lying...'

'Did you think he was lying, Freddie? I didn't. What are we going to do?'

'We *could* take the money.'

'You *are* joking!'

'Mmm.'

'Freddie!'

'I've told him we've got the painting. Or rather, we know where we can lay our hands on it.'

'But we don't...'

'It's what Maurice wants us to say.'

'Yes but Maurice wanted us to say that to find out what Gaillet was up to. See if he had money. But we know now. He's spilled the beans to you anyway.'

'Yes, I know. But I'd mentioned it, hadn't I? I wanted him to think I was going along with him. For the money.'

'How much?'

'I thought a couple of hundred thousand.'

'Francs?'

'Pounds, Florence. Pounds.'

'Two hundred thousand pounds! He never agreed?'

'He did. He said it was a fair price. For a Rubens that's never been on the market and hasn't been stolen.'

'Did you tell him it was a Rubens?'

'He didn't need telling. He knew.'

'He and Maurice, both, then.'

I didn't know what to do. It felt as though some frightful ball of wool was unravelling. Tying us all up in a hopeless tangle. My first instinct had been to tell Freddie to go and make a clean breast of it all to his CO at Finsbury Circus, but we neither of us had much confidence in what the outcome would be. Maurice seemed our only way forward. And we neither of us knew whether to trust him either.

I telephoned my adorable uncle from the call box the next morning on my way to work. He wasn't available.

I tried not to get into a state. Ruby didn't help.

'You look as though you've been up all night, Flo'. Who was it this time? Göring or your old man? The sooner we can get hold of a decent lipstick again, the sooner we can start looking a bit more like it, eh gal? Actually, there's some scent going the rounds in sorting. If you don't want a whole bottle, I'll go shares on a dab or two with you. Either that or we could drink it. You look as though you could do with a pick-me-up.'

I went over the road to the telephone box in the dinner break. I didn't want Ruby quizzing me any more than I could help. I hung on for what seemed ages and then Maurice came on. I took a deep breath, not really knowing where to start. But he beat me to it.

'Have you spoken to Rhoda?'

'Rhoda? No. What about?'

'She's arranged to meet Gaillet somewhere this afternoon. She's told him she can get him the painting. I assumed you and Freddie had roped her in, for some reason. You know…after our chat. I can't get hold of her. I've tried the flat and she's obviously not rehearsing anywhere.'

I was poised to tell him what Freddie had found out, but I bit my tongue.

'So Rhoda didn't tell you any more, then? Just that she was going to meet Gaillet, but not where. That's a bit odd isn't it? When was this?'

There was a brief silence at the other end of the line. I had a picture of Maurice taking a long drag on his cigarette.

'It's a bit complicated, Florence…over the phone. I haven't spoken to Rhoda. I thought you must have done. Let's just say I've been told.'

Yes, I thought. By someone by the name of Raoul Gaillet. It had to be. But Gaillet wasn't telling Maurice everything. Why not? Come to that, why tell Maurice anything at all? My head was spinning. I wanted to scream. Let us out! Let us both out! Freddie and me.

'I'm getting very confused, Uncle Maurice. And a bit

frightened for Freddie, if the truth be told.'

'I know, Florence. Look, I'll fill you in later. But I rather think time's a bit short right now. We really need to know where she's taking him. All I know is, Florence, she's arranged to meet him off the tube at Church End.'

'Finchley?'

'I suppose.'

'That's where the branch line goes out to Edgware. So where in the world?...Coatwood?'

'Coatwood,' said Maurice. 'I'd put good money on it.'

I tried Freddie at Carlton Gardens from the box by the church. But I couldn't get through. Number unobtainable. The operator couldn't do anything either. There'd been a heavy raid the night before, she said. The exchange was out. My heart sank. Freddie hadn't been home for two days either. So I didn't know how things stood with Gaillet. And now this.

Maurice was driving himself in the big Austin, so I sat in the front with him.

'No driver today?'

'Thought we'd keep it in the family.'

'Have you spoken to Freddie? I can't get him…'

Maurice hadn't.

I asked him what he was going to do, if we found Gaillet and Rhoda at Coatwood.

'Not quite sure, Florence. Play it by ear. Depends.'

'Depends on what?'

'Whether they've got the painting, for one thing.'

That did it. I saw red. It all came tumbling out. Everything. Guttman. Phoney representatives. Dead men's bank accounts. The lot. And a few tears of rage for good measure.

'And there's Freddie,' I finished, 'made to look like a thief, an international fraudster. What was it you called it…trading with the enemy? He could quite probably be shot…and all you can bloody think about is a damn painting that most likely doesn't even exist. You know what I think, Maurice? I think you're every bit as bad as Gaillet. Looking to line your pockets even though there's a war on,'

Maurice took one hand off the steering wheel and started to pat his pockets for his cigarettes. He located his case and handed it to me.

'Be a sport. Fish out one of those and light it for me, would you? There's a lighter in the glove. You don't, do you?'

He took a long drag and held it while he wound down his window a couple of inches to let the smoke out.

'Let me tell you about Raoul Gaillet,' he said. 'We're almost certain, now, he's working for Vichy and against de Gaulle. It's a very murky business at the best of times. Carlton Gardens are using the Vichy consuls here to get money into France. Supposedly no questions asked. But friend Gaillet is giving them more than that. And getting stuff back as well. All old pals from the London embassy before the war, you see.'

'What do you mean...getting stuff back?'

'Information about people's families in France. Things that could be used to persuade useful French ex-patriots not to throw their lot in with de Gaulle. Even to find roundabout ways to get home. We've lost an important scientist from New York that way. Just when he was all set up to go to Canada. And I'm certain your French doctor's patient list found its way into his hands the same way.'

'They're Jews. The doctor and his family. His wife and daughter were arrested trying to get into Switzerland.'

Maurice blew a double smoke ring. I didn't know whether it was deliberate. They collapsed and were sucked out in the draught from the window.

'How the devil did the doctor find that out, Florence?'

'Gaillet told him.'

'And somebody paid the clinic a visit. Went through the files. Sent the list to Gaillet. In the Vichy diplomatic bag very probably.'

'Yes, and what's become of his poor family? They're Jews, for God's sake, Maurice. And all because you told Gaillet about Rhoda.'

Maurice took a long, long drag on his cigarette and flicked it, only half finished, out of the window.

'Right now, I'm trying not to think about that possibility.'

'Why did you tell him?'

'I wanted to see what he would do with the information. Being so close to Freddie, I thought Gaillet wouldn't be able to resist using it, if he thought it would get him somewhere. And I was right, wasn't I?'

'Well I think it was a shabby thing to do, damn shabby, Maurice, if you want to know. Look what a mess we're in, now. Freddie...'

'Look, old girl. I didn't know the bloody quack was going to turn up doctoring for the Free French, did I? That was one of those amazing coincidences.'

'Just bad luck, is that what you're saying, Maurice?'

'Well, not entirely, Florence, if you think about it. It's flushed Gaillet out, well and truly. I rather think we won't have any difficulty turning him.'

'What does that mean? Aren't you going to have him arrested?'

'I can't see that he's broken the law, Florence. Still, that's not my main concern. Light me another gasper, would you?'

I fished a cigarette out his case and stuck it between his lips.

'Not broken the law? What about these phoney accounts and things?'

Maurice laughed out of the corner of his mouth.

'Much too political, old girl. And useful too, I should think. Handy mechanism for routing funds here and there. I should think my lot will want to take them over. No, I fear the only one who might look as though he's broken the law is poor old Freddie.'

There was nothing I could think of, to say. I just sat there, staring at the road in front, wondering whether to scratch his face instead.

In a short while we turned up the hill towards Little Stanmore and after a quarter of a mile or so came to the end of the street where the house was. It was blocked off with a low wall of sandbags. A notice said 'Danger. Unexploded Bomb.

Maurice pulled up on the opposite side and walked over. I got out and followed him. A boy of about twelve stuck his head up on the other side of the sandbags.

'You can't come in. There's a bomb,' he said importantly.

'Who says?' said Maurice, 'Just William?'

The warden had, it seemed, gone for his tea, leaving the boy waiting for the sappers. Maurice asked whereabouts the bomb was and was told 'that was careless talk.' Maurice told him he was 'official' and in any case he'd clip his ear.

It appeared the street had been hit by two bombs the night before. One house had been hit but the other bomb had failed to go off and was in a crater in the road a little further down. After a bit more argy-bargy, sixpence saw us through the barrier. As we walked up the road, Maurice called back to the boy and asked if anyone else had been through. He said 'a Frenchie and a lady had' and when Maurice asked why he hadn't said so, the boy said 'he'd been given a bob not to.'

We couldn't see the damage because the road had a right-angled bend about fifty yards down.

'I don't want it to be Coatwood. Please let me go round the corner and see Coatwood still standing. And the middle room.' I thought.

36

'I shall have to go back to Coatwood, *ma chérie*. To my middle room.'

'Why, what's the matter? We're having a lovely time. Aren't we?'

'I don't know, Florence. I don't know. I feel…I feel as if something has to finish now and I don't want it to be here.'

'You don't mean your history, Grandmother?'

We looked at one another in alarm.

'There! You see Florence? You see…'

'See what?'

'You called me "Grandmother".'

'Well?' I said. But she knew.

'You never call me that when I am telling my *histoire*. It all goes wrong, away from my middle room.'

I knew she was right, of course. Josephine Lucie had more or less clammed up after the walk into Ryde. But I didn't want her to take it into her head to up sticks and go home. I was beginning to enjoy the prospect of another week or so at Seaview, as Pa seemed content for us to go our own ways during the day. I tried to talk her out of raising with him the idea of cutting short the holiday. I was fairly sure he would just fly off the handle at the idea of calling it off for 'no good reason that I can see'. To say nothing of the teeth grinding over the wasted expense. Mrs Browne-with-an-ee would hardly be likely to give us a refund.

There was a very tense scene when Grandmother announced her intentions to Pa. He wanted to know if she was ill, of course, but she wouldn't say she was and wouldn't say she wasn't. This exasperated Pa.

'Well you can't go home on your own. You're hopeless on the train, *Madame*. And I don't see why I should cut short the first holiday I've had in years, for no good reason that I can see.'

Considering how far she had travelled on trains and balloons, I thought this was rather unfair, but I could say nothing of that to Pa, being strictly between Josephine Lucie and me. She then said that, in any case, I should accompany her. Pa wouldn't hear of it. He was determined to thwart her, come what may.

'I'm not having the pair of you gallivanting off home on your own. You're not safe. If you're so set on it, *Madame*, you will have to ask that blessed son of yours to come and fetch you from Portsmouth in his motor car. But Florence stays here with me.'

'But why, Charles?'

'Because...Because I need her.'

So that was that. A telegram was sent to Maurice, which Grandmother paid for. I thought she would have caved in, if only for my sake, but she was as adamant as Pa was. She and I sat in, waiting for the reply while Pa stalked off on his own. So much for needing me, I thought.

'Tell me what happened after you met my grandfather Burnell.' I felt rather angry with her for insisting on going and not standing up to Pa about my having to stay. So I was in no mood to accept her misgivings about being away from the middle room, even though I would normally have shared them. Anyway, in my current mood I was prepared to convince myself that the best front parlour at Ferndown had the same vintage air about it as the middle room at Coatwood.

Grandmother, and try as I might I couldn't think of her as Josephine Lucie here, sighed in a giving-in kind of way. Not like her at all. I half felt I shouldn't press her. But what would have been the difference if I hadn't? Perhaps there would have been the chance of a different ending. You never know afterwards, do you, if you hadn't done something, whether everything that happened next would have been the same as if you had done it?

'Edward Burnell and I went to live on the coast near Boulogne. I told you. There was a very grand casino there. Much bigger than the ones in Monte Carlo or Cannes. It was very new and very popular with the English, who are addicted to the *tables*. Your grandfather had devised a system of playing roulette, which meant that after a very short while we had lost all the money he had made with his deals in Paris.'

'What did you do?'

'I went to work in the casino to pay off our debts, so that we could eventually come to England. I told you I had learned to work the roulette wheel at Monsieur Adolphe's.'

'But you were in love with him? With Grandfather Burnell? Had you forgotten all about Augustin?'

I don't know why I had to ask her that, at that precise moment. I needed to know, I suppose. But over our thousand and one nights, I had by now learned not to hurry her along like that. Not to try and push her along ways she wasn't ready to take just then.

There was a loud knock at the front door. It was the telegraph boy with Maurice's reply. The maid-of-all-work brought it in, while Mrs Browne-with-an-ee, herself, hovered in the doorway trying to look snootily as if the telegram's contents were not of the slightest interest to her. Maurice said that he couldn't get down to Portsmouth until the following day. Grandmother was a little put out at this, even though if he had arrived any sooner, she would not have got to Coatwood until the small hours.

'I might have been ill, for all he knows. I might have been dying.'

'But you're not, are you, Grandmother?'

'Don't do it, Florence. Don't do it.'

'What, Grandmother?'

'Make excuses for men. They make them easily enough for themselves. But women always have to do it for them. Husbands, sons, lovers. We make excuses for them, even though they do not ask us to. It is so we can pretend they deserve us more than they do. And then, and then, Florence. You know what happens then?'

'No.'

'Yes, you do, Florence. I have told you often. Then you stop taking the path of your own choosing and start taking the one men choose for you. I did with Edward Burnell and I did with Augustin.'

'With Augustin? But I thought he disappeared. Didn't he…die?'

She stood up abruptly, seized me by the hand and strode out the room, into the hall and, hatless, out of the front door into the sunshine. She almost ran down to the seafront, with me still firmly in her grasp, trying to keep up, half a pace behind. When we came to one of the seats facing out across the Solent, that wasn't occupied, she dumped herself down, very breathless and rather grey in the face.

'It all went wrong. Things were started that were never finished.'

This time I had the presence of mind to say nothing. I don't think she was really talking to me, anyhow.

'Now, opening it all over again, none of it has ever been finished. Always started, and never finished. Still going wrong. Opening it like an old biscuit tin one has forgotten and discovered again, wondering what might be inside it after all these years...' She stopped.

I waited, still unsure whether to prompt her from her silence. That biscuit tin was hovering in my mind now. It was in the left-hand cupboard of her chiffonier in the middle room and had a print on the lid of a lady in a bustle, with a parasol and a little dog. Both were gazing along a seafront very much grander than this one at Seaview, under the legend, 'Chemin de fer du nord'. Ages ago when I'd asked what was in it she'd said 'it was just old bills and receipts'. I'd looked once and it seemed she was right, so I hadn't bothered again.

Her silence became almost audible the longer it went on. Then she said, 'How many years do you have now, Florence? I forget, you know.'

'Nearly fourteen,' I said, hopefully inflating it in the expectation of a seriously adult revelation. I'd not long had my thirteenth birthday. I was not disappointed either.

'Before the telegram, you asked me about love, Florence. You asked me about Edward Burnell and Augustin.'

'Did I?'

'Don't play, *ma chère*. Don't play. Listen and be dumb! You understand me? Your grandfather and I were lovers at first. It was *de rigueur*, expected, in France at the seaside. That was when I should have finished what we had started. I still have not, not even now, *chérie*. *Because* we came to England and *because* we were married. *Because* that was what was expected in England. *Because* I imagined I loved him. He certainly loved me. Sometimes we had money, sometimes we didn't. He bought me the shop in Billericay as an *assurance*, in case he would lose his money from his business dealing, which he did often. Because I could not work at the roulette wheel in England, could I?'

It wasn't a real question, but I shook my head.

'Then after Charlotte was born, when she was about two years, Edward decided to go to Egypt. Everyone was talking about the tombs and treasures and he thought he would make some money. I didn't go with him. I had the shop, and the baby, and he was not going to be away a long time, he said. Three months. Perhaps four.'

About a month after Edward Burnell had departed for Egypt via Gibraltar and Malta, Augustin Montel walked into the little general store in Billericay.

Josephine Lucie came through from the back at the sound of the bell and they stood gazing at one another on opposite sides of the counter in silence. For her it was a moment of sudden realisation which she tried to suppress instantly, but with no success. She said it was like putting the flat of your hand under a running tap and expecting the water to stop flowing.

At that moment Josephine Lucie knew, not only that she no longer loved the man in front of her, but that she had never loved Edward Burnell either.

Augustin, too, could find nothing to say. The speech he had prepared had dried on his lips, he told her afterwards. He had begun to compose it in Paris, when César Machin had given him Josephine Lucie's address at the French channel resort. Augustin had not really expected to find her there. He had written first but had no reply. The letter was not returned, just silence. After kicking his heels in Paris for a while he had decided to take the train from the Gare du Nord to the coast, convincing himself that a seaside holiday was his real reason for going. The concierge at the address the chef had given him was inclined to be unhelpful. There had been a dispute, apparently, about an unpaid bill, which although it had been eventually settled meant she and Josephine Lucie had parted on frosty terms. Augustin inquired about his letter. Did she recall it arriving and, if so, was it before or after Josephine Lucie had left? The concierge could not at first be bothered to remember a letter. But when Augustin tempted her with enough francs to buy a large cheese, she grumbled about until she found it. It seemed the letter had not been delivered in time to Josephine Lucie and had probably only been read by the concierge. And no, she did not have a forwarding address, not even for the price of several bottles of sweet wine to go with the cheese, although for a quart of St Omer beer she volunteered that Josephine Lucie had had a job at the casino 'after her fancy man couldn't clear his slate.'

The introduction of a 'fancy man' came as a sharp blow in the ribs for Augustin. César Machin had not mentioned a man. He, it was, had found Burnell, but perhaps that had made him shy away from revealing that fact to Augustin. Machin had told Augustin that Josephine Lucie feared him dead. He said, too, she had been to visit old Papa Montel but found him gone south and his house shuttered and abandoned. Perhaps Machin thought that Augustin could read enough into that. Her lingering hope of his survival. Or its final extinguishing. What interest should the great César Machin have taken, anyway? He who had been the *chef formidable* at the *hôtel* of Monsieur Adolphe de Marquise, where gentlemen and ladies had always come and gone.

Although no-one at the Casino knew where Josephine Lucie had gone, either, the *chef de tables* had been prepared, for a consideration, to reveal Edward Burnell's address in England from the registration book. Augustin pondered for a week or so, trying to convince himself he was merely indulging his curiosity to while away the holiday hours. Who was to say Josephine Lucie and Edward Burnell had not gone their separate ways? And if they had not, where would that leave him? So, not finding a satisfactory answer to either of these questions, he packed his bag, paid his bill, took a cab into Boulogne and booked himself on the evening steam packet to Folkestone.

'I thought you had died. I thought the Prussians had shot you.' Josephine Lucie tried to staunch with anger the sudden haemorrhaging of all her pent up love. 'Where have you been? Why did you not write? I searched and searched. I waited at Orgelets. A year I waited for you.'

'The Prussians took me to Sedan. I nearly died on the way. I was unconscious or I think they would have shot me as a spy then and there. But they would not shoot me before I had faced a field court and they would not shoot me, even then until I could stand. It was when we got to Sedan a Prussian doctor took charge of me and all thoughts of shooting me seemed to evaporate. I think the doctor told them I would not survive the amputation. The gangrene had taken quite a hold by then. But I did, as you see, Josephine Lucie…'

Augustin tapped his left leg with his cane. Josephine Lucie had not seen him move until then. He had already been standing in front of the counter when she had come through from the back, and it obscured him from the waist down.

'Prussian engineering. The latest thing. Birch wood and aluminium alloy. Very light where it needs to be and very well balanced. So I only have to wear one extra set of braces. It has a proper foot that moves up and down. So I am not like a pirate with a peg-leg, you see, Josephine Lucie. I was a hospital prisoner for a while and then when the war was all forgotten, just a patient convalescing. I did, eventually, go back to Orgelets. But no-one had heard of Josephine Lucie Simon. I found your parents' house but they seemed bemused when I asked about you.'

She felt the final flood of her ebbing love come to an end.

'I felt perhaps there was enough left. Just enough, Florence. And then, afterwards, I thought it might have been pity.'

'Because of his leg, you mean?'

'Yes, I suppose. He had come a long way on it, when you think about it. For my sake. And it was not easy for him, in spite of what he said. It hurt him a lot.'

There was something else. I could tell. But I knew I had come almost as far as I dared on my own. Anything else would be a tangle of things probably still in a mess, even after all these years. I wasn't going to ask her if she had decided to be unfaithful to Grandfather Burnell. And in any case I'd already decided she'd been unfaithful to Augustin. So whatever the answer, it was always a circle, as far as I could see. But I was barely beyond the Carnegie Library view of life.

Then for a brief moment by the sea wall there, looking at the sunlight on the Solent, my grandmother became Josephine Lucie again, one last time.

'We should be cooking something, you know, *ma chérie*. Shall we have some imaginary éclairs? What shall we put in them? Chocolate and some of Signor Minghella's ice cream?'

'Or some animals from the Noah's Ark. Some biscuit rats.'

'There were never biscuit rats. I told you, *chérie*. But there. I suppose there would have been two rats, at least on the Ark. And thank you...for not asking what is without doubt in your mind...'

Then after a moment she said, 'Augustin stayed for a little while. And then he went back to Paris. It was for the best. I have never seen or heard from him since. Edward came back from Egypt, only a little poorer than when he went, and my life went on, with him. I had your poor, dear mother to take care of...'

'And then Uncle Maurice.'

Josephine Lucie pulled my head down and whispered in my ear, 'Maurice was Augustin's. Edward never suspected. And I never told him. Nor Maurice. Only you, *ma chère*, only you, now.'

Pa and I saw her to the ferry at Ryde Pier the next morning. I hoped up to the very last minute she would change her mind, or that Pa would. But she was determined and so was he. So we waved her goodbye as the little steamer moved off towards Portsmouth and the waiting Maurice.

I didn't see her again. Mrs Croucher found her dead in the

middle room a couple of days before we were due home.
'Damn!' said Pa. 'Damn! Damn! Damn!'

37

'Damn!' said Maurice.

'Oh no, Maurice! Oh damn and blast!' I was numb and sick.

'Where's your father? Where's Charles? Would he have been at home?'

Pa? Yes. No. Where was Pa, for God's sake? I couldn't think.

'He's not here. He's in Liverpool or Blackpool or somewhere. With the school. They got evacuated.'

'Thank Christ for that!'

I didn't. I felt a wave of anger come over me. It was his fault. Pa's. If he'd been at home, indoors at Coatwood, this would never have happened. The other one would have gone off. There'd be a big hole in the road, but Coatwood would be all right. And now, instead…

'What a blessing my mother wasn't here. To see this. She loved this house.'

I wanted to scream. She didn't, she didn't! She hated it, she loathed it! She only came here because of mother. And she was dying. The house was full of my father. Full of Leonard and Rhoda. She didn't love Coatwood. She lived in the middle room, because it was somewhere else. Somewhere in between her past and my future. She let me live there too. And now look at it.

'So where are they then?' Maurice reached for a cigarette.

'Don't. There might be gas. It said at the sandbags.'

He reluctantly put the silver case back in his coat pocket. 'Do you think they've gone off the other way? We'd have seen them otherwise. Or are they still here somewhere? Inside? Where's the rest of the street? Evacuated down the pub, I suppose, until that dud's been seen to. Or gone to work.'

It was eerily quiet. Not another soul to be seen. The house was still standing. But it was as if it had been taken to pieces and then hastily put back together again. Not quite straight. Not quite all there.

Perhaps it had been a direct hit. You know…straight through the roof. Sometimes they actually did less damage than the ones that went off in the next street and flattened everything around. You could never tell. Mr Webber said that at his sister's house in Kilburn, when the house over the road was hit, the windows and doors in her house had all opened and shut and were still locked afterwards.

A big piece of Coatwood's roof had gone, anyway. And all the windows upstairs had been blown out. The front door was half open and at an angle. I made my way up the short front path towards it, over the broken window glass, splintered wood and putty.

'Careful, old girl.' Maurice paused at the gate behind me to light up anyway. 'You should have a tin hat on really.'

I couldn't smell gas. It must have been turned off at the main by now. I pushed gingerly at the front door, but it resisted. A large part of the hall ceiling and the one on the floor above had come down, blocking it. Maurice came up with his fag in the side of his mouth, like Humphrey Bogart, and put his shoulder to it. He squeezed past me.

'Rhoda?' he called. 'Raoul? Anyone at home?'

Oh yes, I thought. *Raoul.* Uncle Maurice must think I was born yesterday.

There was a scrabbling noise from upstairs. Then Rhoda's voice, sounding rather flat, I thought. Not like Rhoda at all.

'We're up here, Maurice. On the landing, or what's left of it.'

'Are you all right, old girl? Is Gaillet with you?'

'You'd better come and see. The stairs seem to be safe enough.'

Maurice clambered over the bits of fallen ceiling to the foot of the stairs and began to go up, moving more bits of wreckage out of the way as he went. When he reached the landing and disappeared round the corner, I began to go up too. The stairs were intact, it seemed. The main mess of fallen ceilings and floors was from the top floor higher up, Pa's and mother's room. When I reached the first landing, Rhoda and Maurice were standing outside the door to the middle room, which was closed. Slightly beyond it, Captain Gaillet sat on the floor in his uniform, his back to the wall and his legs straight out in front of him.

'What's happened to him?' I said. 'Did something fall on him?' I pushed past Rhoda. 'Are you all right, Captain Gaillet?' I said, but got no reply. I bent over and touched his shoulder. He seemed to be asleep. He was breathing quite rapidly and his eyes were closed.

Something made me take his cap off.

'Don't look,' said Rhoda. 'I put it back on him.' Her voice was still odd. Agitated.

Gaillet's greying hair was matted with blood which had begun to dry.

'This looks bad,' I said. 'He needs to get this seen to. What happened, Rhoda?'

Rhoda seemed as though she was about to fall over. She steadied herself on Maurice, who had said nothing. He still had his cigarette in the side of his mouth. The ash had not fallen from it, in spite of his having to clear the partly-blocked staircase.

'I hit him,' said Rhoda. 'With that.' She pointed to a round metal container with a handle at the side and a hinged lid. It was mother's spittoon. Pa had fashioned it in his garden workshop from a quart milk churn after the doctor had told him he needed to keep what mother coughed up to show him on his visits. It was quite heavy. I suppose Pa was too proud to buy a proper one from the chemist's. It must have fallen through from the upstairs bedroom onto the landing when the bomb hit.

'Hit him?' I said. 'What on earth for?'

'He kept saying, if he couldn't have the painting after all, he wouldn't let me have that wretched list. Said he would need it to keep Freddie in line after I'd double-crossed him. I didn't know what he was talking about. What's Freddie got to do with the painting? He doesn't know where it is, so how could I have double-crossed him?'

A ghastly thought entered my head.

'Were you trying to *kill* him, Rhoda?'

She didn't reply.

'Well?' said Maurice.

'I just wanted to take the list and be done with it.'

'You don't mean he's got it with him?' I said

Maurice frisked him. There were three or four handwritten pages in Gaillet's tunic pocket, obviously taken from something like a ledger book. I'd have thought he would have kept them locked up somewhere safe.

Maurice must have been thinking the same thing. 'I suppose he didn't want Freddie picking the lock to his desk, while he was gone. I can't believe he was actually going to hand them over for the painting, right here, even supposing he believed Rhoda could lay her hands on it.'

We passed the pages from one to another, running our fingers down the columns of names and dates, as if to make sure we had the right ones. Rhoda's and mine were there all right.

'Some of these others are very interesting.' Maurice reached for a cigarette: his other one had finally given up the ghost. 'I wonder...'

'Forget it, Uncle Maurice. We're going to burn it. Right now,' I said.

Maurice reluctantly handed the pages back to me. 'So...Were you always planning to bash him on the head, Rhoda? Was that your plan? I mean, there's no Rubens here, is there? Be honest.'

'It's in there. At least it was. It's locked, though, for some reason. I don't have a key.' Rhoda pointed to the door of the middle room.

'Unlocking a door in a bombed-out house hardly presents an insuperable problem,' said Maurice, 'It's not exactly breaking and entering.'

I wasn't having this. Not by a long chalk, I wasn't. After Josephine Lucie's funeral and after Maurice had rummaged around fruitlessly for anything of any value, I had been the one who had locked the door. Pa had raised not one word of protest. It was as if he wanted to forget his mother-in-law had ever been there. Leonard had briefly, very briefly, raised the possibility of its being let, but one look from both Pa and me had put paid to that. Rhoda went off to RADA and digs in Kentish Town and I had become the undisputed chatelaine of the middle room.

I wasn't about to relinquish the post now, just because of Rhoda and the Luftwaffe. Anyway, weren't they overlooking something?

'What about Gaillet? He *will* be dead if we don't get him some help. Or were you proposing to chuck him over the banisters, Rhoda, to finish him off? Would look more respectable at the Old Bailey than being charged with clobbering him with a home-made spittoon.'

Maurice blew one of his smoke rings. 'Look old girl, this is technically an empty house. Unless you propose to take up residence, in your father's absence, it'll be secured by the ARP, which means, as like as not, it'll be looted, you know that. If there is a Rubens here or anything else of value, we'll need to be quick. I think Captain Gaillet should sit there a bit longer. The rest will do him good.'

'Who told you it was a Rubens, Uncle Maurice? Was it him?' I pointed down at Gaillet.

Maurice blew another smoke ring. 'Apparently his father knew about it. He was some kind of a dealer in Paris. Shall I break the door down?'

I reached for my shoulder bag. 'I have the key.' My mind was clear. It was all coming together. Rather to my surprise, when it was unlocked the door opened easily. The middle room was thick with dust and there was no glass in the windows. Most of that was in the front garden below. Otherwise it was relatively unscathed. The first thing that caught my eye was the box of Noah's Ark animal shapes. I remembered I'd had them out when I'd been in here last, months and months ago, in those last weeks before the war. I'd come for a bit of peace and quiet before my wedding.

'You see, Rhoda,' I said. 'He's not here, the man with the lace collar. He's never been here. I should know.'

'Yes he is.' Rhoda went over to the far side of the room to where the framed photograph of Josephine Lucie's wedding group hung rather skew-whiff on the wall.

She took it down and turned it over. It had never occurred to me, before then, how much larger the mount and frame were than the photograph itself.

Maurice took the frame from her and carefully straightened out the half dozen pins holding the backing cardboard in place. Very gingerly he pushed the glass from the front. The wedding party and whatever it was concealing, came free. Ever so slowly he removed the glass and the mount. The photograph came away with it.

Underneath, stuck to the cardboard backing, was a painting in oils. The head and shoulders of a young cavalier, his long brown hair falling in ringlets to a wide lace collar. The collar seemed to fold outwards from either side of his beautifully pointed beard, and then, following the line of his jaw to his ringed ear and round behind his neck, it curved smoothly upwards, so that it looked as if his head did not belong on his richly clothed shoulders, but was being presented separately, on an intricate, oblong plate of delicate bone china.

It wasn't how I had imagined the Cambrai collar all these years. I'd pictured it more like a flat, lacy shawl, covering his shoulders. The startling contrast with the demure and lady-like confection I had been imagining, made me annoyed with myself.

But not half as annoyed as I was with Rhoda. The middle room was my place, not hers. I'd made sure she'd been kept out and so had Josephine Lucie.

'How the hell did you know this was here?'

'It was that time when I was looking for props for the play we were doing at school. You remember. Josephine Lucie…'

'Grandmother. She's our grandmother, Rhoda…'

'What does it matter? The old terror's dead and gone…'

'…And my mother,' said Maurice.

'Anyway, she gave me all kinds of grief when she found I'd been in here. In fact I think this is the first time I've been in here since. I knew she'd be absolutely foaming at the mouth if she knew I'd broken the glass in this frame. I had to high tail it down to the broadway with the measurements and just managed to put the new piece in and get it back on the wall when she came in. She'd been to the sanatorium with you in the car, Maurice. It was touch and go.'

'And you've never said anything about the painting under the photograph.'

'Well, would you, Florence? I was in enough trouble for being in here, let alone admitting to breaking things. I assumed she knew about the picture. It couldn't be anything special, if she'd used the frame for her wedding picture. Or Grandfather Burnell had.'

There was a crunching noise on the debris on the landing. Captain Gaillet was leaning in the doorway looking like the ghost of Banquo, shaking his gory locks.

'Ah, there you are, old man,' said Maurice. 'You look a bit seedy, though, I must say. We've found my picture, you see.'

'Yours?' Rhoda and I chorused together, as if we'd been rehearsing.

'Naturally,' said Maurice. 'My mother's effects. Apart from the bits and pieces she left to you Florence. But I don't recall the man in the lace collar being included in them, do you?'

Captain Gaillet made a supreme effort to pull himself together. 'My father, Louis Gaillet had a financial interest in this painting, I believe. Someone here has already been through my pockets today. I do not propose to let them do it a second time.'

I thought this was quite a speech for a man with a blood-caked face and a huge gash on the side of his head. Maurice was unimpressed, however.

'I don't see that you're holding any good cards, at the moment, Raoul. Everything's been rumbled, bank accounts, gold shipments, phoney representatives in West Africa. I don't think you'll be able to make anything stick to Freddie, now. What on earth possessed you to bring that list of names with you? That was your trump. Without that it all just falls apart.'

Captain Gaillet sat down heavily in the doorway. 'But Maurice, we agreed. I thought you were a man after my own heart. But now, I don't know. Who are you? I don't know any more.'

'Exactly so, old man. Who am I? You of all people shouldn't assume people are what they seem. Now, I suggest we get you patched up and then there are some people I know, who want to have a good long chat with you. A little co-operation, Monsieur, instead of collaboration, could make all the difference.'

From outside we could here noises indicating the sappers had arrived and were preparing to move the unexploded bomb from the street. Maurice went to the empty window and called down to them. A surprised officer shouted something about 'authorised personnel'. Maurice took some kind of identification out of his pocket and waved it. 'I am authorised,' he called back.

Two of the sappers were detailed to help Captain Gaillet down the stairs. Outside in the street and safely behind the sandbag barricade, the officer examined Maurice's credentials. He seemed impressed enough.

'This French officer needs to go to hospital, sir. As you can see, I'm rather busy here…'

'My car's at the end,' said Maurice, 'I'll see to him.'

He dropped Rhoda and me at the station. 'I'll deal with friend Gaillet here and then we must talk. Will you go back to Florence's, Rhoda?'

'No,' said Rhoda flatly. 'I'm going home for a bath. You can look in later and scrub my back.'

The two of us stood on the platform waiting for the little train to Church End. We must have cut a sorry picture, covered in dust and plaster. Neither of us really cared. There was no one else in the 'Ladies Only' compartment.

'Was Maurice the baby's father?' I said.

'What on earth gave you that idea? Maurice? He's our uncle.'

'Yes. But he always was adorable, Rhoda. I don't really care any more. It was just a passing thought.'

'Well let it go on passing.'

We relapsed into silence until we went to go our separate ways on the tube at Church End.

'Who's got the painting,' I said.

'Maurice has. Says it's his.'

He's welcome to it, I thought. Josephine Lucie said it brought nothing but bad luck. Is that why she'd never told me it was hanging on the wall in the middle room?

I phoned Freddie from the box by the shelters. There was no reply. I went home and had an unpatriotic bath, nearly up to the top. Freddy didn't come home and I heard nothing more from Maurice that night, either. Nor the next day. Nothing from either of them. I got through to Carlton Gardens on the way to work, but all they would say was that Corporal Draper was 'not in today.' I tried unsuccessfully not to worry. This happened sometimes, I told myself. There was a war on.

38

The following dinner time, I was just putting on my hat and coat to go out to the phone when Mr Webber called me in.

'I might as well have this telephone installed on your desk, Florence.' He didn't seem too put out for once that I'd got a call.

'I'm sorry Mr Webber. Perhaps it's about my husband. I haven't heard from him for a while.'

'We were bombed out last night, Florence. We shall have to go to her sister's in Kentish Town.'

I couldn't believe he'd still come in to the office. 'My father's copped it a few nights ago. He wasn't there, though,' I said. It was all so bloody ordinary.

Freddie was already talking at me before I'd put the phone to my ear.

'...and I got picked up by the MPs. Said I'd been reported awol. So I spent a night in the guard house and then got escorted back to Finsbury Circus because they weren't too keen on sending me back to Carlton Gardens for the French to deal with. I think Gaillet had something to do with it, getting me reported I mean. Wanted me out of the way for a while. I'll tell you why when I see you. Not on the phone.'

Mr Webber was still hovering about, so I couldn't tell Freddie about the events at Coatwood. Much too Sexton Blake for Mr Webber. It would keep until the evening. I was just relieved to hear Freddie's voice.

'Everything all right, Florence?' The Luftwaffe had obviously managed to turn up Mr Webber's human side. I thought I might push my luck in the circumstances.

'Might I make one call, Mr Webber? It's kind of official.'

He couldn't actually bring himself to say the words, but he made an acquiescent gesture towards the phone. I dialled Maurice's number. The switchboard answered.

'Mr Burnell is away.'
'Away, away, or just out?'
'I couldn't say.'
'Well, shall I try later?'
'That's up to you, madam.'
I hung up.

On the way home in the evening I tried from the box by the shelters. The night shift had taken over the switchboard and there was a new voice. I tried a different tack.

'Maurice Burnell asked me to telephone him earlier, but I couldn't get away. Is he still there? It's his niece.' I waited, while they checked.

'Mr Burnell has left apparently.'

'Oh dear. Never mind, I'll try in the morning.'

For once Freddie's half-completed conversation, as he opened the door, was stopped dead in mid-flow.

'God's teeth, Florrie Dee! What on earth's that smell?'

'It's your tea. It's fricassee of tripe. It's had about three days.'

'It needs a bit longer. Did the Luftwaffe drop it? Is it their new secret weapon?'

'As a matter of fact, Old Webber gave it to me. He's been bombed out and he didn't want to take it all the way to Mrs Webber's sister's on the tube.'

'I should think not. What have you been doing to upset him?'

'He let me phone Maurice from the office.'

'Not adorable Maurice, otherwise known as the Scarlet Pimpernel?'

'Why do you say that?'

There had been no sign of Raoul Gaillet at Carlton Gardens when Freddie had eventually returned there from the clutches of the military police. He settled down half-heartedly to his in-tray, but when there was still no word by mid-morning, he went to see if the *française libre* from the typing pool, who acted as Gaillet's secretary, knew anything. She didn't. Freddie went back to his desk and waited. After about ten minutes one of the senior officers looked in. He started to address Freddie in French and then recollecting who Freddie was, switched to English.

'Captain Gaillet is not here?'

Freddie said he hadn't seen him for some time. The officer looked slightly put out, and then he clearly remembered something.

'But of course, he has gone before the *Général.*'

Freddie's heart missed a beat. Could this mean that Gaillet had been discovered and de Gaulle was already interrogating him personally?

'Before the General, Sir?'

But the officer would not be drawn.

When he had gone, Freddie telephoned de Gaulle's adjutant's office and spoke to one of the secretaries he knew well. He asked if Captain Gaillet was still with the General. The girl sounded surprised.

'Captain Gaillet is not with the General. He won't be in today, he's going on ahead. Didn't you know, Freddie?'

The penny dropped. Gaillet was the advance party for one of de Gaulle's trips. He hadn't mentioned it to Freddie. It must have been a last minute plan. Freddie told her he hadn't been in the office for a few days. She didn't appear to know why and he didn't say.

'Where are they off to again? Somewhere up north, wasn't it?'

It usually was. Newcastle or Glasgow. Keeping the Free French navy sweet.

'No. It's the North African thing. Raoul's going to Lisbon to meet some people to fix it up. I think he's flying out from Northholt tonight. But it's not certain the General will go now, so he may have a wasted journey. Still, a few days in Lisbon at this time of the year cannot be bad.'

'She shouldn't have told you all that, Freddie, should she?'

'They all think I'm like Gaillet's private secretary. And as far as he's concerned I am. He's always saying "it's all right, Freddie sees everything". Now we know why, don't we? It's all been part of his fiendish plan to make it look as though I'm in the know.'

I must say this all sounded fantastic to me. Gaillet had hardly looked like a man about to embark on secret business in Lisbon when he'd been escorted off by Maurice, virtually under arrest, apparently, and with a gash on the side of his head that had laid him out cold. I said so to Freddie.

'Maurice? I was nearly forgetting Maurice. It must be the smell of that tripe. He came in.'

'To Carlton Gardens? Didn't he say anything about what happened out at Coatwood, then?'

Maurice had put his head round the door of the office about five minutes after Freddie's indiscreet conversation with de Gaulle's junior secretary. The first thing he asked was how were Florence and Rhoda. Freddie said he hadn't spoken to either of us for a while, which was true at the time. He and I hadn't spoken on the telephone until later.

'Gaillet's not around then, Freddie?'

Freddie hesitated. Should he tell Maurice about Lisbon? Better wait and see. Why had Maurice turned up suddenly and unannounced at Carlton Gardens? These days he was careful not to be seen to be too pally with Gaillet. Hardly ever saw him alone in the office.

'I hear you got into a spot of bother with the Military Police, old man. Everything cleared up?'

'Mmm. Gaillet's not going to be in for some time, apparently. Suits me. The bastard's got me by the short and curlies.'

'About the phoney accounts?'

'How the hell…?'

'I told you, Freddie. We've been keeping tabs on him too, you know.'

'I told him I could get hold of that painting, like you said. Well, I had to, really.'

'Did you? What did he say?'

'He said it was a Rubens, too.'

'Did he?'

'I mean, Maurice, that's what you said, too. How do you both know?'

'He must have said something when he first came looking for me, I suppose. I can't remember. Look, Freddie, first things first. I need to get you in the clear over these phoney accounts. Where does he keep the details, do you know?'

Freddie said they were kept locked in the steel cabinet, but only Gaillet had a key.

'I'm quite good with locks,' said Maurice. 'It's all part of the training, you know. Something here should fit one of these old Ministry of Works jobs.' He produced a bunch of keys and went over to the cabinet, with his back to Freddie.

'There we are. First time. Look at that. Didn't have to force it at all.'

Freddie went through the files for him until he found the one with the account details.

'What will you do with them? He'll spot they're missing.'

'I'll get them copied and pop these back before he gets back. He'll be gone for some time, I imagine.'

'So off he went with all the accounts, Florence Duck, and the phoney representatives details, including mine. And not a word about all this shenanigans going on with you and Gaillet and Rhoda out at Coatwood. It's as if none of it had ever happened. What would he have said if I'd already spoken to you, I wonder? I suppose he'd have had some story ready.'

I said I thought it was probably Maurice, and not Gaillet, who'd had Freddie picked up by the military police, to make sure he was out of the way at the crucial time.'

'Or both of them,' said Freddie. 'And then Rhoda put her oar in at the last minute and Gaillet decided to go it alone. I bet Maurice never thought the painting would ever turn up at all. It was the phoney accounts he wanted. But does he want them for King and Country, like he said? I can't see what else he could do with them, just by himself, do you? He's a bloody mystery your adorable Uncle Maurice. They seek him here, they seek him there.'

In the morning Freddie went back to Carlton Gardens, but with considerable trepidation. Everything felt ominously up in the air. We'd both been putting what reliance we could in Maurice to resolve the threats from Gaillet. Despite his deviousness and the unexplained loose ends in his stories, we didn't doubt that he *was* some kind of secret policeman. The Primrose switchboard, the ATS drivers, the Elstree hotel. They were all real enough. But there was still no word of explanation from him.

And nothing of Gaillet either. Gaillet who was supposed to have taken a flight to Lisbon the previous night. But he couldn't have done in the groggy state he was in when I'd last seen him being lugged off down the road from Coatwood by Maurice and put in the back of his big Austin.

'So if he didn't catch his plane, Florrie Dee, there are bound to be questions at Carlton Gardens about where he's got to. A big stink, I should imagine. He'll have to show up and explain himself and I can't imagine that's going to be very easy for him. Or for yours truly, Corporal Freddie Draper.'

But nothing did happen that day, or the next. Life went on as normal at Carlton Gardens. Captain Gaillet was not mentioned and there was still nothing from Maurice.

On the third or fourth night Freddie came home very late. I'd virtually given him up, although there was no air raid on. He opened the front door with, 'He turned up, Florence, bold as brass.'

'Which one? Gaillet or Maurice?'

'Both, in a manner of speaking.'

A typed note had been delivered by hand for Freddie. It was from Captain Schiffman asking Freddie to meet him in the dinner hour at St Anne's church in Wardour Street where we had gone with him before. It was urgent, the note said. Come alone.

When he entered, the church was empty except for one or two people on their knees or sitting with bowed heads. Schiffman was not one of them. Freddie sat in a pew at the side, away from them, and waited. After a little while he became aware of a presence behind him. Schiffman had slipped in. Freddie felt he must have been there for a while, presumably watching to make sure he was on his own.

'Come into the garden,' he said, leading the way.

There on a bench at the side of the church, out of sight of the street sat Captain Gaillet. He was in civilian clothes and had a bandage round his head.

'I won't waste time, Freddie. It is quite simple. Captain Guttman's family are being watched in France. Perhaps you knew this. They are Jews. Life is difficult for them. It could become even more difficult, or it could become much, much easier. I can make it happen either way. It's up to you, Freddie.'

'Up to me? How can it be up to me?'

'I want you to bring me some papers from Carlton Gardens. If you do this and tell nobody, Captain Guttman's family will be allowed to travel into unoccupied France unhindered and from there they may be allowed into Switzerland.'

'What do you mean, "may be"?'

'The documents you will bring me, will provide me with an identity to get me back into France. If you do anything to prevent that happening, then I shall be unable to make the arrangements for Guttman's family and you will have been responsible.'

'How do you know you aren't being watched too? Something must have happened with you and Maurice Burnell? His people didn't just let you go, surely?'

Gaillet looked genuinely nonplussed. 'His people? What people? Maurice Burnell is a petty crook and a double-crosser. There are no people.'

'What happened, then, after he took you away from Coatwood?'

'I kept passing out. It was serious concussion, you know. He took me to a hospital and left me there. When I was recovered enough to get out of bed, I'd been locked in. I don't know what he'd told the nurses. They said I was not allowed to leave and must wait until I was collected. He'd taken my uniform, my identity papers, my keys, travel papers. Everything. It took me hours to talk my way out.'

'What travel papers? Papers for your Lisbon trip?'

'Clever Freddie. He has taken my place on the plane. I phoned Northolt and said I was from Carlton Gardens. I remembered the flight password at least. They said I was already on the flight. That was my ticket home. If I meet up with Maurice Burnell, he is a dead man. So now you understand why you must do as I say. I am very, very serious Freddie.'

'So what's Maurice done now, Freddie?'

'I should say, Florence my love, that your adorable uncle has done a bunk to Lisbon with details of some very lucrative and untraceable bank accounts, some of which have been receiving payments for gold sales our Government doesn't want anyone to know about. And on top of it all, he's either got a genuine lost Rubens or a very, very passable copy.'

'So he is just a crook, then?'

'Or a spy, or both. I still wouldn't put money on which. But now Gaillet is completely wrong-footed. He's lost all his insurance and he can't be certain what Maurice may have left behind by way of a ticking time bomb. He must suspect Maurice is a policeman. After all he must have had some authority to get the hospital to lock him in, mustn't he?'

'I don't know Freddie. Must he? So what are you going to do now, about Dr Guttman or Schiffman, I mean?'

'I've done what he said, Florence. That's why I was so late tonight. What else could I do? If I'd shopped Gaillet, the result would have been just the same. And poor old Guttman-Schiffman just sat there in the churchyard, looking like some poor old, wet dog waiting to be let in out of the rain. Anyway, Gaillet's chances of making it back to France won't be great. He's getting repatriated on a dead compatriot's papers. That means he'll be in some rusting convoy to Gibraltar, taking the long way round by the Azores and a prey to all the U-boats in the Atlantic, with no guarantee of getting across to Spain, if and when he gets there. No wonder he's vowing revenge on the adorable Maurice. Maurice should have finished what Rhoda tried to start, while he had the chance. Gaillet could be snug as a bug in Lisbon by now, going through his bank statements and checking his investments. Instead of which, if he's discovered using someone else's papers, he'll be treated as a deserter and handed back to the Free French, probably in some crumbling shanty town in West Africa.'

It was quite a speech for Freddie. I wouldn't have bet my week's meat ration my pig-headed darling would have done what Captain Gaillet wanted, but I wasn't sorry. At least Gaillet would be out of the way now and with any luck Freddie wouldn't find himself at the receiving end of some very awkward questions.

'What do you think will happen about Maurice in Lisbon, Freddie? He can't go on being Captain Gaillet, can he? Someone's bound to tell Carlton Gardens they've sent an impostor.'

'He could just disappear, I suppose. Then poor old Gaillet really would be *persona non grata* with the Free French, if it looked as though he'd done a bunk the minute he reached neutral territory. Especially if the real him subsequently turns up in Gibraltar with a false identity. Whatever happens, it looks as though my days at Carlton Gardens are numbered, Florrie Dee. I can't see them keeping me if they think my boss has gone missing with a bagful of de Gaulle's intentions for the future of France.'

Three days later Freddie came home with the news that Carlton Gardens was seething with rumour, although the higher echelons were saying nothing. It seemed the car Captain Gaillet was travelling in from the aerodrome in Lisbon, where his plane had touched down, had exploded and burnt out. There was talk of a hand grenade having been thrown: that Gaillet had been assassinated for the documents he was carrying, by Vichy agents or other Free French factions opposed to de Gaulle. It was even being whispered that it might have been the Americans, who weren't too keen on the General's ambitions.

The word was Gaillet had been collected by a local civilian driver he had apparently arranged himself, even though the Portuguese at the aerodrome had offered him transport into the city. It was being said, too, that there were no remains of the driver and that Captain Gaillet's body had been burnt beyond all recognition.

'My God, Freddie! How ghastly! Poor Uncle Maurice.'

'Don't you believe a word of it,' said Freddie. 'I don't. He's staged it. I bet his driver was one of his old business cronies who can fix anything. Typewriters with accents, some unclaimed corpse from the morgue in the boot. Easy. Dress him up in Gaillet's uniform, and Boom! Raoul's your dead uncle. By the way, I was right. I am being posted back to my unit.'

Epilogue – 1992

'So Grandad went back to his unit, then? And was that it for the rest of the war? Didn't you hear from the adorable Maurice, Grandma? Was he killed or was it all a set-up, like Grandad said? And what happened to Coatwood and the middle room? Did they have to pull it down? And did anyone find out about Great Aunt Rhoda's...you know?' I couldn't bare the thought of her stopping there.

'Don't you let on to Rhoda I've told you all that stuff. That really is just for you, me, and our middle room.'

'Our middle room? We don't have one.'

'Yes we do, my girl, as a matter of fact. They may have pulled Coatwood down and built flats, but the middle room is in my head and yours, when we are talking together like this. You know that by now.'

She pursed her lips, just as I imagine Josephine Lucie, my namesake, used to do.

'Anyway, all those unanswered questions? Yes, Freddie went back to his unit and shortly afterwards they were moved down to Brighton, which wasn't so bad, because I got down there once or twice at weekends. But then he went up north somewhere. Lancashire. Bury, I think it was. I know he got a bit fed up with interminable black pudding at his billet. It wasn't on the ration. And don't keep calling me Grandma, when there's just the two of us. I've told you.'

Florence told me she hadn't seen much of Freddie after that. She tried to see if she could get a transfer to the post office in Bury, when it looked as though he might be there for a while. But it was not approved. Pa stayed up in Liverpool and Freddie did manage to see him a few times.

The war ground on, the news getting worse and worse before

it started to get better. My great uncle Leonard became a prisoner of the Japanese after the fall of Singapore and was put to work on the Burma Railway. After it was all over he was sent to Australia to recuperate and didn't make it back home until nearly 1947, the year my dad was born. He doesn't talk about his experience, except to say the prospect of once again having a drag on a Players Weight, kept him going.

In 1944 Freddie volunteered for 'special duties'. They were asking for people who spoke passable French or German, or both, to make themselves known. Grandad reckoned anything had to be less dangerous than dying a slow, agonising death by boredom and black pudding in Bury.

He reported to a closed camp somewhere in Essex, where he discovered he was to land in Normandy with an intelligence unit. He told Florence it was a good job they wanted him for his fluent French and not his prowess with a rifle and bayonet. The unit he was with landed on Sword Beach less than forty-eight hours after the first assault. Their task was to make contact with the mayors and French bigwigs, as villages and towns were taken from the Germans, and to try and sort out whether any 'sleepers' had been left behind by them.

Florence didn't hear from Freddie for a while, of course, and it was many weeks before eventually a letter did arrive via, of all people, the hero of the tea pot, Harry Bayliss, who was home on leave. Freddie had bumped into him in Belgium, by sheer chance. This letter contained more than the usual 'I am well/ sick/ wounded/ seriously/ not seriously' information crossed out as appropriate. Grandma's still got it. She hunted around in her chiffonier and dug it out for me to read.

By this time Grandad and his unit had moved up through Northern France and come to a semi-permanent halt just over the Belgian border near Mons.

'At last we have settled down for a longish spell here, having come up from Cambrai,' Freddie wrote. *'When we were about to leave, three of us were given a "requisitioned" German station wagon – a rather flashy Mercedes – and told to stay behind to pack up the officers' non-essential kit, the contents of a couple of filing cabinets of documents, and the booze from the officers' mess. This last task was particularly handy, as we were told only to pack up the full bottles and not to bother with the ones that had already been opened. We took our time, needless to say, seeing to the opened bottles, and followed on at a very leisurely pace through the French countryside. So leisurely, that we had to find somewhere to stay*

the night.

We found ourselves at a place called Catillon-sur-Sambre where the bridge over the canal was still intact. It had been fought for fiercely by our chaps apparently. We stayed the night in a café there and I got chatting to the locals, as usual. They were talking about the fighting along the banks of the "Sambre-Oise", meaning the canal, and mentioned a village nearby called Orgelets. This rang a bell with me and I remembered you had said several times that was where your French grandmother came from. Next morning, the others were in no rush to catch up with the unit, so I said I was going to have a walk along the canal to Orgelets and they could drive round by the road in a couple of hours and pick me up.

The point of all this, Florence Duck, is that when I got to Orgelets I needed a cup of what passes for coffee these days and I went into the Café de la Mairie in the village square. It was not much of a place, as you can imagine, except that over the bar there hung a rather interesting oil painting. It was a bit blackened, from cigarette smoke and the wood stove, I guess, but it was definitely a man in a lace collar. I asked the café owner about it, but he didn't seem to know much, except there was a bit of verse he couldn't remember on the back. His grandfather who'd owned the café before his father had hung it up there. The story was that the village priest, at that time, liked a bit of a tipple and sometimes ran up a bit of a slate. Not being too flush on one occasion, he'd settled up with this painting, which he'd unearthed in the vestry.

What a coincidence, Florence Duck! A portrait of a man in a lace collar in the very village your grandmother came from. It cannot be a coincidence, can it? We know Maurice went off with one of them, but did your grandmother ever say what happened to the other one? Perhaps she went back to Orgelets and left it there. But then, how did she come by it in the first place? I suppose we'll never know. It's probably all a coincidence, anyway. Perhaps she knew about this one from when she was a girl and made up a story about it.

I gave her the letter back. 'And the adorable Maurice? Was he ever heard of again, or was he blown up in Lisbon, after all? And Captain Gaillet, what about him? I like to think he and Maurice were in it together and are sitting in the sun on their ill-gotten gains, sipping rum punch. But perhaps the U-boats did get him. He wasn't very nice about those poor Jewish people, was he?'

'Your grandad is still convinced it was all a put-up job. And he still doesn't know the half of what I've told you. Josephine Lucie wouldn't have wanted that. We drove down to Orgelets about ten years ago, you know. He wanted to show me all the places he'd been to in the war. But the Café de la Mairie had changed hands. It was all different from how he remembered it. And there was no picture over the bar any more. But he doesn't let it rest. He saw something in the *Telegraph* very recently. You must ask him to show it to you when he comes in. It was an advertisement for an auction somewhere and it listed a painting in oils, *Portrait of a man in a lace collar*. It said it was 'in the Flemish style, possibly 18th Century.' Freddie's sent off for the catalogue. But I don't know. I think he's barking up the wrong tree. These men in their old lace collars are probably two a penny. Still, I would like to see the adorable Maurice again. I half expected him to turn up at Pa's funeral. I never did get to tell him what a bastard he really was.'

Acknowledgements
∞ ∞

The author would like to thank Simon Dugdale and Jayne Bassham for their invaluable help with editing, Roger Birchall, as ever, for his artistic advice, Chris and David Hughes for their staircase on the cover, and not least, Constantine Lourdas for his production expertise with the image.

The author

Stephen Reardon was born in High Barnet, England, in 1947. He spent thirty years working in government in London's Whitehall, culminating his career there in 1997 as a senior ministerial press secretary. Following a further three years as Director of Communications at the Institute of Directors, he took up writing full-time on his own account. His first novel, *The Equal Sky,* was published by Lulu in 2007. He and his wife, Jane, live in south west London and the Pas de Calais. They have two grown-up children and a grandson.

996032

Printed in Great Britain by
Amazon.co.uk, Ltd.,
Marston Gate.